Brothers

A NOVEL

MANJU KAPUR

PENGUIN
VIKING

VIKING

USA | Canada | UK | Ireland | Australia
New Zealand | India | South Africa | China

Viking is part of the Penguin Random House group of companies
whose addresses can be found at global.penguinrandomhouse.com

Published by Penguin Random House India Pvt. Ltd
7th Floor, Infinity Tower C, DLF Cyber City,
Gurgaon 122 002, Haryana, India

Penguin
Random House
India

First published in Viking by Penguin Random House India 2016

ISBN 9780670089376

For sale in the Indian Subcontinent only

Typeset in RequiemText by Manipal Digital Systems, Manipal
Printed at Replika Press Pvt. Ltd, India

www.penguinbooksindia.com

SECTION I
Tapti

I

2010

For Tapti Gaina, wife of the newest prisoner in the Jaipur Central Jail, what time of day is best?

It had to be morning, the brief flickering seconds that fell between her half open eyes and the cruelty of full consciousness; the quiet, somnolent moment when her mind could preserve the illusion that this was going to be a day like any other.

A few seconds and the best was over. As her present circumstances rushed to attack her, the anguish in her heart kept her in bed with the sheet pulled over her like a shroud, while birds twittered and the sky lightened into soft pale grey.

The thickly leaved branches of the mulberry tree outside her window became more visible. Her reluctant vision took in the light green of a parrot's wings as it darted among the foliage, eating the fruit that would even now be staining the ground with purple splotches.

She was used to sleeping alone. If you collected all the nights of her married life that her husband had been away, it would amount to years and years. This state would be permanent now.

Yesterday she had gone to Fateh Tibba during visiting hours, only to be turned away. Mangal did not wish to see anyone. She stood before the prison walls, absorbing the implications. He had never once not wanted to see her. Since their marriage she had been used to his face lighting up when she entered the room, to the softening of his features when he looked at her, even when angry. This rejection was what divorce must feel like.

As they left the car park, she began to cry, her nose buried in a wad of tissue so that the driver would not hear. The minute she reached home she would have to resume a façade that would convey courage and strength to her family.

Home was A-1/43 Mahavir Udyan, one of the best addresses in town. She had been able to acquire this land in a lottery because of her brother-in-law, get the loan to build a double storeyed house because of him. It was a small white bungalow. Around it was a garden, with one lemon tree, one pink guava tree, one mulberry tree, a night jasmine, multiple flowering hibiscus and a vegetable patch towards the back. In the veranda was a metal framed swing sofa. Inside, apart from the drawing-dining, were four bedrooms, the mezzanine for her mother, and the three upstairs ones for her daughters and herself.

She had spent years in government flats, dreaming of the day when she would own just such a place, surrounded by the comfort of the modern, free of the peeling plaster walls, shoddy construction and unimaginative architecture that marked the allotted quarters of junior staff in the Rajasthan administration. Now the home she had struggled to build, the home that represented success, stability and security, that home was being destroyed by the rottenness within.

Her eyes open to the sudden brightness of day. Soon her mother would appear with a cup of tea, her face wearing the tight, resigned look that was now permanent to them all. Then nag, nag, nag. Why wasn't she up, taking leave did not mean spending days in bed, it was important for the girls to see their mother functional.

Her poor chastened daughters who would be dogged by the consequences of their parent's action all their lives. Mridula didn't want to go to college, everybody kept gawking, asking questions. Why couldn't they emigrate to Australia?

'Don't talk nonsense, Mridu,' said her mother, but why, why was it nonsense?

'Nothing lasts forever. This time next year, nobody will even remember.'

Her daughters stared at her. Everything else might be forgotten, but not this.

But the day had to come when their family drama would cease to be of such interest. Till then she couldn't let Mridu know how much she identified with her. When she returned to her office, it would be to the greedy curiosity of her colleagues, to questions disguised as concern. What was the inside story? There must have been some jealousy, some secret animosity, some depression at the very least? And they would go on talking, talking, assuming her interest in how they felt when they received the news, so surprised, so astonished, so disbelieving, but TV cannot lie.

They fancied their sympathy would be welcome, their inquiries, their condolences. Somewhere too there would be satisfaction that a highly placed officer had been stricken by tragedy, that all were equal before the devilish workings of fate.

For her connections had intimidated people, she could take leave with impunity, she could arrange for the transfers of those that displeased her, she remained unaffected by rumours that she took money for the projects she approved.

If they could see her now! It took all her will to get out
of bed and go downstairs. Then to turn on the TV and flick
through the news channels. That was her sole occupation.
Every image agitated her, yet she could not keep away. It took
her into even more awful territory, but what was not awful
these days?

To think of him so close to death drove her mad with
helplessness. Despite her efforts she had not been able to see
him.

The first time she had gone to the hospital she had been
turned away. 'No one can visit,' said the guard, in the face of her
official ID. 'Those are orders.'

TV crew, reporters, party workers, politicians swarmed the
steps, pressed against the barricade. As she pushed her way out
she could hear excited commentary on what had happened: Jan
Sunwai, his own brother, gave himself up, fight over money,
bribed security, this can happen, look at the Mahabharat, Jats
are like this only, quick to kill.

Again and again she phones the family but no one picks up.
For them she had always been suspect, now in the eyes of the
world they are the righteous, she the tainted. To be forced to
see things from their point of view adds to her trauma.

This morning too begins with her holding her second cup of
tea in front of the TV. Her caftan is rumpled, her mouth stale,
her body heavy from the night. So and so has come from Delhi
to visit the chief minister. Names follow. This alarms her. Is
his condition deteriorating, that such visits are in order? She
fidgets with the remote.

'Must you stare at that thing all day?' demands her mother
harshly. 'It just spoils your mood.'

'What do you want me to do?'

'Go anywhere. Go to the temple. God is our only support now. Even your friends have dropped you.'

'It is I who don't answer their calls. These reporters who dog me, they are my friends. I should talk to them. Make them happy.'

'By now they know they can get nothing more here, they are all sitting at the hospital.'

Tapti waits till her daughters come home, till lunch is served, then leaves the house. There is no point going anywhere when her heart is with him in the ICU. She asks her driver to drive down to Hospital Road. As she alights from her car she can make out the many party workers loitering aimlessly in scattered groups. Young men there to be noticed, to be made use of, to pass the time.

This is her third attempt to see him. She uses a different entrance to arrive at a similar situation.

Visitor pass, demands the guard at the foot of the stairs.

'CM Sahib – I want to see CM Sahib – I am family.'

'Arre Madam, that is what everybody says.'

'I am real family – real – his brother's –'

Her voice falters and the guard's suspicions increase.

'Only one visitor allowed. With pass.'

Standing to one side she sends another hopeless text to his wife, his children, I am waiting downstairs. Is it possible to send me an entry pass?

There is no response, and she senses the curious, patronizing gaze of the guard. She has exposed herself to the pity of a social inferior, and that makes her angry.

Having achieved nothing she is free to leave the building. Outside she comes across women crying near an ambulance. Thin steady low wails emerge from their cloth covered faces. This is the sound of her future. If anything should happen to

HSG, she too would throw her palla over her head, and hidden from the world, cry and cry.

Two steps away she crosses a man lying moaning and ignored on the ground. His surprisingly plump shoulder quivers through the ragged tear in his shirt.

In the space next to the underground parking yajnas for the health of the chief minister are being conducted under a shamiana. People stand around, sweating, staring. Taking off her sandals, Tapti hops over the low sandstone lattice grill on to the dusty grass, pulls her sari over her head and bows, trying desperately to place her faith in the Above. Because it is a hospital there is no microphone, and she can hear nothing, only see the pandits with their beads, and an image of a god, surrounded by incense sticks on a raised dais. The paraphernalia is too distracting for prayer and she walks out slowly, searching for her driver among the waiting cars. There he is, standing among the watchers, along with the other drivers, talking, laughing. He sees her and runs to get the car. She waits among the debris of various small businesses that have sprung up around these gates. Where there are crowds there is money to be made, especially true if waiting is involved. Behind her large sunglasses, her gaze flickers over the fresh juice sellers, flower wallahs, the little temple, the many stalls offering samosas, bhel puri, mathri and chaat. Bystanders eat vigorously, then toss their silver foil plates on to the road. The fumes of a million passing vehicles hang thickly over everything.

It takes fifteen minutes for Tapti to reach home. Gaina is etched in the inset marble plaque next to the gate. Her life has been shaped by that name. The security man she has hired stares at her. Briefly she reiterates that he must not let a single journalist near her house. 'Madam,' he says, 'these people are shameless, they keep coming, asking. This morning one man threatened to report me if I stopped him from standing on public property. But like you advised I told him we could also report for harassing.'

The man is animated, he repeats himself, looking at her for approval.

'You have done well,' she replies, the words dragged from her. There is no point hating the press. She is newsworthy, and it is their trade to sell the latest item of interest.

'How is he?' ask her daughters as soon as she enters. 'Did you see him? Did he recognize you?'

'They didn't let me in.'

'Why do you keep going, Mama? If this is the way they treat us why should we care if Uncle lives or dies?'

Her daughters are young and do not understand the nature of guilt and recrimination.

'Rules are very strict for ICU,' said Mrs Ahlawat quickly. 'On TV they are showing so much press, so many party workers. All probably want to meet the family.'

'I saw pandits doing a yajna near the car park.'

'They allow that in a hospital?'

'He is chief minister. Why shouldn't they allow?'

Tapti slumps in a chair, while the three stare at her. Mridula again produces Australia. If they can't emigrate, her only ambition is to drop her surname, flee Jaipur, go to a hostel in Delhi, register in a new college, good, bad, doesn't matter. She is sick of girls, teachers even, asking her what happened, how did it happen, was there no warning? Pretending to care, when they only wanted food for gossip, she despised them all.

Mansi looks on, her eyes big with a similar anguish. 'Poor Papa,' she said, 'he too must be really suffering. Is it possible to visit him? He must wonder why we haven't.'

'I don't think he has the luxury to wonder that,' said her grandmother.

'Don't worry,' said their mother harshly. 'I have tried.'

When? Alone? Why didn't she inform anybody? How was it? What did he say?

'Yesterday. He doesn't want visitors. Not even family. Those are his instructions.'

'It is just as well. Clearly he knows we can have nothing more to do with him,' says the grandmother.

'Poor Papa,' repeats Mansi, but more uncertainly, while her elder sister shouts, 'Poor Papa! Did he think of us? Even once? He could have talked about it – to Uncle – to Mama – to anybody. Who asked him to go and do this? Who?'

Tapti looks at their tears, thinks of her own bouts of crying, and wonders how she is ever going to be a support to her children. Yes, he had no right to do this to them. At sixteen and eighteen, her girls are on the threshold of life, a threshold now marked by malevolence and blood.

Mrs Ahlawat thinks of the karma that had led her beautiful daughter to marry a man who was essentially a villager. Who, despite all his years in the city, had a villager's way of dealing with problems, whip out a gun and shoot. Animals in the jungle were better. They had all been taken in by an important politician proposing the match, taken in by promises of a security that would last their lives.

Finally the exhausted sleep of the emotionally bereft.

Another day. It is late afternoon when the need to dispel her anxiety leads Tapti to Birla Mandir. The driver parks and she looks up the hill towards Moti Doongri, its dark, time coloured stones obscured intermittently by small random trees. The mellow evening light gilds both the pristine marble of the modern temple and the dulled red sandstone of the ancient fort above.

She climbs the steps. Across the road she can see her office, with *Rajasthan Rural Development Board* in big green letters spread above the building. At night those letters shone with fluorescent iridescence, dominating every sign in the area.

'Every time you pass by,' she had told him, 'you will think of me.'

As though he needed reminders, he replied.

'You never know, anything can happen.'

She had sanctioned the sign after due protocol, but enemies in her office claimed kickbacks; she had ignored the cheapest bid, they alleged. Wastage of public resources, inadequate tenders, reported the newspapers. Why pay thirty lakh rupees for a sign? Incensed she had written a letter to the minister, offering to resign if any wrongdoing on her part could be proved. The noise died down, and in the end she got what she had wanted, another link between him and her.

She sits on the parapet next to some scooters in order to unbuckle her sandals. A priest hoists up his pious saffron dhoti to reveal muscular hairy legs, straddles the seat of his motorcycle, revs the engine, and rides off, secure in his holiness, the wind brushing against his long grey hair.

Temple donations had probably paid for his motorcycle, her donations. She has lost count of the rupees she has put in the daan patra. Always with the same prayer, make him well. Please, please.

Bhajans magnified over loudspeakers assail her as she joins the line inching towards the images of Lakshmi and Narayan clustered at one end of a large hall. The incense filled atmosphere of the temple is soothing. She drops to the floor, leans against one of the pillars near the west exit and gazes at the cool white marble expanse around her. The height of the temple allows her an illusory distance from the nightmare of her life.

She prays, then thinks about her husband. Shouldn't she entreat the gods on his behalf? A pause while she searches her heart for words, honest true words, for the divine sees through all hypocrisy. She tries but her own resentment, grief and anger overshadow any compassion. She resumes her contemplation of the deities, serenely smiling at their supplicants. As she leaves, she presses her forehead to the floor. Just let him live, let him live, let him live. The rest can come later.

A week later her mobile rings. She recognizes his wife's number, and immediately her head begins to pound with fear. 'Yes?' she croaks. He is a bit better she is told, if she would like to see him, she can appear during visiting hours that evening. The line is cut before she can ask questions or show concern.

Tapti sits unseeing in the back of her car, while her driver negotiates the traffic on JLN Marg. Had he asked for her? Her sister-in-law would hardly phone voluntarily, not after ruthlessly ignoring her calls, not after rubbing her nose into the fact that from now on only she would decide who could visit her husband.

She gives her name to the guard on duty with confidence. Doors that had hitherto been closed, smoothly open. Once in the ICU waiting room, she lowers her head before those she recognizes, his children Amar and Shweta, their in-laws, myriad other relatives, everybody represented except her branch of the family. She touches her sister-in-law's feet. How was he? The answers are many. 'You can meet him, but only for five minutes,' says her sister-in-law eventually. 'I will accompany you.' She had not expected so much. Perhaps her presence there was his wife's own bargain with god.

In a little side room they are swathed in masks and hospital gowns, green cloth bags envelop their shoes. Hands rinsed in Dettol, they go towards the cubicle at the end.

'One at a time,' says the attendant.

Irritably her sister-in-law nods. 'Five minutes,' she repeats.

Quickly Tapti slides around the curtain.

The first shock. If anything, the reports had not been pessimistic enough. Around the bed machines blink and beep, needles with nubbly white heads link various tubes to his body, overhead fluorescent lights scream into his face. This man who possessed the dynamism that ensured he never lost a single election, whose words conquered the attention of thousands, this man lies before her, dormant, still, stuporous. As she bends over him, his eyes flicker, and the gleam she had seen so often when he looked at her came for the most fleeting second. Her face twists. She detects a slight movement of his head, he was telling her not to cry. She picks up his hand, the IV free one and notices how cold it is. Why is the air conditioning so high? But to point out anything will be construed as interference.

Slowly she places the fingers against her lips and kisses them, rapid, small kisses. An imperceptible pressure against her mouth, he was responding. A cough outside, five minutes are over. Gently she lets go of his hand.

Her sister-in-law scans her face as she emerges.

'He looks well, considering what he has been through,' lies Tapti.

The wife enters the cubicle, she will be the last family person to see him that day.

'Yes, he is improving,' she remarks two minutes later as they walk down the hall to de-robe in the antechamber. 'He opened his eyes in the morning, frowned a little, looked disturbed. Maybe he was thinking of his brother. That is why I called you. Even though it was your —'

'I will never forget this kindness,' Tapti responds hastily. 'My whole family is praying for him. We only want his recovery, nothing else.'

The wife nods coldly. Long experience has inured Tapti to shifts in her emotional temperature and she knows it is time to leave. Already she has been given more than she had imagined possible.

As she exits she mentally exhorts the devotees under the shamiana to continue their efforts. Earlier she may have questioned their sincerity, today she can only be grateful that so many people across the country are praying for him. There was strength in such concentrated appeals to god, there was.

Outside the gates she notices an increase in the number of banners strung from trees, Get Well Soon, Rajasthan Needs You, India Needs You.

For the next three days the newspapers publish hopeful reports. The TV anchor allows herself a cautious optimism. Tapti follows the medical updates eagerly, sensing in each the hand pressed against her lips. Obsessively she keeps checking her mobile, knowing that as soon as he regains consciousness he will send for her.

Though she waits with an impatience that weighs down each minute with the slowness of hours, there is no call. How long can she live on that moment in the hospital? Contact with the family, medical updates, this is what she craves.

Five evenings later she tells her driver to take her to the CM's mansion. She will see Uncle Virpal. She will fall at his feet, ask for forgiveness. Uncle had always been kind to her, it was criminal to ignore him during these fear filled days. They cannot stop her. He is her relative as well.

The guards at the gates recognize her and let her in. Her steps slow down. This was where he had lived, this garden where he had been shot. For years the coldness between the families meant the house was out of bounds. Now, gathering courage, she enters the great central hall and starts to climb the steps to Uncle's room.

In this she is arrested.

'What are you doing here?' The wife.

'I have come to see Uncle.'

'Why?'

'To seek his blessings.'

'You talk of blessings? There can be no blessings after what you have done.'

'Bhabhi, please! I have done nothing. I knew nothing. Don't punish us more than we are being punished.'

'Nobody sent for you, nobody wants to see your face. Your whole family is namak haram.'

Tapti advanced two steps. 'I will leave if Uncle tells me to. Not before.'

Her sister-in-law's voice rose. 'And what will you tell him? That your husband shot the man who contained all his dreams? Do you know what that will do to him? He is living only because Himmatji told him repeatedly that his blessings were needed for him to reach the highest pinnacle. Then he would release him. That was their pact – and now? Any thinking – feeling person would bury their head in shame. But not you. From the moment I saw you, I knew –'

Her children come rushing out. The mother's acrimony grew more virulent. Tapti stood there, both listening and not listening. Whatever she said to herself in the dark watches of the night was as mordant. Nothing came as a surprise.

'Uncle will wonder why, after so much time, you have come. He does not know what has happened.' explained the son. 'At ninety-four, too much shock.'

How thoughtless, how wrapped up in her own torment had she been to not realize that of course Uncle would not be able to tolerate it. Himmat was his pride and joy, his more-than-son, the golden boy, whose feet he had initially guided when, fresh from the village, he had come to take the place of his own dead son.

'Papa sat with Uncle every evening when he was home,' added the daughter sadly, 'he cared so much.'

'And we do not want to kill him, understand? He thinks he is on tour,' hissed the mother.

'Still, can I please see him? I won't mention anything.'

'You? How can we trust you? All this venom, this envy has come from your family. We have had enough of you. Beta, please see Mrs Tapti out.'

'There is no need, I will go myself.'

'No, no, Chachi, I will escort you,' said the son in a simulacrum of politeness as he walked his aunt out. 'It is lucky we happened to be home. We return to the hospital in five minutes.'

'I wish I could be of help. But your mother –'

'Of course. I understand,' said Amar as he opened the car door for her.

'Thank you, beta. You know I would give my life to change things. But he never listened to me, never, not from the day we married. You think I am suffering less? I have nothing, only disgrace. On my daughters' heads I tell you, we did not know he had so much hate in his heart.'

There was nothing the son could say. It did cross his mind as he watched the car drive away that his aunt was a very good looking woman and still young. What would happen to her was anybody's guess. And then she left his mind as he returned to the all-consuming grief in the house.

He found his mother rocking back and forth, crying with rage. Seeing her sister-in-law had taken her to the past. How was she to know that in looking after Mangal she had nursed a viper, a viper. But he was her husband's brother and it had been her duty. So sweet he was, always Bhabhiji this, Bhabhiji that.

Everybody loved him because he was Papa's younger brother. Couldn't walk one step without consulting your father, not one step. And so much he did for him, cement dealership, arranged his marriage, factory, petrol pump. 'I kept saying, don't do so much, you are only teaching him to expect more and more. But with such a loving heart, with his great sense of duty, your father would not listen. Always they were full of poison, jealousy, hatred.'

Such treachery, unexpected, unforeseen and unguarded against, could only produce more tears and it was a while before they recovered enough to give instructions that Tapti Madam must never be allowed entrance into the house. Never, ever. No exoneration could be possible, no bridge built between the families. They were as divided as the North and South Poles.

One month to the day of being admitted into ICU, HSG slips into a deeper coma and dies. Journalists converge in even greater numbers on the hospital. This raised breaking news to another level. Never before had a chief minister been killed while in office. Comparisons to the Mahatma were made, comparisons that some said were excessive. But faced with murder excess was deemed only polite.

Tapti gets to know of his death from TV. Briskly the broadcaster assures her that she is now the wife of an assassin. Stunned, her mother and daughters huddle together. Every image blasting into the room encourages weeping. Finally the grandmother takes the remote, points it towards the flat LCD screen (such excitement when it was bought, such clarity of picture, such invitation to view) and switches off the news. The plastic lace draped over the TV gleams in the evening light. 'I suppose they will have the funeral tomorrow?' she remarks.

'What will happen to Papa?' asks Mansi.

Tapti shakes her head. From TV they later learn that the CM will lie in state at Raj Bhavan. Ambassadors, politicians, party workers, industrialists, dignitaries are expected to congregate from all over India.

Increasingly uncertain of her status, Tapti only knows she has to see him one more time, to say farewell, to ask for absolution. At a public function no one can stop her. The next day she makes her way to Raj Bhavan without informing her family. Their love will prevent her from going anywhere.

The area in front of the governor's residence is cordoned off, the mourners stretching from the gate all the way down the road and around the block. Ordinarily, such a sight would have made her turn back, but pulling out her dark glasses, covering her head with her sari, she stands in line, drowned in the stench of sweat, inching forward as insignificant, as lowly, as the least of them. When she finally reaches the body, all she finds lying before her is a corpse, the skin pallid, eyes shut, the head ringed by jasmine garlands. His face is smooth and still, is this what is known as peace, she wonders.

'You have gone,' she mutters, 'but what about me?' That is all she has time to say before she is ushered forward. So much for her goodbye. What had she imagined? That there would be a connection between the corpse and herself, amid the crowds, the incense, the flowers, the bhajans, the sound of scattered sobs? He was already far away, seeing him like this further established the distance.

Was there a single one among all these people, who had been as close to him as she? He had once told her the connection between them was so strong he was sure it would last life after life. She didn't care about other lives stretching till eternity, she had told him, all she cared about was the present. Now this statement surfaces in her memory, and how she wished she could throw it back at him, as comfort it was worth nothing.

That evening, her mother raises the issue of the funeral. 'Of course there is no question of our going. They haven't even called. No courtesy, no manners. How is any of this our fault? They should also understand our position.'

'And what position is that? Surely no special effort is required to understand a pariah.'

'Don't say such things.'

'Why not? It's me they are blaming. Because I am the one who poisoned Mangal over the years, made him jealous of his elder brother, telling him he too deserves success. I sent him off to rival parties, I suggested he stand for elections from the Amberi constituency, I manipulated him into hatred. The man didn't have a thought that I didn't put there. Till I came on the scene he was so, so devoted, you see.'

'But they know you. Surely they can't think all this.'

'Leave it, Mummy, how does it matter? He is gone. Let them blame me if it makes them feel better.'

'So there is no need for you to attend the funeral. We know when we are not wanted.'

Tapti looked at her mother, still trying to protect her daughter, despite the odds. She pressed her sari palla to her face and wept softly into the cloth.

Out came the well-known tropes used to deal with suffering. Fate, destiny, karma, have to accept. 'Who knew what was in his mind? For years he must have felt small in the shadow of his brother, such things matter to men. Beta, you have your children, you cannot afford to break down.'

Tapti's tears multiply with each word. She has no defence against her karma.

The funeral is a monumental affair. TV cameras zoom in and out among the white clad mourners, politicians in their Gandhi caps, industrialists, celebrities. For an instant they also capture a middle aged villager breaking through the cordon, shouting I am the eldest son, I will light my father's funeral pyre. Security men surround him, the camera swerves towards the many spectators, when it swivels back to the body, there is only Amar on the platform, igniting the ghee soaked wood. His elder sister Shweta watches from the side, her mother's arm around her.

As the body burns the newscaster recounts the story of Himmat Singh Gaina. His early village days, his stint in Rajasthan University, his introduction to politics while still a student, his rise in the Indian Progressive People's Party, his being elected head of the Rajasthan unit after the debacle of the 2000 elections.

Then followed a list of some of his major achievements: the first computer programme for rural children, the scheme to relieve the debt that was inducing farmers to kill themselves, the compulsory employment for villagers, the cash endowment of fifteen thousand rupees to girls who completed their education up to class ten, the dialogue he initiated among Marwari industrialists, persuading them to invest in the state. Jats would remember him as the one who had ended upper caste hegemony by giving them OBC status in 2003. With reservation, their numbers in the state Assembly had increased to almost thirty per cent.

Tapti's family, glued to the TV, gloomily comment on the action. There is a flash of excitement when a villager starts shouting about his birthrights. 'Did he say he was the eldest son?' asks Mrs Ahlawat glancing at her daughter.

She does not reply. It is her own first glimpse of the child her husband had talked about so much. Grown up Ram Babu, he must be around forty. Watching him being hustled off the funeral platform made her think of tragedies other than hers, associated with HSG's death. As soon as he heard the news, this man must have travelled from his village to perform his father's last rites as was his moral duty. To no avail. That privilege, that attention belonged to the other son, the only son so far as everybody was concerned.

Who will tell Mangal that Ram Babu had managed to come to the funeral, managed to lay forth his claims for all the world to see, if only for one incomprehensible second?

After Himmat Singh Gaina's death, the charges against his brother are updated to murder. There is speculation that Mangal might plead insanity in order to escape punishment.

Overcome with rage, party supporters congregate outside the Jaipur prison. Stones are thrown, slogans shouted. Mangal should be awarded the death sentence immediately. Some young IPPP party workers threaten to immolate themselves in front of the prison gates if their demands are not favourably considered.

The director of the jail meets the young men, gives them tea, reassures them and sends them home. He wants no martyrs. In the dead of night Mangal is driven in an armoured car to the greater anonymity of South East Asia's largest prison, Tihar Jail. In time the case will be shifted to Delhi, also for security reasons.

Next day newspapers publish a picture of Mangal looking dishevelled and unshaven. He has been told of his brother's death but he expresses neither grief nor remorse. We get what we deserve, he is reported to have said.

Tapti hears of her husband's relocation on TV. Didn't she have to be informed? In Tihar would he feel differently about receiving visitors? Would he consent to put her on a list, so that she could spend exhausting hours travelling from Jaipur to

Delhi and back? What would they talk about? But if he called
she would go.

Delhi was also where her brother, Ram Pratap Ahlawat,
practised law. His comforting presence hovers around future
trips, someone from her own side to help navigate this
unfamiliar world.

'Your brother will know what to do,' remarked the mother.
'It is a blessing he went to Delhi.'

Yes, supposed Tapti, it was a good thing that her dissatisfied
brother had pulled up his Rajasthani stakes and moved to Delhi
where the big legal lights glittered. Every time he came home
it was with stories of how much top lawyers charged, one lakh
minimum per appearance. With hard work that eminence
would be his as well.

It was Mangal who interjected disillusion into these
certainties. 'Hard work! As though that gets you anywhere by
itself. I tell you, Ramuji, you need contacts.'

And it was Mangal who proved prescient as, over the
years, Ramu's hard work went unnoticed. The firm took all the
credit, his salary increased, but he was still a cog in the larger
wheel. Mangal Singh Gaina, accused of fratricide, might be the
opportunity he was waiting for.

'People will get to know your brother,' said Mrs Ahlawat.
'It is such a well-known case his picture will come in the papers.
Of course he will have to work for free –'

'Hoon,' assented Tapti dully. Family gratitude would be
Ram Pratap's only reward. And he would more than prove
his brilliance if he managed to palliate Mangal's crimes with
mitigating circumstances. She owes it to her daughters to
arrange a legal defence, to create an air of innocence around
one so manifestly guilty.

'Did you know they would shift Mangal to Delhi?' asks the
mother. 'Wouldn't it have made more sense to send him to

Jodhpur? The high court is there. What does Delhi have to do with it?'

'I don't know, Mama. Maybe they wanted him out of Rajasthan. Security reasons.'

'What will happen now? How will you visit?'

'Train. Bus.'

'Going all the way each time? Oh my poor child.'

'Stop it, Mama, pity makes it harder.'

Her mother looks at her, helpless against the scale of her daughter's trauma. If even her concern is construed as objectionable, what can she say?

Instead she silently curses that long ago day when her lovely child had been selected to welcome an up and coming politician. The fact that Tapti had never joined her in bemoaning that event, made it all the more tragic in her eyes.

II

1987–1989

Seventeen-year-old Tapti was looking at old college magazines dug out from library archives. A first year representative and a Jat, she had been chosen to garland Himmat Singh Gaina, alumnus, and chief guest at the coming Annual Day. The union secretary, a second year Jat boy, will later on deliver the vote of thanks in an English that would be loud, impetuous and ungrammatical.

It had been Tapti's idea to present the chief guest with a booklet composed of photographs from his student years. There he is, Himmat Singh Gaina, from the Law Faculty, after he has been elected president of the student union. His head emerges from an avalanche of garlands, an elongated red tilak decorates his forehead. He wears the smile of a conqueror, vast, brilliant and happy.

Quickly she scanned the interview. The usual: service to the college, the academic community. She imagined these statements segueing into service to the people, the nation. How empty was such rhetoric? She would see and judge. If he retained his idealism after years of power, he would be rare indeed.

While Tapti deftly drew rosettes around the photocopied pictures, threading pink and green ribbons through the holes that would bind the pages, she wondered how this man had travelled so far in so short a time. He must have indulged in underhand practices. Otherwise was it possible to go from student to deputy minister of tourism and civil aviation in a mere thirteen–fourteen years? She tried to calculate his age, perhaps thirty-five.

In one of his interviews he had stated that he was a son of the soil, not metaphorically, but literally, since his father was a farmer. Well, she would never know what he was really like. He would come, the smiling public man, and say his bit. Bouquets and adulation would follow.

Annual Day. He was two hours late. The garland in Tapti's hands had grown limp in the heat of the auditorium. She could smell the perfume from the jasmine in her long plait; she could imagine their browning petals. Her face was shiny with sweat, she wished she had not honoured the occasion by wearing a silk sari.

As she felt herself wilting, she directed her irritation towards the dilatory politician. Like all the others, once they became important their heads were turned by a willing world at their feet.

Finally he came, a man of medium height, sharp features, aquiline nose, full lips, even white teeth, a dimpled smile that despite herself, she couldn't help being charmed by. He was thin, his cheeks caved in slightly, and he had a boyish air about him, unusual in a man so important.

During the function he reminisced about his college days. When the bouquet presenting was over, he demanded to be taken to the canteen. He had many memories he wanted to relive.

It was just as well the canteen was not prepared for a rising young politician's visit; he might not have been able to relive his youth in a place that was less noisy, less ramshackle, less paan-splattered.

The tea that arrived in stained thick mugs was sweet and flavoured with cardamom, the fresh hot samosas were stuffed with crumbly spicy potato.

'Is it as you remember, sir?' Tapti asked, reminding herself that she was part of the welcome committee.

He nodded. They were introduced.

'Tapti Ahlawat?' he repeated, pleased that nothing had changed in the caste equations. In all his years in college he had never addressed a Rajput girl. 'Jat?'

She nodded. Jat like him. Everyone needed to be sure of everyone's caste. She had heard that in big cities such things did not matter, though it was hard to see how that was possible.

Himmat tried to ask another question but her embarrassment would not allow her to engage with him. Public attention was not welcome to girls of Tapti's upbringing. After her father died, the fact that circumstances made her vulnerable had been dinned into her head morning, noon and night. She had to be careful, careful, careful.

This hadn't always been so. There had been a carefree time, when she was growing up in a place that was paradise, known to the outside world as the Railway Colony. The house she lived in had a veranda, and in the evenings the family sat there to watch the light of the sun slowly fade from the hills beyond as they sipped their tea. Water shortages meant that the garden surrounding their bungalow was left wild and overgrown. Butterflies danced through unruly shrubs, bougainvillaea tossed their brilliance over boundary walls.

Her world was wrapped up in all the colony had to offer, cycling about the lanes with friends, free as the birds that wheeled about in the sky every evening, before settling down for the night in the surrounding trees. She was enveloped by happiness and love, but this was not something she knew until it was taken away.

Their lives changed after their father dropped dead of a heart attack when he was only thirty-nine. The railways offered the wife a job on compassionate grounds, but it could not be an officer's post, and she could not continue to inhabit an officer's quarters.

The family had to consider themselves lucky that they had enough money for a tiny domed house in Christian Colony. The building they were now forced to consider home had once stored supplies for the TB hospital run by the British. Clearly a storehouse needed neither a view of the hills nor a garden, and all they got was a step from the gate to the porch to a large airless room divided into two. The toilet and kitchen were arranged around a tiny angan.

Sometimes Tapti heard her mother cursing her father for dying young and leaving them so un-provided for. It was her kismet, otherwise men die and their wives continue to live in comfort; what happened here? At these moments Tapti put her arm around her mother's shoulder to offer words of consolation so inadequate that the mother had to smile.

Such was her situation when Himmat Singh Gaina phoned and asked to visit.

Two days later found him in the drawing room of Tapti's modest home. Her mother's agreement had contained an element of fear. Why was a politician paying them attention? Had Tapti encouraged him in some way?

The girl was outraged at this assumption, while her exasperation with Himmat Singh Gaina grew. Why couldn't

he keep himself to himself? Anyway he would be late. They
needn't bother laying out a lavish tea, everything would get cold
by the time he deigned to come.

But nothing had been allowed to get cold. He was there
on time, and that too without his deputy ministerial trappings.
They received him with some trepidation. Initially he focused
attention on the brother, a taller, more masculine version of the
sister. What was he doing? Law? A very good subject, always
jobs for lawyers, always people fighting.

Towards the end of the meeting Himmat casually
mentioned that it had been Tapti's downcast face that had
drawn his attention. Was she angry with him? He had found
out where she lived only because he didn't want to alienate even
one voter.

She said she didn't believe him. A politician could stand
disappointing people. That was proved by the two hours he had
kept them waiting. In the heat what's more.

Mrs Ahlawat exclaimed, the girl was too quick to speak,
she said whatever came into her head. Her brother added that
his sister had yet to realize that in society speech needs to be
carefully deliberated, especially if you were young and female.

But Himmat Singh Gaina merely said, as he looked at her,
'It is good. Otherwise how is it possible to know anybody?'

Her face grew hot and she wished he would go. Throughout
the evening the purpose of the meeting was not revealed,
contributing an edge to every sentence uttered. Finally the
mother said they were honoured by his visit, but they were
small people, he could see for himself how they lived. Since
the deputy minister of civil aviation and tourism must have a
thousand things on his mind, they didn't expect any further
interaction.

He left with an evasive reply that increased their uneasiness.
What was he getting out of it all?

A few weeks later this was made clear to their startled selves when his wife turned up with a proposal of marriage. She came unannounced, and on a horse so high their gazes never met throughout the visit.

How can this woman be his wife, thought Tapti. He was so friendly and she is so formal. Maybe she thinks our house is too modest. If so, she can go back to where she came from. We didn't ask her to come.

Mrs Sonal Gaina refused all offers of tea, biscuits, namkeen, mathri. It was clear that she was not to be fettered by food; this visit was going to be as short as possible. She moved little, and her handbag did not leave the shelter of her lap for a second.

Her husband was like a father to his younger brother. Though so bogged down with work that they hardly saw him, he was still taking the trouble to see his brother settled; his caring heart was one of the reasons people were drawn to him. Now he was the chief minister's right hand man, the youngest deputy cabinet minister in the history of Rajasthan. As to what the boy did, went on Mrs Gaina, answering all the questions she assumed an interested party would ask, he was a cement stockist in Ajmer, Naya Bazaar. They could go see for themselves. *Fine Quality Ajmer Cement* it was called. On top of that Mangal was an ambitious boy and wanted to expand. He had bought land near limestone deposits sixty kilometres beyond Ajmer and had begun to set up a cement factory.

In the pause that followed the mother said they had not been searching for an alliance. Her daughter had barely finished first year. They could commit to nothing.

Before their eyes they saw a stiff lady become stiffer. She would convey their feelings, she said as she rose to leave with the air of someone who had done her duty.

The rest of the day was spent in avid discussion. They had made their reluctance clear. And why would the location of

either the cement outlet or the cement factory interest them?
As though they even wanted to check.

Alone Tapti thought of the way he had looked at her in
the college canteen, the two questions he had asked, her
own misgivings at such direct attention. So, there had been
something behind it after all.

If there was one thing Himmat Singh Gaina knew, it was how
to be persistent. He presented himself as a friend, and came to
the Ahlawat household bearing gifts of fruit, nuts and sweets.
He heard the story of their Railway Colony days, the story of the
father's early death and the mother's struggle to give her children
the best possible education. This tiny house was all they had.

Himmat assured them that he identified with it all. He
himself had come to the city when he was about eleven–twelve,
almost illiterate, struggling for years to catch up with students
from the city. He was the first graduate in his entire village and
if anybody understood hardship it was he.

When Himmat dropped by with Mangal, Tapti became
quite upset. Why has he brought him, she thought, it was not
as though anything had been decided. A visit by the old and
married Himmat need have no particular significance, but
Mangal, young and single, was another story.

'This boy is so busy setting up his cement factory in Amberi,
that I hardly get to see him,' said Himmat, proceeding calmly
into the mother's flustered tea making. 'Never was interested
in studies. Wanted to join the real world as soon as possible.'

Mangal blushed but found little to say. It was up to Himmat
to do the talking, which he did until an hour was up.

'Soon the factory will be running. Another year or so.'

'You also go to Amberi?' asked Tapti shyly.

'Where is the time? I am in politics, he is in business,'
laughed Himmat. 'A good combination, don't you think?'

And they left.

The next time Himmat came, it was alone. 'What did you think of my brother?' he asked.

'It was nice meeting him; he seemed a sincere fellow, devoted to you,' temporized Ram Pratap.

'Yes,' said Himmat, 'Mangal is very conscious of the importance of family. We all are like that.'

And was he really the embryonic industrialist he claimed to be?

'I will take you to see his factory.'

But they could not agree to such a thing; it was showing excessive interest, and that too with nothing settled.

'Clearly he is very dependent on you,' remarked Mrs Ahlawat.

'Arre, it is my duty to help him. After all he is ten years younger. Our uncle brought both of us up. Just as well that Mangal still lives with him. When he is alone he starts to brood over his dead son.'

'Dead son?'

'Lost his only child at twenty-one. But let's not talk of that   it is too sad,' said Himmat. 'I'm here to tell you about my brother. Mangal's heart is pure gold. He is willing to work hard. In business that goes a long way, better than degrees. Look at the Marwaris, smart, successful, they don't bother with MBAs, they hire them instead.'

'I too want to do something significant. Why should I sit around doing nothing just because I am a woman?' said Tapti, showing little interest in Mangal.

'Beta, first comes family, then the outside world,' pointed out the mother, anxious to show that proper values were observed in her home.

'Don't worry. When the time comes, we will see to it,' said Himmat before he left.

After he was gone, the family went over the conversation in detail. They were beginning to feel hemmed in. Another visit by the politician and the mother's alarm grew proportionally.

They were not thinking of marriage right now. And Himmat must not come to the house so often. Ajmer was not a place where casual acquaintances could flourish without speculation. Rumours could ruin the reputation of a young girl.

But he was just a friend and he didn't come often.

Did he see the narrow gullies? Every time his car drove in, the neighbours noticed. Already she had heard comments.

He could leave his car some distance away.

Further ground for speculation. So, no, he could not come at all.

It is evening. Himmat Singh Gaina, Ram Pratap and Tapti are strolling through Daulat Bagh, the park that borders the Ana Sagar. Himmat has suggested this as a way of avoiding the rumours that could ruin the reputation of a young girl. They climb the steps to the parapet, and there before them is the broad lake built nine hundred years ago by Anaji Chauhan. They sit under one of the marble chattris; a cool breeze fans their faces, the setting sun gilds the water. Hawkers walk up and down, they buy peanuts.

'This takes me back to when I was young,' said Himmat. 'I would dive into the water, close my eyes and imagine I was in the pond at home. Only the buffaloes were missing.'

Tapti was moved. 'How far you have come,' she sighed.

He looked at her. 'Yes. In the village, I would never be talking to a girl like you.'

She laughed.

Ram Pratap fidgeted. It made him uncomfortable, the attention this man gave his sister. Once she was married, she would be safe.

'I will be away on deputation in Delhi for the next two years,' said Himmat suddenly.

The peanuts Tapti was crunching suddenly tasted like dry sand.

'I will always be your friend,' he continued, staring at the clouds that were tinted with the rosiness of the setting sun. 'But I must know what you think about marrying my brother.'

'My sister,' burst out Ram Pratap, 'is very headstrong. Doesn't listen to anybody.'

Tapti looked down. Was she headstrong? It never felt like that, she only had a keen sense of what she needed to live.

'Whether or not you come into my family, I will help you realize your dreams in whatever way I can,' said Himmat. 'Marriage should not mean the end of public service. Even for women.'

Only later, much later, did Tapti realize the importance of the promise he had made her.

The roka ceremony between Tapti Ahlawat and Mangal Singh Gaina took place a few months later. As Tapti looked at Mangal, garlanded, a red tilak on his forehead, she saw the reflection of the person whose picture she had photocopied so carefully for the Annual Day. That man had been grinning as though he owned the world; this one looked more preoccupied.

Himmat explains the steady absence of his wife by an overwhelming sense of duty. 'Her father doesn't keep well you know, she is like a son to them, especially since her brother is in the US. And she is very particular about Amar and Shweta's studies.'

'Why can't they miss a day or two of school? Father's own brother getting engaged!' cried Mrs Ahlawat.

'Exams,' said Himmat briefly.

'It is all right, Ma, we can get to know each other later,' said Tapti.

'Of course. And I am there, no?' His grin was conspiratorial, and looking at him, Tapti knew that here, above all, was the acceptance that filled her with confidence about the future. His word counted for everything in his family; she already recognized she would live in the shadow of his protection.

Tapti was in third year when her wedding ceremony took place in the neighbourhood, a pandal covered colony park affair. Cooks blocked the slip road, the band with their gas lights blocked another road. Generators roared, and while the pair got married in a corner, interminably through the night, the guests ate, drank and left. Towards morning, the bride rested in her own home before leaving for Jaipur, where the reception was going to be held.

It was a reception that glittered with people who had no personal connection to the newly-weds, glittered with the brief appearance of the chief minister, glittered with politicians and social climbers who flashed importance and consequence as they casually congratulated the couple seated on red velvet thrones, surrounded by the giggling young.

Mrs Ahlawat, dressed in her best widow white sari, watched her daughter smiling for numerous photo ops among people whose faces she had only seen in newspapers. Despite everything, the choice was a good one. If the cement factory succeeded, her daughter would never want for anything. She noticed Himmat's wife study the bride speculatively. Notwithstanding the single unpromising visit to their house, she hoped Sonal would accept her sister-in-law, if only in the interests of family harmony.

The next day Himmat personally escorted the bridal pair back to Ajmer. Your new daughter-in-law, he announced to his uncle and aunt.

Tapti bent to touch their feet, her palla almost down till her eyes out of respect. The uncle is dressed in a white kurta pyjama. His lengthened earlobes dangle with heavy gold earrings. The aunt wears a Rajasthani long skirt, her own head also covered by a dupatta.

They bless her with sons and a long married life.

III

2010

Any thought of the past fills Tapti with anguish. How had she started and how had she ended up. Did her fault lie in her karma or in her character? One step had led to another, as is the nature of steps. Now this.

She had longed for love all her life, and like a famished fledgling abandoned from its nest, had found herself hopping from tree to tree, hoping to find it. But whatever she had found had been sullied.

What about her husband? He had loved her so in the beginning; never stopped saying he wanted her to live like a queen. But when the factory began to run into difficulties, she had studied for the civil services, passed the exams and grown in the bureaucracy. She had minions of her own, she was substantial, but to have a wife with a career had never ceased to be an assault on Mangal's sensibilities.

In life you have to develop a thick skin or you are dead. Hadn't she shrugged off all her sister-in-law's insults? Sonal of the persistent cold and disapproving face, the face no amount of friendliness could ever thaw. It had taken years but now nothing from that direction could wound her.

While there was her husband, brooding over every wrong he felt had been done to him, as though people had set out to hurt him deliberately. Everybody held their interests as primary, their perceptions the prism through which the world was judged. If you only looked at the bad you could end up with your own life decimated.

Her mind drifted back to the many ways Mangal had tried to please her. It wasn't easy, given his background, for a man to try and please a woman, but she knew he had struggled to break through those constraints. Maybe it had been a mistake to marry out of her class and station – but what to do when the junior minister for aviation himself comes to woo?

Mrs Ahlawat wanders after her, as lost, but not as silent. 'Beta, thank god your father is not here to see this. It would have killed him, he would have blamed himself for allowing the marriage to go through. The elder brother was of course very good, but you were not marrying him, were you? You remember, I always felt uneasy?'

As this gentle poisoned stream swirled around Tapti, she roused herself enough to say, 'No I don't. What I remember is all the times you said it was a good match. When things were going well?'

Her mother looked confused. If there was such a time, it had been wiped out of her memory so completely that recollection became a major act of faith.

'Anyway what should I do now? Kill myself?'

'Hai beta, don't talk like that. Think of your children.'

'Let them see how much suffering there is in the world,' cried the angry mother. 'If they expect nothing, they will never be disappointed.'

'They are young, impressionable. You want to harm them more? Be sensible.'

These threats were not easy for Tapti to withstand, and her mother used them in every way she could. Think of your children, think of them, think, think, think.

It was her mother who ultimately took a more sanguine view. The case would definitely go on for years. And in those years anything was possible. Look how long it took Jessica Lal's killer to be convicted, and that too when she was shot in front of two hundred people.

So what if witnesses run into hundreds? In India that meant nothing; it had meant nothing when a train was stopped and passengers set on fire in Godhra; it had meant nothing when a family was trapped and burnt inside Best Bakery in Gujarat before a mob of five hundred, not one of whom had yet been brought to justice; it meant nothing when thousands of innocent Sikhs were killed after Indira Gandhi's assassination, again not one brought to justice. Witnesses turn hostile, evidence vanishes, years pass and nothing is proved.

Tapti on the phone to her brother.

'Have you seen him?'

'I have.'

'How is he?'

'He says he is at peace.'

'I wish I could claim the same for myself.'

'Would he want you to visit, I asked.'

'What did he say?'

'Something that made no sense.'

'Which was?'

'He said you were your own mistress. What did that mean?'

'I don't know.'

'And it made no difference what you did. But I know how much he cares for you, we all know.'

For a moment she felt humiliated. Her husband was exposing the fractures in her marriage, which meant that Ramu would pity her.

'How long are the visiting hours?'

'Thirty minutes. He hasn't yet put you on the visitor list. Probably unused to all this. Who can blame him? Should I tell him you want to see him? Maybe he feels ashamed, so it's up to you.'

Up to you, up to you, what did that mean? If anything had really been up to her, she would have cut and run years ago, cut and run when the misery in her marriage grew, cut and run when she became financially secure, cut and run when her feelings led her elsewhere. But escape only remained a fantasy, frequent but inert.

'Maybe it will boost his morale if he sees you,' continued Ram Pratap. 'He seems to be in no mood to even defend himself. In our half an hour together he had very little to say.'

'I'm not sure. The last time I saw him was not so good –'

'Arre, what is there? This up and down between husbands and wives is just daily life. But when something happens, who else is there to stand by you?'

'Yes, I suppose you are right.'

Three months later Tapti catches the morning Shatabdi for Delhi. Alone and free of the concern of others, she stares at the landscape, the distant Aravalli hills, the fields in the foreground. She can see a white figure against the darkness of the earth; a farmer striding along purposefully, his dhoti billowing with the movement of his legs, arms swinging, figure straight. The pagri around his head gleams pale yellow and voluminous. Her husband's ancestors had walked like this over land they loved. Some people cannot survive once

uprooted. Had marrying her led Mangal to jail? In many ways
he had already seemed imprisoned, especially once he moved
to his petrol pump. Till then there had been hope. They were
young, there was time for things to get better. Once the money
started to flow, his ambition resurrected until it became a
wedge between them, then a wall, then a fortress as sturdy and
as strong as the ones built by the kings of Rajputana, which
despite centuries could be seen, still standing, on various
hilltops through the state.

Delhi Cantonment, fifteen minutes away from Tihar Jail.
The sight of her brother distracts her from her apprehension.
She links her arm through his for a moment, before he takes the
bag with things meant for the prisoner.

'Tapti. Trip all right? Children? Ma?'

'All fine. And he?'

'He. You will see.'

So. It was bad. She said no more as they pushed their way
up the stairs, across the platform, down the stairs, jostling
with the crowds, her eyes fixed on his back to make sure
she did not lose him in the human mass that wove between
them.

As their car joins the line of exiting vehicles she asks, 'You
are certain he has put me on the visitor list?'

'I wouldn't have called you otherwise.'

'How is he? Living conditions? I don't suppose you
know?'

'Of course I do, I am a criminal lawyer, remember. He
will have been put in with other undertrials, forty or fifty to a
barrack, ten barracks to each unit, about five hundred men in
one building. His company will be addicts, rapists, murderers,
thieves, though each one claims innocence. It was someone
else, the police just picked on me. It is always like that – only
Mangal is different – admitting to what he did. He has told the

other prisoners he is there because of a family feud – they don't know his face, haven't seen the news.'

Tihar Jail. Tapti hangs behind Ram Pratap as he negotiates formalities through a small barred opening in the heavy gate. Standing on the pavement she notices the thick petalled orange flowers of the silk cotton tree caught in coils of barbed wire above the massive brick walls. Finally they are allowed in. Now she has a connection with Tihar, a place that has had no reason to exist in her consciousness, a place in which over thirteen thousand prisoners are compressed; double the original capacity.

From window to window she follows her brother, booking counter, entry counter, checking counter, a second checking counter, father's name, name of the accused, visitor's name, relationship with accused, which ward, which barrack, what status (undertrial). Ladies body search, gents body search, cell phone confiscated, handbag investigated, clothes and food for the prisoner scrutinized, money for the prisoner taken with receipt issued.

They walk down the path towards the interview room of Ward 3. There the whole process is repeated. Registration, thumb impression, body inspection, items for the prisoner examined.

They sit silently on the benches against the wall of the outer room, waiting for their prisoner to be called. When their turn comes, the time they enter is inked on one of their palms, no argument about the number of minutes spent. It will be over in half an hour, thinks Tapti. Half an hour.

They are ushered towards a window with a one foot wall jutting out from either side. There he is behind the grill. He has lost weight, his clothes are limp and somewhat soiled. From where would he get fresh ones? She herself has not sent any, not even thought of it. Her brother pushes her forward. She rests her hands on the ledge, and stares at this man who has become a murderer. Where is the peace he claims the deed has given him; there is no evidence of it.

What could she do now, what hope could she offer, what solace, when every moment of the day she felt in need of these very things? He would either get the death sentence or spend the rest of his life in jail. How could she see him and hang on to her anger?

Ram Pratap clears his throat. Husband and wife are not talking and time is passing. 'My sister is very worried about you,' he starts.

Tapti fiddles with her purse. The prisoner can see the slight movement of her shoulders; the rest of her is hidden.

'It would help if she knew why you did it. Right now it is very difficult. Journalists always wanting to interview her, to know if this was planned, what does she think, many things like that.'

Tapti starts to speak, then stops and looks at her husband. He pushes his hair behind his ears. It is longer than usual, and his cheekbones are in relief.

'Forgive me,' she mouths.

He says something, but she cannot make out the words.

'What?' shouts Ram Pratap. 'We cannot hear.'

But he just shakes his head and gazes unspeaking at his wife. She drops her eyes to focus on her fists clenched over her handbag. Finally Ram Pratap begins talking of legal remedies. It is a relief to both brother and sister when the guard standing near them announces their time is up.

'There are a lot of drug addicts in Ward 3,' says Ramu to break the silence, as they walk down the high walled path towards the heavy barred gates of the entrance. 'They used to get drugs from outside, injected into fruit or sweets that visitors brought.

That's why they don't allow outside food any more; you have to buy it from the prison canteen or their bakery.'

Tapti looks around. Outside this compound are the usual Delhi crowds, noise, traffic, vendors, shops, pavement sellers, buildings and shacks all piled together; here it is quiet and ordered, pleasant, almost rural. There is a neem tree next to an armed guard standing on a small covered platform. They walk by and a small wind dislodges the delicate yellow leaves from the branches, they whirl about frantically before resting on the broad concrete path. In the distance the caught flowers in the barbed wire are still visible.

As they leave they register their exit, once, twice. They are ushered out through a small door set within massive gates, metal clad, so that no one can see in, no one can see out. In the car Tapti starts sobbing; heavy breathless sobs. To see her husband like this was to comprehend the meaning of prison for the first time. He was only forty-eight, with years, decades ahead of him, all spent in Tihar, overcrowded, confined and observed. Was anything worth it, this terrible loss of autonomy, all freedom, all hope?

'It is not so bad,' says her brother awkwardly.

She shakes her head and continues with her tears.

'What did he say to you?'

'I couldn't make out.'

'He's probably getting used to it.'

'Do you think he is suffering? Do you think they treat him kindly?'

'He does not complain.'

Ram Pratap drops her to Bikaner House, so she can catch the coach back home.

By now it is almost night and she can no longer see outside. She stares at the reflection of her face in the darkened window.

How unsubstantial she looked. To distract herself she forces
herself to leaf through a newspaper. Her eyes scan various
headlines, murder and rape leap out at her. Despite its vaunted
spirituality, India is a bloodthirsty nation. Murder because you
gave money, because you owed money, because you loved, or
didn't love, because you were one religion or another, because
you ate a particular kind of meat, because you were jealous of
another's freedom, or furious at being rejected, or enraged that
you were overtaken on the road, anything served as a pretext.
Yes, murder was the flavour of the day in India. Seen in this
context, what her husband did was not so unusual. Bad yes, but
not extraordinary.

Ram Pratap on the phone to his sister. 'He is talking more.'
    'What is he saying?'
    'He wants to know how he can be seen as a criminal when
he didn't hide what he did. He behaved according to the honour
code of the Jats, allowed the police to record his statement,
assumed responsibility for what he had done.'
    'Did he tell you what honour code he was talking about?'
    'About that he was vague. What he does mind is that there
is no one to pull strings for him so he can get more benefits.
Food, allowances, comparative freedom within the prison, jobs
as lowly administrators, power over other inmates, all this is
beyond his reach. In a way I admire him.'
    'Why?'
    'Whatever drove him to do this – and he is not saying – no
matter how much I probe – at least he had the guts to act on
how he felt.'
    'He has ruined all our lives.'
    'Yes, well. When were you planning your next visit?'
    'Why?'
    'He's been asking.'

Judging by how little they had to say to each other she found that hard to believe. But perhaps silence was of little consequence; perhaps despite everything, he knew he could rely on her. To go on thinking he had brought this upon himself now seemed so limited. If he wanted to see her haggard face, let him. After all there was the question of her penance as well.

'Maybe he just wants to know he is not forgotten,' says her brother, prodding her into speech.

'Hoon.'

'So what should I tell him?'

Indeed, what should he tell him? Tell him she hoped he was happy, now that his brother was dead, now that he had massacred all their lives, their peace, their happiness. That she was glad he was a prisoner, at the mercy of warders and guards.

'Tapti? What should I tell him? You know he is allowed visitors twice a week?'

'Is he saying I should come twice a week?'

'You know he makes no such demands.'

A pause.

'He has met some journalist woman.'

'What did she want?'

'It's more what he wants. He wants her to write a book about the whole thing.'

'Finally he has gone crazy.'

'He feels he has acted in the interests of justice. He wants someone to tell the world that.'

'Naturally. Because he hasn't seen the newspapers, the magazines, the supplements, the TV, he doesn't know how much has already been said about him, about his brother, about his motives, about his village background, about Jat notions of revenge.'

'Well, he wants his story to be told by someone who knows how to convince. People believe him to be guilty. The judges, the prosecuting lawyers will read the book, or at least hear about it.'

'What do you think? Will it help? A book takes a long time to write. The trial may be decided by then.'

Ram Pratap Ahlawat snorted. 'Legally it will make no difference. The case will be argued on merit, not on compassion. And Mangal is not a fool, whatever else he is.'

'Then?'

'Well, he seems to think he has a story to tell. He was very insistent with the journalist. Only if she committed herself to a book would he speak to her. Permanence is what he is looking for.'

Mrs Ahlawat to her daughter. 'What news from Delhi, beta?'

'Ramu says Mangal is very involved in some book about him.'

'Why does he want a book?' demanded Mrs Ahlawat with the suspicion mothers perfect. 'Hasn't enough been said already?'

'He thinks it might help.'

'Has a mad dog bitten him? Nothing can help. What does Ramu think?'

'Won't help, but can't harm. Ramu of course will do everything he can to defend him.'

'With lies.'

'Yes, well, Mama. Only if those lies contain a bit of truth will they be successful.'

'Why doesn't he just die? What is the need to guard him day and night? Such men don't deserve to live.'

Tapti stared at her mother, 'Please don't talk like that. He is the father of my daughters.'

'Look at what he has done.'

'But I too am responsible, do you wish me dead? Don't you remember how he was when we first met? Full of hope, love as well. He wanted to marry me, though I could give him nothing, no dowry, no connections, just a poor girl from nowhere.'

Mrs Ahlawat looked at her sharply, 'What has gone wrong with you? How are you a poor girl from nowhere? Your father was a respectable railway officer, we have always held our heads high. Always. No scandal, nothing, till he came along.'

'He could say the same about me.'

'Oh yes? And you were the one whose finger pulled the trigger? Who went to the Jan Sunwai with a pistol? He is not the only one who is mad. You are too.'

But even this taunt could not rouse Tapti to anger. She sat there looking so lifeless that her mother wanted to slap her. Each succeeding day leached the spirit out of her. If the act hadn't been so public, if he had just disappeared quietly, her poor daughter would still have managed to piece together her life. Now they were forced to think about him all the time. If this book was ever published, she would not read it. 'You don't have to go to Delhi,' she told her daughter for the hundredth time, 'you owe him nothing.'

Tapti sighed. Her mother hated Mangal. As far as she was concerned, the death sentence could not come a minute too soon. But she had lost so much, it made no sense to lose more. She blamed him, as did the whole world, but she blamed herself too. Seeing him in prison was a sign of her loyalty.

~

Tapti on her way to jail, this time more prepared: the night bus, the taxi, meeting Ram Pratap outside the prison gates, identity

verification, visitor slip, body search, buying coupons, the dry
fruit, biscuits, sweets and namkeen opened and checked and
ultimately slid into the funnel that separated the visitor from
the prisoner.

She didn't mind that she had to meet him in that dreadful
room and shout across the grill, didn't mind that words got lost.
She saw him because he was her husband, not out of a desire to
communicate. Now more than ever she was linked to him.

Mangal Singh Gaina stares at his wife through the wire
mesh and notices the changes in her. For the first time her age
is apparent; she had always appeared so young. He can see the
faint line from her nose to her mouth, the frown line between
her eyebrows partly obscured by her neat round red bindi. He
looks at the sindhoor in her parting; imagines the fine body
that he would never know again. When he was given the death
penalty her sindhoor would have to go.

When she speaks her voice is so low he has to strain to hear.
'The children keep wanting to know what will happen. Will
Ramu Mama succeed in getting you out? They don't even want
to meet their friends.'

'They will marry, change their names, they will be all right.'

After a pause, he says 'Are you helping that journalist?'

'No.'

'Did she get in touch with you?'

'She tried.'

'Then?'

'I don't want any more people prying into my life.'

'She is doing her best,' said Ram Pratap, 'only so many
journalists are after her, you do not know. All wanting to know
what really happened, what was the history, she is totally fed
up, has to hire a guard to keep them away. Naturally the topic
upsets her. You must not take tension, everything is being
done.'

Mangal looked dissatisfied, but when you are in jail, there is little you can do about your situation. He shrugged, then turned to the lawyer.

Why couldn't he go back to Jaipur, he asked. The crime was committed there. This was an overcrowded brutal place. He needed money, money for the warders, the munshis, the subedars just to be treated as a normal human being.

Conciliatory words followed. He mustn't get impatient, it would not be possible to move back to Jaipur. IPPP rage against him was greater in Rajasthan, and more security meant more expense. Even in Delhi, the last time Mangal had gone to court, IPPP supporters had attacked the arriving van with stones. There were other prisoners destined for Tees Hazari along with him and there had been complaints.

Once the case had been transferred to Delhi, no judge would agree to shift the venue again. Besides he had a better chance of getting a fair trial here.

The legal discussion takes a while. Murder is a non-bailable offence, but still the lawyer has put in an application. It was up to the discretion of the court. If doctors declared his health to be poor, that could be a consideration. Then there was the matter of the bond, the money required would be considerable.

'Finish, finish,' said the warder near them. Ram Pratap looked at the time penned on his palm. Yes, half an hour was over. Tapti nods silently at her husband as they turn to go. She can feel his eyes following her; seconds later he too would be taken away. No more forced conversation, no more forced cheerfulness.

All around she can see families of prisoners, children, women, men, old and young. Some were well dressed like her, some judging from their clothes seemed lower middle class, many appeared poor. There were women who had babies, babies they carried on their hips down the long pathways of the jail complex, deposited on cement floors to play while their

mothers waited. She could draw no comfort from knowing
she was not alone, only misery. Misery for herself and for all
these others, who in fact didn't look so miserable. They were
chatting to their companions, chatting as though it was normal
to embed prison visits into their routine. But how could anyone
know another's life?

One month later.

Delhi Cantt. Ram Pratap is waiting on the platform. No
matter how much Tapti tried not to impose on him, when the
time came, she could not bear to make the Tihar visit alone,
could not bear the scrutiny, the registry, the curious stares,
stares that saw her life history stamped on her face. She smiles
a smile of careful cheerfulness.

'How is Sonal Bhabhi?' asks Ram Pratap searching for
another topic besides the man in jail.

'I really wouldn't know.'

'No contact yet?'

'None.'

'Must be hard for her.'

'Not harder than it is for me. She is still living in the CM's
house, she doesn't have to run up and down between Jaipur and
Delhi, no journalists are bothering her.'

'You don't know that.'

'Oh, what does anything matter?'

'Tapti, don't be bitter. How does it help?'

'I haven't told you how she treated me when I went to see
Uncle. Threw me out of the house. Started raving and ranting,
as though all this was my fault. Am I the one who shot him?
Does she think I wanted him dead? But no, the wife has to be
blamed for whatever the husband does.'

'She has lost everything.'

'So have I.'

Ram Pratap said nothing.

'Do you know what he used to say?'

'What?' He was always the brother-in-law, never any need to ask.

'"Once I retire I will write my history. How many stories have there been like mine? From dung heap to chief minister?" He wanted me to help him. Of course I said I would – and now –'

'Yes, yes, maybe you can still do it,' murmured the brother.

'After this whoever writes about him will focus on his death. What is the truth, the inside story; it can never be a simple account of rise from village to CM, can it? It will always be about Mangal as well . . . and me . . .'

'Bas, bas,' murmured Ram Pratap, trying to soothe and drive at the same time, grateful that it would not take long to reach prison.

Silence while Tapti slipped one of her brother's CDs into the player, the best of A.R. Rahman. The words from 'Arziyan', *Delhi 6* dropped into the car. 'Repair my fortunes my Lord, At Your door, I bow, I am vanquished, I am made, Repair my fortunes my Lord.'

Tears started rolling down her cheeks. At her sobs her brother pulled over to the side of the road, while cars veered and honked around them. 'What is it, has anything happened, anything more than usual?' 'No, nothing, come on, let's go.' Ram Pratap edged back into the traffic, looking at his sister worriedly. Women were too delicate to go through this kind of thing. Almost every trip to Mangal involved tears, but at least with him she was able to release her feelings. After which he would return to his own life, whereas for her there was never any escape.

The mulaqaat room. Tapti puts on the headphones, newly installed, possible now to hear without shouting. With Ramu there, her own time is cut short, something she is glad of. Out of the one hour she spends face to face with him every month, fifteen to twenty minutes are shaved off in this way.

'How are you?'

'Fine.'

'Food?'

'All right.'

'What is it?'

'One dal, one sabzi, rice, roti.'

'Same, every day?'

He smiles, 'Not a hotel after all.'

She makes her own attempt at smiling, 'No, not a hotel.' Pause. 'What are the other prisoners like?'

'Not prisoners. Undertrials.'

'Have you made friends?'

'Very low people. No values.'

'Ramu says you are working with the cows.'

'Yes.'

'That is nice?'

'Cows are what I am used to.'

'Do you like that?'

'I've ended where I started. As though I never left, never did anything. Maybe that was my karma.'

'Yes. Well.'

'How is your office? Is it – do they – is it all right?'

In another place, at another time, she might have wept with gratitude to hear this question from him; he who never asked about her work, who never wanted to know what exactly she was doing.

Now she tried to gauge his sincerity, but she could make out nothing from his expression. 'To my face they don't dare say anything,' she said carefully. 'As to what goes on behind my back, how does that concern me? People talk. You can't stop them. I would be dead long ago if I bothered about such things.'

They stare at each other, the words they don't say reverberating between them, echoes heard by both, understood differently by both. Then the time is up and another jail visit over.

Conflicting feelings jostling about in her heart as usual, Tapti takes the metro to the New Delhi Railway Station, to pick her way through crowds rushing along the overhead platform, sidestepping metal boxes, holdalls, bags, baskets, suitcases. With just a backpack she is without a coolie, nudged and pushed by the masses pouring along stairs as dense as molten lava. As she hurries along the waiting carriages of the Jaipur Shatabdi, looking for her bogey, she realizes the paving stones on the platform have been relaid; it is now grey kota which gives the dirt a certain cachet.

Finally her carriage, and a seat next to a grimy green paned window. It takes her hours to recover from a visit to Tihar. Sorrow bubbles in her heart like water in a fountain, recycled endlessly. Not only was there Mangal, there were all the other inmates, caged like animals, with expressions meek and mild, prey to any violence dished out. Did Mangal cringe when an official approached him? Could he swear at imagined insults as he had done at home, object to the ways in which people spoke to him, vow that he would show so and so? Would he last one day in prison with this attitude?

As she gazes at the Rajasthani landscape rushing past, she wonders, what does it take to rise from a village, what? The people there are as tied to the earth as the scrubby trees, as fed and watered by it as the cattle.

The Gaina dislocation had started with Virpal Uncle leaving his home eighty years ago, swearing to never return till he had made something of himself, no matter how long it took nor how hard he had to work.

Virpal may not have realized that when he left his village, he left it with a rope tied around his waist, a rope that lengthened with every step without showing signs of fraying. Like a cord attached to a bucket in a well, it served to pull and pull and pull. It had to be strong enough to stretch from brother to brother, from generation to generation.

Uncle. Would they manage to keep the news from him till the day he died? Maybe they were lying when they said he hadn't been told, using this as an excuse to not let her see him. How would she ever know the truth about anything? What was clear was that he too was lost to her. He had been a giant, with a life that was rich and colourful, but since he had not achieved worldly success, he was little talked of. But his had been the first step, his the shoulders on which Himmat had stood.

SECTION II
Virpal/Himmat

I

1930–1940

Virpal (caste: Jat, subcaste: Gaina) belonged to the village of Lalbanga, east of Ajmer. The raja of Kishangarh owned both the land and the produce. Out of ten bags of grain, three were returned to the farmer and on that he had to live. Famines periodically sweep the region, villagers periodically starve. The land here is dry, the earth a light powdery brown. In order to facilitate irrigation, the raja builds the Taj Sarovar, a huge lake that feeds canals in eight of his surrounding villages. Much depends on this precious water. When the rain is plentiful, the lake fills, the wells rise, and crops are planted twice in the year. When rainfall is scanty, there is only enough water for one sowing, and consequently less to eat. In these years men take their cattle further south, where the soil is fertile, foraging there until the next rains make the land green again.

Braided twig fences divide the properties, the huts are made of mud and cow dung. The villagers live, eat, cook, sleep on the floor, their clothes and bedding are slung around pegs in the wall, suspended too are their few tin trunks. Cows share their living space. The earth is their mother, animals their benefactors.

Caste lines divide the village. There are Jats, Rajputs, Bhils, Yadavs, Gujjars, Malis, who largely live as rivals, doing their duty to god by preserving the distinctions he had created with all the vigour at their disposal.

The day that saw Virpal's life shifting from its usual course began with an altercation over a few dusty leaves. While minding the family cattle, the boy had allowed them to munch from bushes some Rajputs claimed were theirs. In the ensuing fight a cow was seized, and Lal Singh, his father, attacked. For this Virpal was blamed, abused and thrashed. It was the natural order of things for beatings to flow from the stronger to the weaker, from older to younger, from male to female.

'You are too sensitive, like a girl,' says his mother as she rubs ghee on his bruises. 'We cannot afford to lose anything, no rain for a year or two and we will starve. Now to get the cow back we will have to involve the panchayat, it's a long business.' Virpal shrugs off her hand, and she is too busy to coax him further.

Dhanpal creeps up to him, all interest in playing lost if his brother cannot join. There he remains, still as the earth he squats upon. The silence is broken by the faint rustle and click of broad peepul leaves brushing against each other. He only moves when his father demands to know if he has turned into the boy's mother.

As the night wears on, Virpal is overcome by a great disgust at the way he lives. Only recently a visiting minstrel had relayed news of Gandhiji and the march to Dandi. Standing on a small platform around a giant banyan tree he had spoken loud and clear of the thousands who had joined him, of the salt laws that were broken, of lathi charges, of the courage it took to go on collecting seawater to make salt. Now the prisons are full, not with criminals, but with people who sacrificed everything for their ideals.

All Virpal knew about Gandhiji was that he dressed in a simple dhoti, like any peasant, and that this was the man leading the fight against the British. He would go to Ajmer, the biggest place within his reach and participate in the struggle.

He gets up before dawn, his stiff body gradually relaxing as he moves. No one sees him go. It will take him three days to reach his destination. Towards evening of the first day, as the sun begins to sink, he walks across fields until he comes to a village. He only has to appear at the doorway of a Jat home for a mat to be laid and food to be served: roti with a dollop of ghee, a little dal, garlic-chilli chutney and a glass of thin sour-salty buttermilk. He sleeps on the floor in the angan. At dawn he pushes on, with a dry roti from the night before.

No one will miss him, he thinks, except Dhanpal. Two years younger, this boy was his shadow, following him to the pond, the fields, to where the cattle grazed. When there was nothing more important to do, the brothers amused themselves by listening to the pandit give lessons under a tree. Such sporadic attendance was not unusual. The pandit received his fees in grain and ghee, and accepted the low priority studying had in the lives of his students.

We must learn, Virpal would urge Dhanpal, but Dhanpal saw no point in it. There were pandits and letter writers to deal with the written word, why waste hours over such a useless enterprise? Their father, a sarpanch, was illiterate, and he was the most powerful man they knew.

Already Virpal had begun to feel lonely, so used was he to his brother trotting after him. Dhanpal would be hurt that he had been left behind. One day, he vowed, when he had worked beside Gandhiji and made something of himself, he would call his brother and teach him all he knew. That is, if he didn't die first. Under his breath he began to mutter the Hanuman Chalisa as protection. It lay beyond him to imagine that in the

succeeding years Dhanpal would travel much further than he
himself would ever go.

On the third day Virpal reaches Martindale Bridge. He is
bewildered by the view of the city from this height, the number
of buildings, the rows of shops, the many tongas, the people.
He sinks to the pavement and, not knowing what to do, shuts
his eyes, his chador around him. An hour later a stranger will
poke him with his shoe.

Gaur Sahib takes a walk every evening. As he climbs the gentle
incline towards the haveli he has bought with his life's savings,
accumulated as a clerk in the British railway offices in Ajmer, he
can hear dogs barking, and because he has a poetic bent of mind
he likens them to the barking of the nation when confronted
with Gandhiji, the present day Messiah.

He finds this man disturbing. At the moment he is in
prison, having broken British salt laws. Gaur Sahib sees this as
implicit criticism of his own service to the imperial master. Of
course the poor suffer because of the salt tax, but in marching to
the sea so publicly, this man has drawn attention to everyone's
moral frailties.

The Mahatma would want all government jobs boycotted so
that the non-violent struggle of the Indian National Congress
is carried into every sphere of life. Who would feed his family
then? When it was India's destiny to be free, the British would
leave and not a day before.

Besides Gandhiji was always going on about Muslims, toilets,
scavenging, Harijans, temple entries. Gaur Sahib shudders at
this horrible mixing of castes. Social change may be inevitable,
but cleaning toilets should be left to those born to do it.

Gaur Sahib is a Brahmin and he thinks there are other ways
to protect the motherland. The nascent organization he is part
of, the Bharat Jagrit Sabha, sees itself as the preserver of Hindu

tradition, teaching young men to be proud of their heritage. Their bodies are built through yoga, surya namaskar, archery, kabaddi and pure vegetarian food.

Now as he prods the inert body in front of him, he wonders whether the day will ever come when the poor of this country don't have to sleep on pavements. The boy opens his eyes, good he is alive. He leads him to his house situated in one of the gullies leading off Naya Bazaar.

Virpal sits on the floor, listening to the hiss and pump of the kerosene stove inside the kitchen, the scratch of a thali against the floor as dough is kneaded. Four thick hot rotis with a blob of white butter slowly pooling in the middle are put before him, with a small bowl of dal, green chillies, and some spicy mango chutney. He eats slowly.

Gaur Sahib's wife is used to her husband's eccentricities, but he has never picked up waifs from the street before. 'Who is he?' she ventures.

'Found him on the bridge.'

'We can't take in anyone just like that. What is his caste? You hear of so many bad things happening.'

'Arre, he is just a child. How old are you, beta?'

The boy looks at his glass of tea.

'They don't know their age.'

He looks up. 'Twelve.'

'How do you know?'

Every year their vanshavalli came to record the births, deaths and marriages in their caste, mumbled the boy to the floor. For the first time in his life he was in a Brahmin home. Everything about the haveli overwhelmed him, the marble floors, the cement walls, a miraculous pump, and the fact that he was being fed.

'I have come to fight alongside Gandhiji,' he now said.

'How will you find him? He is in prison after breaking the salt laws. Is that where you want to go?'

Gaur Sahib's wife tittered. 'Arre, you have to be important to be arrested.'

Virpal carefully put the big steel glass down. 'If I can stay here,' he said, 'I will work for you.'

Before he could stay, they wanted the truth. Why had he left his home?

The boy remained silent. 'See what happens when you pick up vagrants from the street. Suppose he is a thief, a murderer?' demanded Gaur Sahib's wife.

'If we don't look after these children, the missionaries will. They will say Yesu Crist has sent them. You want that?'

It is decided that the boy will sleep on the roof, the door leading to it will be bolted, so he can neither escape nor harm them. The very next day Gaur Sahib will take him to the temple where the Bharat Jagrit Sabha has built a complex large enough to house a boy indefinitely. Of course the boy will have to work, but he has already offered to do that.

∽

The priest associated with this temple does not think of philanthropy as part of his religious duties. The care of humans is left to god, destiny and karma. His role is to interpret the scriptures and to provide the knowledge needed to perform various pujas.

'I can't keep him here,' he said. If every runaway was to be looked after, what would happen to the sanctity of the temple? The boy could be some outcaste, hoping to escape into the anonymity a city provides.

Gaur Sahib frowned. Why was the spirit of social service so absent in their pandits? Look at Christian preachers, embracing every low caste, setting up schools, spreading their religion through education and charity. Left to themselves they would convert all of Hindustan.

It was not as though the kitchen would be polluted, he said. The boy would stay in one of the outhouses, cook his own food and run errands for the priest when he came back from school.

At the thought of a free servant, the priest brightened. 'Why bother with education?' he remarked. 'Village boys, and Jats at that, are not capable of brain work.'

Impatiently Gaur Sahib got up. As he turned to go, the boy hastily touched his feet. He is a simple, sincere child thought the older man, the priest will soon realize that. 'Come to the haveli in the morning, I will take you to school,' he said as he left.

Virpal wondered whether his caste was the reason the Brahmin wouldn't keep him in his household. He could always run away again if living in the temple became intolerable.

Once alone, the priest glared at the boy.

'Don't expect to be swaddled in velvet here.'

The boy said nothing.

'Where are you from?'

No reply.

'You think somebody or the other is bound to look after you. No?'

Silence.

'What's your name?'

'Virpal.'

'Caste?'

'Gaina.'

'You say you are a Jat?'

'Yes.'

He lifted his head up a bit, showing the aggressive traits that marked a Jat. Such tendencies had to be stamped out. 'There is the broom. Start sweeping. And run any errand my wife tells you to. All right? You will sleep in that storeroom there. Once you have finished the chores, you can cook your own meals. We are not running a dharamshala. Understand?'

'Yes.'

'So – you want to go to school? Become a big man?'

Virpal's downward gaze galvanized the priest to greater fury.

'Just be glad you met a man like him. Otherwise the police would have picked you up and thrown you in jail. This place is run by the English. They don't tolerate vagabonds.'

Let the priest go on talking, Virpal did not care. To share his living quarters with the temple cow was to be in familiar surroundings. As he lay in the shed, with the smell of fresh dung around him, he wondered at how different Brahmins could be from each other.

Things grew worse for Virpal in the coming months. Back from school, he would be put to work like any servant boy. Look after the child, milk the cow, swab the floors, carry water from the tank, run to the market. Once he had done all this he had to sit by while the priest's wife whipped out her scales to weigh his purchases, suspiciously staring as each potato or tomato trembled with the readiness of accusation.

Nobody would have dared insult him like this in his village. Every day he thought of taking the steps that would lead him home. Once in Lalbanga, all would come running from far and near, asking, asking, what had he done, how had he managed. But he would disappoint Gaur Sahib, a Brahmin who had taken so much trouble over him.

So he continued to bear the insults, the accusations, the occasional beating. Even if he did take a tomato, so what? The pandit family ate constantly; when they finished, a cold unappetizing scrap occasionally came his way.

The boy visited Gaur Sahib on holidays, swallowing with wistful mouthfuls the food his wife made for him, while he listened to Gaur Sahib hold forth – India had to change – too much illiteracy – look at the West – scientific education – superior knowledge led to conquest – when they were living in caves, we had a glorious civilization, now we are backward – after you are educated you must help your village – this will be your guru dakshina.

Virpal was silent about the treatment he received at the temple, complaining would change little. On rare occasions when he was free, he would walk towards the lake. At the Ajmer Club, he would stop to stare at all the grass, never a cow or a goat grazing on it. Then to the Ana Sagar, a larger version of the lake at home. Sometimes he swam at night, his water-enclosed body absorbing the beauty of the moon and stars.

One afternoon when Virpal was walking home from school, brooding over his menial status, an insect dropped on his shoulder. He brushed it off, to find another, another and another, red-eyed, hopping, large, hungry, a locust advance guard. Soon a moving jagged mass of insects had fallen upon every leaf, twig, bush, branch and tree in sight. The air was full of their noise, within seconds all traces of green had been eradicated.

Though the city could talk of nothing else, its buildings obscured the actual brutality of a ravaged landscape. Uneasily Virpal imagined the consequences of a locust raid on his village. If all vegetation were destroyed, what would the cattle eat?

They would have to migrate in search of pasture, as they did in times of hardship, hiring themselves out as labour.

'I want to go home,' he told Gaur Sahib, at last the chance he had been looking for.

'Why? Are you returning with sacks of grain on your back? Am I taking all this trouble, so you go running off the minute a locust drops from the sky? Education is a serious business. Many boys would kill for your chances.'

Virpal was forced to settle back into his lonely routine, with an anxiety in his heart that replicated almost exactly his family's anxiety about him.

By fifteen Virpal had had enough. Though he learned more than he did in the village, school never became pleasant. While the city employed the same pedagogic tools of rote learning and repetition, they were accompanied by greater violence and abuse. The thrashings given to aid his memory were frequent. Complaints occurred.

'Apparently even with punishment you know no shame,' said Gaur Sahib.

'The teachers don't like me, Baoji,' said Virpal. 'They say I am a lazy country idiot. The other boys also taunt me. I hit back to protect myself, why should a Rajput mistreat me? The Brahmin boys are as bad.'

'What about the Jats?'

Virpal didn't say it was they who encouraged him to fight. Nor that, in order to make friends, he did as he was told.

When Virpal failed his class eight exams, for the second time, Gaur Sahib sat him down for a talk in the inner angan of his haveli. As the bright warm sun cooled into the chilliness of a December evening they discussed his future. How exactly did he visualize it?

Virpal said he was a patriot, he had left the village to serve his country. This studying business was not for him, he wanted to offer civil disobedience. Even as they spoke Gandhiji was in prison again in Yerwada.

Gaur Sahib looked at him. Perhaps the priest was right, it was difficult to take a village boy and thrust an education down his gullet. 'Is going to jail a profession?' he now demanded. 'Following Gandhiji blindly, right or wrong. And what is he doing in prison? Fasting for the upliftment of Harijans. Harijans, Harijans, put them on your head and worship them. Say the thousands dead in the Bihar earthquake is divine retribution for untouchability, is this a scientific approach to social problems?'

'Baoji, how long can I wait? Everywhere people are resisting. Even swamis. And not only against the British. In the south they are agitating against their kings.'

'Arre, to protest is easy. Are Indians ready to rule themselves? The best schools, hospitals, railways, roads are here in Ajmer, not in the neighbouring princely states. If you have to have a ruler, what is wrong with the British? They are fair, efficient, there is no corruption.'

'They say Germany is going to be the next big power. The Angrez are finished. Now is the time to throw them out, once and for all. All I do is sit and fail in school. What glory in that?'

'Who are you? Nobody. If you end up in jail, are they going to publish bulletins of your health in the newspaper? The poor cannot afford the luxury of satyagrah.'

'Lakhs are going to jail. Why shouldn't I?'

'First stand on your own two feet. After that what you do is your responsibility.'

Gaur Sahib found Virpal a job in a shop near his haveli. The boy would live in the space behind the storeroom.

Shopkeeping came naturally to Virpal. He fetched, carried, dusted, cleaned, while the owner sat behind a wooden chest and counted his money. Every week he handed him eight annas.

With his first pay he presented a box of sweets to Gaur Sahib and bent to touch his feet. The older man looked at him, perhaps he was going to be a success after all, there were other ways of doing well besides working as a clerk with the British.

When Virpal had collected five rupees, he sent a money order home. They would be amazed he was doing so well. They themselves hardly ever handled cash, every transaction was done on the basis of barter: grain, ghee, or cattle.

He realized they might also be amazed that he was alive.

A year later Gaur Sahib fell ill. A pain in his chest was diagnosed as a heart attack. He had recently retired from the railway administration but inactivity didn't suit Gaur Sahib; he ate more than he should have, walked less than he would have.

For Virpal, the uncertainties of life suddenly seemed to jump into his lap and stare him in the face. Nothing in the city would have any meaning if this man removed his hand from his head. His desire to offer civil disobedience vanished. Let Gaur Sahib live, he would serve him for the rest of his life, serve him as Hanuman had served Lord Ram. Every evening he went to visit him. Afterwards he would walk to Bajrangarh, near Ana Sagar, to offer prayers, flowers, a coconut, a pice or two. As he looked at the glow of the setting sun over the waters, he felt years thrust on him.

When Gaur Sahib died, his weeping wife looked at Virpal and said, 'He gave and gave, with what reward? Now who is going to run after you? Who bothers about those they find on the road?'

Virpal's own tears flowed thick and fast. Should his family see him, they would laugh at a bereavement that went beyond blood and caste. To add to his sense of loss, was the fifty rupees the widow handed him. 'So much caring, such generosity, where will you find? He left this for you,' she sobbed, concealing the other fifty in the depths of a rapidly failing memory. Virpal could only agree. 'Now you will have to be independent. He always said you had some fire in you. Prove him right.'

Over the next few days Virpal walked all over, looking for the best place to open a shop. Naya Bazaar was too expensive, but towards Ana Sagar lay possibilities. He found a spot on the outskirts of the city, where new developments were taking place. On the top of the hill beyond, he could see a small white temple with a white spire. He had developed a distaste for temples, but Gaur Sahib would approve.

The land was cheap, and the shack he put up was made entirely of tin and cost very little. He stocked cigarettes, soap, sweets, churan, biscuits, oil, things that wouldn't spoil.

Gaur Sahib's widow organized the puja that would inaugurate this skeleton. She saw Virpal's rolled up bedding under the counter, the nearby pump that was his bathing place. Perhaps the boy did know how to struggle. Lord Ram was tested in the jungle for fourteen years, why should Virpal have it any easier?

Though not in the jungle like Lord Ram, Virpal in fact did not have it any easier. He stood behind the counter of his shop from eight in the morning till ten at night, in winter hanging a hurricane lantern from a nail in order to prolong business hours. When he could, he sent money home.

His monthly earnings rose steadily, anna by anna, till one day he decided he had fulfilled his promise to himself. If not quite a big man, he was a self-sufficient one. He could afford to shut shop for three–four days and visit home. Perhaps it was time to find out what his wife looked like. Men younger than him were already fathers. And his brother, how would he be doing?

He was anxious about the recruitment drive taking place in Ajmer, indeed all over India. The British were at war, and they needed soldiers for the Indian army. They were promising a salary, promising smart clothes and shoes. Should these people land up in his village, how many youth would sign up? Being under the raja was no protection. Throughout Rajputana rajas were making conspicuous contributions to the war effort, money, planes, material, men, but still the Angrez wanted more and more.

II

1930–1941

After Virpal's disappearance it was Dhanpal who had
shouldered the burden of his father's wrath. Lal Singh
knew of only one way to prevent more absconding, and that
was fear. The vigour with which he beat the younger son
reflected his rage at the elder one's absence. Dhanpal saw
no point in minding. If he had to stand in for his brother,
that was his destiny. Nothing was fair, and karma explained
everything.

To Dhanpal his father was the most powerful man in the
world. If his brother never came back, and as the years went
by, this seemed more and more likely, it would be Dhanpal
who would one day head the clan. His would be the name that
would make everybody quake in their shoes. It was a future he
earnestly looked forward to. His body stored up each blow to
be delivered with interest when his own wrath acquired status
and sanction.

There was one person outside the village for whom Virpal's
existence was of vital interest and that was his father-in-law.
For Virpal to be declared dead would be to pronounce his

daughter a widow, and he was not going to allow that without a fight.

Virpal and Mithari, both children of village sarpanches, had been six and five when they married. Immediately after the ceremony the bride returned to her parent's home to wait out the years until puberty. When the girl became a woman, her father sent word to her husband's village, but to his surprise no reply was forthcoming.

Inquiries revealed that Virpal had disappeared some time earlier.

Where? Where had he gone?

No one knew. They were waiting for him to come back. It hadn't really been that long.

The father-in-law did not believe this for a second. Could a family be so careless as to mislay their eldest son? There was definitely something crooked going on. Just thinking of Mithari's dowry put him in a rage, ten tolas of gold at eighty rupees a tola, thirty tolas of silver, besides household goods.

He looked at his daughter, rolling rotis next to her mother, her brightly coloured skirt pulled up as she squatted on the floor. He would need proof of a corpse before he accepted that Mithari was a widow. If necessary he would appeal to the Jat panchayat.

Some of this was conveyed to Lal Singh whose angry comments were relayed across neighbouring villages. Virpal had gone to become a big man. Was he to come running back because his father-in-law was making noises? Who said they were denying their daughter-in-law her rightful place?

The very next week Mithari was left in her married home. The father departed the same day, it was against all custom to accept even a drop of water in his daughter's house.

That night her mother-in-law pointed to a place on the mud floor. Mithari had a few seconds to stare at the girl next

to her before the mother-in-law turned down the wick in the
hurricane lantern. The quiet darkness grew and so did Mithari's
trembling. A moment later she felt a hand stroking her, closing
about her wrist. Mithari inched closer, an arm wound around
her waist. Like this the sisters-in-law (as would be apparent
later) fell asleep, like this Mithari spent the first night in her
husband's home.

A year passes with no sign of Virpal. Mithari's closest
companion is Gulabi, Dhanpal's wife. Dhanpal often looks at
the two veiled women, and thinks of his own attachment to his
brother, an attachment that becomes more vivid in his memory
as he grows older.

It is the middle of the day, hot like any other, with a dust
laden loo that has been blowing all morning. Cattle move
slowly from bush to bush, flicking their tails to drive off flies.
Mithari swats them from time to time while searching for twigs
and branches that could be used for fuel, enough for a bundle to
carry home on her head.

A shadow grows in the distance. Bemused, the villagers
watch as the patchy moving cloud turns out to be insects.
Misfortune descends swiftly as every plant for miles around is
covered by thousands of red-eyed, sand-coloured bodies, with
long legs, dry papery wings and waving antennae. The sound of
devastation is conveyed by thousands of jaws massacring every
bit of scanty vegetation. When they rise it is to reveal the sad
remains of naked sticks.

How long does it take to destroy lives? In the case of
a locust plague not even half an hour. The family open their
precious store of grain, but this cannot provide for the cattle.
The sarpanch resolves on temporary migration. The elders are
left behind to guard their property.

They move in a convoy, walking beside their cattle, away from the land that has served them so ill. As they walk, their thick leather shoes whirl the powdery earth about. At night they sleep on the sand under the bright stars. In the morning the women start the fires to make tea and roti, then they are off again, walking south, away from the desert.

As they walk Dhanpal thinks of his brother. How can he be in the vicinity and not suffer because of the locusts? Maybe he is dead. Dhanpal stares at the ground moodily and whacks the cow nearest him.

They finally settle down in Malwa in Madhya Pradesh, where the earth is green, where there is enough to feed the goats, the buffaloes and cows, where they hire themselves out as daily labour. In this way they will survive till the next monsoon.

Mithari worries about being away from the village. The swarm of insects that had fallen out of the sky could have attacked him, all alone as he was. But it was unthinkable she even ask a question. Since there was no way of assuaging her fears, she kept them to herself.

Four more years pass. Still nothing has been heard of Virpal.

Mithari carries on with the functions of a daughter-in-law. It is at night that the difference between the other women and herself becomes significant. Except for the babies, all the females in the compound are wives (with the odd widow thrown in). Teenaged Mithari sleeps the sleep of the young. No mysterious disappearances, no angry beatings by a husband when an exhausted wife dozes off.

Once in the early years, when they were back from Malwa, she asked Gulabi, 'Didi, where do you go at night?' Gulabi looked at her pregnant body and sighed. 'When your husband comes back you will find out. For now you are lucky you can sleep without any problem.'

Mithari stared at Gulabi's roundness and wondered if she was indeed lucky. Her sister-in-law would be going to her mother's home to deliver. Mithari wanted to see her mother too, but only a pregnancy would allow her to do this. To be a wife without a husband, that too was no life. She had to hear comments like man-eater, inauspicious, bad karma, etc. No reply was expected to any of this; all she could do was pull her ghunghat lower over her face.

From time to time Mithari wonders whether she is a widow. But no, they would have smashed her bangles and removed her silver. Gulabi keeps reassuring her, you have brought the family luck, she says.

'What luck?' asks the wife doubtfully.

'Wait and see. They know he will come back one day, that is why they do not treat you as a widow, I'm telling you.' Gulabi was the only one offering any reassurance, and for this reason Mithari clung to her all the more.

Then one day a five-rupee money order arrives in Lal Singh's name. In the narrow space meant for a message at the bottom of the form the son has written that he is well, he hopes to visit soon. The news spreads like fire, jumping from house to house, Virpal is alive in Ajmer, sending money, a big man.

Mithari's status inches up a notch. Her bangles rest secure on her wrists. On her ankles the silver lies heavy and legitimate. 'What did I tell you? Soon, very soon,' whispers Gulabi as they settle down for the night. Mithari blushes. Gulabi finds her bashfulness funny, and pinches her. 'Aiee, what do you have to say?'

Mithari pushes her away, 'Leave me.'

The months pass, and Virpal does not come.

September 1939. The Viceroy of India informs his subjects that along with Britain, they too are at war. The Congress

Party protests, they are willing to offer conditional support in order to fight fascism, but they want independence in return. No such assurance is forthcoming, nor do the Indian people speak in one voice. The Muslim League supports the war, the princely states donate heavily, Indian businessmen profit from increased industrialization.

Six months later in Lalbanga, there appears an officer belonging to the raja of Kishangarh. This official was the one who oversaw the crops at harvest time, he is familiar with every household. He now announces the arrival of an English recruiting agent. Able men are needed for the Indian army. The raja expects every family to give a son, in return the lagaan will be reduced from seventy per cent to fifty per cent for the duration of the war. The raja's priest will perform a special puja for each volunteer, guaranteeing both their safety and the preservation of their caste.

Commotion, questions, anxiety. They only knew farming, how would they manage in an army? Arre, said the officer, did they think they were talking to idiots? There would be a training period. They would be equipped with uniforms, they would learn the use of guns, rifles and tanks, they would be paid, they would belong to regiments of their own caste. Jats to the Jat regiment and so on. They would lead a worry free life, no anxiety about whether rain was going to fall, or whether some sick cow or buffalo might die, none of this would matter once they were in the army.

For two hundred years they had been under the British, theirs was a karmic connection. As such it was their duty to join them in their fight against evil. If they refused to do their dharma, who knew what could happen to them in their next life?

Only the officer was aware of the chain of pressure that led from the British to the raja to himself. We expect four hundred men from you, said the collector. For every man that falls short you will have to pay two hundred rupees. As a result the official is told that he has to get at least fifty men per village. The women can farm while the men are away.

The visit is discussed deep into the lantern lit darkness. The officer knew the members of each family, he would make sure that suitable numbers of young men were offered. The poor always had to suffer, no matter who the ruler – was the raja sending his own sons to join the army?

Nobody knew. It was irrelevant. Lal Singh says if he sets eyes on Virpal, he will beat him to death. Now he will have to send Dhanpal, but maybe Dhanpal will not pass the doctor test. Of late he has heard him coughing.

Silence greeted this statement. Dhanpal was built like an ox, his strength was legendary, as was his health. Dhanpal growled, even if Virpal was there they probably wouldn't take him, his blood had always been thin. He himself was neither weak nor a coward.

A week later a British agent appears, accompanied by a doctor and the raja's officer. The male villagers collect under some trees, remove their kurtas and bunch their dhotis around their hips. Those indicated step forward, the doctor examines their teeth, their eyes, listens to their chest. The agent watches as the chosen gather to one side. Their names are noted, with parentage, village, caste and probable ages. Among them is Dhanpal.

Once they are selected, they are taken immediately, walking down the dusty track, their possessions rolled in a bundle on their heads. Boys follow till the outskirts.

It is 1941. Hitler's armies move to take over North Africa. There aren't enough English soldiers to fight in this world arena, so from the colonies they come, thousands and thousands, recruited to fight for the safety and independence of a country that has denied them these very things.

Three months later Dhanpal pays a visit. Sahib-like, suited, booted, hair and moustache trim and military, he sits on a charpai, while his family squat around him. He has been training in Punjab, with both Indian and English officers, the higher the rank, the whiter the face. There he got to hear that the British considered people like the Jats, the Rajputs, the Gurkhas and the Sikhs to be martial races. He speaks of the hours of marches, drills, of rifle practice, trench digging, of the oath they had to take. They would go wherever they were sent, do whatever they were ordered. Otherwise they would be court martialled – what was that? Shot, put in prison, the punishment was heavy. He is part of the 9th Jat Regiment, infantry. He and his comrades have taken a vow that if they had to die, it would be with a bullet in their chests, rather than their backs.

The listening Gulabi trembles. She doesn't quite understand what war means, but from his way of talking, years of absence are in store, perhaps death. Tears trickle unseen down her cheeks. Like Mithari, she too will be a husbandless wife. Through her veil she sees her three little daughters playing about. If her husband leaves how will she ever produce a son? This distant war, so unconnected to her family, threatens all their futures.

He is going to leave the country, Dhanpal goes on. From Ajmer they will go by train to Bombay, from there on a ship to some place in Africa. Or the Middle East, he does not know.

What is that, Afreeka?

It is across the seas, said Dhanpal. Hot and dry like here.

There was a silence. His father turns and spits in the dust, his mother goes on cooking, but her hands are shaking. What kind of karma does she have, that both her sons should leave the village, perhaps never to return?

That night, obeying an imperceptible signal from her husband, Gulabi waits in the bari. As he sits next to her, he pulls the ghunghat from her head and gazes at her face in the moonlight. She looks back at him. 'Don't do anything dangerous,' she whispers.

'It is not in my hands. We are at war.'

'What does that mean?'

'It means fighting. Bombs from the sky, dropped from flying machines, bullets coming at you from every direction. Always on the alert, day and night. They have shown us how to run with so much samaan on your back, it feels like carrying a buffalo.'

'Hai. And you will do all this?'

'No choice.'

'Why do you have to go?'

'I don't know. Our fate.'

'Only promise, promise one thing.'

'What?'

'You will not leave me a widow.'

'You have a woman's brain,' he says. 'What do you understand, that you ask for such promises? This is a war, there will be fighting. The only thing I can promise is that I will dishonour neither my caste nor my name.'

Gulabi fidgets unhappily. Dhanpal says quietly, 'Have I called you here to talk? Lie down. It may be for the last time.'

The next morning Dhanpal leaves along with the other men chosen for the army. He has no idea whether he will see his home again. At least his brother had been spared. Their father will have a son left should anything happen. Everything is ordained, not a leaf falls from a tree that is not directed by the gods.

～

Six months later. It is the day after Mithari's period, she has bathed with special care at the village pond, washing the many

metres of her indigo dyed skirt. She walks home in her thick
shoes, the wet clothes under her arm, the lithe body unburdened
by childbirth, her youth reflected in the glow of her skin. As she
walks a young man carrying a small canvas holdall can be seen
striding through the village lanes. Nobody recognizes this city
person. Children accost him, who are you? Virpal, Lal Singh's
son. By the time he reaches home he has a train consisting of
every walking male child around. Virpal, they shout, Virpal has
come. It was Virpal who gave a figure to his absence, eleven years.

When the news of her husband's arrival greets Mithari, she falls
behind confused. In her nervousness she wants to run back into
the fields, but there is really no place to hide.

In the angan of their compound, Virpal is surrounded by
half the Jats in the village. He tries to locate Dhanpal, where is
he? Has he been so foolish as to enlist?

A hundred voices supply answers: recruitment, the raja's
promise, the lessening of tax, every father had to give a son,
visited after training, Bombay, ship, ocean, Afreeka.

Why had anybody let him go? demanded Virpal. In Ajmer
they talked of how the empire was weakening. Every day of war
cost the Angrez thousands of pounds. Their own soldiers were
dying so fast, they had to come to the villages of Rajputana
to look for replacements. Truly karma had a way of levelling
everything, even the most mighty. And uselessly his brother
had been sent. Uselessly. He was only twenty-two, twenty-
three, twenty-four.

Arre, said Lal Singh, has the city rotted your brains? Where
were you when all this was happening? For years you stayed
away and now you come with your complaints. Dhanpal's
horoscope cast by the pandit said there is only protection in his
stars. So you see?

Virpal had no answer to any of this. He is aware of the faintly sour smell emanating from fresh cow dung stacked near the outer wall. As the sun falls lower he can hear the gentle tinkling bells of cattle on the way home from grazing. It all feels familiar and strange at the same time. He shakes his head. In Ajmer they are fighting for freedom, and here, his own brother has joined the army. Should Dhanpal die, his death would be on his head. If only he had come home sooner, but how was he to know and what could he have done?

He is urged not to brood about what had happened. Slowly Virpal rinses his face and hands with the cool earthy water of the village well, slowly settles down to eat, thoughtfully chewing the thick, butter-soaked rotis, sipping tea from the steel glass by his side. Would Dhanpal be getting enough to eat?

How had he managed after he left, they ask, and out comes the story of Gaur Sahib the Brahmin, his kindness, the school, the city, the pandit, employment, then his own shop, the money he makes, the room he lives in.

His family swallow up his words, wondering at their steady flow. The women on the periphery hear as much as they have time for. In the furthest corner crouches Mithari on her haunches, kneading atta, rolling out rotis, cleaning dishes with sand and fibre. Through her veil she can see his city feet, the skin looks fair and clean. Will he acknowledge her in any way?

Eating over, cleaning over, talking over. Mithari's mother-in-law prods her, leading her out to where the cows are kept at the back of the living quarters. In the corner of the bari is a charpai, propped against the wall. Put it down, says her mother-in-law. Mithari hesitates, the floor is her designated area, but her mother-in-law gives her a slight shove, then turns and leaves.

The moon is almost full, low and red-gold. Around her is the quiet friendly presence of animals she has washed and fed over the years. She hears the sound of footsteps and reflexively pulls her veil further down. As he stands irresolute she shrinks into herself. He clears his throat, hawks, spits, then sits down. The charpai strings squeak. He gropes for her hand. Its softness startles her. Did he not work at all? Her fingers twitch uneasily against his own, he sighs and starts his business. It was easy to get at her, just lift her skirts; his own city clothes were more cumbersome.

When she cries at the piercing unexpectedness of it, he reaches out and removes her ghunghat. Though she can see him, he is unused to such darkness. He traces her features with his hand.

'What is the matter?'

'It hurts.'

These are her first words to him, words of distress and intimacy, words he is helpless against, so he chooses to ignore them, continuing to relieve the urgencies of years spent alone in the city.

Finally he sits up. When he turns to look at her, he can see a crumpled female form, something indecent in the still body and wide apart legs. He can hear the catch in her breath, her first time, the pain she had mentioned, but how could he have done it any differently? She will get used to it. He carefully pulls down her skirt.

His hand on her clothes feels peculiar, this man who has the right to pull her skirts up and down. Her ghunghat is still around her shoulders, he adjusts that too.

She hopes he won't complain to his mother, she will try to not cry next time. He half tugs at her hand; confused, she pulls back. Surely he didn't want that they walk together to the main house? She can imagine the teasing that would greet such a sight. Did he not know how things were done?

'What's your name?' he asks uncertainly. She refuses to answer. Why would he ever use his wife's name? Certainly in all her life she will never use his.

At last he leaves. She waits a bit before following him. The moon is higher in the sky. She can hear a few dogs, their perpetual barking reverberating loudly in the still night. As she passes the cows she pats the nearest one. She can now wonder how many such couplings they have witnessed.

Next day upon waking, she glances shyly at her sister-in-law. Gulabi pokes her. Mithari blushes. Before more can be implied and inferred, her mother-in-law informs her that her husband can no longer manage alone, she has to leave for the city with him.

All the pleasure Mithari feels at her husband's arrival vanishes. For the past ten years she has not set foot outside this village, she has been surrounded by family women night and day, now she is told she has to leave.

'I don't want to go,' she sobs.

'As though it is up to us to decide where we go or don't go.' says Gulabi, trying to comfort her. 'Besides there is no farming in the city. Life is all easy.'

'When will I see you again?'

'You will go to your mother to have your child, think of that,' says Gulabi as she helps her tie her belongings together. 'And then you will forget me.'

Mithari shakes her head.

'What are you shaking your head for? You don't want to be a mother, hain?' She nudges her. 'Now you will have a son. Many sons.'

'You also. When he comes back.'

'Who knows what is in my kismet? Three girls so far. You must make up for it.'

The air was still cool from the night when an hour later Mithari leaves the village, the bundle on her head containing her few clothes. The couple walk silently down the dirt path. Once or twice he turns around to see if she is all right, causing her to slow down in embarrassment. When they reach the main road, they will hitch a ride on any one of the bullock carts slowly creaking along.

'Eleven years ago I walked on this very road to Ajmer,' he said. Her covered head looked up. He smiled but the head bent down again, and he sighed. He thought of the wife of Manikyalal Sahib given a two year prison sentence for picketing shops that sold foreign cloth. The freedom struggle meant that women were more in the public eye. His own wife seemed so backward in comparison.

Still, he was already alert to the sounds that came from her, the clank of silver, the rustle of skirts, the shuffle of feet, the sound of her breath. He had liked what he had been able to make out of her face the previous night, and he wanted to see more. This would never have been possible in the village. Any sign of attention to a wife would provoke ridicule: tied to the wife's palla, are you a suckling child, has she done black magic on you, arre, you think every other person in the world has gone and died?

Villagers knew no better. In the time he had been in Ajmer he had gone to that newest generator of dreams, the film hall. It was there that he saw the glitzy Bombay version of village life in *Kisan Kanya*, there that he drank in the beauty of Devika Rani in *Achhut Kanya*, an untouchable girl far different from any untouchable he had known, there that he witnessed romance, courtship, love. He yearned for some of this in his own life too.

Virpal now had all the pleasure of introducing the wonders of the city to someone as inexperienced as he had been eleven years ago. From the moment they crossed Martindale Bridge he began to talk – see, this is where Gaur Sahib found me, this is the road to his house, this is Naya Bazaar – see how big it is, how many shops – these are tongas – but most people walk – some have bicycles. Look, that is the Ajmer Club – only for white sahibs – see, see, have you ever seen so much grass? They use it for nothing – all waste.

Mithari's eyes are everywhere. She has to see much, but above all she has her husband talk to her, and she is not sure how to respond. When he looks at her, she pretends not to notice, but she registers the pride with which he shows her his home, see, our own two rooms, one the shop, the other for sleeping, cooking, all brick, cement, durable, look, we have electricity, here the bulb and here the switch, here the pump so near the house, and the private shed in which to do your business, you will not have to go in the open.

When her husband was in the shop, or attending political meetings Mithari was left alone with all these marvels. Alone as she had never been in her life, her thoughts bounding emptily against the blank walls of the single room. It frightened her so much that she had to tell him.

'Dar lagat hai.'

'Why?'

Wasn't it obvious, but she struggled with more words.

'Akela hai.'

He moved closer. 'You have me.'

Reflexively she tugged her ghunghat further down.

'We are alone, no need to cover your face, who are you hiding from?' he asked as he gently pulled it back.

She bent her burning face closer to the floor. There was no dark to lose herself in, just an electric bulb (that she still wasn't used to) hanging from a wire, bland flat light illuminating all things equally, so unlike the friendly shadows cast by kerosene lamps.

He stared at her thin pink lips, narrow face, large eyes and even brown skin, a shade lighter than his own.

'Can you talk?' he asked.

She smiled at this, as he had meant her to. Her teeth were large, white, slightly irregular.

'If you don't talk who will be my friend?'

A broader smile as her gaze flickered over him. He was handsome, she allowed herself to think, with the lean face of a Jat farmer, though she was far more farmer than he.

And so it went, courtship by day, and sex at night. Some weeks later, Mithari discovered she was pregnant. She didn't dare say anything. Having fulfilled the duties of a wife, there was every danger of being exiled from her husband's sight for years together.

Three months passed before Virpal's hand over her belly made him joke that Ajmer was making his wife fat. Mithari delivered the news next morning.

Confronted by women's stuff, Virpal looked apprehensive. In the city how was he supposed to deal with such things by himself? He would take her to her mother. When the baby was born he would come to get them.

'It is early days yet,' she replied.

Her eighth month approached, and Virpal's anxiety to send his wife home grew along with her reluctance. The city that had seemed so strange was now familiar, the husband who was only a name now a man to be loved, spoken to, more than she would have ever dared to in the village.

'I want to stay,' she said. By now they had both been to the cinema, and the language of love had ceased to be foreign. How many women get to spend time with their husbands? thought Mithari. Not Gulabi, whose body proclaimed her wifehood year in and year out, without any visible evidence of husbandly attention.

'Who will help you here?'

'Arre, women give birth in the city, or no?'

'Not by themselves. They have their mother, sister, bhabhi, someone.'

'You will forget me.'

'I came to the village to get you didn't I?'

'After how many years? And what all I had to go through?'

'That was different. It won't be so many years now.'

'Who will look after you? Who will cook?'

'Cook! I've been cooking since I was twelve.'

'It's not the same.'

Finally Virpal accused her of indulging in female folly, they were leaving for the village and that was that. Her head sank, the ghunghat he had tried so hard to get her to abandon fell about her shoulders. He squatted next to her and stroked her head with a still clumsy hand. She caught it and said, at least bring my brother back with you. I won't be able to sleep, just thinking — thinking of you alone.

All right, he said, he would come back with her brother. Whether it was her real brother, cousin brother, village brother, caste brother did not matter, but the boy had to be smart.

One week later, Virpal was back in Ajmer along with brother Om Prakash. Om Prakash cooked, shopped, washed clothes, and stood behind the counter when needed. Virpal had lived with Mithari for barely a year but everything resonated with her absence. He had never heard of anyone missing a wife; the city had made him weak and sentimental. Though he reasoned with himself, his loneliness grew, especially at night. Om Prakash's gentle snores rising from the floor further irritated him. He needed action, he needed to prove himself, he needed to remember his duty to his country.

He had once run away in order to join the freedom struggle. To this end he now joined the Ajmer Praja Mandal, their goal complete independence. He was lucky he was not in the neighbouring princely states, where no speech or action against the British was allowed, in case the war effort suffered.

Frequently Virpal imagined his brother before him. He was safe in Ajmer, while Dhanpal was fighting somewhere in Africa. By now there were over a million Indian soldiers all over the world, and every day still more were recruited, trained and sent overseas.

After a lot of discussion the Ajmer Praja Mandal passed a resolution stating that while they fully supported England in its fight against the Nazis, they wanted a commitment that independence would be granted once hostilities ceased. This resolution was sent to the British Resident.

III

1942–1964

I942. Quit India. Gandhiji's message, Do or Die. At last the Mahatma was allowing the Indian people to take matters into their own hands. On the evening of 15th August thousands gathered before the police station in Gol Dak Khana Chowk. They insisted that political prisoners be freed. They were told to go home, or they would join the prisoners they were so keen to release. Some impetuous young men climbed on to the roof of the police station, pulled down the Union Jack and unfurled the Indian flag. The sub-inspector came out, fired a revolver, ordered a lathi charge. By the time the compound was cleared, only those on the roof remained, hands firmly around their flag. The four of them were thrown into jail. Among them was Virpal. He manages to send word to Om Prakash – tell the family – they are not to worry about him, he is happy to die a martyr.

Mithari had been afraid of exactly this, of being abandoned while her husband disappeared into the depths of an unreachable place. He had not even seen his son. What need was there for him to go to jail, was there no one else to heed Gandhiji's call? She turned to Gulabi with her fears.

'Arre, you are the only one who matters?' demanded Gulabi.

'What do you mean?'

'At least he doesn't have bombs fall on him from flying machines, doesn't have bullets coming at him. Nor does he have to watch his comrades die; he gets food, he gets water. Some people might think he is lucky.'

'In prison he can be tortured.'

'He escaped recruitment; in prison he will be even safer. So what is your problem?'

Mithari stared at Gulabi, the woman who had helped her countless times in her early years, given her hope and courage. She has gone mad, she decided, as she turned away. Later she found out that they had not heard from Dhanpal for almost a year.

Her mother-in-law resumed muttering about the bad luck this bride had brought, first Virpal's years in the city, now jail where the British were either starving him or breaking his limbs; perhaps they had even killed him. What kind of man-eater was she? Why didn't she go and die somewhere?

It was clear that every frustration had to be taken out on her. Leaving Ajmer had been the start of all this misery. She was learning the necessity of retaining the power of a wife. If Virpal survived, she would never part from him again, no matter how persuasive the arguments.

Jails have to be emptied, if only to allow room for more. The day did come when Virpal was freed. He made his way home to find his shop vandalized, the shutter broken, the shelves removed along with the light bulb, charpai and the few utensils. He could only imagine what had happened to Om Prakash. Frightened by miscreants, perhaps threatened by loneliness, tired of waiting for him to return, afraid like Mithari had been afraid when she first came.

Standing forlornly on the street, he wondered what his imprisonment had achieved. Congress leaders were still in jail, Jats and Rajputs from Rajputana were still being recruited, independence was still un-promised.

If Dhanpal died, he would redouble his efforts at satyagrah, sacrifice his shop, his family, everything for the cause.

His feet turn towards his village. Home to the sadness of missing men, home to collect his wife and Kishen Singh, his son. He would return to the city and live the life Gaur Sahib had trained him for.

1944. Virpal receives a letter from his brother. He is wounded. The army has discharged him. From Calcutta he will arrive by train. Tears run down Virpal's cheeks. All his prayers have been answered, his weekly fasts, so strict that he will not even drink water, have yielded results. Each time he reads the letter his joy is freshened. Thank god Gulabi will not be a widow, thinks Mithari, now she cannot blame me.

Every day Virpal goes to the station in time for the Calcutta Mail, the letter had been silent as to the actual date of arrival. It has been fifteen years since he last saw him, but Virpal goes in the firm belief that blood will call to blood. His wife insists on coming. Her more recent acquaintance with her brother-in-law's face will serve to support her husband's conviction.

It takes ten days, but at last a number of soldiers alight from the Calcutta Mail. Virpal's faith in blood answering to blood is fleetingly tested, but his wife nudges him, and of course, there he is, a man looking blankly around the station, one arm hanging by his side, his walk slow and stiff, a face gaunt from years of combat, sallow skin and weary eyes. Virpal hurries up to him, falls on his neck, the soldier winces, the veiled woman and child stand to one side. Hoisting his brother's trunk on his shoulder, Virpal leads the way to a tonga.

Dhanpal tells the same stories over and over. The desert,
the first time he saw a bomb explode, the unexpected noise,
heat, range of destruction, the running out of dugouts to man
anti-aircraft guns. You never knew what was going to hit you
or when you were going to die. The fear, the constant fear,
perpetually suppressed. Their living conditions were worse
than those of the British with whom they hardly mixed. Their
first commander, Auchinleck, talked to them in Hindi, it was
so startling. But then the commander changed, and they never
saw the new one.

In 1942, after the battle of Alamein, they were sent to
Burma, the heat and humidity was unbearable, surrounded by
mosquitoes, bombed by the Japanese, hiding in jungles, not
knowing who might attack from where. Bullets, artillery shells,
all day with a dry biscuit. There in Burma he got malaria, which
made everything ten times worse.

Virpal starts to tell him of his tryst with the flag, of jail, of
Do or Die but Dhanpal does not respond, and Virpal feels the
flimsiness of his own attempts to make a difference.

'When I left all those years ago, it was to build a better
life for me, for us,' he said in an effort to span the gap.
'After I made some money, I returned but it was too late. If
anything had happened to you, I do not know what I would
have done. Certainly I would have fought the Angrez in
every way.'

'The Angrez are getting weaker by the day. The German
goras are stronger, and they have the Japanese on their side.
They have already conquered Singapore, now they are in
Burma, soon they will be here.'

'It will be better under the Japanese than the Angrez,' said
Virpal. 'They are like us.'

'Do you know the goras put us in the front, so we can die
like flies, while they save their skins? The Jat regiment was

full of heroes. They had sworn to never turn their backs to the enemy, brave even when dying. The Gurkhas, Sikhs, Marathas, Rajputs, all of them were like that.'

When Dhanpal spoke his brother got a glimpse of a wider arena, which made him feel that for all his years outside the village, he had seen nothing, known nothing.

Kishen Singh follows Dhanpal around from morning to night. He will only eat with him, he will only sleep with him. The man gives him all his attention, while the parents comment indulgently. 'Arre, he knows it is his Chacha, otherwise when does the boy go to strangers? He is so shy. Soon Bhai, you will have your own sons.'

When Dhanpal leaves for Lalbanga Kishen Singh whimpers his dissatisfaction for days.

1945. The war is over. England has won, but England has also been bled dry by six years of fighting around the world. The government knows it is no longer possible to hold on to India. Talks are initiated alongside increasing communal violence.

In Lalbanga, Gulabi moves about with a heavy heart. When her husband returned she had considered herself one of the lucky ones. But the man who has come back is not the man who went away. She knows he is still young, but his talk is all of war, bombs, bullets, wounds, death and the fear that never left him. He talks more to her than he ever did, she attributes this to the lonely years spent abroad. His attempts to farm leave him in pain and bad-tempered.

His survival is a sign that she is meant to bear sons, even though so far her womb has been weak. Dhanpal occasionally gestures to his wife after the evening meal. But it is difficult for him to do anything, his stiffness gets between them and she doesn't know how to help him. At times he gets angry and

pushes her away, at others he just lies and stares at the stars.
The stars in the African desert had been as bright.

When he gets a son, thinks Gulabi, he will look to the
future and forget all this war-shar business. Months turn into
years and still there is no son.

1947. At last the British are leaving. Ninety years have passed
since the first war of independence, and centuries since the first
white man landed on Indian shores.

Mithari stands with her husband near the Ana Sagar, lifting
up five-year-old Kishen Singh, so he can get a better view of
the lights. They rejoice, but who in India can be completely
happy on this first Independence Day? For decades they had
fought for this freedom, fought with courage, non-violence,
restraint and righteousness. Now overnight that spirit has fled.
The new nations play out the divisive legacy left by the British,
unleashing an evil that will continue to stain the relationship
between the two religions on the subcontinent. Hindus flee to
India, Muslims to Pakistan, thousands are raped and murdered
on the way, whole train loads, bus loads, car loads, village loads.
Let's drink the blood of our enemies; drink till our inexhaustible
appetite is temporarily sated.

Refugee camps are set up all over cities in northern India.
Virpal donates tea, biscuits, sugar, ghee and soap. But he wants
to do something more, the desire to lead a larger life has not
left him.

1950. Virpal makes a trip to Delhi to attend a meeting chaired
by Dr Ram Prasad Gopal in the Raghu Mal Arya Kanya
Vidyalaya, a school near Gole Market.

A new party is being proposed, different from the United
India Party that had won India's freedom. It will be called the

IPPP, the Indian Progressive People's Party, and it will have its roots in Hindu culture and identity.

Mithari trusts that this new organization will find a place for her husband, that his sincerity, lack of pretension and capacity for work will be recognized. Virpal hangs around the IPPP offices in Ajmer, expecting that when the time came to distribute tickets for the next election, he would be considered. He had gone to jail, and that should earn him some recognition, but in the new India jail does not carry the moral weight it once did.

They keep him hanging, hoping. Eventually the ticket goes to a Rajput called Prithvi Singh Rathore, a man untested by adversity, whose zamindar father had donated heavily to the party. Though bitterness consumes Virpal, he sees no choice but to continue his work for the party. He campaigns among Jat villagers, among families of soldiers, speaking as one of them. His speeches lack the edge of passion that self-interest might have given them. When the IPPP loses, his wife says, serves them right. Virpal just feels old.

From time to time Mithari worries about a womb that has turned barren. Would her husband hold a single child, albeit a son, against her? Would he beat her, send her back to the village, negotiate for another wife? These fears trembled beneath the surface of her life. 'It is the city water,' she tells her husband, 'it is not pure, it comes from god knows where, it has dried my blood.'

'We don't need more children, one is good enough,' said Virpal. 'Gaur Sahib was childless, then he became my father. I would have died without him. One day I too will repay that debt.'

Mithari remained silent. How would her husband pay a largely imaginary debt to a man who was dead?

Lalbanga, 1952. The birthing rooms lie towards the back of the compound, where the angan narrows into a passageway. It is adjacent to the stall for the cattle. You can hear the thud as a hoof hits the earth, the splash of dung, the clank of a pail as cows are milked. It is here that a woman who gives birth lies for forty days, here too stay those who are menstruating.

At present it is Gulabi's sweating forehead that the dai wipes, her hair that is untied to help the baby emerge faster. There has only been one daughter to show for the seven years Dhanpal has been back. This war-shar has weakened her husband's blood, but not producing a boy is her fault, she knows it is. For this one child, she has conducted every fast the pandit has told her to, made all the offerings he has suggested.

'Aiee, Ma,' she moans, 'let me die.'

'Arre,' says the dai, 'it is a boy, he will take his time, na?'

'Definitely a boy,' murmurs her mother-in-law, 'see the shape of the stomach. All along I have been saying.'

'The head is coming, soon now, sister, very soon.'

The pain is so intense that Gulabi can hardly hear. A final convulsive shudder and the baby slithers out.

It is a boy! A boy! White as milk, with a great future, alert with big black eyes, the image of his father. Tears flow down Gulabi's cheeks. At last all her prayers, her years of waiting have been rewarded. She knows her mother-in-law will ensure that suitable offerings are made at the temple.

For now the grandmother cradles the child. On the tiny wrist she ties a black thread, may the evil eye be averted. With difficulty she leaves him long enough to go through the Jat section of the village banging on a thali, announcing the birth.

Dhanpal's face relaxes momentarily when he gets the news in the fields, but he doesn't stop the rhythm he has set up with the buffalo and the plough. The child who has brought the news wonders whether he has heard correctly.

'It's a boy,' he repeats.

'I have understood,' says Dhanpal. There is no point showing emotion, who knows how long the child will live, and he has a field to finish before it gets dark. As he watches the blade turn over the dry earth, the thought of Kishen Singh comes to his mind, nine-year-old Kishen Singh, who only last year had visited the village to get married. Just seeing that child had filled him with longing, and made him return again and again to his wife, night after night, though his body hurt and he would rather rest.

As the sun falls, the light grows less harsh and long shadows swing around the field as he ploughs furrow after furrow. Tomorrow he will plant mustard seeds and then one family boy or another will spend nights to protect them first from birds, then rabbits.

Despite the dai's predictions, the baby seems weak of life. His mother gathers him close, he turns his tiny face to nuzzle at her breast. She puts her nipple into his mouth, god only knew how much nourishment she was capable of giving the child. She keeps poorly now, coughing incessantly. At least for forty days she won't have to breathe the smoke from her cooking fire. Her mother-in-law gives her ghee and almonds to stimulate her milk. She will do her best to make sure this grandson thrives, if necessary cutting into her own store of food.

In the city, Virpal is overjoyed. At last the good news he has been waiting for has arrived. He makes arrangements to go for the naming ceremony.

Mithari watches him collect money for the occasion. They are in a good position. Though they had spent liberally on Kishen Singh's marriage, the dowry they had received was even more liberal. The new baby will be gifted gold guineas.

'Now the door has opened, now there will be more,' says Virpal referring to the line of male progeny he perceives glimmering on the horizon.

Mithari takes this as a reference to her continued barrenness. She thinks hopefully of the daughter-in-law, still in her village, still pre-pubescent, but who, one day, will augment this lack.

At the naming ceremony the pandit takes out 'h' as the auspicious letter. The child is named Himmat Singh. Gaina, their caste name, will only be used when confronted by strangers.

With the combined devotion and care of every member of the household, the child grows to be sturdy and wilful. He will not sit still, he will run off and play. If he has to gather firewood, he wastes time in the pond; if he has to help his sisters with the cattle, he gets into a fight with other boys. He has even broken an arm and one can see the slightly crooked angle at which the village hakim has set it.

~

1956. Ajmer joins the Indian state of Rajasthan. Virpal anticipates better luck in the new configuration. When the state elections come, he haunts the IPPP office, hoping for a ticket, but he is not seen as a vote getter. The Rajput candidate hadn't worked, now they were thinking of Bishnoi, a Jat from an old Ajmer family, and a man with some financial backing.

When Bishnoi won by four thousand votes, the decision taken by the IPPP seemed justified. At the victory gathering Virpal watched the radiant winner being carried on the shoulders of his young supporters, watched his face on thousands of posters flap in the wind, watched and wondered how he would ever find a place in the sun. Would this man even remember how wholeheartedly he had campaigned, when others could also claim the same level of commitment? He had not been the only one, he was never the only one.

He is almost forty years old. For how long can he go on anticipating a role in politics? In the village there would be no question of changing the future he was born to. In the city it had seemed possible to rise, but the lack of money and connections held him back. When he saw others in the IPPP office push themselves forward, he knew he possessed an innate meekness that held him back. His hopes settle on his son. He would make sure that Kishen Singh was visible. In a few years he would be ready to join the youth wing of the IPPP. Already the boy was doing well in school, displaying an assurance he himself never had.

Meanwhile Mithari becomes obsessed with her future grandchildren. The birth of Himmat Singh has made her want to people her house as well. When her daughter-in-law was about fifteen she judged it time to call her from the village. She had waited way past the girl's puberty only because she wanted to be sure the girl was healthy and ready. The house is empty and she is getting old.

Virpal had succumbed to family pressure once, marrying Kishen Singh off when a bride with a suitable dowry had been suggested. With a sense of foreboding he thinks back to the fighting which had marked his son's wedding. When the boy had entered the bride's village on a horse, some arrogant upper castes had declared it unseemly for a Jat to be higher than a Rajput, and had dragged him off. The Jats retaliated, and through the wedding ceremony violence continued in the background. Virpal had told himself repeatedly that this did not mean that his daughter-in-law was an ill-omened creature, India was beyond such superstition, but still there was no need to saddle his young son with family life just yet.

Kishen Singh himself shows no interest in whether his wife comes to the city or remains in Lalbanga. But eventually Virpal gives in and the daughter-in-law is called to take her place in her married home.

Over the years the raja of Kishangarh's enormous estate has steadily dwindled. The villages he once owned are broken up and transferred into smaller and smaller holdings, the owners spread over the region.

Lal Singh dies and the power of the clan devolves on to Dhanpal. His stick is never far from his hand, there are rumours that a six day absence concerns a trip to Sonagarh, a village west of Ajmer, famous for its pistols. The army has trained him in firearms and he lets it be known that should anybody dare cross him, he will not be afraid to use his weapons.

With the money Virpal now sends home regularly, Dhanpal acquires his first field from a Sarwar Pandit. Bit by bit he accumulates both land and cattle. He tends to favour buffaloes, they are hardier than cows, and easier to feed when rainfall is scanty. Eventually his hundred bighas and seventy livestock make him the most prosperous Jat in the village.

Dhanpal continues to buy what land he can, while claiming even more for his use. First the claim, then the levying of punishments (usually free labour) on those villagers who step into his area foraging for firewood or water. Anybody who rebelled came to a bad end. The latest had been a poor chamar, whose body was found in the fields.

In the 1960s his bighas are threatened. The low castes allege that he has seized some of the fields they are entitled to. A nosy government officer scrutinizes the transfer records in the Ajmer Land Office. Dhanpal feels out of his depth. He can deal with any village dispute within days if not minutes, but the legal action against him takes place in a distant anonymous world of which he has no understanding. Virpal tries to have the relevant file removed by bribing a clerk, the money is taken, the file remains, the clerk transferred.

Rage consumes Dhanpal's soul. These people thought they could do as they pleased, just because they had some education. If there was anything he could achieve by the power of his status, his wealth, his personality, his willingness to confront an enemy and fight, he would do it. Hadn't he fought wherever the Angrez had sent him? Hadn't he proved himself over and over again? But he found it impossible to deal with what he couldn't see.

His son is going to be the one who will sort out the land issue. He doesn't know how he will do it, but that is what sons do, build on what is left them by their fathers.

Nine years after Himmat's birth, Gulabi conceives again. To have this happen in her old age is something of a miracle. Maybe this time too, a son. You look after yourself, the mother-in-law tells Gulabi, I will be the one to fast.

It is Himmat who brings this child in his wake, the women think. Himmat is the one with the luck, the one with the charisma. And when a son is born, a carbon copy of the elder brother, their linked fates are stamped indelibly on everybody's mind.

The pandit takes out 'm' for his name, and they name him Mangal. Luck, fortune, all this would come with his birth. Fame and glory are predicted for him; like his brother he is born under the sun sign. Of the ten children Gulabi has borne, three girls and two boys survive into adulthood.

At Mangal's naming ceremony, Himmat is married. Much money is saved in this manner. As part of the dowry he is presented with a bicycle. It is the first cycle in the village and the object of much admiration. The bridegroom himself is not allowed to ride it.

'Send Himmat to me,' said Virpal to his brother after the wedding. 'I will see that he is educated, same as Kishen Singh. In the city he will have more opportunities to prove himself. There is a spark in him, you can see.'

'Always getting into trouble,' growled Dhanpal. 'Never listens, even after a beating.' Involuntarily his voice softened. His son was growing tall and handsome, the ringleader of all the other Jat boys. If he could shine so in a village, what might he not achieve in a city? But he could not bear to send him away. 'Maybe in a few years, maybe when he is a father.'

'By then it will be too late. Once he gets an education, he will be able to help you with the land cases, he can't do that here.'

'In a bit, Bhai, in a bit,' said Dhanpal. Though Virpal was convinced that city life was the best thing for the boy, in the face of his brother's attachment he could not persist. If it lay in the child's karma to become a big man, he would, otherwise not. He had done what he could.

A few months later, Kishen Singh Gaina dies. What is happening to the world? wonder the villagers. Last week it was Jawaharlal Nehru, now it is Kishen Singh. In Virpal's house the tears are endless. No one can get over the randomness of the accident. A car roars through the town at dusk, a car Kishen Singh does not see, as he steps off the kerb to avoid some dog shit. In his hand are some kachoris, he is in a hurry to get them to his wife while still hot. As the car hits him, it lurches slightly, then speeds away, leaving the boy's inert body bleeding, minutes away from home. That is life. Everything is fine, and in the midst of all that fineness comes death.

Mithari lies slumped against the wall, her wails rising and falling with each new hand on her shoulder. At intervals they force some tea down her, food is clearly impossible, she has no wish to live.

Bitterly she thought of how often she had compared herself to her village sisters, wondering at the kindness of her fate. Now it was clear that her contentment in Ajmer had served only to delude her into thinking happiness was possible.

The only time Mithari shows any life is when she gets up to beat her son's widow. She has brought this tragedy upon the house. It had served no purpose bringing her to the city. The daughter-in-law had allowed her husband to die without fathering a son, practising birth control no doubt. The karma of childlessness in their family was like a snake concealed under a stone, waiting for a quiet moment to pounce.

But her ultimate crime was that she was still alive. 'Die!' screamed Mithari. 'You sucked his life, now he is gone, when you should have been the one.'

The widow did not question the turning of her mother-in-law's love into hatred, it seemed too natural to her. The sorrow she expressed in the privacy of her ghunghat could be of no interest to anyone. Her life was over, she knew that. She had had three years of togetherness with a man who had gradually become interested in her, perhaps that was all one had any right to expect in a lifetime.

She might not have felt her isolation so keenly if she had known that her husband's parents shared the same feelings. Why were they still alive? It was against nature, against everything.

Overnight Virpal ages. The hope of his life, his future, all that has gone. He does not wail like his wife, he does not remain hunched up, silent and still like his daughter-in-law, he greets each visitor with folded hands, dry-eyed, blank and frozen.

Dhanpal gets ready to leave for Ajmer. He thinks of the son he had not been able to part with, and now his heart feels sore as he contemplates the step he must take. How will the boy's mother react? Himmat, her firstborn son, her special one, yet she had to suffer this loss, just as Virpal was suffering his.

It is the end of the day. Those cattle that need to be milked are at the back of the compound, the others tethered further away. Dhanpal comes into the angan and unwinds his pagri. Water is put on for tea while preparations for the night meal go on simultaneously.

'Where has Himmat gone and died?' he asks.

'He is at the pond,' replies Mangal smartly. 'Trying to catch fish. And he wouldn't listen to me, though I kept saying let's go back, let's go back.'

'Get him.'

Gulabi hears this demand and grows nervous. What trouble had the boy gotten himself into now? He would not be wanted otherwise.

'Arre, he behaves as though he is a sahib in a palace, coming and going as he likes,' said Dhanpal. His anger allows no room for other feelings, and now he is angry, angry at fate, angry at Kishen Singh's death. Only two years ago they had seen the boy at Himmat's wedding, tall, healthy, handsome; not a sign of impending mortality. What life would be left his brother, without a son, a grandson, or a future.

Himmat appears.

'Where were you?'

'Milking.'

'The whole world has finished milking, you are still at it. Mangu says you were at the pond.'

'Mangu is lying. I was milking.'

'I was not lying,' shrieked Mangal. 'You were catching fish. I saw you.'

Himmat hit him on the head, Mangal immediately started wailing, Dhanpal raised his stick, but Himmat dashed away. They would not see him for the rest of the night.

'From now on he will live with his uncle in the city. And if they send him back, I will thrash the life out of him. Understand?' said the father to the angan in general. Though nobody said a word, Dhanpal knew this news would be conveyed to his son.

Tears prickled against Gulabi's eyelids. Once people left the village, there was seldom any coming back. Would she have to put a stone on her heart, a stone so big and heavy it would press the life out of her, in order to help Mithari? Dhanpal glared at the shape of his wife, responsible for all the annoyance he felt about his children. 'Just see what I do to him,' he repeated.

His daughter, home for her pregnancy, put his thali on the floor next to him and ladled some water carefully from the matka into a steel glass.

'To have only one child — then this,' said Dhanpal slowly as he smeared pieces of roti with dal and pickle. Who could understand the workings of fate? He had survived a war, when men were dying all around him. His own son was always getting into mischief, an early death could easily be his destiny, but Kishen Singh? Perhaps his wife had brought him bad luck.

Gulabi tapped an adjacent nephew, her anxiety giving her courage, 'Say the city is not a safe place. Here there are many elders to keep an eye on him, he gets into so much trouble as it is.'

'If it is his karma to die, he will die even in a ditch,' announced Dhanpal to the air in general.

Karma could not be argued with, Gulabi saw its cruel and arbitrary ordering all around her. Still it was a question of her son and she persisted in low agitated whispers. 'If Bhaiyya goes, he can have an accident like Kishen Singh,' repeated the nephew.

'What? You are still arguing?' said Dhanpal as he raised his shoe. 'Your whole life you have just seen two villages, what do you know?' The others nodded. Women knew nothing, their opinions were useless. But mothers have a heart, that too has to be recognized.

Even as the thrashing was going on, the words she would kill herself could be heard from within Gulabi's ghunghat. Dhanpal stared at her. No wife in their community dared oppose her husband. 'The boy has to go and that is final. Arre, what do you know that you are sitting here making your brain work overtime? Have you seen the world? Do you know what all goes on there?'

No, Gulabi had not seen the world, but she knew that Himmat was the one who had brought luck to the family. He was the first of her male children to survive, it was because he had to be born that he had brought his father home from the war. Wasn't her husband aware of this? The ache in her heart led her to address further words to the floor, 'I'm not giving my son. Thirty–forty years it took for him to be born. Why should he go to that house of bad kismet?'

'Fool woman, you would be dead if it were thirty–forty.'

'I'm not giving my son. I will eat poison. I will die.'

'Die then.'

Gulabi lay slumped against the wall while various women tried to comfort her. Finally one of the women pushed Mangal into Gulabi's lap. The child at once began to pluck at his mother's blouse, and Gulabi pulled it up to give him her breast. As he suckled, the familiar tugs calmed her. Her hand wandered over the thin legs, the smooth oiled hair tied in a ponytail. Soon he would be three, then he would have his head shaving ceremony. Would Himmat come for that? Would she ever see him again?

Himmat heard about the beating his mother got, heard that he is to go to the city. He finds her in the fields the next day and walks beside her. 'Ma, are you all right?' At this concern on the part of her son, the mother's tears begin again. Who showed any sympathy to anybody after a beating? It was as normal as taking a stick to a buffalo in the fields, to urge the animal forward in straight lines, to pull the plough that was yoked to it, instead of wandering around, following its own inclination as it would if left to itself.

'It doesn't matter about me. Cities are not safe. You saw what happened to your brother.'

Himmat knew his mother's permission was not necessary, yet most of the tender feelings he had experienced in his life centred around her. 'For how long will I go?' he asked.

'Must be forever. To take Kishen's place. Will you return here when your wife arrives?'

'Ma,' and the boy's voice grew firmer. 'In the cities there are big men. Doesn't Uncle keep sending money? If I become a big man, you will never have to work again. One day I too will have light, water, servants, brick house, motorcycle, you will see.'

Her heart felt heavy with her belief in her son, and the tears that had been in her eyes since yesterday began to drip once more.

'Ma, this is the last time you will cry. I promise.'

'Beta, how do you make such big-big promises? Let me see, how old are you? You were born in that year when the cow died, and then we had to get another cow, and that took two more summers, and this cow, let me see, how many summers has it been? Maybe you are eight, nine, ten. Somewhere there. No, maybe ten, eleven, twelve, somewhere there. The vanshavalli doesn't come any more.'

'Never mind, Ma, how old I am. I am old enough to go.'

IV

1964–1966

D ust rose from their thick leather shoes, as father and son walked down the rough uneven path towards the main road in the growing light of day. From time to time Himmat shifted his bundle to distribute its weight. They would walk the ten kilometres to Sarwar to catch a bus.

Silence between them was a usual thing, so Himmat had no idea how painful Dhanpal found each step. Mithari would never know but her husband shared both her fears and her sorrows. How long before he would see the boy again? His only consolation was that his sacrifice would bring some comfort to his brother. His brother who was now childless, with just one daughter-in-law. She would go the way all widows went, unnoticed, discarded, their status gone, though not their usefulness. He sighed, kismet was everything. Images of poor Kishen Singh floated in his mind, increasing the tenderness he felt for his brother, making it easier to part with his own son.

He knew that Virpal would take good care of Himmat. He looked at the boy walking quietly, for once the naughtiness drained out of him. How would he adapt to life in the city? He would have to sit in one place, read and study much of the time. If he gathered enough ability to help him deal with government babus trying to take his land, his altruism would generate its own reward.

'Do what your uncle tells you to, all right? When you come back it has to be as a big man, no wasting your time running around like a junglee in the city. You have to take Kishen Singh's place.'

Himmat nodded. Life away from the village defied his imagination. No point asking his father anything, he would be whacked on the head for insolence. He had heard that before Dhanpal went to fight for the English, he had been a mild man. Now he was angry practically all the time. Whenever his raised voice was heard, people's understanding stretched towards that far off event.

By the time they reached Sarwar, it was fully light. On either side of the road were houses, shops, all made of brick, all painted. Himmat looked around with big eyes. He had never seen pucca brick and cement houses before.

'Are we almost in Ajmer?' he asked.

'Don't be so smart,' replied his father. 'It took your uncle three days to walk to Ajmer. Now you are like a raja, going in a bus, instead of using your feet.'

They continued down the narrow lanes, till they reached an arched gateway with an adjacent one room structure; the man waiting outside was the ticket collector. No, the bus had yet to come, they should wait.

Dhanpal squatted on the ground, his son squatted next to him. Behind the bus stand was a man making tea. Himmat looked longingly at the foamy brown bubbling liquid, but he knew there was no question of spending money. If he was thirsty, he could drink from the pump beside the bus station, if hungry he could eat the rotis they carried.

Other passengers came with their holdalls, their metal cases, their small leather bags, their cloth bundles. Finally they saw the bus lumbering towards them, to stop in the middle of the road while blocked vehicles gathered and honked all around.

How fast they moved. From this height Himmat could see vast stretches of dry land, carrying the memory of hills beneath their undulating surface. Now and then cattle crossed their path, followed by a boy like himself, indifferent to any traffic. Once the bus swerved violently on to the soft side shoulder, and Himmat, unable to bear the nausea any longer, stuck his head out the window to vomit down the side.

Dhanpal too surveys the landscape, a good monsoon meant that normally scrubby bristly trees looked lush and green. Bundles of cut wheat lay in the fields. Women gathered and loaded them on to waiting bullock carts, while further off, more of them were bent double, sorting and tying, their heads covered.

As they approached Ajmer the hills rose higher, sometimes looming ahead, sometimes moving to the right and left as the road twisted. A few bent eucalyptus trees struggled in the alien environment. Small white temples dotted the landscape in greater frequency. As they crossed Martindale Bridge into Ajmer, the buildings grew larger, the traffic denser, till finally they reached the edge of a small bus terminal near Agra Gate.

There were tongas standing by, and rickshaw wallahs who looked them over indifferently, knowing that the villager would walk wherever he needed to. We'll reach in about an hour, said Dhanpal as they set off, the boy hoisting the bundle on his head to relieve his arms.

It was all so different from the village, grand buildings, cycles, tongas, scooters, some cars and buses, paved roads, numerous shops with people hurrying, standing, staring. Nor had Himmat ever seen this much filth lying around before. Piles of garbage lay exposed under clusters of flies that rose and fell, while a ruminative cow wandered here and there.

Dhanpal held his son by the arm, felt the bump near the elbow and shook him. He had to be careful. If he got into any kind of danger, any trouble at all, he would personally come and kill him.

The boy, bewildered by all that he was seeing, could barely answer.

Finally the house of mourning. Scooters and cycles are clustered beside the gate. Dhanpal hurries inside, tears beginning to flow under the influence of memories and sorrow. He clasps his brother, rocking back and forth. 'How did it happen, what went wrong? Your only son, whom the gods loved so much. But Kishen Singh had to go, it was his time. You cannot argue with destiny.'

As explanations follow, the dead boy looks on tenderly from his photograph, garlanded with roses, surrounded by incense sticks planted in brass holders.

'Only two years ago he came to Lalbanga for Mangal's naming ceremony.'

Onlookers gathered around the two men, now would Virpal break down and cry? But still he stared, still he looked glassy-eyed, his body unyielding in the embrace of his brother.

Virpal pushes Himmat towards his uncle's feet. 'Your son, Bhai. He will look after you, care for you, yours for life —'

Virpal looks at the uncomfortable boy staring at him, sees the family resemblance, feels the weight of what he has lost, and his face twists as tears surface in his eyes.

They are taken to wash at the pump outside, then given tea and roti. As they eat, Dhanpal observes various young men, serving snacks, taking care of arrangements concerning the final ceremonies, the pandit, the pandal, the lunch. When his brother tries to thank them, they say, 'Bhai Sahib, don't embarrass us,' and disappear into the warm night. They are all boys belonging to the local youth wing of the IPPP, where Kishen Singh had spent so much time.

In the years since he was here last Virpal had added rooms to a house that now straggled up the hill. Above and beyond was a temple, white spire gleaming, saffron flag fluttering, home of the deity that his brother had hoped would smile benignly over all his enterprises.

Night fell. As no fire could be lit in a house of recent death, food was sent by a neighbour for the bereaved family. Dhanpal watched as Virpal put a few unsteady morsels into his mouth. He knew how grief could settle into your very being, a guest ready to stay forever.

Once the meal ended, Virpal looked mournfully at Himmat. 'You go to school, beta? How much do they teach you in the village?'

'Arre, what does it matter whether he learns or not? Just a waste of time. Will it help the rain to come, or the crops to grow, or cure the cows when they fall sick, or pay the money lender, or win cases filed against you?'

'He likes to study?'

'Is he the son of some raja that we need to ask him what he likes and what he doesn't like?'

'Here education is essential,' added Virpal with the same slow dreariness. He looked at his brother's face, lined with the sun, the large wary eyes, the thin wiry calves revealed through the dhoti, the white pagri on his head. A farmer's clothes but a soldier's bearing, one who had returned from the war to father two living sons. He was rich in the things that mattered, and clearly by bringing this boy he was sharing the wealth he had.

Aware of this scrutiny, Dhanpal said, 'If he misbehaves, send him back.' And turning to his son, 'Your uncle will be like a god to you, do you understand?'

As Virpal looked at the apprehensive expression on the boy's face, he was reminded of his own early days in the city, when everything was so strange. 'Beta, do you want to stay here?'

Himmat stared at the ground. 'Have you grown dumb?' demanded his father. 'Otherwise you are always answering back. You have to do as your uncle tells you, remember you are not to start using your idiotic mind.'

Next morning Dhanpal reiterated, remember your uncle is now your god, and having done as much as possible for his brother, left for Lalbanga.

That night Himmat lay on his allotted place on the floor, an unfamiliar fan cooling him. Street light patterned the walls, light that would not let him sleep. There was a breeze, it was cool and pleasant, but his heart felt empty.

The tears he had controlled all day slid down his cheeks and wet his pillow. In his whole life he had never felt so alone. People died, that didn't mean others were sent to take their place. Already his home seemed unbearably distant. Among the younger boys he was the leader, wherever he went he was followed, everything he did was copied.

The tears continued till he thought he had cried more in this one day than in his whole life. He lay hollowed out and exhausted, with nothing changed.

Inside the house the aunt thought of the boy on the veranda floor. Silently she promised Gulabi she would treat her son like her own. For her husband, they were all vessels of the same blood.

Tomorrow, tomorrow she would train herself to see with the same eyes he did. For she had failed in the most basic duty of a woman, to ensure that her husband's seed was transmitted. She thought of her barren daughter-in-law with hatred, miserable creature, sitting in silence, her ghunghat pulled over her cursed head.

As for the young wife, she lay paralysed by desolation. From now she would be deprived of the protective presence that stood between her and the world. Her life was over, they said. Where does one go, how does one behave if one's life is over? This was the lesson she had to learn.

Eventually the last rite of mourning was over. Though Kishen Singh had contained the family's collective hope, and now their collective despair, their separate ways of grieving divided them from each other as effectively as impenetrable walls.

Till a few days ago Virpal had considered his life to be successful, despite his political disappointments. With the induction of his son into the youth wing of the IPPP, he hoped to be reconciled to that failure. But now his personal life was also destroyed. Didn't having an only child entitle you to some divine protection? It seemed not.

Instead there was now an evil omened widow in the house. Had she given birth, at least his line would have continued. Yet even to think like this was useless. No power on earth could add one breath to his son's allotted time nor alter the karma that decided his own afflictions. His brother had given him Himmat. At his death it would be a nephew who would light his funeral pyre.

As for the nephew himself, no one paid him any attention. His uncle disappeared into the shop, where he remained all day; his grief-ridden aunt lay in bed, where she remained all day. It was the widow who fed him. All he could see of her were thin bare arms, every bangle removed the moment her husband died.

It scared Himmat the way his cousin brother hovered over everything. Death was different in the village. At home he could have roamed around the ponds, the fields, played gulli-danda, kabaddi, kho-kho with a dozen other boys, numerous enough to scare away predatory ghosts.

He tried looking for company rambling up and down the hill. He found small homes, little lanes leading to a room or two, a scooter in an angan, clothes hanging on lines, children gawking at him. Was he trespassing, were they of his caste? Apprehensive, he scuttled away.

Down the hill there was an open maidan. One evening he saw boys doing exercises. An older man in white shorts was shouting instructions, there was a flag hanging from a pole, orange and limp. The man beckoned, but he turned and ran.

He remained curious enough to ask his uncle about it that evening. Yes, his brother had been a member of the local Bharat Jagrit Sabha, said Virpal sadly, maybe he should become one too.

Himmat waited eagerly, but nothing happened. To remind his uncle could be construed as a demand, and he knew that whatever happened he should not impose.

Two weeks later Virpal told his nephew he had found a school for him. It was attached to the local BJS shakha. Tuition was free. Till the boy proved himself worthy, even a rupee was too much to waste on what could be an investment of meagre return.

At seven thirty the next morning they made their way down the colony roads, crossed the main street and entered the gates of a low white building. Before the portico was a small shrine, with a marble statue of Saraswati, goddess of learning, on her swan. A fresh red tilak blazed from the white of her forehead, framed by painted black curls and a glittering stone studded cardboard diadem.

'Do pranam,' nudged the uncle to the boy, who obediently bent his forehead towards the goddess's feet. The man fumbled in his shirt pocket, took out the smallest coin he had and looked at it sadly before offering it. 'For your success.'

Himmat also looked sadly at the coin. In the village, they showed their devotion by offering grain.

'New admission,' said the uncle, once inside. As they waited in the principal's office, Virpal indicated a garlanded photograph on the wall, 'That's Hari Gopal Krishna, the founder of the Bharat Jagrit Sabha.' Himmat looked around. From the open doorway he could see a dusty courtyard, a broken swing, and a rope with a tyre hanging from the neem tree in a corner. The wide veranda extended on three sides of the building, with classrooms on two sides. On the third side small dingy holes gaped in the yellow washed surface of the wall. Toilets. Some boys in light blue shirts and dark grey pants were playing on the steps.

A gong rings for assembly. The names of gods are sung to drums, cymbals and steady hand claps. Rows of children sit before two giant framed portraits of Saraswati and Hari Gopal Krishna.

After reciting Vedic slokas, India's rivers are invoked, her mountains, her saints, her holy places.

Om, shanti, shanti, shanti. Om, Om, Om chant the children in pure uneven voices.

Then pranayam. Hold each nostril in turn, exhale-inhale, inhale-exhale, on and on.

Now fingers over your eyes and hum the mantra for conquering death.

This done, the diya of learning is lit, and the Saraswati Vandana sung so the goddess would grant them the ability to absorb things quickly.

One boy gets up, and vows to make his country proud, to achieve something, no matter how humble his origin.

A teacher clears his throat:

A seth lived in a village, the master of lakhs. For his daughter's wedding, he, swollen with pride and ambition, called the halwai. The food was to be served on big rotis instead of dry leaves. The halwai was uneasy, the seth was insulting grain. He took the leftover rotis to feed his cows.

That night the seth dreamt that Lakshmi, the goddess of wealth, was leaving him for the halwai. Panic stricken he hid his money and jewels in a chest on the roof. A flood came and swept away the chest. It floated past the halwai's shop. The halwai was now rich, the seth poor.

The halwai took pity on him and gave him a box filled with gold coins. The seth carried this box to the river and gave it to the oarsman to take him across, as blind in his poverty as he had been in his wealth.

Now children do you want to become like the seth or the halwai?

The halwai they chorus obediently.

So when you step on crumbs after eating, you know you are dishonouring food.

They swore they would never insult food again. The assembly ends with invoking blessings from various authority figures. Lines of children disappear into adjoining classrooms, teachers pass out books, the day's recitations begin.

Himmat is now presented to the principal as raw material to be moulded into a worthy individual. The principal's eyes drift indifferently over the human scrap in front of him.

Most students come to nothing, but they are a school and he says fitting things about vision, diligence, religion, service, community, dedication and hard work.

The uncle in turn praises the institution. It is free, this alone makes it wonderful.

They know no distinction, says the principal, the sons of clerks, shopkeepers, daily labour, all are welcome. If they didn't take care of their own, Christian missionaries were just waiting to take over. How old was the boy?

Virpal suggested nine.

But the boy was too tall for nine. Ten, said the principal firmly, maybe eleven. Why prolong the years of free education?

A few questions established Himmat's lack of knowledge. He was put in a class with younger children, guaranteed to make him feel even more awkward.

Once he was home, his aunt gazed mournfully at the garlanded picture of her son and murmured how good he had been in studies, and how his teachers had nothing but praise for him, from the first day to the last.

His own experiences were not required.

Virpal, duty done, proceeded to ignore his nephew till one day he saw him in the corner of the veranda, head bent against his knees, arm across his eyes. He shook him. Was he all right?

The boy turned away his head.

'What, now I have to beg you to tell me what the matter is? Don't be a stupid village idiot who has no tongue. I am not going to ask again and again, understand?'

It turned out that the teacher had hit him, and the other students inspired by this had made even more fun of him than usual. He would never be able to fit in. He was older, he had a different way of speaking, he was expected to understand subjects with barely any explanation. He had no desire to go to school, what would he do with an education?

Himmat kept shifting his gaze as he spoke, alternating between the floor and his uncle's chest. He was conscious of not having measured up, his uncle had called him a stupid village idiot, repeating the litany he heard at school.

'I want to go home, Uncle,' he murmured. 'I will not be able to glorify your name, it is too difficult here.'

Virpal rapped him on the back of his head, but it was essentially a feeble gesture. 'Don't talk rubbish,' he said almost to himself. Years ago, he too had wanted to leave school because of trouble with city boys. Now here was his brother's son, eager to commit the same mistakes. Himmat was going to be educated, whether he liked it or not. It was a passport, a passport he was at present too ignorant to value.

He looked at the boy's withdrawn face; if he didn't yet feel comfortable, the fault was his. In giving him Himmat, Dhanpal must have remembered how, two years ago, he had promised to give him opportunities he would never have had in the village. Now it was time to honour his generosity by making sure that his grief for Kishen Singh did not prevent him from carrying out his duties towards this other boy. The pain within told him his life was done, but if he didn't do Himmat justice, he would never be able to hold his head high in front of his brother.

Himmat kept fidgeting. Was his uncle so annoyed that he would not speak? He glanced at him and saw sadness in his face, the same sadness he had seen on his father's face as he was leaving.

'Baoji,' he cried, this time with greater sincerity, 'I will not give up, I will put a stone upon my heart if necessary. They can say what they like.'

Virpal's eyes filled with tears as he remembered the trouble
Gaur Sahib had taken over him. Now it was his turn to make
sure another child acquired the skills to advance.

That night for the first time he really looked at Himmat as
he noisily gulped down his food. Even after some months he
appeared an awkward village boy. If his social skills improved,
his self-assurance would also increase. Confidence was
everything, he knew that.

Next Sunday he led him into a neighbouring gullie, towards
a two roomed pink stucco house, bordered by a veranda, with a
small dirt patch in front. Kishen Singh had gone to this shakha,
and association with it had become painful, perhaps that was
the reason he had forgotten his promise to introduce the boy
to the BJS.

Himmat wondered at his uncle's grim demeanour.
Virpal had done nothing but stare at him since he had
found him crying. He wished he hadn't behaved like a girl.
He wanted to prove himself, it did not matter how, when
or where.

As they opened the gate an advertisement for the shakha
appeared; a young man who emanated confidence, health and
beauty. Himmat remembered him as one of the men in his
uncle's house when he had first arrived in the city, organizing
the pandit, the terevein, the food that would be served. So
this is where he had come from.

'Here is my son from the village,' said Virpal. 'Take him, prepare
him, teach him. Make him like his brother.'

Sandeep's glance flickered over the boy. How old was he?
What were his interests? What did he know?

Himmat remained silent. What did he know? Nothing.

'You must know something? Kho-kho? Kabaddi?'

At the mention of these village games Himmat bridled. Any donkey could play them.

Sandeep smiled his gentle smile. 'Right from childhood we are taught to ape the foreign and despise our own. Arre, look at cricket. You need so much space, so much training, special equipment. What opportunity is there for the humble youth of India, I ask you? In our training camps every boy, rich or poor, can play kho-kho, kabaddi and build their bodies. The British thought we were weak because we didn't eat the polluted flesh of dead animals.

'What they took from us was our self-respect. Our culture, our heritage, our ideals have disappeared. Once India was the teacher of the world. And now?'

Virpal nodded. He never tired of stories of India's vanished greatness, and the effort to get her back on track again.

'People remark that we work on a Sunday. Arre this Sunday-Monday business is all from the West. Do we not eat on Sundays? Bathe on Sundays?'

Himmat tittered. He admired everything about this young man; the black hair brushed back from a high forehead, the clear eyes with the straight, slightly challenging gaze, the white pyjamas he wore with a sleeveless vest that showed his muscular arms.

Under Sandeep's guidance Himmat learned to use his mind. If he played kabaddi, it was to keep alive their traditional games in which everybody could join. If he worked to build his body, it was to establish the power of a vegetarian diet. And so on.

One day, his face flushed with shyness, he told Sandeep, 'I want to be like you.'

'Be patient. It will come.'

'How long?'

'It all depends on you. Your hard work.'

Every morning, before school, Himmat went down the hill where the man in charge had once beckoned him. Now he was one of the flag saluters, a practitioner of surya namaskar, the most elaborate yoga asana. Again and again he lifted his arms to greet the sun, then in a series of movements lay with his heart next to the earth. Alone at home he would flex his muscles and gaze at his puny arms anxiously, hoping to see Sandeep's bulges there. With a tape he measured his chest and shoulders, overjoyed at even an infinitesimal increase.

At home the boy's perceptions grew quick. It became clear to him that the centre of attention was the gilt edged portrait, and he grew as devoted to it as his aunt. He was the first to notice when the incense sticks burnt out, he was the one to filch flowers from wherever he could. A rose, a champa, a quickly wilting bougainvillaea sprig.

He did other things for the photograph. He polished the frame with oil, wiped away the dust from the glass with a careful hand. This was followed by a request to hear about Bhaiyya, after which tender comparisons between himself and his cousin would follow.

In these softer moods the girl with the covered head also crept near. As the days continued, Himmat noticed that the more tolerantly his aunt felt towards him, the less she shouted at her daughter-in-law. This made him feel powerful and protective.

Their spheres were different. The four rooms of his uncle's house were built one behind the other, following the contours of the hill, with small flat terraces in between, facing the lake. Stairs united them.

Himmat's room was on the highest level. Every night he dragged his durrie out to lie under the lustreless stars of the city. When his solitude became unbearable, he chanted the mantras he had learned at the shakha until he fell asleep.

Equalling him in loneliness was the widowed wraith that lurked in the house. Every day that shadow crept to the roof to wash clothes. Her covered shape squatted near the tap by the water storage tank as she soaked, soaped, beat, wrung, squeezed and hung for hours together. Covertly he took in her feet, arms, the bumps of her spine visible through swathes of material. In her shapelessness she was no different from the covered figures in his village, yet she managed to move him in unfamiliar ways. Even to look at her was to cross a barrier he would never have dared to in the village, a shoe would have hit his head. Here there was no such policing.

So far he had not heard her say a single word. If he spoke to her, wouldn't she have to answer? In the village knowing anybody was never a goal. Women were too foreign, he was closer to the cattle than he was to any female. He knew he was special to his mother through the portions of food she covertly fed him. As for that distant creature, his wife, she was a stranger he never thought of.

One cloudy evening as drops of rain begin to fall, the widow emerges running from the stairwell entrance, to pull hours of labour off the line. At her steps he looks up from his books. She darts here and there and the veil slides off her head. She struggles to hold the clothes, undo the pins and drag the sheets so they don't touch the by now quite wet floor. As the sheets fly about, he finds himself dashing to help. He reaches out to take the load from her, his fingers brush against her shoulder. She turns and for the first time he sees her face.

Her lips were full and bloodless, the eyes sad and big, the eyebrows finely arched, the cheeks slightly flushed. Surprisingly she was light coloured, the hands he had seen so far were at least ten shades darker.

She hurries towards the staircase. He follows. When she turns to take the washing from him, he holds back. She goes down a step, then turns back again, will the washing remain with him, or will he give it to her? His feet tell her he will carry it down. Towards the bottom she turns again and now he puts the load into her arms.

All night this little scene played about in his head. He wanted it to rain every day; next time he would collect the sheets before she came rushing from downstairs, she would then look at him once more.

If only he could give her something, but what? Several days passed before he could push his schoolbook towards her and say, his mouth dry, his heart beating, that he could teach her how to read.

She shook her head.

'Why?'

But she would not speak to him.

'Why?' he persisted. 'They won't know.'

Again she shook her head and quickly retreated.

Maybe she didn't quite know what he was offering her. Next time he elaborated further. He would teach her to write also, he said, see, she could learn on his slate. He was so insistent, that at last she whispered into the clothes she was beating on the floor that she was literate and had no use for his gifts.

A village girl and literate? How, where, what level?

Bang, bang went her clothes, but he didn't move out of the way of the splashing water.

Finally she murmured that his brother had taught her at night. That was all she needed to say for him to realize it must have been a secret between the two of them, a pursuit hidden in order to protect it from any annoyance that would be felt at the importance the husband was giving his wife.

He saw a tear fall on her hand and knew he was right.

Tell me – but here he faltered. He didn't know what she could tell him, her history was there to see in the bent head and the constantly working hands.

Tell me – but before he could formulate his inchoate requests, she got up and left. The clothes lay in the bucket, it was clear that she would come back to hang them only when he stopped his questions. But she had said something to him and that was a triumph.

It was Sunday, and he waited till she had finished hanging the clothes, swaying as he studied, one eye on her, bending, straightening, flicking the clothes over the line, repeating the motions until they were all hung.

As she turned to go, he quickly stepped in front of her, 'Here,' proffering a screw of sour churan balls covered in black salt, wrapped in some newspaper. She looked, but did not stretch out her hand.

'For you,' he repeated as he placed it at her feet, and walked back to his books. When he glanced up a few seconds later, she was gone, but so was the twist of paper.

He was forced to use his imagination to get her to look at him, talk to him. Since all his interaction with her took place away from people, there was no abrasive commentary.

~

Virpal had seen Sandeep change from a scrawny slum boy, ridden with aggression, to a calm muscular model of Hindu manhood. So when he said he was certain that Himmat had leadership qualities he believed him.

'I will take Himmat to visit the unfortunates in our city. He will see that the desire to serve and the desire to lead is one and the same thing. Of all the seeds we plant, who knows which will bear fruit?'

The uncle cleared his throat, blew whatever was in his nose inwards, and agreed that the boy's development was the main thing.

'We will remake India person by person,' lectured Sandeep. 'No person is so low that he does not merit attention. Christian missionaries understood this very well. They came with a handful of rice – our god has sent this for you – and what do you see now? Christians all over the country. Look at Assam – full of Christians where they used to be adivasi. Now we are opening our own schools and medical centres there. We give scholarships, bring the bright children to the cities. Villages and towns should mix. India is One, after all.'

Himmat is told his background would enable him to connect to boys, the city dispossessed, the village poor, so that they feel inspired to join shakha programmes. Alongside Sandeep Bhaiyya he sees silent, tongue-tied children, eyes both curious and wary. Just looking at them drags him back to his former self, and the assurance he was meant to display wavered.

'Look at Himmat here,' said Sandeep, 'he was just a farmer's son, but see how confident he has become.' At which point Himmat would say he owed everything to the shakha. Through yoga and discipline, they could develop personalities that would allow them to rise above their circumstances.

To his own ears he sounded like a parrot. Village youth wanted money, jobs, a place in the world. He wasn't sure Hindu culture could provide that.

Sandeep listened to him falter, and lectured him afterwards. 'Be proud of yourself, you have everything. Look at me. My father was a rickshaw puller. All he earned he spent on drink.

Whatever I could steal from him, or from anybody else, I did. My mother encouraged me. She had no choice.

'One day I shouted that my greatest wish was to see him dead. After he had beaten me enough, he took me to the shakha. He was so drunk he could barely speak, but he told them I needed to learn how to respect my elders.

'When he left I cried. "What about his drinking, his beating, his abuses? Day in and day out. Home is hell."

'My father was suffering too, said Bade Bhaiyya, pity was required, not anger. Bade Bhaiyya became my guru, he was like Dronacharya, Bhishampitamah, people who vowed never to marry because they wanted to devote themselves to society. From that day to this I have lived in Mata Mandir, in the shadow of those principles.'

To think of Sandeep as thin and scrawny was beyond Himmat. But in front of him was a man who had known both poverty and violence. After all, there was not much difference between the son of a rickshaw puller and the son of a farmer.

Two years after Himmat's arrival in the city, his uncle decided he was performing well enough in school to justify some expenditure. It was time to prepare him for the DAV admission test; if necessary he would even hire a tutor. A better school would have a better class of people instead of the sons of vegetable sellers and the like. The boy had lost his scrawny look, his watchful expression. The family features that united him to Kishen Singh were more apparent, as was his uncle's desire to see him succeed.

When the school announced Himmat's success in the entrance tests, for the first time Virpal felt that the future might still have something to offer.

V

1967–1971

In the meantime life on the roof had become more nuanced. Despite the pressures of his new school the terrace continued to preoccupy Himmat. He was almost fifteen, much taller than the girl. His face had sprouted a soft fuzz; his voice was cracking.

Though all he wanted was an innocent friendship, he knew that so far as his family was concerned, innocence did not enter the picture.

After his success with the churan, he increased his offerings. He got her the sweets she was not allowed to eat. Money was a problem for him, and because he could buy little, he secreted away anything tasty that was given him. If he was given a samosa, he squashed it into his pocket, likewise a pakora, likewise savoury namak para, kachori and barfi. He kept these gifts in envelopes made out of used notebook paper.

By the time he could produce these delicacies, they were crushed, cold and greasy, but still more palatable than the things she got to eat and often, as she nibbled on these forbidden foods, tears came to her eyes.

The grease spots left on his clothes became more stains for her to wash away.

One day he asked, 'What is your name?'

She didn't say anything.

He persisted, day after day, 'What is your name, what is your name?' Finally she snapped, 'What will you do with my name? You feel no shame in asking?'

He was delighted. This reprimand was a step towards intimacy.

Now it was his turn to indulge in some reproach. 'Why don't you say something? You are always sighing. Our guru says women are equal members of society. In fact more than equal. They are like devis.'

'What does he say about widows?'

Himmat was silent. Widows hadn't figured in his guru's discourse. A conversation with Sandeep came back to him.

'Where is your mother now?'

'Vrindavan.'

'What is she doing there?'

'What is she doing? She is leading the life of a widow, that is what she is doing.'

'She was willing to leave you?' This was not comprehensible to Himmat. Since when did women leave the shelter of their men?

'At first she wanted me to marry. Kept talking about a daughter-in-law to help her in the house. She had to understand that this marriage business was not for me.'

'Then?'

'Then what? I took her on a pilgrimage. We went to Vrindavan where I left her in an ashram. A good place. She won't have to beg. Just some light duties, and they will give her food and a place to sleep. Arre, now she is a widow, she has to lead a holy life and focus on god, not waste her time thinking of daughters-in-law and grandchildren.

'In the shakha they thought I had done a good thing. Vrindavan was where Lord Krishna had spent his youth. What better fortune than to live by the banks of the holy Yamuna, to worship it daily, and then to die in her arms?'

Himmat accepted this without question. Women didn't have many needs. They stayed at home, happy with what their men gave them, whose duty it was to provide protection.

The girl in front of him spoke into the silence. 'See?' she said, 'Even he considers us unworthy of mention. Now will you stop pestering me?'

'How am I pestering you? I am just talking.'

'If anybody sees you, they will be furious.'

'Who is there to see?'

'You know who.'

'Nobody comes to the roof.'

'That means you can do what you like?'

'I will do what you say.'

She half turned towards him, he could see the little smile on her lips, and it made him mad to only see that and nothing else. Involuntarily he pulled the palla from her head. She turned, raised a hand, was she going to slap him? He scurried out of reach, she pulled her palla back and disappeared downstairs.

He would have to wait a whole day to find out how annoyed she was.

To assuage that anger, next morning he laid a paper cone of masala channa in the place where she came to wash clothes. From his room, through the lattice grill, he could see her look around and slowly put the channa one by one into her mouth.

If she were to see him she might stop, so he was careful to remain hidden.

Next day:

'If I have offended you, forgive me.'

She sighed. 'You are a child, you know nothing.'

'Nonsense. I am now a man.'

'If they find out I even speak to you, they will kill me.'

'All the time you are talking like this.'

'Go away, if you don't like it. Who is asking you to have anything to do with me?'

She seemed upset. Then he had to apologize, which also felt strange. The men in his family never apologized. But he was treading on unfamiliar territory, and the precedents were few.

The accidental brushes between them increased, every one of them initiated by him. Sometimes he was driven to squat next to her while she washed clothes. Though she drew away, she never said anything. And so he felt allowed to continue. If only he could get her to the roof at night.

It was summer. The uncle and aunt slept in the angan just outside their bedroom one floor above the kitchen. The girl was always the last to sleep, the first to get up. She slept in the narrow space next to the storeroom, at the lowest level, no lake breezes, no moonlight playing on the surface of the angan for her.

'Don't you feel hot?' he took to asking.

'What does it matter what I feel?'

'It matters. Come to the roof. Come, na.'

'Are you mad? Why should I come? They will kill me.'

'Is there nothing else you can say? No one will kill you. I am here, no?'

'You? You think anybody will listen to such a boy?'

'Once they go to sleep, I am going to stand on the staircase and wait for you until you come. I will wait the whole night if necessary.'

'Don't be silly. Someone will find out.'

'No one will find out. The whole night I will stand there. You'll see.'

The full moon rose dazzling in the sky. The town was silent (only the dogs). The thought of the boy on the roof would not let the girl sleep, though she changed her position a hundred times. Eventually she got up, and on bare feet made her way to the staircase. The silver light, the smell of the raat ki rani and the pleasant touch of the slightly moist air on her face made her restless. She silently climbed the three flights. She hoped he had gone to bed, she would look around once, then go down again.

There he was, his back against the bannisters, his head supported by the bars, eyes closed.

She shook him. 'Go to your bed,' she whispered.

He got up, took her hand and half pulled her up the stairs. On the roof the moonlight touched everything with cool magic. In the distance, the waters glittered and shimmered in the luminous light. She stood staring, her face turned upwards. Her veil fell back, he led her towards the little room where he slept.

His hands were diffident, they sought consent, they sought knowledge. Soon his hesitant wonder quickened into a passion that she answered with a passion of her own. Then came the miraculous moment when she did nothing to prevent him penetrating her. Afterwards she lay shuddering by his side. This time her sobs were different; instead of turning away, she clung to him. Each tear was now an invitation to enter her life, no matter how sad the process. That was what he had wanted, that access, that invitation.

When she could cry no more, he turned her face towards him and dropped a clumsy kiss on the top of her head.

Would he have started anything had he realized that this was only the beginning, and not, as in ignorance he had thought, the end? Did he know how his blood could burn for her? That having known her once, he had to know her again and again and again?

Intuitively he gathered from the way her body moved, that her feelings were also growing. Along with her sorrow. 'What life is there for me?' she used to say, after she had begun to speak to him. 'What happiness can I possibly have?'

He could never give her an answer, because he himself didn't know what life she could lead, besides this one, sitting in the shadows, hugging the walls, eating last, working incessantly day after day, season after season, with never a word of love or appreciation. In all these years, he never saw a good thing given to her to eat, never saw her with anything pretty to adorn herself.

And yet she was so pretty. Till the end of his life, he could conjure her up in his memory in all her youthful slender beauty. He never saw her fully, only bits and pieces as they lay in frightened togetherness on those occasions that he engineered and persuaded her to be complicit in.

When he thought of the girl, he felt he was doing the right thing. Hadn't he been sent to Ajmer to take his brother's place? Uneasily he repeated this argument to himself, over and over, but the secrecy with which he had to cloak all his dealings with her left him guilt-ridden.

Since she was a widow, he was not violating anybody's possession. If only he lived in the time of the great Hindu reformers! They would know what to do. He was willing to marry her, he had read of widow remarriage in his history books, virgin widows it was true, but this was the 1960s and things had changed. He had a wife already, but he didn't see how that was pertinent. It was important to discipline the desires of the body, Sandeep had said time and time again, important to maintain purity. Contact with the girl kept him from self-abuse. Otherwise he was in torment all the time. This kind of yearning didn't dissipate by itself; anyone who said it did was lying. He hoped he was not departing from the principles of the shakha. But if he was, there was nothing he could do.

It was his aunt he was the most scared of. She, who was in the house all day, who was always calling her daughter-in-law to press her legs, to press her head, to press her back, who afternoons and nights had to be massaged into sleep. He waited for those interminable sessions to be over, but the mother-in-law took a masochistic pleasure in her insomnia. He himself pressed the legs of his uncle, but that was over relatively quickly.

Himmat began to notice a change in the girl. She didn't cry so much, gave herself to him more easily, once or twice she even initiated their intimacy. He thought he would faint with joy. He began to talk of marriage. He babbled on about how he would slay the demons that lay between them, she was the one he loved, without her he would die.

She was older than him, she objected, she was his brother's wife. She didn't want to ruin his life. That was not how love functioned.

So what? So what? He was willing to tackle all these problems.

Once or twice she covered her ears. 'What a child you are! Do you even know how to go about all this?'

It was true that no matter how brave he sounded, he could not imagine going to his uncle to ask for the widow in marriage. Marriages were always arranged by others.

'They will throw me out of the house,' she said, 'the minute you mention any such thing. As it is, my life is worthless after he died.'

'Don't talk like that,' he raged, 'nobody's life is worthless.'

'Who treats me with respect? Tell me. Who?'

'I do. After we get married, everybody else will too.'

She said nothing.

It is winter. The nights are freezing. Himmat has managed to coax the girl to share his bed and quilt. At that late hour no one needed her, no one except himself. He had a mud angeethi, which he only lit when she was there, hoarding his allotted share of coal and wood.

One night, after they had spent many hours making love, she began to talk of his remembering her. 'If you do not, my life will have been in vain. No one here cares about me, only you. And whatever happens, you must promise you will never forget me.'

He always got annoyed at such talk. It reminded him unpleasantly of his mother.

At his anger, those inextinguishable tears reappeared. As he tried to get her to stop, for the first time he understood the impulse to hit a weeping woman.

'I will ask my father to come to Ajmer,' he said desperately. 'I will do something. In the village no one gives so much importance to one wife or two. Especially when it is to protect a brother's widow.'

'You are such a child.'

Her tears gradually wore away as they lay still, side by side on the terrace in the lightening darkness, listening to the birds beginning their movement in the trees, hearing the sounds they made in the still silent city.

By morning she had vanished.

Consternation in the house. They searched all the rooms, they searched the streets. They did not call her name, they asked no one if they had seen her, because then their humiliation would be published to the world. People would gossip, ask questions, visit in order to gauge the extent of their disgrace. This certainty made them even more reticent. Night fell, still no sign. The aunt had to cook, which put her in a foul mood.

Days passed. The aunt's tongue loosened to her nephew's distress. 'Good, she had run away to die somewhere,' she remarked. 'She had her eyes on you from the moment you entered. She was a man-eater, a churail. First one brother then the next. It is her shame that has made her run away, after all we have done for her. Kept her when even her own family did not want her, though your uncle kept writing, come, take her.'

Take her? He would have taken her in a heartbeat. She could have lived with him when he became independent. His wife would have adjusted and besides it would be no business of hers. Later, perhaps an ashram in Vrindavan, to live in peace and holiness like Sandeep's mother. But she had removed herself, and with that all possibility of love in his life.

It turned out that her name was Guddo.

Himmat's loneliness took on the edge of agony. To leave in such silence, how could she? Was she ever coming back, was she ill? She probably thought that because he was a boy, he couldn't do much. But he could do more than she, surely that much was obvious even to her. He heard his aunt's invective in silence, bending over his books, his work, his food, trying to shut her out. Mithari was particularly enraged because so much of the household was now in chaos.

As his aunt freely advertised her opinion as to the widow's morals, a new idea struck Himmat. Had Guddo become pregnant?

Of course, of course, that was it. In the village he would have thought of this possibility much faster, surrounded as he was by fertility, both human and animal. How often had he heard, the cow is green, time to get it mated, take her to the bull? He himself had done it countless times.

Again and again he thought of the last time they had been together. Her body had responded to his own urgency with more than usual abandon. Afterwards, when she had made him promise to keep her in a small corner of his heart, he had brushed away her seriousness. They were meant to be together life after life, he had said.

'You will be with your wife one day.'

'Who can force me?'

Then the sighs he was getting immune to. Promise, she had insisted, and so he had promised. And then the next morning her disappearance.

What was he looking so sick about, demanded the aunt. The churail has run off, now who will do the housework, you?

Himmat bent his head to hide his trembling lips.

His uncle intervened. By the grace of god they could afford to hire someone.

But to pay for labour she had been accustomed to get for free did not sit well with Mithari. Family values were being eroded, ties of mutual dependency flouted, and in such conditions she did not wish to live.

Virpal listened with half an ear. His thoughts were with his daughter-in-law, whose face he had never seen. What had driven her from the house? In all the years with them, she had never once set foot outside the gate, how did she have the courage, or was it desperation? He stared at Himmat's bent head, at his trembling hand, at the emotion that was so clearly evident and so clearly inappropriate. His sister-in-law should have been invisible to him. Invisible. Let alone within his reach.

Had she been in the village the surveillance of a hundred eyes would have made any transgression inconceivable, but in a house with only four people, anything was possible. And the boy was old enough.

Was it a pregnancy? A pregnancy when there had been no sign of one in her three years of marriage. The irony of fate. Briefly he shared his wife's outrage.

Where would she go? To a brothel, a dai, a morgue, to Benaras to hide her degraded self in an ashram for the destitute? At political party meetings, the agenda for female empowerment had been frequently discussed. His own home was a good illustration of what could go wrong with the life of a girl.

Although Himmat shone with health, every internal organ hurt. His heart felt weighed down by a sack of stones, when he looked at the tap on the roof the constriction in his lungs made breathing difficult, his stomach no longer aided his digestion, indeed directed him to abjure food altogether, his eyes teared up at night, his mind knew no rest, his head exploded with shooting pains.

At times he hated her. How had her power grown, that he could be so tormented? It wasn't like that when she was here. Then she was just a woman who was always crying, tears that he had grown bored by, so fixed had they been in her unfortunate eyes.

Now he saw the value of being a brahmachari like Sandeep. Desire was the most painful torture. Better discipline than indulgence.

He went to the Bajrangarh temple, climbing steps gouged out of the steep slope. Once at the top he could see the hills that surrounded the lake, stained red by the setting sun. He sat behind the peepul tree, watching gold patches undulate on the water. As soon as she returned, they would make plans to run away together. He would work, and she would have the protection of a man.

Without intending to, he roamed the city for hours trying to find her. The streets near the house, then further and further away, till he reached the bus adda, expecting to see a veiled figure, waiting for him to take her by the hand and lead her to happiness. One week, two weeks, three weeks, how long could he go on hopelessly looking? She had vanished, and that too with no money.

He could ask no one about her whereabouts, no one whether they had seen her. What use would any description be when her face was covered?

Mithari, still brooding over the loss of willing hands, asked her husband to call Himmat's wife from the village. It was not seemly that with so many relatives, she should have to hire help. Virpal resisted. The damage had already been done so far as Guddo was concerned. As for Himmat, he should concentrate on getting ahead. His own son had been excessively distracted by his wife, the kachoris in his hand at the moment of his death must have had something to do with her. He didn't want a repetition of the same thing.

Eventually the household help problem was solved by a part-time maid, old, ugly and buck-toothed. For seventy-five rupees a month she would clean the house and wash the clothes. The low caste sweeper was already there to clean the toilets at twenty rupees a month.

Curses continued to be heaped on the head of the absent daughter-in-law while Himmat continued to pay obeisance to his brother's photograph. In each offered flower he saw her face, her big eyes, her giving body, and his own weakness. Resentment, unhappiness and moral discomfort pervaded the house.

It was now that Himmat told his uncle he wanted to live like Sandeep. Sandeep's talk of a higher calling gave him an alternative perspective. As the Gita said, dharma lay in action. Sandeep had disposed of all family ties, he was a self-proclaimed pracharak, a celibate, whose aim was to devote himself to others.

Irritably, Virpal pointed out that Himmat could start his life of selflessness by helping his father free their ancestral lands. Now an NGO, colluding with a lady IAS officer, was after Dhanpal. The local patwaris were all under Jat control, but this was different. Did he know how much his father was sacrificing in order to make his son a big man?

Himmat acquiesced listlessly. Ever since he could remember he had been hearing about land difficulties. From this distance those extra bighas hardly seemed worth saving, though he knew both his father and his uncle would willingly shed blood for every inch of that earth.

Physical exercise at the shakha gave him temporary relief from his misery. On his way home, he often made a detour to the field in front of the cinema hall in Naya Bazaar. There he stopped to look at the boys playing kabaddi. Two teams crouched in the dust, the players circling each other, murmuring kabaddi, kabaddi under their breath. How enthusiastically he had once played this game! And how heedlessly. The dry land of his home flickered before his eyes. Its precious crops, the threatened bighas, the duties a son was born to. He must never pause in his climb away from the village, away from poverty

BROTHERS   141

that dulled the mind, and forced money and survival to be the
driving force behind everything.

Wryly, he thought that in this he had her blessings, she who
had been fond of saying, make your brother's name shine, make
amends for his short life. Only you can do it. At the time he
had paid little attention. Now those paltry wishes reverberated
in his mind.

His ambition made him focus on his studies, rocking back
and forth on his cot in the little room on the roof, memorizing,
memorizing, book in hand, back to that fatal tap, his gaze on
the hill beyond the house. When he was tired he sat with his
ear glued to a small transistor radio. The Australian cricket
team was visiting India. Here, in the world of sport, there was
no sorrow, no pain, unless India losing almost continually to
Australia could be counted painful. With his uncle he could
share accounts of centuries by Border, Chappell and Viswanath,
discuss Pataudi's captaincy, its pros and cons.

That year Himmat topped the class in his new DAV school.
Virpal insisted they go to the class teacher's house with a box
of sweets. This boy has potential, announced the teacher and
recommended a month-long summer camp held for students
his age. The focus would be on English, maths and general
knowledge.

If money was what it took to help Himmat develop, Virpal
was, by now, more than willing to spend. He himself had been
at a disadvantage because the village touch had never left him,
nor had the self-deprecation that came with it. In a world where
connections were everything, you had to have the confidence to
make them.

A month in the company of boys from other schools
brought Himmat his own depressing knowledge of how far he
still had to go. Useless to say take pride in your language and

culture, useless to rail against Western influences, they were the new reality. Anybody who said English was not essential was lying. Look at the self-assurance of English speakers, see the uneasiness of the non-English ones.

So Himmat struggled to become fluent in the language through *Reader's Digest*, the *Illustrated Weekly*, *Filmfare* (borrowed from the local lending library), reading his English Reader over and over again, memorizing poems so those locutions would stay with him. He committed to memory essays as well; My Holidays (a visit to a holy shrine), My Ambition (serve the country), My Favourite Festival (Diwali), Father of the Nation (Mahatma Gandhi), etc. etc., reproducing essays every child in the entire educational system hoped to get good marks for.

In a few months he would give his school-leaving exams. Now that he was doing well, his uncle was thinking of sending him to college. Were he to go back to his village, matrimony would suck him into its clutches. Dhanpal had once or twice asked if he should send the wife to the city, but he had always said no. Nothing should be allowed to distract the boy. Himmat would be the first in his entire clan to contemplate higher learning. He was nineteen years old.

VI

1971

Summer has given way to the wet uncomfortable heat of monsoon. On the opening day of university, Himmat sets out towards Government College, the oldest, most reputed college in Ajmer. On his forehead is a red tilak, mark of the puja his aunt had performed that morning. In his ears are his cousin's gold earrings; now yours, beta, she had said sadly.

His uncle escorts him, his nephew's first day as an undergraduate requires this much ceremony. 'I hope our Jat kin learn from your example, otherwise they are slow to use their brains,' he says. 'Fighting is all they know' Himmat gives a tight smile. He is more focused on the ragging he might experience, while his uncle's thoughts turn towards his son. He would have been the one to lead the way, but now it is Himmat who assumes that role. He has to remind himself that it is unfair to hold his son's brief life against his nephew. Everybody has their own destiny, useless, useless to compare.

Himmat walks up the driveway towards the long double storeyed white building, and feels all the discomfort an imperial builder would wish him to feel. This institution represents the academic mountain he has to scale. As he crosses the statue of

Prithvi Raj Chauhan two boys appear in front of him. They do not look friendly.

'Fresher?'

He nods.

'Don't you have a tongue? Say yes sir.'

'Yes, sir.'

'Name?'

'Himmat.'

'Caste?'

'Gaina.'

'Gaina – why are you wearing earrings?'

He stares at the gold glinting from the boys' own ears. They are Rajputs, enemies as ancient as the soil he stands on. His mouth felt dry. Where were his own people?

They hustle him off towards some bushes.

'Now Gaina, you can take off your earrings, or we can tear them off. We are giving you a choice because this is a place of learning. Your lesson starts with who you are.'

Himmat's hands tremble as he unscrews the studs. What would his aunt say?

'Fucker, why are you taking so long? Do you think you are some upper-caste boy, that your earrings are glued to your ears?'

A minute later he is on the ground doing sashtang pranam to his betters; that will teach him to look them in the eye. The earth he has smelled so often during surya namaskar is forced into his mouth as a final sign of his humiliation.

'If you report us, see what happens.'

He is a Jat. These boys should be the ones on the ground, begging for mercy, calling him sir.

'What do you say fresher?'

'Yes, sir.'

'Very good. You are a quick learner. You will go far,' they snigger.

He can see their dirty toes sticking out of their sandals. Just before they disappear, the earrings are flung in front of him, the gold discs rolling in the fine dust.

Angry tears trickle from his eyes as he bends to pick them up. Nothing like this has ever happened to him in school. He can see the main administrative building in front of him. To negotiate those few steps to the building now seems impossible, impossible to find his teachers, or take down his timetable. One day he will be avenged. He doesn't care how long it takes nor how he achieves it.

The worst has happened, thought Virpal looking at Himmat, home so early. Ragging could go on for weeks. As the story unfolds, Virpal tries to console. Rajput goondas on the social margins, need to show their muscle, used to thinking they can treat Jats any way they like. In reality every one of the seven hundred Jat gotras as good as the Rajputs.

Such consolation meant nothing to Himmat. In the village months of feuding would have followed such an incident, no problem there with whom to target, nor how wide a net to cast. In the anonymity of the city, injustice was harder to redress.

All night he tossed and turned, tension gathering in his stomach. More than the ragging, it was his own behaviour that bothered him. He should have fought back. He was outnumbered, he was inexperienced, but these things were no excuse. He had prostrated himself before Rajput goondas. What would Sandeep say if he knew? He could not imagine him on the ground before anyone.

Next morning Himmat left early to tackle demons as befitted a Jat, but at the gates of his college he faltered. His feet carried him further down the road till he reached DAV, where his friends were. The day was spent most enjoyably, loafing in the canteen, surrounded by the ambience of cigarette smoke and empty glasses of tea. 'Arre yaar, how is GCA?' asked his friends as they ignored bells for class, curious as to why he was there, he who had done well enough to go to a more prestigious place.

'Ghar ki mitti. You are my brothers,' he replied, and they were pleased, Mani Ram, Indraj and Kartara, from similar backgrounds, village antecedents, sent to the city by families that wanted educated sons.

How was college, they demanded at home that evening. Just fine, responded Himmat, and why wouldn't it be, since he had not entered it?

Three days later, Himmat came home with the announcement that he would rather die than go to GCA, DAV was the place for him. His refusal to elucidate accentuated the images in Virpal's mind of all the indecent things boys could make other boys do.

'Another college means another set of fees. Do you think I can afford to go on sending you, first here, then there, as though we are comparing prices in some bazaar?' he cried at last, exasperated by the problems of the young and their refusal to ever go away. 'You have so little respect for money? If you don't go back to college, you can kiss the buffalo's backside in the fields for the rest of your life, understand?'

The listening aunt was pleased that at last her husband was driving some sense into the boy. He was too soft on him, always too soft, which was why he could fuss so much about a little bit of ragging. Arre, boys get ragged, was Himmat the only prince in town to start objecting?

He may not be a prince, but he was not going to return to that place.

Dinner passed in silence and disapproval. The next morning Himmat disappeared before breakfast, to return only in the evening, exuding defiance. 'Where were you?' asked Virpal, unnecessarily. For the answer would be a lie.

'In college. Where else would I be, Baoji?'

'He has forgotten how to tell the truth,' screamed the aunt, the bitterness that was embedded in her bursting forth at every opportunity.

Uncle and nephew stared at each other. God must now be invoked to solve the problem. 'It's Tuesday. Lord Hanuman's day. Let us go to Bajrangarh.' As they walked towards the temple, Virpal said, 'Open your mind to the deity. Whatever happens, happens for the best. With our human minds we cannot know everything.'

God, who saw all things, would have seen Himmat's disgrace as he lay in the dirt, with his torn off earrings. God would have seen him two days later, seen his pants pulled off, seen the way they handled him, the obscene comments that passed when he had tried to hide himself. Was this what was meant by ragging? If they had wanted to emasculate him, they had succeeded. Not only had they kept him out of GCA, they had silenced him as well.

They reached the base of the temple and started to slowly climb the steps, to the accompaniment of the uncle's laboured breathing. All around them were people clambering up the hill, the young men giggling, holding hands, the girls decorous, the elder ones stopping from time to time to catch their breath and clutch their chests.

This was where Himmat had come a few months earlier to ask for success in his school-leaving exams. It was at the back of this shrine that he had tied a thread to mark the prayer. Now the obstacles in the path of his higher education had evolved into more pernicious ones.

'Beta, when your father gave you to me, it was to fill the gap in my life,' said Virpal as he dabbed his reddened eyes. 'He wants you to be a lawyer to protect our lands. Only our own will be bothered by our difficulties. Who else will care? The faculty of Government College Ajmer is the most respected. Since when does a Jat run away? How will you shine like this?'

After they pay their obeisance to Lord Hanuman, they walk around the sacred area thrice, slip money into the donation box, tie thread on the place of wishes.

'I wish I had gone to DAV college, Uncle, my friends are there. I can still change. They give some of your fees back.'

'What do you think college is? Sweetie – toffee – whenever you want, you spit one out and chew another? This has a better name. You were eager to come here. When it was admission time you didn't talk of friends.'

It was true. In the years Himmat had been in Ajmer, he had noticed how important your institution was. During the leadership camp, boys from well-known English speaking schools were the ones who bristled with importance, that was the springboard from which they leapt ahead.

The uncle sat on the parapet to gaze at the view below. 'All around you, you can see how hard it is to change the condition you were born to. I tried to enter politics. Even though I had gone to jail for my country, it made no difference, and I remained a small shopkeeper. Your father – he fought for the British, went to Afreeka, went to Burma, lost his health, but what did that get him? He is still a farmer. People like us cannot waste a single opportunity. If you make something of your life, it will help Mangal also. Otherwise who is there in the entire khandan? You, Mangal, that's all. Kishen Singh –' Here his voice broke. Himmat hung his head in shame. He would brave anything to make his uncle and his father proud.

Perhaps it was the power of prayer, or rumours that ragging was not going to be tolerated beyond the initial week, or the fact that once teaching started, the classroom became a place of refuge, but within ten days Himmat was successfully installed in Government College. In the routine of lectures, canteen, friends, studies, he passed blameless months under his pleased uncle's eye. The boy has finally seen sense, in many ways he was still innocent, taking too much to heart irritants that the more experienced were able to overlook.

Then came university elections. Fascinated, Himmat participated in discussions, canvassed among friends, inked out leaflets, hung around canteens, college lawns and hostels, ignored his studies and came home as late as possible.

'Will they really give us free education?' demanded a Jat friend, in the DAV hostel. They had just heard a candidate address the students after dinner in the mess, in a speech that swung between tuition subsidies, the war with Pakistan, the necessity of self-protection, minority communities, the need for a strong nation, and what was the student community going to do about all this?

'Free education? If they are promising, they will fulfil. Otherwise who will vote for this party next time? You only tell me,' said Himmat.

'Arre, it's all talk. Last election they promised us free books. Did we get any? All they did was put them in the library and allow us to borrow them for the whole term instead of two weeks. In the end you still have to return them. I just tear the pages out, that's how I make sure the book is free.'

Everybody snickered. Yes, that was how you had to make things work.

'In my time,' said Virpal, disapproving of so much distraction, 'students fought for the independence of their country, now the young only think of themselves. In Delhi it is goonda raj. Sons of leaders behaving as though the country is their own.'

'That's not true, Uncle. The boy yesterday talked of the Indo-Pak war, of Article 370 in Kashmir – how is that only thinking of himself? When I am a graduate, I too am going to stand for elections.'

'What will that get you? You can't study and do dada-giri at the same time.'

That remained to be seen, thought the nephew.

Then came the incident that threw Himmat into prominence.

Cultural Nite at GCA. Because there will be girls on the stage, male guests are not permitted. Himmat's DAV friends ask him to do something, they too want to see the culture that GCA is famous for. It takes some days, but eventually Himmat comes up with passes and fake IDs.

He waits on the front steps of the auditorium, pleased that they have slipped through the security at the gate. There is extra vigilance against boys like them, Jats from other colleges, out to create trouble. On their part, these very boys take such precautions as challenges, and wish to show signs of their presence.

Halfway into the show, the DAV students decide to have some fun. They whistle their appreciation. One of them throws coins on the stage at the end of a song. Such lumpen behaviour causes suspicion. Are their girls to be humiliated by suggestions that their performances, and by extension, they themselves, are for hire?

An interval is announced, the lights go on. The DAV boys are asked for their IDs. When they prove faulty, they are hustled outside. Sensing trouble, other boys quickly gather. Stories of what has happened grow wilder by the second. The fight blooms into knives, fists and stones, all the way down the driveway. Himmat tries to protect his friends by shouting insults and looking ferocious, but the excitement of the moment doesn't allow for protection. Katara from the Jat Chhatra Nivas, who had only come along for the fun of seeing the girls of Government College, a junior boy, the son of a farmer, like himself, is wounded so severely that he has to be taken to the railway hospital, down the road, where his head injury demands that he be admitted into ICU.

For Himmat, some kind of discovered honour is at stake. These are his friends, he has to show that he is capable of action, or he will never be able to live with himself. There are not many Jats in his college, but they draw support from the growing number of DAV students standing outside the gates, shouting. Led by Himmat, they gherao the principal's office, demanding justice.

What was the boy doing at the Cultural Nite in the first place? demanded the college authorities. Outsiders had not been invited for a reason. Anybody who broke the rules did so at his own risk.

This feeble excuse cuts no ice with the Jat contingent. It had been a harmless infraction of rules, harmless, harmless. If the boy was doing wrong, punish him by all means. They were not denying that he was culpable, but should you try and kill him? The boy was still in ICU, they were looking at a possible case of murder.

The gheraoing goes on for days. Students sit in the foyer outside the staff section. From time to time Himmat (among others) kept the fires of indignation burning by addressing the crowd. If students cannot be safe in an institution of higher learning, then of what worth is it? Rajputs thought they were the lords of the universe, nothing they did would have any consequences.

'We want rustication, rustication,' they shouted. 'The culprits should be rusticated.'

As the boy continued in ICU, the situation grew increasingly
volatile. Talks were initiated. Himmat was among the Jat
representatives. Eventually the demonstration was suspended,
the attackers had to publicly apologize, and agree to bear the
boy's hospital expenses. Once Katara was declared out of
danger, the Jats could afford to appear magnanimous by not
involving the police.

Students outside his batch began to recognize Himmat, both
in his own college as well as in DAV. Himmat liked the sense
of importance this gave him. How could he sustain such
recognition? People had short memories.

'Arre, Himmat,' said Maniraj, 'tu leader ban ja. So much
dada-giri you did when Katara was in ICU.'

Become a leader. Be known, and in the cauldron of college,
where varying ambitions seethed and churned, it was possible.
By now Himmat was sure that the key to success lay in student
politics. If you were the kind of person who could get votes,
your life was made. Then you didn't have to bother with studies,
there were different exams out there in the world. In classes
he slept, in anything to do with politics, he was wide awake. In
school he had innocently believed that academic excellence was
the only way to rise. But in the long run, what would studying
bring him? It would fry his brains, that was all.

At home, his uncle notices how little time he spends on his
books. He tries to remonstrate, but to no effect. All kinds of·
boys have begun to drop by, and Virpal sees how they revolve
around Himmat. What is it about him, he wonders, that attracts
so much attention? Maybe he is a natural leader, although he
finds this hard to believe.

The following year. Student elections. Rajputs versus Jats. Over
the past several months, the Jat candidate had worked to build a

support base, not only among his own caste, but among Gujjars, Meenas and Muslims as well. The Rajput candidate, lazy, arrogant, preferred to rely on his contacts in the police force. These he had used to get the Jat boy arrested under MISA. He was finally released after a week of agitation, a week in which his supporters gheraoed the police station, the principal, the vice chancellor. When the sincere Jat lost the elections, his followers were filled with fury. They had to do something about this defeat, their pride was at stake, as well as the need to issue warnings.

But the Jats had to be circumspect. College authorities had warned students repeatedly that any disorderly conduct would be taken very seriously, expulsion was going to be the mildest punishment.

This particular warning was planned for the middle of the night. Himmat was invited by a senior Jat to accompany them to the hostel, just to teach these bastards a lesson, yaar, we don't want anyone to know. That Rajputs in general needed to be taught lessons was as clear to Himmat as the earrings he still wore, and his face brightened at the prospect. His heart was pounding as he stealthily followed the boys up the stairs. This was the moment, longed for, over two years. Best of all was the fact that he wasn't alone, and therefore he needed to justify nothing to himself.

An hour later, it was all over. It hadn't taken long, and he had not been one of the main players. The Rajput boy had been dragged from his bed, his pyjamas ripped off and tied around his neck, pulled tight and still more tight, his strangulated face growing deeper and deeper red, his clawing hands, ten boys around him, watching, till a dead body lay in front of them, all its life and youth gone. They threw it over the gate, where it lay for morning to discover.

As Himmat left the college, despite his stern injunctions to himself, he could feel the nausea rising, could feel his legs unsteady and his face sweating. He walked through the main gates and threw up in the drain outside, heavy deep retches. When he could look up, he glanced around. There was no one he could see. Nor, since it was late, and he was standing in the shadow of a tree, could he be detected.

The news of what happened, and rumours of who were responsible, spread even while the body was being cremated. Every Rajput in every college in the city is part of the ensuing ruckus. They stand outside the shut gates of GCA, throw stones and yell. They want justice, they want revenge, and they are going to take it out on every Jat in the city.

Violence erupts, wrapping its arms around the hostel, jumping from room to room, from class to class, like sparks lighting on the tinder of the constant simmering hostility between Rajputs and Jats. Fire breaks out in the auditorium.

GCA is declared shut till further notice, the mess suspended, the hostel closed. The police question the boys but nobody says anything. Nobody trusts the police, they are too riddled with caste considerations themselves. The killers are never found.

Meanwhile Virpal accosts his nephew. 'Did you have anything to do with this incident?'

'Why would I? It happened at night.'

'You were not at home. Where were you? Can you be implicated?'

'I am innocent. I did nothing.'

'Don't be a fool,' snapped Virpal. 'Once you are in the police station, they can torture you to extract a confession. Innocent, guilty doesn't matter. Do you understand? This is kaliyug.'

Himmat hated it when his uncle talked like this. Kaliyug was hardly an adequate explanation for all that was wrong with the world. One might as well lie down and die because it was kaliyug.

They sat in silence in the small angan behind the shop. In the distance, the light of the little temple on top of the hill glimmered. Except for the sporadic barking of dogs, all was quiet.

Virpal decided it was safest for Himmat to leave the city. He suspected the boy was more involved than he let on.

Himmat is to go home after an absence of nine years. He had never once returned, not in the planting season, not during harvest, not for festivals, nor during the summer holidays. His uncle had made sure that every moment was involved with self-improvement, studies, shakha, body building, spirit building, determined that the gift his brother had given him yield dividends.

Though anxious that Himmat put down roots in his new home, Virpal had kept the village alive in his nephew's memory with stories, told with the purpose of cementing the boy's bond with his absent parent. Virpal talked of how close his brother had been to him, taking his place on British battlefields, something he could never forget. 'Your father is a great man,' he told Himmat repeatedly, 'He has carried the burden of the family on his shoulders, it was his big heart that made him part with you. This is a debt that someday you will have to repay.'

This debt rested lightly on Himmat. His desire to go home was weak. He was afraid of being sucked back into the earth from which he had emerged, afraid of an embrace that only death could free him from. His parents, his wife, sickness, an accident, anything could pin him to the mud floors of his childhood.

VII

1972–1975

Himmat left the house early next morning with a small suitcase. As he walked down the road, past the Ajmer Club, towards Naya Bazaar and the bus depot, his mind was full of the image of the boy who died. They had given him no time to scream, covering his mouth before he was even awake. The boys in the rooms on either side had remained oblivious from beginning to end, so quick and skilled had they been. There would be an inquiry, the chowkidar would probably be blamed, perhaps fired to satisfy the need for action.

Himmat was sure they would never be found out, a certainty based on nothing but a feeling that retribution could not happen to him. He had just gone along because he sensed that the revenge he had wanted for so long was about to take place. He was grateful to his Jat kin. They had guts, they were fearless, they had wiped the shame from his heart. He had a lot to learn from them.

The soothing journey home was already putting some distance between him and the event. With a mind less preoccupied than usual, he gazed out the window, at the remnants of forts crawling up various rocky slopes, at the small temples perched on top of them. Almost nothing grows on these stony hillocks, remnants of prehistoric mountains, interspersed with boulders. Ancient walls disintegrate into pools of rubble. Goats nibble at dry scrub, women with heads covered, bellies showing stand, stick in hand.

Here and there is a ploughed field, with a crude one room hut near the edge, the crops demanding day and night vigilance. How could anyone eke a living from these bravely planted meagre fields, set within the desert, dotted with kikar trees, their gnarled and knotted branches thrust against the sky?

What difference did it make whether you were near the city or far? As long as you were chained to the land, there was no escape. For every year of a munificent monsoon, there were two of scanty rainfall. How could anyone fight against that?

A few hours later the bus dropped him on the road that branched off into Sarwar. He walked a kilometre before turning right on to the dirt path leading to his village, moving through landscape that hadn't altered in hundreds of years. He had changed though, and the quiver of identification he felt with the villagers slowly meandering along on bullock carts troubled him. Almost he wished to turn back.

There was so much stacked against a boy trying to break through the barriers of his birth. Hadn't his uncle also thought he would be a big man, gone to jail in order to prove his value in a life that was poor and obscure? Hadn't the shakha shown him that it was necessary to work tirelessly if you wanted to influence people? GCA was no different. He had taken political science as one of his subjects, but the real science of politics was the one practised in the halls of the college every day.

It is getting on to four as he passes the reservoir, the water as green as ever. He can hear the chink of bells as cattle return from grazing, can see them step their delicate way down to the pond, see the dust rise gently from their hooves to hang in the evening gold lit air. On the far end of the ghat women pound clothes. His steps grow heavy with accumulated thoughts. This would still have been his home if not for the death of his cousin, and his father's desire to alleviate a brother's suffering.

To be a Jat headman like his father and grandfather would not have been a bad life. They were landowners, and the love they bore their land would bind them to it forever. Living close to it, tending it, nurturing it. But now that he had moved away, both worlds jangled in him, he was neither fully one nor the other.

He reaches the village, to be accosted by the first wayward boy he meets. Should he hold his suitcase? Where had he come from? Whom has he come to meet? At each word there is a giggle.

Himmat is going to the Gaina section, his suitcase can be held if it is done carefully. More boys gather, till the line that follows him stretches down the gullies. By now the news has reached his home. Himmat has returned. You won't recognize him, he is like a sahib, a sahib.

The inner section of the Gaina home lies beyond an outer courtyard linked by a narrow passageway. It is here that the family gathers, here that the cooking takes place, here that Himmat's mother has spent most of her life. In the dim light of evening, her lined face is lit by the fire over which she crouches. Children and women surround her. She hears the news, and her hands begin to tremble, her silver clad arms feel uncharacteristically burdened.

Gulabi watches her son bend to touch the feet of his father. Dhanpal rises unsteadily from his charpai, his white turban framing his lean handsome face, furrowed like the earth he has spent practically his whole life working with. Some of his teeth are missing, his earlobes are weighed down by heavy gold earrings. Whether it was in the fields of Lalbanga or the fields of war, he has only known hardship. Now, to see his son after years means happiness is his, pure, unalloyed happiness. Tears come to his eyes as he takes in his city manner, his city pants, shirt, shoes, city suitcase. He looks like those government babus who have made his life hell for so many years. Maybe he can become an IAS officer instead of a lawyer, those were the ones with the power, the ones whom every poor litigant had to bribe.

'Look what a sahib he has become,' says Dhanpal to all who gathered in their angan to stare at the newly returned.

They want to know how it was in Ajmer. What was he doing? After so long, still studying? Arre, they laughed, if he was here, he would be a father.

'This lawyer business takes a long time, otherwise what was there to stop you or me from becoming one?' demands Dhanpal.

Again they all nodded.

'Baoji, I want to become a leader. This lawyer business is not for me,' said Himmat.

'Don't you want to free our lands?'

'As a leader I can do much more than that. Much more. Baoji, you will see.'

'Your uncle said you were studying for law.'

It was too difficult to explain. In the end Himmat let them believe he was studying for a law degree, which in a sense he was. Only with different intentions.

Dhanpal doesn't speak of the years he has missed his son, doesn't speak of the years the son has waited before coming home. Once he had given him to his brother, the giving was complete. It had no strings attached, no claims to contest. But seeing Himmat, tall and citified, he knew that his sacrifice had been worth it; the boy was going to make something of himself, he could see it clearly in his face.

Himmat feels the smooth cow-dung floors, cool beneath his bare feet, smells the smoke whirling up from sticks thrust into mud stoves, sees the string cots scattered around the angan. For the first time it is clear to him how far he has come.

Gulabi puts her hands up to touch him, her lips trembling. Her age means she doesn't have to cover her face any more, Himmat can see the white hair peeping out from the edge of her gilt edged veil. She looks so much older than his aunt in Ajmer, what was this place that sucked all your youth? And his younger brother, there he was, spindly legs, oil slicked hair, he was sure he only went to school when he felt like it, and fooled away the hours when he didn't. He could predict every minute of his future if he stayed in the village. Maybe a time would come when he could do something for him, blood of his blood, and therefore his responsibility now and forever.

He is fed, rotis smeared with ghee, onions, some radishes from the fields, green chillies, a glass of sweetened buttermilk by his side. He eats alone, within a circle of twenty people who observe every gesture. Perhaps, they comment, this food is not to his liking any more. It is the food of home, he replies, its taste is in his blood.

Ghar ki mitti, they murmur at this appropriate response. Who can forget it?

A charpai is pulled out for him to sleep on. All is dark, dark as velvet, dark as only a village night can be. The stars above shine thickly and take him to his childhood. Tears no one can see swim about, but then he closes his eyes, and falls asleep.

There is no fan, no electricity, it will take him a while to get used to this. He also has to get used to getting up early in the morning and going to the fields with a precious pot of water. His father tells him that it was because the low castes wanted to use their fields in the morning for the same purpose that tension has increased in the village. These low castes were getting above themselves. If they had nowhere to go, how was it their problem? They could do it outside their own homes for all it mattered.

Himmat spends his first day walking slowly from place to place, listening to echoes of his youth emanate from the landscape, unable to feel more than a vague connection. Was that really his younger self, thin, barefoot, knobby kneed with spiky oiled hair, whacking a cow, staring at him expressionlessly, a face startled into a shy grin when Himmat looked at him. For of course, they all knew who he was.

Dust got into his chappals as he walked down the mud paths, past a few shacks functioning as shops, a low neglected building that was the school, a dusty maidan used as a playing field, the odd tractor, a few cycles and rows of neat mud dwellings. Everything filled him with a sad nostalgia. He desperately wished for the objective gaze of a stranger, but that was not possible. In the myriad eyes focused on every step he took, on every gesture he made, he could feel the collective desire to claim him. But he could no longer be one of them. The issues that occupied his family were so petty, who was shitting where, whose cow ate what leaf. It was disloyal to experience his home like this, but he could not help it, and to feel so torn exasperated him.

Finally the night. Himmat is bone tired, but sleep doesn't come. He turns to see a figure curled on the floor beside his bed. Who is it? 'Aiee,' he whispers. No response. He pokes the bundle with his foot. 'Aiee,' he says again.

The figure sits up. 'Bhai,' it says. Mangal.

'What are you doing on the floor?'

'Nothing.'

'Is this where you sleep?'

Mangal did not know how to answer this question. He slept wherever he happened to feel sleepy. All the boys did that.

'Don't you have a voice in your head?'

Mangal bridled. For the past nine years he had been nurtured on stories of his brother, stories of valour and courage, along with stories of amusing naughty deeds, and the emptiness all had felt when his father had taken him to Ajmer.

Now the hero himself was here, and he wanted to savour each moment by his side. The brother though seemed to not notice his presence in any marked way, as if he were just one of the many cousins he had been introduced to. Nothing specific had been directed towards him, the younger brother, the closest brother. This made no sense to Mangal.

'Don't you have a voice in your head?' repeated Himmat.

'Why did you take so long to come back?' stuttered Mangal. 'They kept saying I had to take your place.'

There was a pause.

'Come here,' said Himmat at last.

The boy gingerly sat on the edge of the bed.

'Closer. What are you afraid of?'

Himmat pulled Mangal towards himself. He stroked him lightly, and felt some of the stiffness leave his brother's body.

'What do you do all day?'

'This only –' Mangal waves his arm around. Cows, fields, family.

'Don't you study?'

Himmat could feel him shaking his head.

'How will you be a big man?'

'When you take me to the city.'

'You want to leave Baoji?'

'You did.'

'That was different.'

'How old are you?'

'Ten-twelve.'

'Let me see,' and he slipped his hand into the boy's loosely tied drawers and cradled his testicles. Mangal parted his legs slightly. 'Still some time to go.'

'Hair is growing,' said Mangal defensively.

'Little walnuts. Now go to sleep.'

The boy squirmed with delight next to his brother, close enough to smell the faint perfume that enveloped him, wondering what it must be like to be so sophisticated. Himmat, not used to accommodating his body to another's, eventually deposited the boy back on to the floor.

Another day passes. Himmat wonders about his wife, but will not ask. A particular woman serves him, veiled, young, work roughened hands, nails smeared with bright red iridescent polish. When she bends to pour dal or to refill his tall steel glass with water the odour of her sweat reaches him. He feels only indifference towards her and, that night, when his mother leads him away from the main living quarters towards the back, where the cattle are kept, he stops to resist outside the rim of light.

'Where are we going?' he asks, though he knows.

'To your wife.'

'She is nothing to me.'

His mother giggles, 'Afraid of your wife?'

'I don't want a village girl.'

'Are these your city ways? You have to be with her, otherwise there is only shame for us. Her family will say things.'

'What things?'

'Your son doesn't know how to be a man.'

'It is not their business.'

'Then whose business is it?'

The son was silent. He had seen the girl working next to her mother-in-law, cooking, fetching, carrying, doing the thousand things village women did from morning to night. Now it was his turn to fulfil his role.

The mother tries to placate him, 'You will be happy when you have a son. That is what she is here for. She is a good girl, all these years she has not said a word. She is your wife, you want to be a brahmachari all your life?'

This grates on his nerves. Is there only one way to have a wife? He, who had broken out of the village mould, was now expected to cohabit with shadows. The mother sensed the change in his mood. She stroked his arm a few times, urging him towards her world, which had once been his own, before turning back towards the main compound. What followed would be decided by the girl's karma, there was nothing more she could do.

As Himmat advanced, he could make out his wife's covered shape on the charpai. At his footsteps she straightened, half turned towards him, he could hear the silver on her arms as she moved. He sat down next to her. The cot sagged and the ropes sighed. He tried to turn her face towards him, to see her eyes, her expression. Instead she bent her head. His fingers against her chest could feel the beating of her heart. Village girl.

Tentatively he put his hand under her skirts. She didn't stop him, but neither did she lie down obligingly. Impatiently he pushed her down, fumbled with his own clothes. When she cried out, when her flesh involuntarily shrank from his thrusts, when he heard the stifled sob in her throat, he thought of that other woman, her shy willingness, and in his anger he grew more savage.

Abruptly he finished and left. He had told Guddo that he hated his wife, told her casually and with no knowledge of the girl. If she could see him now, with this meaningless ritual behind him, she would know that he had not lied.

Yet, despite himself, the memory of the night lingered. He had done it once, he could not think of a single reason to not do it again. To have a woman so easily available was a novelty.

But she never spoke, just allowed him to do what he wanted. Did she mind he was away so long, he asked. She did not answer. It had taken him almost a year to make Guddo speak to him, but that was because she was not his wife. What was the problem with this one?

Gulabi watching, sees how often he gets up once the lanterns are out. She is glad. She has told the girl to go to the bari every night, Himmat's experience in such procedures is new. Once he became a father, his ties to his home would be strengthened. She remembered how easily Mithari became a city wife, why should the same thing not happen to her daughter-in-law?

By now Dhanpal had lost the cases he had been fighting for ten years. Other people had legal issues that stretched into lifetimes, but here, some interfering NGO and that dog of an IAS woman, made sure that his court hearings were hurried in the name of social justice. Papers, papers, he was sick of being told that he had no claim over land that had always been his. As far as he was concerned that was nonsense. The low castes had been put on earth to work the fields of the upper castes, not to fancy themselves by claiming ownership rights. Even if a few of them were killed as a warning, what good could that do against the government?

Himmat tries to relate to what his father is telling him, but in the nine years that have passed, his notions of social justice have assumed a more personal aspect. What do you do when one caste tramples on you unchecked? What do you do when your earrings are snatched from you, when you are forced to the ground, when your pants are removed, and your member touched? Insults which remained without redress didn't fade with time, they could ambush you at any moment for years together.

Meanwhile he develops a certain affection for the fraternal creature who never leaves his side. The child had been two when he left and in the years he has been away, he has never thought of him. Now when he looks at Mangal, he sees his own features mirrored, reminding him of what he used to be. There is much of himself in the boy, the same restlessness, the same propensity for getting into trouble.

Mangal barely talks, it is Himmat who initiates conversation, conversations which focus on his studies, for he feels disinclined to discuss cows, buffaloes, grazing, fields, planting, those essentials of a farmer's life.

'What is six times eight?'

Silence.

'Five times ten?'

Silence.

'You don't know five times ten? What kind of student are you?'

Mangal looks confused.

'What is two times two? If you don't know what two times two is, I am going to talk to your teacher tomorrow. Either he is a stupid idiot or you are.'

'Four.'

'Chalo. At least you know something.'

'Arre,' said Dhanpal, who was listening. 'You don't expect schools here to be like city ones, do you? If you are so concerned about his education, take him back with you.'

The onlookers giggled. How can you ask a village boy what six times eight is? It was unreasonable. None of them knew. They had their own method of calculation, which was all they needed.

'Whatever you become, a leader, a lawyer, I don't know, but you have to remember your family. A Jat never forgets.'

By now Mangal's whole foot is white with dust, so vigorously has he twitched his splayed toes in the soft earth. Normally he can talk quite well, he just didn't know how to talk to this man, his brother, who is actually a sahib.

'In the city everybody is only for themselves. That is what we have heard. Is it true?'

Before Himmat could apply himself to this question, Dhanpal broke in angrily, 'How can it be true? Arre, do you not see how Virpal is looking after him?'

But Virpal was blood, what about the others?

'What others?' demanded Dhanpal. Only blood mattered. In the end only blood was left.

As if to emphasize this point, for the two weeks Himmat is there, people comment, freely and liberally, as people are wont to do, see how Mangu loves his brother, see how he follows him, arre, his own blood after all.

Buoyed by these comments, getting used to his presence, towards the end of the visit, Mangal begins to ask his own questions. Himmat was surprised and pleased. 'So you have a brain after all?' he said.

'Just like yours,' retorts Mangal. Had Himmat really gone to two-two, three-three schools, was he going to become a sahib, work in an office?

No, laughs Himmat, he doesn't want to become some office babu, whose importance comes from the files he could block if you did not bribe him. Where is the achievement in that? He wants to be of service.

'Service? To whom?'

'The people.'

'What people?'

'Everybody.'

'Then stay in the village, what's wrong with the people here. Not important enough?'

'You are too young to understand.'

'Make me a babu everybody wants to bribe, Bhai, if you don't want this kind of work. Money for free. Better than following a buffalo all your life.'

'Before I call you I have to make something of myself, no?'

'If you wait another ten years, I do not know what will happen to me.'

'Why?'

'They are talking of my marriage,' said Mangal shyly.

'Arre, now they consult the groom or what?' Himmat started laughing. Mangal laughed too.

'No, Bhai. Of course not. I heard them talking, that's all.' As usual, his big toe was frantically going wiggle-wiggle in the dust.

So. At eleven his brother's future has been decided. Ploughing fields in the day, planting his seed in his wife at night. If there was one thing he could do for Mangal, it would be to prevent his marriage.

College reopens, his uncle sends word that he is to come back. Briefly, he thought about the body thrown over the gates before he pushed the Rajput from his mind. He had done nothing, seen nothing.

As he got ready to leave, he wondered whether his wife had become pregnant. She too had been green, she too had been taken to the bull to be mated. If he saw her in daylight, he would not recognize her. Hopefully he had performed his duty effectively enough so that no one could accuse him of not being a man.

On the day of his departure he was up at four. Everybody gathered to see him off, escorting him through the village. Mangal stays close to him, holding his suitcase as they walked all the way to the main road. 'When will you return? Can't you take me with you? You were as old as me when you left.'

'How do you think our father will feel if you also leave? Besides what will you do? You can only go to school, and even for me it was awful in the beginning. Sit in one place, study, study, study.'

'I can also sit with a book,' said Mangal. 'What is there in that?'

'The city is lonely unlike the village, not this togetherness, knowing everybody. People have no time for you.'

'But here too everybody keeps working from morning to night. At least in the city there is none of this field-cattle business.'

This statement jarred on Himmat and he whacked his brother hard, 'Arre, this earth is your mother, don't you know anything? Feeds you, clothes you, and you show disrespect.'

Mangal rubbed his head, more in reproach than injury. 'If the earth is your mother, why don't you come back, huh? Every Diwali, every Holi they wait for you; but you never come. They say it is because you are busy becoming a big man. Well, are you?'

'I can't come back – there is Uncle – there is –' Himmat stopped. Once you left, there was no return, it was like sliding backwards into a hole. He himself did not know what lay in his future, but he knew it would not be the one prescribed by his origins.

At the main road Mangal hides the suitcase behind his back – there is a small tussle – a little laughter – and finally annoyance before Mangal reluctantly hands it over, touches his brother's feet and turns back, almost running. Himmat looks at the dust his feet raise, the thin legs pumping away, and his old self again comes to mind. At least his father had promised to postpone the boy's wedding. In return it was understood that it was up to Himmat to shape that future he had already interfered with.

In Lalbanga, nine months after Himmat's departure, a son is born. Messages are sent to the city, the naming ceremony will be held in forty days. Presence essential.

Virpal announces the birth to the new father, news which is received in silence. The boy is only twenty-one, thought Virpal, too busy with studies to realize how important it is that his line be carried on, that his wife is fruitful.

Himmat continued resistant to any suggestion that he assume the role of fatherhood, even the nominal one of being there for the naming ceremony. There was no question of his going, he said. He had done his duty, kept the honour of his family, produced a son, but he could not be actively involved in the child. One thing would lead to another and this was not a journey he wished to make.

So it was left to Virpal to temporize, to go to the village in his stead, to lie and say that the pressure of exams did not allow the father to return to his home, they must understand, these things were considered very important, no, not more important than a son, but there was a time for everything.

Mangal was very disappointed that Himmat did not return for the ceremony. It seemed that his brother could do anything, even be absent for the rituals surrounding his own son's naming.

'I want to go back with Uncle,' he told his father.

'To do what?'

'Meet Bhaiyya.'

'And hang around his neck? Your place is here.'

How could his father be so sure? His brother had been his age when he had left to take Kishen Singh's place. Who could die, whose place could he take? At this thought he quickly spat three times, spitting at the evil spirits who had drawn near his family, attracted by his thoughts. May his brother be protected forever. Still, a tragedy in the family had turned out to be anything but a tragedy for his brother. That had to be recognized.

If Himmat ever thought of his son growing up in the village, he didn't say. From time to time Virpal tried to send him back, something he had never done in all these years. Don't look at the mother, but the son you should look at, no? The aunt stared on drearily. Ever since Kishen Singh died, there was a bitterness in her soul that made her anticipate misery everywhere.

Virpal tries again at Diwali, 'You have holidays, go for a few days.' At Holi he says the same, but always Himmat claims work and then disappears from the house.

Virpal thinks sadly that he had never thought the boy's roots would weaken if not refreshed by frequent visits. This lack in Himmat is a burden on his heart.

Three years pass. Exam time arrives, exams that should have been studied more for, but college seniors had taught them that there were many ways to pass, studying was not the only one.

This was proved when they sat in the exam hall and copied down the relevant answers from chits secreted in their hands.

This was the ultimate triumph; to find loopholes in the system that would allow you to beat it.

BA in hand, Himmat joins the Law Faculty. He hangs out with his friends in the dhaba outside the gates. They start with tea, pakoras and cigarettes, and move on to rum and charas as the evening wears on. They talk and talk, suggest the changes they would make if they could, and among them, Himmat unfolds his own dreams, centred on one thing and one thing only: a political life.

As a senior he is eligible for the post of union president. A nomination from the IPPP student wing was what he needed to make him a significant candidate. But how to get it? Tickets were given to sons of politicians or to sons of big landlords. Besides which, there were caste considerations, Rajputs and Brahmins dominated. But if his uncle talked to Rash Behari Bishnoi, a party nomination might be possible? How many stories had Uncle told about helping him win his first election? Maybe now was the time to use this contact. It was not as though they had many.

'Don't even think of it,' said his uncle. 'I refuse to be one of the sycophants around him.'

'Please, Uncle.'

'Beta, this politics is very difficult to get into. Limited seats and so much competition.'

Himmat was silent. He thought of a CPI man he had encountered the other day, come to gather support for the Communist Party in the university. He had been on the university rolls for fifteen years, moving from one course to another, all so he could remain in student politics, while waiting for a chance on the regional level. Politics was not a field where the old made way for the young.

'Beta, listen to me, concentrate on your studies, don't waste your life chasing shadows.'

'I want to waste my life.'

'Is this any way to talk to your elders? This politics has poisoned your brain.'

'Sorry, Uncle, sorry. Just once talk to him. Please. He is a Jat, he will be sympathetic.'

'What about money?'

'The party gives.'

'The party? They will not give you a khota dhela.'

'Not the UIP, it is true, but definitely the IPPP, at least something.'

Uncle snorted. The foolishness of youth was beyond him. They thought money grew on trees. They only needed to find the one specific ladder tall enough to enable them to reach out and pluck thick wads of cash. That's what youth thought.

Had his father sent him to the city, he said, to exchange one set of uncertainties for another? What madness has gotten into his nephew that he thinks politics is a citadel he can scale? It is birth, pedigree, connections all the way. Look at the Son, the Rising Son. His only qualification was his birth, and that enabled him to hold the country in his hands. If politics was so easy wouldn't everybody line up to do it? He himself had failed.

'Please, Uncle,' begged Himmat again and again, 'I am only asking for an opportunity, that's all. Those sons who have so much power, they had fathers, grandfathers who took the first step. You helped Bishnoi Sahib when he was unknown, he will keep that in mind when he sees me.'

'Arre, that was eighteen years ago. Now he is a minister, too high. We cannot expect anything.'

'He is a Jat, he knows how to be faithful. At his weekly darshans he is available to everybody.'

Rash Behari Bishnoi: They could still see his face, round, moustached, smiling, plastered on thousands of posters pasted on the city walls during the recent elections, now frayed and tearing. In the world of posters, so far as Rash Behari Bishnoi was concerned, nothing had changed. He continued to decorate the walls of Ajmer on a periodic basis.

'So what do you want me to do? Stand outside his office and beg?'

'No, Uncle. I will be the one to stand outside his office and beg.'

'I can write a letter, no more. If it is your kismet, he will deign to look at you.'

His uncle accompanied him to the inter-city bus terminal early next morning. Two and a half hours later when Himmat finally made it to the bungalow of Minister Sahib, he was startled by the number of supplicants clustered under an awning stretched out behind a small two roomed office complex, adjacent to the main house. Jats, waiting to see what one of their own could do for them, young men flanked by elders; you did not walk by yourself in this country. As they were ushered in, they hauled out boxes of sweets and kilos of fruit from cloth bags.

He handed his letter to the clerk who was taking down names and assigning numbers, 'My uncle, an old friend of Bishnoi Sahib's, please be sure to give this to him. They are very good friends.' The clerk's indifferent gaze slid past his face, suggesting this fabrication was not even worth addressing.

An hour passed, then another. The benches lined against the wall were full, he was tired, impatient, upset and hungry. In one corner was a matka of water, he had already dipped the metal mug into it and drunk from his palm several times. He noticed the privileged ones, the ones who came later and were seen earlier. The hierarchy that allowed you to jump queues was impenetrable to such as him.

Restlessly he left the gate, he needed a wall against which to pee. He walked down the broad street, the branches of its old trees meeting overhead. He gazed at the large plots, the smooth grassy lawns, the set-back houses, the driveways within the gates. This is what it was like to be a minister. It was quiet too, no hawkers, scooters, or rickshaws, only the oiled wheels of government cars going in and out of those gated entries.

Soon it would be dark, he would have to catch the night bus back to Ajmer. There was hardly anybody left under the awning by the time he was gestured inside. Cool air touched his sweaty face as he opened the door. He looked shyly at the man behind the table, dressed in a crisp white kurta pyjama. On his feet were white chappals, he wore blue tinted glasses. His belly strained the roominess of his loosely fitted clothes, his hands were broad, the ringed fingers stubby. 'Sirji,' he stammered, 'my uncle, Virpal Singh Gaina, sends you his respects. He also wrote to you, I gave his letter to the clerk outside. I hope you got it, sir?'

The politician looked at Himmat. 'Come, come. And how is my friend Virpalji?'

Before Himmat could elaborate, he must bend to touch the elder man's feet, he must offer his own weary box of sweets, he must suggest that without Bishnoi Sahib his life could not begin.

'Tell me, what is the problem?'

The phone rang. An assistant handed it over. 'Choudhary Sahib is asking, what about that contract?'

As Rash Behari talked, he gestured Himmat towards his assistant. Phone call over, the assistant explained, 'Ji, he wants the IPPP nomination for student union president. Studying in Government College, Ajmer.'

Bishnoi Sahib sighed. Morning to night he was visited by Jats who saw him as their entry point into a system overrun by multiple community interests. The assistant was told to phone their local man, find out the situation, was anybody else being considered? Who were the opposing candidates? Their background?

While this was being done, Himmat said, 'My uncle, Virpal Singh Gainaji, was very sure you would look back on your youth and encourage someone like me. From the village. Wanting to work for the country.'

'That's all very well, but how will you pay for this? Nothing is for free here. You have to raise a certain amount yourself, otherwise the party will choose another person, someone with money, with connections, with some strength in their bones. There are how many like you? Thousands, thousands all over the country.'

'Sirji, please, I can raise some –'

'You think party leaders are going to give you just like that? Even if I ask. They will say who is he? How do we know he can deliver? Has he ever won an election?'

'Sirji, please, I just need one chance.'

'And this is a university election, not a college one. How will you campaign in Jaipur for instance?'

'I will tap all the Jat networks, sirji. I am willing to work. If necessary I will walk all over Rajasthan.'

Bishnoi Sahib allowed himself a small laugh. 'Did you hear that?' he asked his assistant. Turning to the boy he added, 'The days of Gandhiji are gone, beta, when walking all over the country meant something. But I will see what I can do.' Himmat darted forward to touch Bishnoi Sahib's feet once more, and the minister tapped his head. 'Remember I promise nothing. If you get this chance, it will be the only one. Should you lose, no one will bet on you again.'

'Yes, sirji.'

On the night bus. Himmat's first contact with power left him unable to close his eyes. It was true then, Rash Behariji was a man who did meet the common people, did give them hope. What did it matter that he had to wait so long, or that the secretary was making money by fiddling the sequence of appointments? If nothing came of this visit, he would return to Jaipur again and again. Now he had seen Bishnoi Sahib, his awe of him morphed into a determination to get that nomination.

Some campaigning, some political influence, some luck and Himmat was nominated the IPPP candidate for the post of student union president, with a budget sanction of five thousand rupees. Now he and his friends could start campaigning in earnest.

GCA was his base. From there he spiralled out. Going by cycle from college to college, arranging meetings, making speeches in hostels, cafeterias, marching into classrooms, to talk about concessions, hostel subsidies, scholarships and the necessity for a committed student leadership. The '71 war with Pakistan had shown that the country needed to be strong; the world over students were demonstrating their power, why should India be any different? He tried to keep his speeches brief, punchy and patriotic, knowing how quickly he himself had become bored whenever candidates addressed classrooms.

Himmat approaches his uncle for money. 'From somewhere the NSUI has found a Jat candidate, some big-big landlord's son. Otherwise they always nominate Rajputs. They want to split the Jat vote. I need to travel, contact our boys in other places. I will have to give money for posters, for tea-samosas, for liquor. The communists, Congress, all the other parties are doing this.'

Grudgingly the uncle parts with cash. A hundred rupees at a time, hundred by hundred by hundred, each hundred accompanied by an equal number of questions. Patiently Himmat described how he was saving money by travelling on the top of buses, muscling his way into trains for free, staying with Jat students across the state. What was not for free was food for his cohorts, election materials, alcohol. He stretched each paisa to new limits.

Every moment of political activity confirmed to Himmat that the struggle for supremacy was least loaded against him here. Otherwise, what opportunities were available to a boy like him? Educated, but with few contacts? A government job as a clerk in some dingy office? A lawyer hanging about in courts waiting for clients?

Election day. Classes are suspended. Outside the polling booths young men swarm like bees around a hive. Young girls, eyes lowered, walk decorously inside. The ground is coloured with squares of cheap coloured paper, ballot numbers, candidate names and election manifestos. Observers from the faculty and various parties are grouped inside. Voting finishes at 5 p.m.; the results will be announced two days later.

For two days Himmat felt worse than he ever had in his entire life. He didn't want to meet his uncle's anxious eyes, he didn't want to meet his friends, those Jat boys whom he would be letting down if he lost. Both evenings he walked up to Bajrangarh and stared moodily at the lake beneath him. Beyond those hills lay his village and the life of the land. After a point it was all destiny. It took an hour of such contemplation before he felt calm enough to walk down, sit on a bench and allow himself to eat something alone, in itself an anomaly.

The announcement of his victory left him dazed, elated and unsteady. His work had paid off. He was the first Jat president of the student union. Firecrackers were let off near the union office, garlands thrown around his head, there were interviews in the press, and photos. A huge tilak adorns his forehead, his smile splashes across the page, but the feeling of unreality persists.

Across the state the IPPP celebrates. Their candidate has won. Day and night supporters come to the house, come to congratulate, to proffer sweets, to talk and celebrate.

Success even in this minor key had eluded Virpal all his life. Now his predictions fly fast and furious. The boy will go far, he has the dedication, the capacity to win people. He has to go to Jaipur and seek Bishnoi Sahib's blessings. It is his hand on his head that has enabled this.

That Sunday afternoon Himmat caught the bus to Jaipur. In his jhola was a box of special Ajmer milk cake. If he was unable to meet the minister after a few hours, he would leave the sweets, along with a note containing gratitude and devotion.

Once he reached the house, he hesitated. Without the structure of an official gathering it seemed intimidating. The gates were shut, the guard stared suspiciously at him. He slowed down in front of Minister Sahib's residence, before hurrying on to calm himself.

As he walked, Himmat barely registered dusk falling, or the birds wheeling about in the pink Jaipur sky, or the green lawns gleaming with their unreachable expanses, or the white walls of the spacious bungalows, or the girl veering towards him on her cycle. She had to brake suddenly, her bike toppled and she would have hit the ground had Himmat not grabbed her.

It was a Hindi movie scenario, faithful down to the last detail. The pair, now staring at each other, embodied every single difference there could possibly be in class, education and status.

Himmat at this stage of his life was handsome. Life in the city had given a sheen to his smooth skin, his height was above average, he was slender, his colour was pale brown and the reddishness of his cheeks shone through. The features were sharp, and full lips could be seen under a carefully cultivated moustache. At the moment his expression suggested a melancholy closer to a poet's than a farmer's frustrated son.

As for her, she was her father's only daughter. Unfortunately nature had endowed her with little beauty, her face was round, her nose broad, eyes smallish and forehead narrow. But she was fair, and her gaze direct enough to move him.

'You will think I am blind,' said Himmat. 'Please forgive me. I hope you are all right?'

She looked down, twitched her handlebars about, murmured she was all right.

Her willingness to remain there, even for a few seconds, emboldened him. 'I am so sorry. You see I have come all the way from Ajmer to see Minister Sahib. I have just been elected president of the student union and I wanted his blessings. He knows me, my family. My uncle campaigned for him in his first election in '56.'

'You've won?'

'Yes.'

'Then your work is done. What more do you want? You think he doesn't see enough people, that now he has to see them twice?' She tossed her head, while looking at him out of the corner of her eye.

'Arre, to show I am grateful. He put in a word, I got the IPPP nomination, you think I should be so shameless as to not even seek his blessings?'

'Everyone else is shameless, why not you?'

He could indulge in repartee as well as the next person, but a) she was a girl, and b) whose girl was she? He could not function in a vacuum.

'Forgive me, you are related?'

She was his daughter, she said, looking away, as though it were a merit she did not wish to insist upon.

He bent slightly, his hand on his heart, in homage to one who was his superior. 'Forgive me if I have said anything to offend.'

It was all right. She was not offended.

Half an hour later he was on the road again, happy, elated, triumphant. Not only had Minister Sahib seen him, but he had personally congratulated him on a job well done, indicated that this was a good way to enter politics, had handed the box of sweets to the girl, who had sat there the whole time. What was it like to be Bishnoi Sahib's daughter, to enjoy the freedom she seemed to enjoy? She may not be pretty, but she was something more, she was smart, smart like city girls, the ones he would ordinarily never dare approach. He had shot one or two shy looks at her and when she noticed, she giggled, which made him turn a deep red. He should have said something, now she would think he was a tongue-tied village idiot. Should he write to her, thanking her for entrance into the house? He had never written to a girl before, and after much hesitant composition, sent a letter, then waited anxiously for a reply to his hinted feelings. Nothing, nothing, every day nothing, and he withdrew into himself. Why should a girl like that look at him, he had overreached, and at the thought he felt humiliated and angry.

As the year went on Himmat's profile grew more visible. Of all the concessions the IPPP had promised, they had actually managed to implement one without any trouble (an increase in scholarships) and for the bus concessions they had gheraoed the Rajasthan State Transport Office day after day, until their demands were met. Bus passes would be available to any student for ten rupees a month. Then the exam break came, and all activity died down.

May 1975. A time of unrest. Jayaprakash Narayan launches nationwide protests against the government. A rally is planned in Jaipur, the state capital of Rajasthan. It is going to be massive, all sections of the Opposition are involved.

Student leaders mobilize numbers, among them Himmat Singh Gaina. Night buses, night trains, they must use everything they can to get the required masses into Jaipur by three o'clock, the time the leaders are scheduled to speak. Before Himmat starts planning, he pays a visit to Bajrangarh. God must know that he is willing to work hard, he has always been willing, but he must be recognized. Please, god.

Every contact he has ever made in the university is called upon. As for transportation costs, his friends will take care of any ticket collector who makes unreasonable demands. Their campaign experience means they are old hands at this.

The purpose of the rally was to ensure maximum visibility, aka maximum traffic disturbance, to ensure media coverage, to make a splash large enough to counter the ruling party's hegemony.

The leaders, the speeches. JP, the most charismatic, touched on freedom, violated rights, the sanctity of the judiciary, and how the guilty would have to step down, no matter who they were. He spoke of corruption in the leadership, the need for complete probity. At a time when people were afraid of being thrown into prison under MISA for so-called violations to internal security, there was nothing he did not dare say. Total revolution was what he called for.

The massive crowd, filling the huge square before the state Parliament, cheered and waved their red, red flags, the IPPP flags, Marxist-Leninist party flags, the BJS flags (Bharat Jagrit Sabha). There were student unions, trade unions, worker unions, there was the CPI (Communist Party of India), the CPM (Communist Party of India [Marxist]), the SOP (Socialist Party), the SP (Swatantra Party) and the BKD (Bhartiya Kranti Dal). For all his experience of university politics, this was the first time Himmat fully realized how rich the dividends of planning down to the last detail could be, particularly for those out of power.

The national dailies focused on the speeches, while the local newspapers added articles describing unruly students beating up ticket collectors, while bus conductors were forced to let students ride for free. If this was the concern for law, thundered the editorials, the centre was justified in the stringent measures they took to impose order.

Rally over, Himmat returns to being a student. The mid-term exams are approaching. He wishes to put an LLB after his name, though he has no desire to be a lawyer, doesn't want to sit in an office, or ever fight a case.

He has a long road to travel if he is to become anything, and clearly, being in student politics is no more than a speck of sand upon the shore of the Ganges. What did he expect, a call from Bishnoi Sahib's office, congratulations, your efforts for the rally marked you as exceptional among student leaders, now please come to Jaipur and be my right hand man? Did he expect that the girl he had written to, would persuade her father to see his qualities? When she hadn't even replied?

There were many like him. He was nothing but an insect crawling in the gutter, scrambling over other insects in order to survive.

'You are young, it takes time to rise, time, time. Patience, perseverance. Look at me,' said the uncle in a tone meant to be encouraging.

But that was where Himmat was afraid to look. A life of frustrated hope was not for him. It was clear that without a mentor he was going to get nowhere.

'I just want to be part of Bishnoi Sahib's retinue,' he told his uncle. 'I want to learn from him. How can I do that if I can never get near him, or anybody else for that matter. Who am I?'

He didn't want to remain a student forever, going from course to course so he could continue in university politics. But if there was no other way to gain his heart's desire, he would do exactly that. How many years before he became visible and valued?

12 June 1975. The Allahabad High Court pronounces the prime minister's 1971 Lok Sabha election invalid. Justice Jagmohan Lal Sinha declares that Indira Gandhi cannot contest elections for six years.

Days of agitation and uncertainty follow. There are demands for the PM to resign. Bishnoi Sahib's voice is prominent among these. Himmat decides it is time to contact the girl again. Maybe the earlier letter had been misplaced, maybe she had been too shy to write back, these aspects needed to be considered.

He wanted to assure her, he wrote, that if he could be of any help in the present situation, she should just let him know. He didn't want to boast, but he had mobilized the greatest number of students for the protest rally. She should not take offence at anything he said, just think of him as a brother and direct him accordingly.

His tone is a mixture of the impetuous and the tentative. In the world he came from, for a man and a woman to be friends was a daring activity, fraught with anxiety, secrecy and tension.

But anxiety and tension were now operating on a larger scale, and perhaps this was the reason that Bishnoi Sahib's daughter did reply, a terse letter, which he read and reread till it was engraved in his memory. Her father was in danger. They did not know what was going to happen, she could think of nothing else. She would keep his offer of help in mind. He wrote back immediately, trying to restrain himself from expressing all he was feeling. He was into his third letter when a state of Emergency was imposed on the nation at midnight, 25th June 1975. India's darkest hour had begun.

Within a day news came that Bishnoi Sahib had been arrested under MISA. Immediately Himmat set off for Jaipur, he didn't care if he had to hang around jail for the rest of his life. Let him be useless, let him be turned away, let him be beaten up by party workers, hounded by police, but this was the place to be, and be seen.

VIII

1972–1977

The years did not lessen Mangal's longing to be like his brother, suited, booted and sahib-like. Living in the city will work this wonder, and to this end he pesters his father to let him go.

'And who is going to see to these fields when I am gone? My ghost?'

'There are others, Baoji, I am begging you. He wanted me to come.'

'And leave what son here? Do you see any more around?'

'Ram Babu. He is almost three.'

At this argument, Dhanpal raised his shoe. Mangal is as afraid of his father as his father meant him to be. He returns to the idea of just upping and leaving, it seemed the only way to achieve his goal.

But he neither ran, nor settled down. Offers continued to come for his marriage. As the son of a man with extensive landholdings, he was intensely eligible. But Dhanpal had promised Himmat he would wait, and for the time being, he wanted to keep his promise. The elder one's marriage had not turned out well. Quite clearly the boy wanted nothing to do with his wife, even after she had provided him with a son. This made him uneasy. Why couldn't he be like Virpal, who had taken his woman back to the city? That was the way things should be done.

One night. Mangal was sitting by the cooking fire, eating. A kerosene lamp hung from a nail on the rafters above, and in the dim light his father's voluminous white pagri stood out.

'Baoji,' he said hesitantly.

Observing the anxious gaze and chewed lip, the father wondered what it would take to make this boy a man. He had beaten him countless times trying to instil courage and strength, and look at the result, a snivelling girl, probably in a fight with some Rajput that he couldn't handle.

'We need to be careful.'

'Why? What have you gone and done?'

It turned out that Mangal had beaten a Rajput boy who claimed that his cows had eaten the young wheat in their fields. This was when the cows were on their way home, clearly the boy was looking for an excuse to fight. Which he shouldn't have done, because he was so weak that a few knocks had left him flat on his back. Whether he was dead or unconscious he hadn't bothered to find out. But best they be on guard.

'You think we don't have enough difficulties without you killing Rajput boys?' demanded his father.

Everybody could tell the demand was a rhetorical one. If Rajputs troubled you, what could you do? Dhanpal sighed, as he gave orders for vigilance. Their compound walls were low, anyone could easily jump over them.

It was dark when they came with sticks and stones. The Jats, ready and waiting, managed to push them away. The next morning, while on his way to the fields, Mangal was attacked, this time with a knife. When he ran home, blood pouring down

his face, for the first time Dhanpal was afraid. He could not
afford to have anything happen to Mangal. And the boy was
such a baby that it would be easy for anyone to knock him about
a few times, wound or kill him.

That night he discussed the issue with the others; nobody
put it past the Rajputs to not murder Mangal, and nobody had
any faith in Mangal being able to resist an attack. Send him
to his uncle for a while, then we can sort this out through the
panchayat. Otherwise he will never be safe.

Dhanpal would be better able to deal with the Rajputs if
he didn't have to worry about his son. They set out that very
afternoon for the city, catching the bus from Sarwar. At last the
boy was getting his wish, thought the father grimly, let him see
what city life was really like.

It was night by the time they arrived at Virpal's. The door
opened, and Mangal fell at his brother's feet. All the way he had
dreamt of this meeting, smiling to himself as he stared out of
the window.

'You didn't want him to marry. Now here he is. Make
something of him.'

Mangal looked expectant, but Himmat remained silent.
'I am here, Bhaiyya,' he said, 'remember you wanted me to
come.'

'It took you three years?'

'It was not in my hands, Bhaiyya.'

It was Virpal who welcomed them, Virpal who asked for
the story, Virpal who condemned the Rajputs, who said of
course, this was the only thing they could do, something like
this had made him run away all those years ago, it went without
saying that their home was Mangal's home. Life and safety were
the most important things.

Dhanpal returned to Lalbanga the next day.

'When will you learn that you can't settle everything by fighting?' demanded Himmat once they were alone. 'Especially since you can't handle matters yourself.'

'What could I do?' demanded Mangal, who seemed to have found his tongue on the journey from Lalbanga to Ajmer. 'Sit back and let them insult me?'

'Learn how to keep out of trouble.'

'Look.' Mangal pushed his sleeves up to show him the scratches still visible, pointed to the gashes on his face. 'They might have blinded me.'

'It's fights like this that keep villages backward. Rajputs-Jats, fighting for centuries. Has it improved anything?'

What had happened to his brother, thought Mangal. Nobody ever questioned the value of fighting, it was something everyone did. It was the only way to prove yourself, and though he kept getting thrashed, the day would come when he would thrash others. His brother was a good example of how possible it was to change.

In these three years the village was stamped out of him. His early morning stints at the shakha meant that his shoulders were broad and his arms muscular, like those of a pehlwan. In the city his colour had become clean and fair. His hair was cut long at the sides and back, filmi style he said when asked.

The days passed. Mangal would not leave Himmat's side, whether inside or outside the house.

'You stay here and study. There are my old schoolbooks. Try and learn something.'

'If I had wanted to study, I could have done that with Masterji in the village.'

'I have to go to various places for work, I can't take you every time, what will people think? As it is, it has taken me so long to not be seen as a village boy.'

'What is there to think? You are looking after your younger brother. That's good, no?'

For the first time Himmat understood his uncle's impatience with him when he had first arrived, but younger and more malleable. 'You won't understand,' he said curtly and left the house.

Mangal grew more miserable by the day, besides looking sulkier. The city which had appeared so wonderful to him, the running water, the flush, the toilets, all of it meant nothing if he was left alone with some worthless books. He had imagined the interest his brother would take in grooming him, but the opportunities he had visualized falling into his lap the minute he arrived, remained well hidden.

'Baoji was right,' he said one evening. 'There is nothing for me here. Bhaiyya has no time. If I have to stare at books all day, I can do that in the village.'

'And be killed?' said Virpal. 'These feuds can last forever. They will want blood, your blood, they say you murdered the boy.'

'They are lying. I only pushed him.'

'They are saying you threw a stone at his head.'

'He started it. How was I to know he was so weak? He tried to take our cow.'

'That is all villagers think about. Cows. Feuds,' said Himmat.

'Beta, you have to take an interest in your brother. Go with him to the Bharat Jagrit Sabha school. They will remember you as one of their bright students, they will take him.'

'He doesn't know anything.'

Mangal looked at the ground. Had he taken so much trouble with his tables for nothing? He knew them all, forwards and backwards. 'Ask me any table,' he now said.

'Nine times nine?'

'Eighty-one.'

'Twelve times eight?'

'Ninety-six.'

'Beta, bas. He has a sharp mind. Tomorrow take him to the BJS school. Now you are better qualified than me to talk to the principal.'

His uncle's praise made Mangal glow; there was hope for him. His brother would be speaking to the principal of his former school, tomorrow they would go together, perhaps he could prove himself there.

Early next morning, they walk to the BJS, located so conveniently at the edge of the colony. 'I will do the talking,' said Himmat.

Mangal hadn't imagined otherwise.

Himmat sighed. His brother would appear backward, but at least not ignorant, and they understood shyness. This school where all the losers of the world went. Where you had to get out as quickly as possible if you wanted to make anything of yourself.

They entered the metal gates. There, in front, was the goddess Saraswati, there were the boys, so clearly from the lower classes, hair slicked with oil, loose and baggy trousers held up by belts, their scuffed shoes carefully polished, the same classrooms, with no tables or chairs, merely durries on the floor, the same hole in the wall for a toilet.

Himmat was greeted with great joy. An alumnus, in a manner of speaking, one who had made them proud. He must come and talk to the students, motivate them, show them it was possible to succeed.

Mangal was admitted provisionally. Standards were more rigorous these days, they told Himmat, but since he came from such a family, he would have the brains to succeed.

'Now, sala, make us proud,' said Himmat as he left a puzzled Mangal behind.

All day Mangal sat quietly in the class he was assigned to. 'Your brother was so smart, very quickly he topped, now you have to follow in his footsteps,' he was told at every possible moment.

Indeed that was all Mangal himself wanted. Learning through osmosis was a favourite pedagogic tool in the school, and he understood nothing of what was going on. It was difficult for him to do the work assigned, he was forced to copy from a friendly Jat boy, and could this really be the road to greatness?

Mangal noticed how little time Himmat spent on his own college work, while he himself was supposed to sit with his head in a book all day, killing his brain. If studies were that important, why wasn't his brother studying? All he did was run up and down between Jaipur and Ajmer.

So Mangal was left to sink or swim as the tide took him. Some mugging, some cheating, some luck, and the reluctance of the teachers to keep back a relatively older child, carried him forward. At home if anybody noticed his attention wandering, they shouted, 'How will you pass? Do you want to stay in one class all your life?'

The best part of Mangal's days were the nights, when he crept next to Himmat who would put a heavy careless arm around him. Often he stayed awake as long as he could, just for the pleasure of feeling his brother's breath rise and fall next to his own.

Himmat's frequent absences were the cause of many fights between Virpal and him. 'You are making a fool of yourself, these people will do nothing for you – finish your studies, become a lawyer – enough money has been spent on your education.' Inwardly Mangal cheered his uncle on, Yes, tell him – he can't be leaving us all the time, it's not right.

'I have to go,' said Himmat looking agitated. 'Bishnoi Sahib is in prison.'

'So what? Is he your father? Is he holding durbar in Jaipur Jail that you are dancing attendance? Or have you established an adda outside the gates, and all the waiting police are your honoured guests?'

'He is like my father. More than. Who got me the IPPP ticket? My father couldn't have done that.'

'Sala – now you are insulting the man who gave you life?'

'Uncle, I am not. I am only saying, a man has to have many mentors in order to rise. In the village, in Ajmer, in Jaipur. Where would I be otherwise?'

Mangal, listening with all his might, wondered what they were talking about. Had his brother reached somewhere? If so, where was that – everything still looked the same, and money was tight as usual.

'Bhaiyya, where have you reached?' he asked Himmat.

'Nowhere,' replied his brother gloomily.

'I hear you are a president?'

'What is that? You can't be a student forever. Bishnoi Sahib is in prison, now is the time to do seva, now, when he will remember me. Uncle does not understand. He thinks I am making a fool of myself. Arre, I have to make myself useful, or no? Otherwise why should anyone care about me? Naturally I will do anything party workers or the Bishnoi family ask me to. We are trying to get him released on compassionate grounds, he has sugar, and his pressure is too, too high.'

'Who is this we?'

'Why aren't you studying, sala? Always asking questions.'

Mangal was dissatisfied. He wanted more of his brother's life, because he wanted more of his attention. In the village, boys did everything together, but he knew that to expect that of

Himmat was unreasonable, after all he was ten years older. All
he could do was catch up as fast as he could.

A few months later the family heard that Bishnoi Sahib had
been shifted to the State Guest House where better medical
care was available. 'Now will you stop running to Jaipur?'
demanded Virpal. 'Do you see the situation in the country?
You think a few – or even many – visits to Bishnoi Sahib will
get you anywhere? Power is only in the hands of those who have
the trust of the Family. Nothing else is allowed.'

   Himmat looked stubborn, and the trips to Jaipur continued.
Finally he got his heart's desire. He was arrested under MISA
for holding a demonstration against MISA. He had been
part of a group clutching placards outside the state legislature
demanding the release of all prisoners thrown into jail without
a reason, without a trial, without a case. This was a time of fear
and cowardice, why had Himmat rushed in where angels fear
to tread? Did he have a death wish? This is what Virpal wanted
to know when the secretary of the student union brought him
the news.

   'They hit him with lathis when he resisted, that much
I heard, Uncleji. He was with other students from Jaipur.
I wanted to tell you before you heard it from some other
source.'

   'Always acts without thinking. Doesn't listen.'

   'He is too small for them to care much. It is just a warning.'

   'Arre, it is because he is too small that they can do what
they like. I kept telling him, kept telling him, be careful.
What mad dog has bitten him that he must demonstrate
against the government in these times? I am going to tell
his father, take him back, make him a farmer. Being student
union president is not enough for him, always running after
something bigger.'

'Uncleji, your nephew was brave enough to court arrest. Today everybody is scared. We all admire him.'

Virpal grunted.

'He doesn't want to remain mired in the mud, he wants to soar.'

'All this soaring-shoring. Now he is eating the dirt of jail. Is he happy?'

'He wants to do seva for the country. Now is the time, he said.'

'Fool. People are tortured in prison, they die in custody. This is not British rule, when there was respect for the law. This is kaliyug, anything can happen. And what about his LLB exams, how will he do them?'

'I will get you news as soon as I can, Uncleji.'

But news was slow in coming. Gloom and accompanying fury struck the family. What was the need for the boy to behave so recklessly? Had he taken anybody's permission? Now they were all suffering.

Mangal said maybe he too should demonstrate against MISA, that might help his brother. Demonstrations appeared to be the way things were done.

Uncle hit him on the back of his head. 'I have had enough foolishness in this house,' he cried. 'Why don't you both go and die in front of the jail – why are you here at all?'

'He is just trying to copy you,' said the aunt in tears. 'Did he even discuss his plan? Just like that, runs off, does what he likes, as though he were an orphan.'

After a few months Himmat was released. Go eat your own dal-roti, they said as they kicked him out.

At the Ajmer station, friends gathered to garland him. He had proved himself, and the halo of his months in jail shone brightly. All day students and local IPPP people streamed into his house.

Although public demonstration was muted, and the absence of the cowardly press noted, there was plenty of private rejoicing.

'What were you thinking, beta?' demanded Virpal. 'If something had happened to you, what face would I show your father? He would have said any child who comes to this house is cursed.'

'Nothing would have happened to me, Baoji. Besides, what should I do? Hide in the house to save my skin? That's what the teachers did. They refused to join me, only students came. Then they give us moral lectures in class. Fight against injustice, blah, blah.'

'They don't cause their parents the worry you do.'

'You want me to sit by, with my mentor in jail?'

'Since when is Bishnoi Sahib your mentor?'

'He helped with my nomination for president, doesn't that make him my mentor?'

'You and how many thousand others?'

'Doesn't matter. Mentor is mentor.'

There was no arguing with the boy's stubbornness.

When Mangal saw all the pumping his brother had got for going to jail, all the importance, he was filled with admiration. Talking back to Uncle, with no subsequent beating, meant that Uncle acknowledged Bhaiyya was right. Books were useless. It wasn't degrees that got you consequence, it was how cleverly you moved the world in your direction.

~

January 1977. Elections are declared. The prime minister, who had experienced no real opposition during the entire twenty-one months of the Emergency, was sure of victory.

Himmat announced his involvement in the ensuing campaign. Again Uncle objected. 'These are national elections. Not some college thing, where you can cycle around and gather votes.'

'Everybody's effort is important.'

'Why? What about your studies? You want to fail or what? The LLB exams start in April.'

'What is there in passing? But this chance won't come again.'

'What chance? What chance? Bishnoi Sahib is still in the State Guest House, not allowed to go anywhere, meet anyone. Like Bharat you will put his chappals on your head and ask for votes in his name?'

'Soon he will be released. Any day now.'

'How do you know so much about him?'

'In Jaipur everybody knows.'

'For this campaigning business you have to take Mangal.'

'And his studies?'

'You are so good at studies, you teach him. As it is, we can't sleep at night thinking of the trouble you can get in. With him, at least you will be careful.'

'While we wait for Bishnoi Sahib to get out of jail, I will address the student communities in Ajmer, Jaipur, Alwar, Udaipur. I have Jat contacts in all these places.'

Mangal's heart leapt up. At last a glimpse of the world outside, the world that had been tantalizingly dangled in front of him by his brother's comings and goings. By now even he had developed an interest in Bishnoi Sahib, his name was mentioned so often. What was he like?

'Because of him I am union president. People look up to me, come with their problems. You have seen that, no?'

Yes, Mangal had seen that.

A few weeks before the elections it was announced that all political prisoners would be freed.

'Sala, Jaipur chalna?' asked Himmat. 'Come and see who I am campaigning for.'

They went by bus straight to the State Guest House. Was this a jail, wondered Mangal, but he was careful not to ask anything, careful to be a silent presence, so that his brother would realize how unobtrusive he could be, and take him next time too. Whenever his brother glanced at him, he smiled.

By the time Bishnoi Sahib appeared, two hours had passed.

'Why, he looks just like a farmer,' exclaimed Mangal, as they jostled among the crowds, trying to touch the politician's feet.

'He has become so thin,' said Himmat sadly.

'How will he travel anywhere? He looks as though he should be in the hospital rather than the road. Arre, if I touch him, he will fall down.'

'Mind your tongue. He is the IPPP candidate, and the IPPP has decided to back the Janata coalition. Nobody else has such a chance to win as he does. We have to help him all we can.'

We, Himmat had said we. They were going to travel together, do things together. It was all Mangal wanted.

'He doesn't care about his health, but his family does, I have promised them I will look after him.'

'You have got to know them so well? Because they are Jats?'

'His daughter trusts me to look after her father.'

'Aiee. His daughter. Are you doing love-shove with her?'

'Sala, don't talk when you know nothing. She is a friend, nothing else.'

On what basis could you be friends with a girl? How did you even begin to talk? Where did you meet, who all would be looking, how could you be natural? This baffled Mangal so much that he couldn't even think of what more to ask.

Instead he said, 'In school they said I was lying when I told them I was campaigning.'

'When we win, our names will be mentioned in the papers.'

'Can't you come to school, Bhaiyya, and tell them?'
'Wait till the elections are over.'

The day before they left, Mangal kept asking Himmat, what is
it like, where all are we going?

'Don't expect anything great. We will travel in buses, jeeps,
sometimes on top if we don't get space. Nobody cares for you
on these campaigns. There are so many just trying to be noticed,
trying to make out they are important.'

'But you are important. You said his daughter is relying on
you.'

'Bishnoi Sahib doesn't know that.'

'Then?'

'Why are you always asking, then? I have to make him see
how much I can do for him. And when the time comes —'

'Bhaiyya, when you are in politics, don't forget me, huh?'

'First let me reach somewhere myself.'

In the hilly dusty swathes of the Ajmer constituency, they
travelled in the IPPP convoy. All day Himmat looked for
opportunities to present Bishnoi Sahib cups of tea that were
sugar free, to give him snacks that were not fried. Every day
he went to houses of sympathizers, touched the feet of elder
women, pleaded for home cooked meals with very little salt or
oil, all for the cause of democracy. He had even come equipped
with a five-container steel tiffin carrier.

From time to time Himmat would collect branches of
green channa roasted in a fire, peel the pods and gather them
in a bowl for Bishnoi Sahib. 'This is a very good snack, sirji,
very healthy.' And the man would take the bowl without even
looking at Himmat.

'Is this what campaigning means?' asked Mangal, unable to
see his brother reduced to such a menial position.

Himmat sighed. 'Don't tell Uncle. This is the way things work. You don't know what all you have to do to get noticed. Even president of the student union doesn't matter here.'

'Then why don't we campaign in the university, where it does matter?'

'Because this is a bigger stage. The minute I leave, there will be twenty others to take my place. At least you and me are fingers of one hand. I trust you because you are my blood.'

Mangal blushed with pleasure. His brother may not show his love, but that was just his way. How can the fingers of one hand ever be separated? He mumbled, 'When you are like Bishnoi Sahib, I will be like you – I will bring you tea without sugar.'

Himmat laughed. 'I hope I never need that.'

Villages, towns, mohallas. Each stop represented thousands of votes. Everywhere people were talking of how India was going to change. Look, said Himmat, at the poverty. Indira Gandhi had proclaimed *Garíbi Hatao*, but garibi was everywhere. Did she think that by saying remove poverty it would get removed? Arre, what money is spent in saying?

But Mangal was not paying attention. He was thinking of all the eunuchs they had met.

'Not eunuchs, you donkey. Sterilized men. Some boss in Delhi thinks India should control her population, so grab every man you can find, mostly among the poor, uneducated and unsuspecting, and sterilize him, either by force or by bribes. If they don't have their manhood, what do they have? Good, now they will vote for us.'

As they bumped along on top of buses, at the back of jeeps, Mangal wondered at the life Himmat had chosen. He never saw Bishnoi Sahib look at Himmat even once. Yet Himmat claimed he was responsible for his meals, his transport, his accommodation.

March 1977. Victory for the Janata Party! Indira Gandhi defeated! Congress defeated for the first time since Independence! Victory for Bishnoi Sahib, the Indian Progressive People's Party's candidate from West Ajmer! When the cabinet is announced, he gets a ministership! Jubilation!

In one photograph Himmat Singh can be seen in a corner, behind many of the influential. In an interview Bishnoi Sahib thanks the student community for their support. Himmat took this as recognition and continued going to Jaipur.

'Half your life you spend there,' complained his uncle. 'Is Bishnoi Sahib going to reward you in some way? Does he even know of your existence? Once you do your exams, you can settle down as a lawyer, call your wife and son. You have never even seen your child. What is he going to feel?'

For a moment Himmat's face twisted. But all he said was that politics was a game of patience and he knew how to wait.

Himmat cleared his LLB papers, thus proving the existence of miracles. He had hardly attended any classes and knew next to nothing. His uncle kept pressuring him to begin his internship, while Himmat clearly felt his future could be found on the Ajmer–Jaipur highway.

How will he ever settle down after tasting the blood of politics? thought Virpal. He hoped Bishnoi Sahib, now set to shuttle between Delhi and Jaipur, would find the time to recompense the boy who insisted on regarding himself as his protégé.

Then one day Himmat announced casually that Uncle should pay a visit to Bishnoi Sahib.

'Bishnoi Sahib has asked for me?'

No, not exactly.

Then what?

Himmat looked embarrassed. His uncle became suspicious. What had the boy been doing? He didn't want to hear any complaints. He kept telling him to settle down, no good could come of this constant roaming about.

It was nothing like that. Only good news. It was his daughter who wanted Uncle to talk to her father.

Why? asked Virpal.

They had been meeting, said Himmat, only innocently of course, but a visit by Virpal would make his intentions clear. Her parents were insisting she get married, otherwise Himmat only wanted to approach Bishnoi Sahib when he had made something of himself. It was she who didn't want to go on seeing him without her father's consent. So could Uncle please go to Jaipur, and make their involvement public. Then a roka could follow.

Virpal's jaw continued to drop during this speech. He was not sure he understood what his nephew was saying. He had never thought of Himmat as a stupid boy. That perhaps was a mistake, the young are nearly always stupid. In this case ungrateful as well. Bishnoi Sahib had recommended him for the post of student union president, welcomed him into his house, and he had taken advantage, gross advantage. He grew so agitated that for the first time he slapped Himmat. Mangal started. This was the slap he had been waiting for ever since he had entered the house. He had almost given up, it was so clear that Himmat led a charmed life, with his own wishes at the centre.

'Uncle, what have I done?'

'Since when have you become so brazen? You meet Bishnoi Sahib's daughter, secretly-secretly when the man is in prison. People will say you did this behind his back.'

'Uncle —'

'So this is why you keep running off to Jaipur? Where is your sense of honour? Your decency? I myself will tell her father what kind of boy you are. I myself. Do you hear?'

'Uncle, please listen.'

'Is this the way you treat the man who made sure you got money for the union elections? Who referred to you in the press? Who will he blame? Me.'

The aunt began to cry. 'He looks innocent like milk, but is poisonous like a scorpion. So many years he has eaten our salt. What is the use now, even if you send him back to his village, they will still come with lathis and kill us. They are Jats too.'

'I have done nothing,' said Himmat desperately. 'I only talked to her, that's all. Why is that such a crime?'

'Where did you talk to her? In her house?'

'No.'

'Was anybody else there?'

'No.'

'Have you told her you are married?'

'I am not married. That is no marriage.'

'Don't fool yourself. You are married, right and tight. You have a son.'

'So what? I did it for them. All the time they kept saying, it is your duty. Otherwise you are not a man.'

The uncle was silent. Himmat was too shy to initiate anything on his own. The girl must have been one of those forward city types. Finally he said, whether he considered himself married or not, the fact was that he had a wife. They were not Mussalmans who could have four-four wives at one time. It was illegal to marry in this situation, and he would not go to Bishnoi Sahib. Did he think Ajmer was a village, where nobody knew the law and anybody could do anything?

Mangal was thoughtful too. So Bhaiyya had lied to him, she was not just a friend. This was why he never came home.

'Wives are not like dolls,' continued Uncle. 'You can't buy another when you get tired of one. Has she been unsuitable in any way? She has given you a son, she has never disobeyed you.'

'Obedience? Is that all I want from a wife? As for the son, I keep telling you, I was forced to do that.'

'You think this is how family life is conducted? What about the ones who arranged the match, you want to blacken their faces? What about the years she has lived in your house? Do you think whims and fancies can change all that? Your father will never allow it. Never.'

'Bhaiyya,' asked Mangal that night, 'are you going to have two wives? Can you do that in the city? In the village you have to go to the panchayat.'

'Just shut up, all right? How is any of this your business?'

'What about Ram Babu? He looks like you.'

'So?'

'I am just saying. The child lives in our father's lap. He cries when he goes to the fields, sticks to him like glue when he comes back, sleeps in his bed at night. Other men have many grandsons, he just has Ram Babu.'

'Should I be kept back from all I want, just because they insisted I go with that girl? That is why I can never go back. Never. Even Uncle doesn't understand. This is a chance of a lifetime. For months and months I had to plead with her just to look at me.'

Yes, thought Mangal, Uncle did not understand, and thinking of his uncle's incapacity, he felt superior and close to his brother. He had seen Himmat on the campaign trail. He sympathized with his ambition, with his frustration at how difficult it was to get noticed. This was a game played by thousands of players, all waiting to pounce like tigers at a chance. Once the chance came, it was seized, even if it meant trampling over everybody else, because there was hardly ever another opportunity.

'What's she like?'

'Who?'

'The girl.'

'Like girls are.'

'Arre, very clever, doing love-shove with Bishnoi Sahib's daughter. Now future is made.'

'You think I did it for that?'

'What else? When you have a wife – son – everything.'

'Hold your tongue, if you know what's good for you.'

'Why taking so much tension, yaar? Am I saying anything wrong?'

'You don't understand how things work.'

'Uncle is complaining. Saying you are playing with family honour.'

'Nobody thinks of honour these days. It is all about network. Look at our leaders. Who is the most important man? The PM's son. No position, but everybody at his beck and call. Even his friends are powerful. Why do you think Uncle never got a ticket though he did so much for the country? He had no connections, that's why. I do not wish to be like that.'

'Of course, Bhai, of course. You are doing the right thing. Uncle will realize. He is old. Emotional.'

The brothers went on talking into the night. As Mangal listened, he saw the figure of Ram Babu recede into the distance, this boy who had been his tail, whom he had played with to make up for the father's absence. Sacrifices had to be made if you wanted to be somebody important, he was not such a fool that he didn't realize that. He hoped for his brother's sake that everybody in the family realized it too.

~

A year later, Dhanpal died. Virpal was devastated. It was the war that killed him, he was convinced of it, and he remained convinced of it even when they told him he had gone suddenly, shortness of breath in the evening, tightness in the chest. After playing with his grandson, he had lain down to sleep and never gotten up.

Virpal went on crying. 'Younger and gone first. Who is there for me now?'

Himmat and Mangal cried along with him. Their grief continued as they got ready to go to Lalbanga, continued through the arguments of how long Himmat would stay. His fear of the village shone through with greater force than grief for a father he had only seen occasionally over the last many years. 'I am just going for one day. This is my duty I know. As for the pagri ceremony, someone else can take on the mantle of the Jat clan, I cannot do justice to it. How will I be able to, if I am never there?'

Before the cremation, Mangal, Himmat and Virpal shaved their heads as was customary. Himmat performed the last rites and left the next day. There was no mention of his taking back his wife, an expectation he could decipher on many faces, including his mother's. He refused to acknowledge her, as she hovered on the periphery, a hopeful covered figure, similarly he averted his eyes from the small boy who clung to her side.

Virpal observes all this, sitting gloomily on the charpai. The little boy is clearly the darling of his grandmother. There is only this one child at home to lighten her age. The bloodline of the family was weak. Boys Mangal's age had children, children he could see all around him. But Himmat refused to be with his wife, and Mangal's marriage was still pending.

The minute Himmat left, Mangal relaxed. He was going to be in Lalbanga for the full thirteen days of mourning. Young Jat boys clustered around him, tell us what it is like, is it true Bhai is going to become a famous politician, is it true you were part of the elections, how come you didn't come here to campaign, your own village.

Mangal, squatting on his haunches, said, 'You voted for us, didn't you?' 'Haan, haan,' chorused the older ones, 'Jats not vote for a Jat, what are you saying, of course we did.'

'Well then? Campaigning is not like going to your friend's house. You have to convince the uncertain. We even had to visit the outcaste section, what to do, we are in politics, we had to go where no Jat has ever set foot. They looked as dirty as they always do, worse than dogs. But we needed their votes against the Rajputs, we have to give out daru, we have to arrange free films, what to do, each person is one vote, whether chamar, or gujjar, or Rajput, Jat or Brahmin.

'With our own people we could talk of setting, how to make sure those low castes voted the way they were supposed to.'

'What about Himmat Bhai? What was he doing? Is he really such a big-big man?'

'Arre, you have no idea Bhaiyya — he knows everything, strategy, donations, reporters, media, campaign promises, posters, transport to rallies. Arre, if he could, he would have talked while sleeping.

'I was the one who stayed near him, the one who massaged his legs, pressed his feet when he couldn't sleep, made sure he got his tea the minute he woke up.

'After that he would be the one running after Bishnoi Sahib. Looking after his food, his tea, his comfort. In politics you can't say I will only do this, I will only do that. Whatever has to be done, you do.

'And then there are other things.'

Mangal lowered his voice, his hearers edged closer, what did Mangal mean?

It turned out Mangal had experienced women for the first time when they were travelling.

They were sitting outside the compound wall, under the shade of the peepul tree, where Virpal had lain fifty years ago when he had been beaten. Now the same rustling could be heard as Mangal continued with his story to eager listeners.

How was it done? Did he arrange it himself?

'Arre, why should I arrange anything? No, Bhaiyya did it all. He always handled anything to do with money.

'"Make sure the whore is clean," he told some hanger-on. "Get a young one, full of juice. It is his first, should be something he will remember."

'I could hardly wait. "Remember you are the man – she has to please you – just give her a kick if she fails to satisfy, we will find you another," he said.

'It was strange, everybody knowing what lay ahead of me. There were jokes, the bull is ready, huh, one man said, and another man said, look how ready he already is, it's standing and another said let's feel, he tried to grope me and I had to give him one push.

'For them it was all a big tamasha.

'That night I had to pretend to eat, so tense was my stomach. Was this how heroes felt on their wedding night in the films? And the heroines, all fair and lovely, with red-red lips, would the one they were going to bring me be like that? After all I was the brother of a man who was going to be a neta.

'After dinner Bhai offered me some daru.

'"Le, pee."

'"Why make him drunk," they said, "he will be drunk before long as it is –"

'Bhai held a glass to my lips. One more, one more, one more, he kept insisting, as though I were a baby. I pushed away his hand, it was not daru that I wanted. When I yawned, pretending to be sleepy, they said, "Arre, sleep later, for now your rod has to be awake. Go to the shed in the back."

'I left, glad to be away from their stupidity.

'The shed had a tin door. Inside I knew there was a bulb hanging from a wire. I found the switch but when I pressed it, no light. I felt around. At the back were some rolled up durries, I spread them out. Squatting, waiting, fidgeting, behind the barely visible bulk of the scooter, its front wheel at an angle, raised a few inches off the ground.

'Why was it taking so long? If they were making a fool out of me, I would leave for the village next morning.

'The amount Bhai had forced down my throat was making me drowsy, maybe this too they had done on purpose, fill the boy with nasha so he won't know what happened, then we can tell him anything. Conspiring behind my back.

'A noise outside. "Half an hour, no extras," and then the sound of the door shutting.

'The rustle of her skirt as she edged her way to the back, no need for me to think how will she find her way, she found it quicker than I had. Then I felt her next to me, her hand on my pyjamas, her hand slipping inside, actually touching me, stroking me, though there was no need, I was perfectly ready, but still she went on. I reached out, and through the cloth felt her thighs. Was she pretty, I wondered, I wanted her to be pretty and young. Why had they sent me to this shed where I could see nothing? I could only hear her breathing. Was she waiting for me to say I loved her? But I felt too shy.

'Then she undid my pyjamas, and her weight was on me. She smelt of sweat, her skirt was bunched against my chest, then she pushed me inside her and all of me went blank. It was like a madness in me, rising, rising. Hundred times more intoxicating than what Bhaiyya made me drink.

'Once it was over, she got up and left. As the door shut I heard some talking, but to me there had not been a word. It no longer mattered whether she was young or old, pretty or ugly. I lay there, panting, feeling more light and happy than I had in my entire life. She had done shameful things, it was better that they were done in the dark. That was probably why the light hadn't worked.'

The boys surrounding him listened with their mouths open. 'Arre, yaar, this is why you are not yet married, now we know. You have to get your women like this only.'

'Don't be stupid. This is a village idiot way of thinking.'

'Arre, yaar, get us women like that. Ones that will sit on you.'

'Stupid,' said Mangal, 'you think such women grow on trees? You have to have contacts.'

'Oye, Mangal, when should we come and visit you?'

'Mangal, you don't have a wife, you have to do it like this only.'

'Stupid, I will get a wife one day, a fair, lovely, rich wife. That is why Bhaiyya insists I don't marry yet.' There was a brief silence among the other boys. They were all, without exception, married.

Mangal on the bus to Ajmer. He stared out of the window, observing the colours of the landscape soften as the light over the fields grew less harsh. Trees cast lengthening patterns across the road. Farmers were getting ready to plant the winter crop of wheat, the rains had been good that year. He could see myriad plots of turned earth, the recently ploughed ones dark against the light brown of the bordering hillocks. They looked pretty, interspersed by the fresh green spikiness of the acacia trees that were scattered randomly throughout. There were ponds, some bordering the roads, some at a distance, covered with green scum, black patches of water revealed through rents here and there.

This was the earth from which he had come, this land was in his blood. It was only after he left that he realized its role in shaping him. On his first visit Himmat had scolded him for valuing it lightly, that was not an accusation he would be able to make again.

When Mangal came back, he looked at Himmat with even greater respect. He would never have been able to command the deference he had in the village, if it had not been for his association with him. The story of how he had lost his virginity, the attention he had received during the telling, still lingered. In retrospect he realized how much of a man of the world he had become.

'How was the pagri ceremony?' asked Himmat.

'They thought you should have been there.'

'They will think that till the day I die. They would suck my blood if I let them.'

'No, Bhaiyya, that is not true. They feel you are one of them; it is love, that's all.'

'Love? This is not love. This is ownership.'

Ownership, what was that? But as always, better to be safe and silent. He never knew what his brother would mind or not mind.

A few days later Himmat came home with a legal-looking document. 'You have to help me,' he told Mangal. 'Uncle thinks I want a divorce because I am involved with a girl. But even if I weren't, I don't want to be shackled to a villager.

'Threaten her if you need to. It was very difficult for me to get this piece of paper, otherwise the woman has to be present for the hearing. There is an x where she has to put her thumbprint. Here is the bus money.'

Mangal stared at the papers. 'Arre, you want a thumbprint so badly? I will put mine, why go all the way to the village? Who will find out?'

Himmat reacted violently to this. 'You know nothing,' he said. 'Do you have any idea of the trouble I went through? How much I had to bribe? Otherwise the girl has to appear before a judge. Divorce has to be done properly, otherwise why get one?'

Exactly, why get one? Did Himmat think his wife was going to come to Ajmer, go to court and start talking of whose thumbprint was whose? He was the one who knew nothing.

As Mangal got ready to return to the village, he wondered what they would say. And what about Ram Babu, what would happen to him, the boy who had been the light of Dhanpal's eyes? Himmat would never have been able to do all this if their father had been alive, of that he was sure.

Nobody would understand this whole business with signatures, and court, and stamp money, and bribes. Himmat was bypassing the panchayat completely, they would not like that. His was a different way, the modern way.

In Lalbanga Mangal was greeted with some alarm. Was everything all right? Why had he returned so soon? And what about the money spent running up and down?

'Some work of Bhaiyya's.'

'What work?'

In the end he just blurted out, 'A very important girl wants to marry him, she will not tolerate any of this co-wife business.'

After much talking, Gulabi insisted that her daughter-in-law sign with her thumbprint, but there was no question of getting rid of the girl. 'This has been her place since she married. Her child is our blood. God only knows where both of you are going to end up, or what children you are going to give me.'

He too was going to be a big man, Mangal assured his mother before he left, there would be not one hero in the family, but two.

Now that Himmat had the divorce papers in his hand, a roka could be arranged between Bishnoi Sahib's daughter and himself. By this time, he had won his future father-in-law's trust completely. Once in a meeting MP Sahib said, 'You all are looking after your interests, this fellow is looking after mine.'

As part of the governing coalition, the writing on the wall was that Bishnoi Sahib was not going to be a minister for long. For three years, the various parties involved had fought among themselves, till finally the whole government collapsed. In 1980 fresh elections were called.

'When are we going to campaign, Bhaiyya?' asked Mangal. 'Why is Bishnoi Sahib standing, now you are going to be his son-in-law, you should stand.'

Himmat looked worried. 'We have to make sure he wins,' he said.

'Isn't he campaigning?'

'Have you seen him? Jail has ruined his health, he is too-too weak. Then being minister, so much tension, stress, people jealous that he got the position. Home minister is one of the most important posts in the country. Of course Jats will vote for him, they are always loyal.'

'Even though he might fall down dead any moment?'

'Even then.'

Back to campaigning, back to a night in each place, back to helping Bishnoi Sahib win. In 1977 there had been hope, this time there was only disillusion. That Bishnoi Sahib might lose soon became obvious.

'It's all because of the tamasha at the Centre,' said Himmat. 'Politicians only wanting ministership for themselves. Few are like Bishnoi Sahib – a saint.'

'Will she still marry you if you are not able to help her father win?'

'Of course. She loves me. Don't you know anything?'

'She loves you? She said?'

'Certainly not. You think she has no shame?'

'Then how do you know?'

'She said she could not meet me any more without her father's knowledge. That's when I asked Uncle to speak to Bishnoi Sahib.'

Mangal looked confused. Himmat rubbed his head. 'You are still young, wait till it is your turn. In the meantime there are always other women. There, you will find them behind the petrol pumps. Twenty rupees a shot. Here's the money. Ask the petrol pump dealer to arrange one. I have to meet the Jat sarpanch in the village.' And Himmat disappeared, leaving Mangal to his own devices.

'How was it?' he later asked.

'Fine.'

'Sala, you have nothing more to say?'

'Why should I say anything more? You know what it is like.'

'Calm down. I thought you would be happier. Don't tell me this is twenty rupees wasted.'

'No, no,' mumbled Mangal. 'Not wasted at all.'

'Good. Now cheer up.'

What could Mangal say that would make his brother respect him? That he had preferred the first time, with the lights out in a garage? That here he was reminded of the women in his own village and he found this painful? That in this short span of time he wanted something more from the experience? No, he couldn't say any of this. His manhood was in question.

Meanwhile Himmat continued to struggle against the palpable indifference to the IPPP that he encountered everywhere. People should not forget, he shouted into the mike, what it was like to function without true democracy, what it was like to be forcibly sterilized, what it was like to be poor; he hoped they knew the difference between empty promises and reality. The IPPP had always been with them, through thick and thin. It was they who had worked for the people's welfare.

Vote for the IPPP. Put your chhaap on the bird, Jai Hind.

The people were not interested. All politicians talked like this. 'What have you done for us in these three years?' they asked.

'Is three years such a long time? If we have made mistakes, please forgive us. You have given the Congress decades, I am just asking for one more term. Then you see what we will do.'

But there had been too much infighting, too much political turmoil for people to want another coalition. The voters who had punished Indira Gandhi earlier on, now chose to reward her with her biggest victory ever. The Congress gained more than two hundred seats. Only the fools were surprised.

Discussions, discussions day and night; who had won, who had lost and why, why, why. 'People aren't donkeys,' said Virpal. 'They are not going to continue to vote for the IPPP, no matter what the government does. Arre, in three years you have two PMs, and endless uncertainty. No governing, only jostling for power, how does it look?'

In the middle of all this Himmat got married. Virpal and Mangal were the only guests from the boy's side.

'Shouldn't the baraat be bigger?' asked Mangal in the bus.

'Small wedding. Registry.'

'What's that?'

'You sign a paper and you are married.'

'Why is Bhaiyya letting them do things so cheaply? His father-in-law is an important man and god only knows how much seva Bhaiyya had done. There should be some shor-shar, some band-baja, some celebrations, some sign that something is happening.'

'The girl insists. She wants no strain on her parents especially after her father's defeat in the elections.'

'Doesn't the boy decide how things are done?'

Virpal snorted, 'This is not that type of marriage. Understand that from now only. Besides he is going to live with them.'

Mangal was silent for the rest of the trip. On the one hand, he was impressed with the way Himmat had broken new ground. He had gotten a divorce, chosen a bride himself, saved lakhs by doing registry, and then moved in with his in-laws, so that he could benefit even more.

On the other hand, his brother was leaving without a word. They had campaigned twice together, it had been understood that he was going to follow in his footsteps. He had been sent to the city to be made into a big man. Now who was going to help him? Uncle?

SECTION III
Mangal

I

1982–1987

Mangal was almost twenty when he graduated from school, with a pass mark of forty-three per cent. In the year since his brother had married, he had missed him more than he had thought possible.

'When can I join you in Jaipur?' he demanded on the phone.

'First do a BA. Then we will talk.'

'All this reading-sheading is good for what? Bishnoi Sahib is only tenth class pass.'

'That was in another day and age.'

'Bhaiyya, you can be the only one in the family to graduate, that is fine by me. If I have to look at another book, I will die, I tell you, die.'

'Listen, Mangu, I am promising you the best three years of your life. In DAV you will find real friends, Jat friends, who will always stand by you.'

'If you couldn't use your brains to get more than forty-three per cent,' offered the listening uncle, 'there is no need to use them with your brother. There is always farming if you don't want a degree.'

To his surprise, Mangal took to DAV, passing without too much difficulty, cheating without too much difficulty. After three years he graduated, amid much rejoicing. Himmat and Mangal, sons of a farmer, the first graduates in the entire village. The books had done their job. Mangal stared at them in disgust before selling the stained and tattered texts to a second-hand bookshop. The notebooks were sold by weight to the kabaari wallah.

Mangal now felt he had proved himself, and his dreams of joining Himmat in Jaipur became more vivid. He knew one entered politics as someone's sidekick. Who better than a brother to be a sidekick to? 'Bhai,' he said, when the call he was waiting for did not come. 'I want to be a leader. One day. From you I have learned. I can also talk of being a son of the soil, the sword of the Jats, what is there in that? Together we will be stronger.'

This was so self-evident that he was not prepared for Himmat's response. Did he think politics was like going to the temple and eating prasad? He himself had still not got a ticket. His only hope was his father-in-law, and he had no wish to burden him with another Gaina. When he was in a strong position, he would call him, but not before.

That night Mangal tossed and turned, refuting his brother's points one by one. He had only expressed a desire to serve him. How did his father-in-law enter the picture? Was Himmat wilfully refusing to see his brother's heart, refusing to recognize his esteem and devotion?

In Jaipur Himmat also tossed and turned. His brother was wanting what he himself did not have. But clearly the boy needed some direction, otherwise he would go on with his pestering.

A few days later Uncle said, 'Your brother is thinking of setting you up as a cement stockist.'

'Cement stockist? I know nothing of cement.'

'There is nothing much to learn. Construction is always going on – always demand outstripping supply – can't go wrong.'

'Is this what he wants for me?'

'He wants a secure future for you. Arre, beta, look at me. I could never make it. There should be just one family member involved in the uncertain game of politics.'

'But why cement?'

'Always asking questions. Someone in Jaipur wants to open an outlet in Ajmer. Satisfied?'

A shop was set up in Naya Bazaar. *Fine Quality Ajmer Cement*, it said on the board above, and underneath, *Rajasthan Ruia*, the brand name.

Mangal had to make sure the sacks of cement, black, white, red, fine and coarse, were stored properly. He had to count the bags when they arrived, count them when they were loaded on to tempos, all the while breathing so much of that dust that his eyes kept watering and his hands were covered with grime.

His best times were when his college friends drop by. He seated them on a bench under the shade of a tamarind tree that grew beside the pavement, while he sent the boy for tea and kachoris.

How much money was he making? asked his friends.

Enough, said Mangal coyly.

Now the next thing on the agenda was a wedding invitation, they tittered.

Mangal blushed and ordered paan. It was not easy, he told them, not like sitting in an office, ordering peons about. Here he had to do everything himself, be there when the cement trucks make their delivery, keep the inventory, keep multiple copies of deliveries, make sure the official account book is in absolute order.

But business was this only, and if Mangal wanted to, they would be willing to exchange their jobs for his, and be masters of their day, not answerable to anyone else, huh, Mangal, are you willing to do that? Then they all laughed because, of course, Mangal was not willing, and they had caught him out.

~

1985. Election year. Bishnoi Sahib's health has finally given way completely. Out of respect for him, the party agrees to nominate his son-in-law from his usual constituency, the I P P P MLA seat from Ajmer West. This is the moment Himmat has spent years waiting for.

'Sala,' said Himmat on the phone to Mangal, 'at last I can campaign for myself. You have to be by my side.'

'Really?'

'Really.'

'And afterwards?'

'Before you even take one step, you want to draw up a lawyer's contract? There are plenty of others who would be happy to come with me, but I thought of you.'

And so Mangal was taken along and could, among other things, watch Himmat evolve into a man of the people. Standing in the jeep, his voice amplified through loudspeakers attached to the roof, he delivered the same message over and over. He knew what it was like to be without water, electricity, to toil the whole day in the fields, to not have money for festivities, for marriage, death, birth, illness, to face the cruel rates of the moneylender. The I P P P were the ones who had worked on roads, schools, health clinics and farmer subsidies during times of drought. The country needed development, farmers needed better seeds, fertilizer, easier loans. Help us continue our good work, put your chhaap on the bird. Jai Hind, he ended.

Mangal noticed how, in the limelight, Himmat grew in confidence, connecting with crowds, doing his best to seem indispensable to them. Everywhere there were people waiting with grievances, and no matter what the hour, he met them all. Next morning, by eight they would be on the road, to see, hear, be seen, be heard. Himmat could not stop talking and his brother drank it all in, as he pressed his feet and massaged his legs.

'These people have seen me before, they know I am one of them, not some stranger from outside, saying vote for me. No, I am their friend, and will keep my promises.'

'I hope you win, Bhaiyya, if not, I will come back here, to every constituency, and ask why. I will come with my stick.'

'Arre, this is politics, there are other methods we must use. But even if we capture booths, even if we make up voter lists, how long can all this work? Bishnoi Sahib always says, don't let the gap between what you promise and what you deliver be too great. Sooner or later your constituency will punish you. The voter has a long memory.'

From Jaipur, Bishnoi Sahib directed him towards influential locals, to union bosses, to prominent Muslims, to various Jat leaders. Son-in-law was the operative word.

'Father-in law seriously promoting you, yaar, you have it made. No tension, no headache,' said Mangal admiringly.

'You blind or what?' he replied. 'Can't you see those young men near the IPPP office nosing around, just waiting for me to lose? What is so special about me, born as I was in a village gutter, in the company of cows and buffaloes?'

When Himmat had had something to drink, these ravings increased, while his followers looked sympathetic. There would be about fifteen of them crammed into the room,

Himmat giving everybody drinks, whisky, not country stuff, ordering seekh kababs if they were in a town, pakoras if they were in a village. Mangal was the one running and fetching. The most junior and clearly the most trusted. He felt proud. Everybody could see the way he opened the bottles, the way Himmat casually handed him his wallet, the way he served his brother, anticipating all his needs, doing everything as silently and unobtrusively as Himmat had once done for Bishnoi Sahib.

Himmat won. There he was with his picture in the papers, the local boy made good. Two days after the result, he was in Ajmer to touch Uncle's feet and assert that it was all his blessings.

Mangal was overjoyed. My brother, MLA from Ajmer West. This is just the beginning, see how far we go. His heart was filled with a pride he could barely contain.

Anxiously he thought of his cement outlet; he was making steady profits there, but if his brother called him, duty came first. If he had won, surely it had been partly due to him. Hadn't he repeatedly said they were fingers of the same hand?

But, said Himmat, no question of joining him for now, what would happen to the cement outlet? Even Mangal could see the sense in that. Uncle had sat at the shop for the duration of the campaign, but the profits, particularly the no. 2, had suffered while he was away.

Now that Himmat was an MLA, now that he was Bishnoi Sahib's son-in-law, now that he was part of a political family, now that his talents could be noticed, now his rewards began to come.

It took just a year after the elections for him to phone his family in Ajmer to inform them that he had been made deputy minister, civil aviation.

'Beta, beta,' said Uncle with tears pouring down his cheeks, 'soon we will all stand in your shade. Your brother wants to talk to you.'

'Bhaiyya,' said Mangal, his voice choking, 'congratulations, congratulations. You are truly great.'

Pride flowed through the house, their son's foot was at last firmly placed on the political ladder, his circle of influence widening. Phone calls were made, boxes of mithai distributed, letters flew to the village. Our son is officially a big man.

When things quietened down, Uncle said to Mangal, 'Your time will come. With your brother in politics, business is the best thing for you. Every single businessman in the country queues up in front of politicians for permits, licences and quotas, all in government control. And if they are related, there is no end to the benefits they receive.'

Yes, thought Mangal, everybody benefited when a family member went into politics. You just had to be patient. He returned to Naya Bazaar, carrying in his heart those days of togetherness with his brother.

In Naya Bazaar, the no. 2 continued to flow. Those customers whose need for cement could not be filled by the bags the government allowed them, what were they to do? Bundles of cash changed hands, turning from white to black, unaccounted, untaxed, unreceipted and all belonging to *Fine Quality Ajmer Cement.*

As Mangal grew flush with money, he became less afraid of spending it. Gone were the days when he would dutifully hand over the extra amounts to Uncle. His clothes turned more fashionable, as did his shoes, to his uncle's horror he even went in for a motorcycle.

'Save, you should save, what is this spending? If you have so much you should send more to the village.'

Mangal was saving, but for himself. Let Uncle and his brother send, they were his elders, theirs was the responsibility. The Gainas in Lalbanga never had to borrow, they were able to substitute a brick house for their mud one, able to place a down payment on a tractor, able to cover illnesses and ceremonies with ease. Sala, when are you going to contribute, demanded Himmat, and just as Mangal was debating this issue, there came an opportunity that would at last pull him out of the smallness of a cement outlet, into the big-time of Rajasthan industry.

His friend Suraj Prakash called. Did he know that the government was developing an industrial zone beyond Ajmer? Land at subsidized rates, loans for equipment, emphasis on regional prosperity. Near Amberi there were good limestone deposits, why not expand into cement production? Become an industrialist rather than a petty shopkeeper. He himself was going into steel, they were going to specialize in farming tools.

Uncle looked doubtful when told of Mangal's plans. It was a risk, agreed Mangal, but then what wasn't? He was the brother of a junior minister, hadn't Uncle himself said business and politics went together? All he wanted was help in getting the land and the loans, with his contacts it would be a day's work.

Before anything more could happen, the long arm of the family in Lalbanga reached out to encircle the two brothers. Ram Babu was getting married.

It was taken for granted that the money for this wedding would come from the father. Besides that, his presence was expected. It was a question of loyalty and prestige, of renewing ties with the earth that produced you, of showing the whole village how far this one family had travelled. And it was a question of his son.

As Mangal thought of home, his heart grew tender towards the young Ram Babu, who had followed him around so assiduously. How old would he be? Twelve? Thirteen? Once he returned, they would put pressure on him to marry as well, but with his years in the city, his ideas of married life have expanded. When the time came, he knew Uncle or Himmat would arrange his wedding.

But it turned out that Himmat refused to go. He came to Ajmer to tell them so.

'You will be a father-in-law,' teased Mangal.

'How old is he?'

'You don't remember how old you were when you went to the village and did it?'

'Watch your mouth.'

'Eleven years younger than me.'

'Child marriage is against the law,' said Himmat, a statement no one took any notice of. The villagers had their own traditions, their own panchayat, how could they relate to laws so far from them? 'I cannot be associated with it. If it was ever found out –'

'Who will find out? Your wife must know about your first marriage?'

'This has nothing to do with her.'

'Bhai, it's the most important moment in Ram Babu's life,' said Mangal. 'He is not so young that he will not be aware of his father's absence.'

'You can represent me.'

'It's not the same.'

'I want nothing to do with him, I made that clear long ago. If I go back even once, they will try to make me feel responsible.'

Himmat put his head in his hands. How casually he had been trapped all those years ago by demands he was too young to understand. He now knew what being a father meant, knew the tenderness of holding his son, tiny, vulnerable and sweet. Such a father-son equation could never be him and Ram Babu. He would not allow it.

His wife must be making things difficult, thought Mangal, otherwise why would Himmat deny even this much to his son. He would be going to Lalbanga in any case, he would represent him on the wedding mandap in any case, as for explaining why Himmat couldn't come, he would prepare some lies. Himmat should rest tranquil on that score.

Himmat put his arm around Mangal and whispered, 'Sala, it is much better you go rather than I, you will know how to handle things. He only saw me once when Baoji died, and he was too young. What is there to miss? You are far more important to him than me.'

Uncle watched the two, almost twins, and sent up a prayer, may they always be together, together was strength.

'Just make sure they don't marry you off as well, they will not be able to tolerate that you are single at twenty-three.'

Mangal tittered. 'I have already told them you are saving me for someone special.'

'Come back and we will find the most beautiful girl in Rajasthan for you, and of course see about the loan and the land.'

'I always told you politics and business go together,' said Virpal. 'If anybody can help you, it will be your brother.'

It was the afternoon of two days later when Mangal set out. At the fork that led to his village, he whacked the side of the bus, it slowed down, he jumped off, and turned on to the dirt road. Now that the sun was low, the brightness was going from the fields, soon it would be dusk. From time to time he passed cows plodding along, the gold brown of their coats just a shade darker than the turned fields. The dust these cattle raised was so high it reached above the head of the man leading them home. An occasional passing tractor shook and lurched beside him, adding to the dustiness.

The raw pitted countryside, with its scrubby dry bushes and sprawling acacia trees, aroused in Mangal a vague yearning. Everything had to struggle to survive, no tall trees here, but a country of low vegetation, with roots tenaciously delving into the earth.

By the time Mangal reaches home he is exhausted. The city has weakened him, he thinks, at one point walking five kilometres would mean nothing.

He rests in his angan, all around him the excitement and chatter of welcome. People cluster next to him, explanations about Himmat and Virpal demanded and pondered over.

Ram Babu is nearby, Mangal grabs him, chucks the child under the chin. 'Who is getting married?' he asks playfully.

'I am,' shouts the twelve-year-old, throwing himself on his uncle's back and gripping him with his legs. Mangal tickles him till he runs away.

There were many jokes at Mangal's expense, Arre, not married yet, what are they keeping you for, some princess? Etc., etc.

To which Mangal, equally jovial, Wait and see who I bring home. Bhaiyya is arranging it all for me.

Next evening they walk to the main road, where a hired bus awaits them. From there it is a short ride to Sempla, the bride's village. A band is waiting on the outskirts, along with a horse, and they set off with as much noise as possible. Dogs bark hysterically as they chase them. The marriage party dances, dances with greater and greater abandon, as they approach the wedding arena draped with shiny white and red cloth. Green and blue lights glitter above. A small open drain runs down the middle, the water stagnant. Mosquitoes as big as flies hover around, steadily nagging at their prey. People encircle the dancers' heads with fistfuls of money, the band wallah stretches his hand out for the ten-rupee notes. The lights go, the generator comes on. Some little boys go wild, throwing their limbs about with increasing energy. Seated on the horse, his arms around his nephew, Mangal remembers his own one time fervour on such occasions.

The wedding takes several hours; the welcome, the escorting inside, the settling down in front of the pandit. Mangal takes the place of the father. Halfway through, Ram Babu falls asleep and has to be woken for the pheras.

Now you are married, little one, whispers the uncle, may you always be happy. He thinks of Himmat's two wives, and his own still unmarried state, and the women he occasionally had. How complicated marriage had become. It used to be so simple. For Ram Babu it would still be so.

Wedding over, the baraat troops to a nearby school. Here, in the playground, are two awnings, one covering the cooks and one the guests. Mangal sits on a long thin durrie. Across from him, he can see the big karhais mounted on low mud blocks over burning wood, hear the slap of hands flattening out dough before tossing it into hot oil.

Lights are strung on a wire across the field. Some children ride around on bicycles. The moon gleams in the starry sky. He can the smell the dirt, moist from the water used to keep the dust of so many feet down.

He caresses Ram Babu, still half asleep in his lap. His father's refusal to accept him means that nothing will take him away from the security of the familiar.

After two days Mangal returned to Ajmer.

Uncle. 'How was it?'

'Everything went smoothly. Now Bhaiyya has a daughter-in-law.'

'Besides that? The arrangements? The eating?'

'It was fine – all as usual. Ram Babu was excited.'

Thinking about the boy, feeling his arms around his neck, made Mangal uneasy. All that wasted love. If only he could have taken him back with him, so he could meet his father just once. Himmat might relent with the sweet and lively face in front of him.

But without his brother's permission, he hadn't dared. He too was a coward. Though these thoughts were strong, they flared only to sputter and die, as the loans and the land allotment came through, and he became totally absorbed in his new venture.

Once construction on the site starts, Mangal has time to think of nothing else. He falls asleep at night, exhausted, at daybreak he is at his site. Depending on the traffic, he spends two to three hours a day commuting, that much less time for his work. He cannot afford it. He builds a room for the nights. When it was completed, Virpal came for the puja. Mangal bent to touch his uncle's feet and get his blessings. Tears came to Virpal's eyes as he thought of his brother, and how proud he would have been of his sons. I am here in his stead, he murmured, it is for him you must succeed.

Now all that remained to settle the boy was to get him married.

The sight of his towering unit filled Mangal with exultation. Some might call it ugly, those high and intricate, massive structures, rising from the soft hilly ancient earth, but he could only see the beauty of blasting rocks to extract limestone that would go towards making something useful. Sometimes he would stand under the rotating kiln, a hundred and sixty metres long, the giant dust coloured tube turning steadily round and round, night and day, three hundred and sixty-five days of the year, as it had to, if he was to make profits.

He mouthed silent prayers to it, imagining the fire inside this revolving cylinder, heating limestone to 1400 degrees

centigrade, and he understood worship in a richer sense, as
something that could materially control his destiny.

As he prayed, he found it hard to breathe. The air was full
of dust, limestone dust, clinker dust, fly ash dust, laterite dust,
gypsum dust, the dust raised by each passing truck. Every tree,
every shrub, every leaf in the vicinity was coated white and
thick, their green only faintly visible.

His staff lived in Brij Nagar, the nearest town, five
kilometres away. The workers came from nearby villages. He
imagined the day when he could accommodate everybody
in quarters on the campus, thus building a strong sense of
solidarity among his employees.

In the morning he supervised the trucks leaving for the
quarry. The mines, where blasts shook the limestone from
the earth, were a kilometre away from the factory; should this
source ever dry up, he would have to go further afield, and the
further he went, the more it would cost him.

When he went to sleep at night in the little room, he could
not believe how far he had come, and without any help. Now he
was glad he hadn't gone into politics, where would be the glory
in standing in his brother's shadow? Satisfaction flooded his
heart. For the first time in his life he thought it would be nice
to have someone to share this with. Suraj Prakash, on the same
highway, working as hard, had a wife with a child on the way.
Sometimes the two got together for a drink.

II

1987–1988

Despite being the MLA for Ajmer West, Himmat found it more convenient to stay in Jaipur with his in-laws. Hence Mangal was surprised when his brother phoned, make sure you are in Ajmer this weekend, I am coming especially to see you.

Anticipation seized him. He had been waiting for this moment when Himmat saw the plant, the moment when the grandeur of his project would strike him, the moment when he said well done. Who could say otherwise, when they saw the mammoth machines, saw the limestone being tested, observed the bags of cement being produced?

Himmat came to his usual welcome. Uncle fell on his neck, Aunt went off to fry pakoras and make tea, and Mangal stayed smiling in the background, waiting for so, you have started manufacture, how is it going, when can I see, tell me if you have any problems.

Instead Himmat said, 'I have found your wife.' His eyes glittered.

Uncle shifted in his seat, Aunt demanded a photo, while Mangal looked confused. How had his brother managed to

figure out what was in his heart, how had he known his lonely
nights in the semi-desert? Although Uncle had announced he
needed to get married, he hadn't expected evidence so soon.

'Who is she?' asked Aunt. 'Does she have money? Now he
is a factory owner, we are not going to give him cheap.'

Yes, thought Mangal, it was true, one could always do with
a rich wife. He was making it on his own, but the rich have
influence and connections that are always convenient.

'Material status cannot always be a factor,' replied Himmat
stiffly.

Uncle looked surprised and Mangal grew suspicious.
Money was everything. It created your place in the world. As
sons of a farmer they knew that better than anybody.

Uncle said, glancing at Mangal, 'Bhai has chosen her,
must be for a reason. Otherwise who is going to arrange your
marriage? It's not as though you are going to do love.'

'Arre, why should he do love,' said Aunt, 'when he has so
many people to care for him? This girl, is she beautiful? Fair?
She must be something to make you come all the way.'

'They want to see him,' said Himmat.

'A modern girl. We never got married with all this seeing-
sheeing. You think I saw your uncle, or he saw me?'

'Things are different in the city. After all Himmat has also
done love marriage,' remarked Uncle.

'That was different,' said Himmat.

'What about dowry?'

'It's against the law.'

They stared at him, flabbergasted. Himmat had taken to
invoking the law when it suited him. The law against dowry was
disregarded on a daily basis, as he well knew.

'They have nothing and they want to see me? Am I a girl?'
asked Mangal indignantly. Even in the village he would get a
dowry, Ram Babu certainly had. With his rise in status, the

money that came with his bride should increase, not dwindle to zero. Didn't his brother think he was worth anything?

'Be sure to buy some new clothes,' said Himmat before he left. 'Shoes also. You must look smart.'

'I'm not going.'

'Enough foolishness.'

'I'm not going,' repeated Mangal later to Aunt and Uncle. 'No dowry! Is this why I am still not married? Look how carefully he arranged his own match, look where it got him.'

'At least see the girl, he has promised the family, you cannot make your brother's word meaningless,' said Uncle.

'All right. Then let us get married. Why do I need to see her?'

'It is they who want to see you beta, modern people think like this only.'

'I hope Bhaiyya is not trying to palm me off. With Ram Babu married, he might feel it's high time he did something about me. Everybody in the village asked this one thing only, when are you getting married, why aren't you married, nephew married, uncle bachelor, how does it look?'

'Trust your brother. He hasn't reached where he has without deep thought.'

The day before Mangal was to see the girl, Himmat arrived. He went over Mangal's clothes and what he would say when they were introduced.

'You would think I was the bride,' joked Mangal.

'Take off your earrings.' Mangal noticed he had stopped wearing his own.

'Why are we doing all this? She doesn't even have any money.'

'She is an educated girl.'

'And I? Am I not BA pass? And a factory owner? One day I will be the richest industrialist in Rajasthan.'

'You can't talk like this in front of her.'

'You always said with women I had to remember I was the man?'

'Sala, that was with whores. You can't tell the difference or what?'

'I haven't even seen her. Why are you acting so strange? If she doesn't like me – too bad – what is it to me?'

'Mind your tongue.'

'Why? You keep her for yourself if you like her so much.'

Himmat gripped Mangal's arm and twisted the flesh. Mangal stared at him, daring him to hurt him further, when he backed off.

On their way to her house in Himmat's official car, he ventured, 'Why aren't you telling me what's so special about the girl? You think I am mentally deficient? At least this much I need to know.'

'These people don't think like villagers, willing to marry whoever their parents choose. They want to be sure the boy and girl like each other, that there is a chance for future happiness.'

'Like each other? That is only with film hero and heroine.'

'Not always.'

'You chose so carefully, but me you are throwing away on a poor girl. Why don't you marry her if you are so keen? Present Bhabhi with a souten.'

A small giggle emerged from Mangal as he thought of the girl as a co-wife. Then his head lurched forward as his brother hit him sharply on the back of his shoulders.

'Talk with respect. I have not brought you here to insult women. The age of co-wives has gone.'

'How have I insulted her? Are you crazy? What do you want?'

'That you behave like a civilized human being. Ever since you have come, I have tried to teach you sense. Look at me –'

'I didn't ask you to arrange my marriage,' said Mangal, almost in tears. 'I could do one like this myself. Girls were after me in college.'

'Don't talk rubbish.'

'They were. They would stare and not look away. Now for some girl you are willing to beat me. Do what you like, Bhaiyya, I don't care.'

Himmat stared at his younger reflection, sulking and ungrateful. 'You have choices I didn't have. This girl, because she is poor, will always be grateful. You will be king in your house. The age difference too is right, seven –eight years.'

The Gaina brothers meet the Ahlawats. Mangal finds it hard to look directly at the girl.

'You have a cement dealership, I believe?' asks the brother.

'Had. Now factory.'

'Oh? Why the change? Isn't running a factory a lot of trouble?'

Running a dealership was also a problem. That was why he had wanted to get into manufacture. It was a big headache dealing with customers who wanted to bribe in order to get more than their allotted share. Cement was sold at a controlled price, given out in fixed quantities, what could he do? His shop was inspected, and even when everything was above board, the babus negotiated their price for giving a clean report. He was sick of the whole dirty business.

The girl looked at him with some interest. When he spoke, she was reminded of Himmat.

Before they left Mangal permitted himself one last look. To make sure that indeed she was fair, her eyes large, her mouth full, her plait long and lustrous.

'Well?' asked Himmat when they were in the car.

'What?'

'Did you like her?'

'She's all right.'

'Is that all? You think you will get a girl like Tapti on your own?'

'Just now we have seen, and just now you want me to agree?'

'Where have you come from, that you are taking your time saying yes? This is how marriages are arranged.'

Mangal felt it advisable to hide how immediately he had been attracted to this girl he had looked at so briefly. Himmat tousled the hair on his brother's head. 'Have it your way. Think about it.'

A few weeks passed. Mangal waited for Himmat to pursue him. Boys never sounded eager about marriage, he knew that, it put them in a vulnerable position. But every day he woke up with the expectation that Himmat would call, would suggest seeing the girl again. He imagined the lack of interest he would show, imagined how his brother would have to beg, cajole and plead.

Where had he found this girl, he wondered. Was it through advertisement, word of mouth, or had they contacted him? It all seemed so unlikely, especially since she didn't have a father.

A month later, Mangal finally heard from Himmat, and that too in person. 'They are pressing for an answer. Girl's reputation is at stake.'

'How can I harm her reputation by seeing her once? Maybe I should meet her more.' The month's delay had annoyed him.

He was further bewildered by the lack of any special attempt to woo him, despite no dowry.

'What more is there to see? She is young, she is pretty. In the village you would not even see this much, you know that.'

'And the dowry?'

'There are things in life where money is not a consideration.'

'If you are so clear about everything, tell them what you like,' said Mangal. 'Why are you asking me?'

Himmat turned severe. 'You cannot be half-hearted. Once things are settled they want a roka. The wedding itself can wait till her studies are over.'

'You are my elder brother,' said Mangal, making a great show of giving in. 'How can I go against your wishes?'

'You will not regret. That I promise.' Himmat put his arms around Mangal's shoulders and drew him close. For the moment the younger brother felt entirely enclosed by his brother's strength and certainty. He bent to touch his feet. At the end of it all, his brother knew what would benefit him. And then, the girl was fair, white as an unripe mango. Their children would reflect this.

He began to think of his wedding with anticipation. Ever since Tapti had been suggested as his wife, his imagination had shyly revolved around her. When thinking of his future, her face floated above the cement that was now his daily life. He shivered as he imagined this girl in his bed, when all he had had were those women who cost twenty to thirty rupees.

After the engagement, a visit to the cement factory is arranged. Himmat will drive the Ahlawats down. They will meet Mangal at the site.

As they negotiate the sixty kilometres of narrow road, weaving in and out of traffic, swerving and bumping, Tapti gazed eagerly out of the window. On either side of the road barren land intermingled with hopeful fields. With every kilometre travelled, she feels her destiny coming closer. She leans towards the half open window and closes her eyes, feeling the rushing wind twist her hair. To leave the city behind, to live among these rocks, far from civilization, would be like having an adventure every day. She glanced at her mother and smiled. Himmat caught the look and was pleased.

As they turned into the side road towards the village Amberi, Tapti could see on the top of a small hill some huge metal equipment towering above everything, dominating the landscape, an anomaly among these low dry stony hills and scrubby trees.

As they inch cautiously along the unpaved road, the car rocks with each dip in the surface, jolts over every stone. It takes twenty minutes to travel the next five kilometres.

Ram Pratap remarks, 'Must be unpassable in the rains?'

Himmat nods. 'He will get it paved once he has the money. He has just started.'

'Of course,' agreed Ram Pratap. 'How many things can one man do?'

At the gates they were gestured towards a small room on the right. Tea was waiting for them. The guard would tell Sahib that they were here.

When Mangal stepped into the room, Tapti suddenly felt shy, the man seemed so much more substantial here. In Ajmer the elder brother dominated, now it was this man's turn to shine. He continued to shine during the tour they took of the place. His priority was the plant, explained Mangal, as they walked in the powdery dust of the unpaved paths, but he would tar these roads very soon. It was difficult for the trucks to come and go as well. Each second of wasted time cost him money.

Everything about the factory moved Tapti, all unfamiliar, strange and exciting. There the limestone quarries towards the back, there the trucks that bring the limestone to the plant, here it is broken, here tested, here the kilns, here made into clinker.

In this equipment she saw her future cemented together with that of her husband's, cemented together for better or for worse, in a future where they strode along together doing good and making a difference. What a brave vision this man had. How much courage to do something like this alone. He could easily have chosen to tread in his brother's footsteps. Maybe she could set up a school for the workers' children.

Mrs Ahlawat looked around her with satisfaction. Any doubt she might have had about the suitability of the union vanished under the pressure of the revolving kilns. And to think such a good match had come knocking at their door, without any effort on their part. To be associated in one fell swoop with two such successful brothers, was recompense for years of privation.

As they left the premises, Mangal accompanied them. They were all going to stop at a wayside restaurant for lunch. 'Sagar has a good reputation,' said Mangal, 'I eat there often.'

As they settled down to chola-kulcha, they talked of the factory. 'Now you can only climb,' said Himmat.

Mrs Ahlawat agreed, yes beta, it is very impressive. In this only is the progress of our country.

Ram Pratap, who till now had no idea of how imposing a cement plant could be, added his praise. It was going to be difficult to condescend to this man after their visit, but he was large-hearted enough not to mind.

Mangal glanced at Tapti. In showing her his factory, he was showing her himself. Would she understand him? At that moment she glanced up, their eyes met, and she neither looked down nor away. Mangal flushed with happiness, and to hide his embarrassment quickly began harassing the boy, how long was he going to take with their bill? And didn't they have finger bowls?

What finger bowls? There was the tap, right in front of them, replied the boy cheekily, as he threw their plates briskly into his greasy aluminium tray.

They parted company outside the restaurant, Mangal to return to his work. Rocking along the dirt road to the plant he thought he must get it paved, it was intolerable to think that she would have to bump around in this way every time she went in and out. He would have to divert funds, but no one should know the real reason for this hurry.

Over the next few months whenever Mangal felt discouraged, he thought of his fiancée; when the babus of the Rajasthan Electricity Board demanded repeated bribes for giving him an uninterrupted supply of electricity, when the engineer misread the board which controlled the machines and precious time was wasted in breakdowns, when the laboratory technician took forever to measure the composition of limestone, when villagers absconded during harvest and planting and there was not enough labour to load the trucks. Each such moment translated into thousands of rupees, and for solace he turned to that exchange of glances which had become enshrined in his heart.

The year passed, with only infrequent meetings between the engaged couple. On the occasions they do meet, the talk is of cement. Now that Tapti has visited the factory, she listens with interest. He had started tarring the roads, but it all took time, so much time. And he had begun adding to the guest house. Space was not a problem, so he was planning an extra bedroom, a large kitchen, a bathroom, a drawing-dining around an angan. Hopefully the water connections would all be sorted out by the time they married. What did she think? She smiled and murmured, whatever he decided was all right by her.

This was a new industrial zone the government was developing, in order to attract business to Rajasthan. The factory was so far from anything because it had to be near limestone, between one and five kilometres, any further was fatal to profits. Had she noticed the other factories, some still being built, on the way to Amberi? Had she noticed the marble sites, the brick making units, had she noticed the pen with goats and cows? There was a steel unit that belonged to his friend, Suraj Prakash, had she noticed that?

She had been too busy noticing the hills, the trees, the sky, and how pretty it all was, she said, but next time she would make sure she saw the bricks, the marble site, the steel unit, for it was of equal importance.

'My brother helped me get this land and the permissions,' said Mangal. 'Together we will be a force to reckon with in Rajasthan, he the politician, and me the industrialist – god willing. All my equipment is the latest – I got it in Bombay, from FLSmidth, Copenhagen. These kilns and grinders are not manufactured in India. With collaboration – maybe one day –'

'Yours is a remarkable family. How many people have come as far as both of you? And without contacts. My friends think I am very lucky. All of them have settled for boring-boring matches. They are not exciting like mine,' said Tapti.

Her admiration encouraged him. Did she know, he said, that when he went to buy an excavation machine from the Larsen and Toubro dealer, the man had offered to make an inflated bill and keep a percentage of the difference?

'What?' exclaimed Tapti. 'He was offering you black money? Shameless!'

'This is the way people do business. How do you think our country functions?'

There was a silence. Tapti had never known anybody who dealt with black money. The daughter of salaried parents, every paisa they earned was taxed at source, not once had they to cross the boundaries of the permissible. When her mother talked of black money, it was with moral horror and a sense of superiority. 'I'm glad you have nothing to do with it,' she said now. 'It's dirty.'

Women didn't understand the real world, thought Mangal. Black was how he had generated income as a dealer in Ajmer, when people had begged him to give them extra bags of cement under the counter, he could name his price, so desperate were they to finish construction. That black was how he had met the conditions governing the loan he had got. He had to make her realize how basic it was to every transaction.

'I can't have nothing to do with it. What other option is there when some clerk demands money to make sure I get a steady supply of electricity? If I refuse, he will make my life hell by letting it become erratic. How will I run my factory, pay my salaries?'

Tapti was silent as she fiddled with her chunni.

'The factory has to make profits, in business that's the bottom line. With profits you can assure the workers of a steady income, provide housing, roads, schools, clinics, all the things the government promises but doesn't deliver.'

His fiancée brightened. Visions of the future were what she identified with.

III

1989–1991

The wedding took place just before Tapti's final year exams. Unlike Himmat's, this one was carried out with a certain amount of ostentation, despite the austerity move in the government that limited the number of guests, as well as the items of food.

'Why can't they get married in court like we did?' demanded Sonal Gaina. 'We are Gandhians after all, against vulgar display. Our whole family should set an example, not just us.'

'Not everybody is you, Sona,' said Himmat. 'I want Mangal happy. Even in the village we do not do weddings on a small scale. The food might be simple, three–four sweets, dal, sabzi, puris, but the whole village is fed, even the lower castes, fifteen hundred to two thousand people. Sometimes, we boys would eat two–three times. They would catch us, make us help, clearing up the banana leaves guests ate on, setting out fresh ones, pouring water, serving the food, from four in the afternoon to four in the morning it would go on.'

Sonal stared. He never talked about his village, refused to either go or to take her. Now what had happened? 'You sound wistful,' she said in a neutral tone.

'Not really, just passing thoughts.'

'Do you want Mangal to get married in the village? We can escort the bride there.' At the thought of Tapti eating off banana leaves Sonal smiled.

'No. That part of my life is finished.'

Tears came to Sonal's eyes. 'You will do for that boy what you don't do for yourself.'

'What is the option? I am like his father. I am the one who arranged this. With your help.'

Sonal remained silent. Her help had been a frank appraisal of the girl's character and situation. The fact that she was young, fatherless and poor meant she would adjust easily, that her family was small meant there would not be too many hangers-on. To this extent her husband had chosen wisely, but had he considered that she was too smart, too pretty and too educated? How homely or simple would she actually be? She had given her opinion, and though it had been ignored, it was now her duty to welcome the bride, which she did by buying her a brocade Benarsi sari to wear for the reception Himmat was hosting. After the event, the couple would return to their home in Ajmer.

~

Wedding night. Rose petals are strewn on the white sheets of the bed, strings of jasmine are wound around the headboard. Mangal looks at his wife sitting in the midst of this, young, beautiful and all his. He lunges at her. Startled, she draws away. He pulls at her lehnga.

'What are you doing?' Panic edges her words.

'You are my wife,' he replies by way of explanation.

'So?'

Mangal had no inclination for words. She was his wife and he wanted to get near her. In his eagerness, he pulled more forcefully at her clothes. 'Come here. Don't you know anything? Didn't your mother explain your duties to you?'

'What duties?'

'You must know what marriage means. Come here. Don't make me keep asking.'

This was more than she could handle. As she slithered off the bed, her lehnga brushed the petals to the floor, and she stepped on them as she ran into the bathroom, newly constructed for the occasion. The bridegroom could hear the latch being bolted.

Fifteen minutes passed. He got up and pushed at the door. It was locked. He tried some soft banging. Still nothing. What on earth was the matter with her? 'Come out,' he semi-shouted, 'I won't do anything.'

Still no answer. He returned to the resplendently decorated bed. The wedding night was turning out all wrong, but who was to explain the concept to his wretched bride?

By the time she ventured out, he had fallen asleep. She spent the night on the floor.

They woke almost together. He stared at her, married and still so distant. She stared back. It was quite clear he had no idea of what he had done.

'You are my wife,' he started, 'You can't do all this.'

'What about love?'

At his blank look, her face crumpled. Some tears dampened her cheeks. All his anger left as he crouched tentatively next to her. She shifted, he shifted too, careful not to go too near. Really, she was like one of those wild creatures they had tried to catch as children.

'I am your husband,' he started.

'So?'

Why did she keep saying, so? Wasn't it obvious? His face grew red. The first time alone with her and he was losing face.

He thought of the conversation he had had with his brother a few days earlier.

She is not like the women you have known, he had said.

Mangal stared at him. 'What are you trying to say?'

'Don't hurry. Be gentle. It will all be new to her.'

Mangal found it hard to read the expression on his brother's face, normally so open. Besides this girl was going to be his wife, what went on between them was nobody's business but theirs. He knew his brother would not think so, and partly to provoke him, he murmured, 'How do you know? These city girls . . .'

'Don't be a fool. It will not pay. Wives are different.'

Mangal said no more, feeling possessive about something for the first time in his life. Of course he was going to be gentle with his bride. But first he had to get near her, no?

'I won't hurt you,' he now said.

She blushed again. 'It can't be just like that,' she swallowed, then whispered, 'like animals.'

Was she calling him an animal? 'This is no way to speak to your husband.'

'I want to go home,' she sobbed.

Just looking at her, her hair dishevelled, her eyes red from lack of sleep, filled him with a terrible hunger. He leaned forward and gingerly took her heavily hennaed hand. He felt the hand stiffen, but at least she did not withdraw it. He looked at her palm, the slender fingers, the red tipped nails, the orange patterns vivid against the fair skin. Everything about this hand was news to him. As he stroked it in wonder, he could feel the rigidity going. Obviously holding her hand was the right thing to do. Next he lifted it to his mouth and kissed it. She didn't pull back, again the right thing to do.

'You want to wait?' he asked, a bit more confident.

She nodded.

He drew closer, but she leapt up. 'I have to greet Uncle and Aunt,' she said as she hastily left the room. He followed to see her bend to touch their feet in morning obeisance.

As the day continued, Mangal was met with more upsets to his established notions. Instead of his bride sitting in the kitchen there was a maid he had never seen.

'Arre,' smirked his aunt, 'your brother was very keen that Madam not dirty her hands. She is a student, she has to study. He asked his friend's wife to look for a maid, and when you were in Jaipur for the reception, she arrived. He is paying her salary too. You know our habits, beta, we do everything ourselves, now we have to waste money on keeping someone for the top work. She may steal; I will have to keep my eye on her all day long.'

Mangal didn't know what to think. Did his wife know anything about this? It turned out she did. And so did he, she pointed out. Before the wedding, Bhaiyyaji had said he would hire someone for the domestic work so she could have time for her studies. Her mother had been very pleased that her daughter was marrying into such an enlightened family. She had thought Bhaiyyaji was speaking for both of them. Was that not the case?

The large eyes in the pale face seemed ready to fill with fresh tears. No, said Mangal quickly, or yes, yes of course. Otherwise he would have said so at the time.

The following night she said, door closed, bed waiting, 'Tell me about your family. Your aunt, uncle, how you came to Ajmer, tell me about your mother. Will I meet her?'

'You will not survive one day in the village.'

'You don't know me,' she laughed. 'I can be happy anywhere. Take me and see.'

She had no idea of what the village was like. No water, no
electricity, toilet in the open, inconvenient and uncomfortable.
It was so different from anything she knew, it wasn't like in
the films. Then everybody would stare at her. Especially if she
didn't keep purdah. Was she willing to keep purdah?

Tapti was silent. Purdah was beyond her.

'See?' he challenged.

'All right, tell me about your brother.'

'Hasn't he talked enough about himself?'

'You tell me. I want to hear what you have to say.'

A little more coaxing and he found himself telling her
about his brother's first marriage. She was amazed. A year of
friendship and never a hint that he had been married before.

'You thought you knew him?' said Mangal. 'He didn't tell
you he had a son, did he?'

'Only Amar,' said Tapti in a low voice, feeling betrayed,
then angry with herself. Why should anybody tell her anything,
they were not obliged. It was only necessary to know about her
husband, and no one else.

'His name is Ram Babu. How old would he be now, let me
see. Fifteen–sixteen? I went for his wedding three–four years
ago.'

'What? He's married?'

'Village boy. Happens like this only.'

'His father also went? What did Sonal Bhabhi say?'

'Bhaiyya refused to come. Arre, Ram Babu would follow
me around, whole day. Night also he wanted to sleep with me.
Everybody said just like you, just like you. We look alike, you
know, Bhaiyya and me.'

'I know. But didn't the mother mind? That the father never
wanted to see the boy?' Himmat had seemed so transparent.
How wrong she had been. He had a son practically her own age.

'What are you thinking?'

'I am sorry for that poor child.'

'His mother also minded. But what could she do? Bhaiyya sent me to get the papers signed, divorce papers you know.'

'And she signed them? Just like that?'

'Well, my mother made her.'

'Oh! Poor, poor thing.'

'She had no choice, you know. Bhaiyya would have done what he wanted anyway. He never lets anything stand in his way.'

'But what about her? What's her name?'

'How would I know? We don't take names in the village. Disrespectful. And this was my elder sister-in-law.'

'Well, what did she say? She must have said something.'

'Yes, she did, of course she did. But first she had to find me alone. Even that was difficult. Early one morning, as I was about to leave for the fields, there was his wife waiting for me. This was quite daring of her. We had never talked. I had never seen her face. I would not recognize her if she was standing before me now.'

'Then?'

'She said if she had annoyed him in some way, she was sorry, she begged forgiveness. She would learn city ways, she would change her style of dressing; all she wanted was a chance.

'But if it was her fate to be discarded, there should be some consideration for his son. He was very intelligent, he needed to be educated in the city like his father. I could take him back with me, he was five years old, able to take care of himself.

'Of course she was lying. I had already seen the boy scramble countless times into her lap, pull at her blouse, and begin nursing.

'"You may never see your son again," I said.

'She was prepared for that, she said.

'I did not know what to say. Bhaiyya would be furious if I brought him back. It would definitely interfere with his marriage.

'In the end I just walked away. It was cruel, I know, and I was attached to Ram Babu, but my hands were tied.

'Indeed nobody thought of asking how a divorce was being got in this way. They didn't even know how illegal it was. But it was Bhaiyya's contacts, always Bhaiyya's contacts.'

'So that is how he married Sonal Bhabhi,' said Tapti slowly.

'Yes. I was the only one of my family who was not married off before I could think.'

'The only one?' asked Tapti with wonder. 'How come?'

'With Bhaiyya it had been a bad experience. Costing money and all. Her father was a very cunning man. Came to Ajmer in his pagri, dhoti, earrings, a typical Jat farmer. There had to be another woman, he said, there could be no other reason. Bhaiyya shouldn't get him wrong, he was not objecting, but he had spent a lot of money on his daughter's marriage, then more money on the gauna, then money when the son was born, and now what was all that worth? He hoped he wouldn't have to come to the city to explain things to the new wife.

'He addressed Uncle but it was Bhaiyya who answered. How much, he asked. In the end the price settled on was one lakh, more money than any of us had ever seen. Uncle just sat there looking unhappy. So much for a divorce! Where was he going to get that kind of money from?

'It took Bhaiyya six months to appear with half the cash, no one knew from where. The other half would be given when the decree was final. They should appreciate that he was trying to do things legally, he said. But nobody could appreciate anything, least of all why he was bothering so much. He needed to be free, he said, with nothing clandestine tucked away in the village. Even here he was far-sighted. Later no one could blackmail him by threatening to reveal hidden secrets from his past. By the time he got his precious divorce, his son was seven. Poor Ram Babu. My mother didn't understand that divorce meant she was supposed to part with the daughter-in-law who had worked by her side for so many years. As for the child, he was her grandson, blood of her blood, she was not going to let him go. Bhaiyya had to accept that, but he knew his mother would make sure they never bothered him. And they never did.'

The story of this divorce took half the night and many don't tell anybodys. By morning, Tapti felt more part of the family, their secrets now her secrets. It was all so strange, so different from anything she was used to. She kept asking more questions. To distract her from this village saga, Mangal began to talk about the factory, a subject which always got her attention. He had already started building a home on the premises.

As he talked, he played with her fingers, running his hand up and down her arm, putting her fingertips against his lips, kissing them one by one. Inch by inch he made his way towards her. In all his life he had never been so careful with anything. If he was too sudden, she withdrew, but she did respond to caresses that were accompanied by plenty of talk. Each night he saw evidence that she was willing to love him, and when their marriage was finally consummated, it was with a triumph both shared. Mangal felt he had conquered, while Tapti felt bathed in a glow of womanhood. Her chosen husband would be the one to fulfil her dreams.

Mangal couldn't wait for them to move to the factory premises. There, he promised, she would reign like a queen.

'All I want is to be your queen,' she said, and he said that his body was her kingdom, for her to do as she pleased.

Tapti blushed. How beautiful she is, thought Mangal, he had never really appreciated this before his marriage, and it was only now he realized how rightly his brother had chosen.

A wave of love and gratitude rose in him, gratitude for every moment of happiness with his wife.

Perhaps he should tell his brother this. But Himmat was far away in Jaipur. Once he saw them together, he would understand on his own.

After he married, Mangal stopped spending nights at the plant, preferring his wife's company even if it meant commuting a hundred and twenty kilometres on the congested highway. Each morning he got up at five thirty, to leave the house by seven. Though he starts early, it still takes him a while to leave the city. He reaches Martindale Bridge, drives alongside it, past the Sai Baba temple, past Government College, where his brother had studied, past the DAV hostel where he had hung out with his friends, past DAV college where he himself had studied. There, on the pavement, he had eaten gol gappa, drunk green coconut water, watched people haggle over school uniforms. Further down he could see pilgrims climbing up to Taragarh towards a dargah, where prayers were answered. His own have been answered, he is happier than he has ever been, a wife he loves, work he loves.

Despite all his efforts, the house he was building for Tapti was not yet ready. His earlier optimism about sorting out the water connections proved unfounded. And laying the sewage pipes was taking longer than anticipated, the ground was so rocky, and then of course there was all the wiring.

Tapti loved hearing him talk about anything to do with the factory. Her husband was an entrepreneur, full of initiative. He had given jobs to the poor. He was going to make the desert bloom. Just listening to his wife's praise made Mangal even more determined to succeed.

Finally the guest house was fully constructed. A pandit came from Ajmer for the grih pravesh, even Himmat came from

Jaipur for the ceremony, blessing them with all the happiness
in the world. A feast was prepared in the new kitchen.

The most significant moment of Mangal's workday came when
it was dark, and he felt he had done enough at the factory to
be able to join his wife with a clear conscience. All day he had
worried about how she had occupied herself. She was so young,
only twenty-one, she must miss the city, her friends. 'Why
don't you take up gardening,' he said.
  'Gardening? Where's the garden?'
  'You like flowers, don't you?'
  'I do.'
  'Then plant some.'
  'What about water?'
  'Plant ones that don't need much.'
She saw the Railway Colony before her eyes, and the
brilliant bougainvillaea lambent against the dust coloured
earth. She would plant masses of them. Colour everywhere you
turned. Magenta, orange, white, pink, purple, mauve.
  'When can I start?'
He drew her into his arms. 'Day after. Tomorrow I will
arrange somebody from the village. He won't know anything
about flowers. You will have to teach him.'
  The bougainvillaea was bought and planted. 'You must make
sure they don't die,' she said to the villager who accompanied
her around the compound. 'Cattle won't eat them because of
the thorns, so it will be easy for them to survive. And here,' she
said taking him towards the inside angan, 'we will plant grass.
You must use water from the kitchen, grass needs a lot of care,
and this is the only place we will grow it.'
  Planting and growing was happening within her as well.
Two years into their marriage, a delighted Mangal learned that
his wife had conceived. 'My son will inherit all this,' he said.

'Whatever happens is in the hands of the gods,' temporized his wife.

Much of her pregnancy Tapti spent in the angan with its still patchy grass, enjoying the mildness of the winter sun, marvelling at how it was possible to be so content.

It was on Diwali that Tapti got an inkling of how much Sonal Bhabhi disliked her. Bhaiyya had insisted they come to Jaipur; she was to be a mother soon, there was much to celebrate. Through the day, visitors swept through Bishnoi Sahib's house, carrying sweets, dry fruit, gifts for both politicians. There was so much, that it had only seemed natural that Bhaiyyaji present them with some boxes of dry fruits, a silver diya she had admired. Had Sonal minded? Or had she minded her holding sparklers with Shweta and Amar, minded that Bhaiyya was laughing with them? Whatever it was, in the midst of all this, she heard Sonal Bhabhi say to Mangal, 'I am glad that your wife and your brother are such good friends, after all he arranged the marriage, so there can be no tension.'

Tapti glanced at her husband, who was looking blank, but the poison was now out in the open. At that moment she hated her sister-in-law so intensely, she could have stabbed her.

'Yes, she is like a younger sister,' replied Mangal, oblivious to the barb. He was not used to taking anything a woman said seriously.

Sonal's face darkened, but to object openly to younger sisters makes you seem jealous and un-family minded.

Tapti's heart went out to her husband, he was so straight, so simple, it took him a while to even understand people's contemptible insinuations. Dealing in cement all day, what would he know of how people functioned, how they could say one thing and mean the exact opposite? I am not some sahib, he often said, but a man of the earth.

Mangal liked to talk like this, but his simplicity, she had discovered, was also a pose. He never forgot things once he understood them.

A few days later Tapti said, 'Bhabhi doesn't like me.'

'Don't be silly. She hardly knows you.'

'You have to trust me. Because she is MP Sahib's daughter, she thinks she is too high for us.'

Mangal frowned. 'How do you know? Did she say anything?'

'She doesn't have to. I am not a fool.'

This was beyond her husband. His brother had often said, women feel a lot, and depending on the circumstances, you had to either ignore or indulge these feelings. Now he said, 'It might take time but Bhabhi is full of love. She has always been very fond of me.' To comfort her, he took her hand in his, an activity that was new to him. There was a particular charm in his wife's hand, delicate, white and soft, that made him want to cling to it.

Tapti's faith in Mangal's predictions ebbed as time passed. Far from exhibiting any love, Sonal Bhabhi found countless ways of shutting her out, even when she was standing right before her. She is jealous that my husband pays me so much attention, thought Tapti carelessly, let her be jealous.

The only fly in Tapti's ointment was Suraj Prakash. His factory was close by, and he visited often. Sometimes the men sat and drank in the front room, sometimes they drove out. When he came back, Mangal invariably lunged at her, his breath stinking of alcohol, onions and meat. She couldn't bear it. She would push him away and they would fight, and she would cry, and he would shout.

Next day he would apologize, shouldn't drink so much he would say mournfully, holding his head, don't know what happens to me. With the hope of youth she would smile, glad that her world was back to normal.

IV

1992–1995

When Tapti was nine months pregnant, she moved to Ajmer for the delivery. Mridula Gaina was born on 30 January 1992.

'Never mind,' said Mangal.

'Mind what?'

'A girl.'

'Why on earth should I mind? Do you? You have hardly looked at her.'

'The next one will be a boy.'

'You love me so much, but you are not willing to give some of that love to your daughter.'

'Don't be silly. You can't compare,' and off he went.

Ever since Tapti had moved to Ajmer, he had been driving up and down the highway, once, twice, three times a week. He was tired of the commute, but he had grown used to his wife, and a night without her was a disturbed one. He understood that circumstances were difficult, the baby small, and she needed to be near her doctor. He tried to be patient, but when it seemed no amount of patience was enough, he started to persist, when are you coming, come na, it's so lonely without you. And she, looking at his tired face, the lines of fatigue perceptible even in the morning, agreed to return to Amberi, despite her mother's reluctance to let her go.

As they drove down, her baby in her lap, a new maid beside her, she remembered the first time she had travelled this road and how hopeful she had felt. Now she was a woman, responsible for many things, with her girlhood firmly behind her.

'Nothing here,' remarked the maid chattily. 'No shops, nothing.'

'No,' replied Tapti.

'Then?'

'Then what? The car goes to Brij Nagar for supplies. It takes time for places to develop,' said Tapti, conceiving a dislike for her maid for the first time.

They turned on to the potholed dirt road and began the slow, bumpy journey to the guest house. Tapti could see the bougainvillaea she had planted, now small shrubs, putting out their brilliantly coloured petals. Those flowers were there because of her, linking her to the landscape.

To her surprise, Mangal was waiting.

'You're back,' he said and then reddened.

'Here,' she said, holding out Mridula. He took her clumsily, acutely aware of his staff looking on. No woman would dare hand a baby over in the village. It made him feel awkward, the master of this entire complex doing women's work, and his embarrassed happiness at seeing his wife dimmed a little.

Mangal beckoned to a waiting servant. 'Help Madam. I will see you later,' he said striding off.

Tapti could tell he was upset, probably because she had given him the baby, something she had done dozens of times in Ajmer. It was a small thing, and she made an effort to push it out of her mind, but for the first time, it occurred to her that the Mangal of the factory might be a different man from Mangal in the city.

These moments of misinterpretation continued. What should have brought them closer, instead became a source of tension. He was quick to feel belittled, often by casual gestures or remarks. Tapti could not understand it. Was there trouble in the factory, why did he have to work so hard, why was she alone all day and practically half the night. Who did she have for company? She had come back for him and she felt this should be more appreciated.

'You have the baby,' he said.

'It is not enough.'

'The trouble with you is that you have nothing to do. Do you have to cook? No. Clean the house? No. Shop? No.'

His way of thinking seemed foreign to her. Was she supposed to be happy because she didn't have to work? Maybe that satisfied the women in his family but she was different. She knew that if she were to make any reference to the village, he would immediately feel insulted and accuse her of thinking she was better than him. She didn't want to conclude he was incapable of understanding her, but what else was she to assume?

As for him, it took some hours in the factory to settle his feelings, and to look forward to seeing his wife and daughter in the house. Again and again his thoughts turned there, and he hurried back as early as he could.

Himmat came to visit.

'Lovely place you have here.'

'Come more often then.'

'I was passing on my way to my constituency, so I thought why not drop in? Haven't seen Mridula in a long time. How is she?'

'As you see,' said Tapti, indicating the child sleeping in her lap. 'Not a care in the world.'

Himmat looked around. It was the first time he was seeing Mangal's quarters after he had gotten married. The angan where they were sitting was a cosy, colourful place, floors of yellow Jaisalmer, around an open square of thick green grass, pillars of black polished granite, with palms and shrubs in pots. For Mangal to maintain such an establishment, the factory must be making money.

'Where do you get the water for this?'

'From a bore well. It is difficult getting enough water.'

'Mangal is living better than I am.'

She gave a light laugh. 'Don't be silly. This is your house too, you know that.'

'Yes. Of course. Where is he?'

'He didn't know you were coming. He is out at the quarry. There was some problem with the blasting, a worker got hurt yesterday, and they are making outrageous demands as compensation. If not met, they will go on strike.'

'He has to stand firm.'

'That's what he says.'

'And also to be careful before he makes his workers permanent,' Himmat said. 'He will never be able to fire them. And there will be their pension scheme, provident fund, earned leave, half pay leave, sick leave, casual leave.'

'You must tell him all that,' said Tapti, slightly surprised. 'He doesn't discuss his work with me.'

Himmat sat looking at her and she, feeling his gaze, flushed. 'Will you stay for lunch?' she asked.

No, he had to go.

Now Tapti was really astonished. She stared at him, her mouth slightly open. 'The whole factory knows you have come. They will think the brothers have had some fight – or, even worse, that I have sent you away. No, no,' she said, relaxing into some flirtation. 'You have to see him, if necessary, I will tie you to this chair.'

'All right. Here I am, tie me to the chair.'

She giggled, 'Don't be silly.'

Finally, he got up, bent over the baby in her lap, and caressing it, rested his fingers against her arm. She did not move, again he stroked the baby's head, again his hand brushed against hers.

Footsteps in the outer room. 'Oh good, there is your brother,' she murmured, 'someone must have told him you are here.'

The atmosphere in the room settled back to normal. Before long Mangal took Himmat for a factory inspection. When he came back it was alone, giving Tapti some respite from her confusion. Not that anything had happened, it was all innocent.

～

Mridula was only eighteen months old when Tapti conceived again. Mangal was delighted, this time a boy for sure. The news inspired in him an insatiable appetite for his wife, she wondered whether he thought so much sex would influence the gender of the child? She tried to reason, but he was beyond reason, accusing her in one horrible moment of not doing her duty by him.

It was easier to give in.

The result was spotting. She was not prepared to be so far from her gynaecologist. At the sight of blood even Mangal became alarmed. He agreed that she had to return to Ajmer, though the baby wasn't due for a while.

Her mother noticed her depressed spirits. What was it, what was it? she persisted. Nothing, nothing, she was just tired.

'Two children in two and a half years, is the man mad?' said the mother conversationally.

'He wants a son.'

'And if you don't produce one?'

'I don't know. And right now I don't care. He is very keen, which you should understand. Many people are hung up on sons.' And she changed the subject. She was not going to be disloyal to her husband by complaining to her mother. It would turn her against him, besides when things changed for the better, could she rely on her mother to forget her daughter's one time unhappiness?

For now, she was consumed by the weight of the growing child inside her, while the child outside her, catching her mood, cried persistently, and refused to let anybody else do anything for her. It had to be her mother who fed her, bathed her, entertained her, put her to sleep and took her to the park, there to sit at some distance from the other ayahs.

Fatigue was her constant companion. Boy or girl, there was no question of her getting pregnant again. How she would tackle Mangal, she had no idea. One girl, one boy, and the family is complete, he kept saying, while she remained silent. Why argue over the unknown?

Himmat came to visit at her mother's house, just before the baby was due. Despite herself, her spirits lifted when she saw him.

'Nice brother-in-law,' she said, 'to be away so long.'

'Forgive me, Madam,' said Himmat, 'forgive this humble politician who only lives to serve you. I have come as soon as I could. Here, here is a gift from your sister-in-law. She sends her love.'

'You are too generous with your gifts. We cannot go on taking like this,' said Tapti.

'It is nothing. We are your elders. It is our right to give.'

'I wish I could thank Sonal Bhabhi myself.'

'That will happen, don't worry,' said Himmat who saw no reason to share his wife's opinion of her sister-in-law.

Tapti turned over the gold embossed envelope, heavy with money that would buy the baby anything that was needed.

'Being an elder doesn't mean you have to look after me for the rest of my life.'

'To look after you is my pleasure. I just want to be sure you are all right.'

When Tapti didn't reply, he repeated, 'Is anything the matter, tell me, you will feel better; is it Mangal, is it the factory?'

She hesitated, then said, things were difficult for her husband. He had to keep visiting the electricity board, then finally, when he got fed up and spent twenty-five lakh rupees to buy a diesel generator, the problem wasn't solved, as he had to sometimes run it eight–nine hours at a stretch, and then his costs mounted. But he couldn't allow the kiln to cool either.

Himmat could imagine the money spent on bribes, on diesel, the tension at such continuing cash outflows.

'Then there is SP,' went on Tapti, 'who always comes with a bottle.'

'I see.'

'Naturally he likes to share a drink, but afterwards he becomes moody. He wasn't like that in Ajmer. He started with so much hope, Bhai Sahib, you know that better than I do. If anything happens to the factory –'

'Do not worry, I am here, no?' Before he left, he said, 'Always better to think ahead. What happened to your desire to serve the country?'

Her mother who was listening, said, 'Beta, once the baby is born, her husband wants her back in the factory quickly. He keeps phoning to say this one thing only.'

'Well, maybe, but there is no harm if you take the civil services exams. The state ones. We can't let your education or your gold medal go to waste, can we?'

He smiled and departed. The door shut behind him, but he had opened another door in the edifice of her marriage. He had suggested working, implied that she should have something to fall back on that wasn't a husband.

Another daughter is born, with all the attendant consolation a second girl brings. 'Never mind,' said Mangal, his arm around his wife's neck, 'you are still young, there is always a next time.'

The birth had been difficult, and Tapti was exhausted. 'I don't think I can go through this again,' she murmured. 'It will kill me.'

'Ha, ha, that is what you are saying now. You will change your mind soon enough. My mother had to try many times before she gave birth to a boy that lived.'

Through the ceremonies attending the birth and the naming, Mangal remained unshakeable in his belief that this was just the beginning. By the end of it Tapti couldn't wait for him to go away. She needed space to distance herself from Mangal's desires. Like an oyster reacting to a grain of sand, she vowed to establish a professional life, become someone who could not even remotely be construed as a stay-at-home breeder of male children.

Months pass, and still Tapti does not return to the factory. The baby was delicate, she said, till she got a bit older she needed the assurance of a paediatrician nearby.

Mangal tried to be patient. It wasn't as though he wanted his wife and daughter to be far from medical care. But wasn't Tapti being extreme? What she had gone through was a process of nature, he knew no woman who fussed like this. To say anything, though, produces tears and 'You don't understand what I have gone through.' So he remains silent, but continues to fret over her absence.

'Sometimes women suffer from depression after their children,' remarks Mrs Ahlawat.

Tapti didn't think post-partum depression existed in villages, nor did she think this was something her husband would give credence too. Above all, she didn't want him to think she was making excuses to not return to Amberi. She couldn't bear for him to be hurt in any way. While he was with her, she showered him with love. Despite himself he responds, lingering in her presence in the mornings, enjoying the breakfast she serves him, the attentiveness to all his needs, the small passing caresses. It is nine before he can bring himself to leave. Nine, and it will take him two hours to drive to Amberi. He will have to make up for it by staying late.

Finally he is out of the city, on to the straight road that leads to his factory. The Aravallis rise to his right, to the left is a train depot, and the muted hills tapering into the land. Mercifully the traffic is thinner here, occasionally he overtakes a tractor or a tempo filled with brightly dressed village folk.

He loved these hills, the sight of cattle grazing, the low thorny trees, ponds with silty green water, even the men standing aimlessly around, the cows wandering on to the road. All this was him, the soil from which he had emerged, the place where he would make it big.

From time to time he passes an ad for his own product, Gaina Cement in big yellow letters painted on the side of a village shop. His name stamped on the landscape. One day it will be everywhere.

Here and there he can see marble quarries and brick kilns, low mean buildings, squat against the earth, so different from his magnificent plant rising tall and majestic into the sky.

For a moment he imagined himself the owner of a marble unit. Just hack the stone out, cut it, polish it. An activity with no glory, no need of talent, dedication or enterprise. Who remembered any name associated with the marble industry?

He was building a future for his son. He must try and convince Tapti of the necessity. He could do that once she came back to live here. In the city there were too many influences working against him.

Foolishly she thought he didn't care for his daughters. It was not that at all. But how could daughters take on the responsibility of a business, or carry on the Gaina name? When the time came, he would give them the biggest, grandest weddings anybody had ever seen. Not like his brother's, or even his own. There will be pictures in the society pages of the newspapers, he will fly down film stars from Bombay to add glamour, his politician brother would call his influential friends.

For now, though, it is his son who will make his toil worthwhile, his son who will work beside him, who will stretch the fruits of his endeavour into the future, and give his struggle meaning and continuity.

Tapti's refusal to see things his way made Mangal nervous and drove him to mention his son more often than he might have otherwise.

'Two daughters are enough,' she said as she nursed Mansi, with Mridula climbing over her back.

'That is for me to decide.'

Tears gathered in Tapti's eyes. What was she, a machine that would go on producing children until he got a son? At twenty-four she felt there was nothing left of her youth, so swallowed up by babies was she, and it hurt her that he saw nothing of how she was feeling, his main concern not her, but his seed, his line, his name.

'The doctor says I became pregnant too quickly. Hence this weakness.'

'You should see village women. Have babies, return to the fields almost instantly.'

'She also said two children were enough,' lied Tapti.

'Who is this doctor to give her opinion? Village women have ten-ten children. Are you so superior to them?'

Not superior, nor inferior, just different. Was that a crime? He had courted her under false pretences, claiming to be interested in her, in her plans for the future. What he really, really wanted was a village woman.

Would she please talk sense? What he really, really wanted was to have her back at the factory. Everything was wilting without her, the house, the garden, the bougainvillaea on the hillside. His own staff was beginning to slacken, taking advantage of his absences.

Just a little more time, begged Tapti, just a little more.

Every day Mangal thinks that this situation cannot continue, and every day it does.

Finally the day came when Tapti could put off her return to the factory no longer. The first time Mangal broached the topic of his son after her return, Tapti said, 'If you say anything more about this, I shall simply go back to Ajmer.'

'It's my son and my right.'

There was not much she could say that she had not said already.

'Are you on the pill?'

'Of course not.'

He looked in her toilet bag.

'How suspicious you are.'

'Why aren't you conceiving then?'

'How should I know? I had such a difficult time with Mansi, maybe that's why. Too much too soon.'

'Hah! Too much too soon! What are you? Some kind of mem?'

'No. Just not an animal.'

Once before, on their wedding night, she had accused him of being an animal. Then he could take it, he was young and inexperienced. But now?

He turned away. She looked at that back, sick at heart. Was this any marriage? If they could be open to each other's point of view, how much happier she would be. As things stood, he had a right to be suspicious. Though she was not on the pill, she had done something worse, she had had a tubectomy. She could never tell him this. He would kill her.

As Tapti hung around in the factory, with a husband so consumed by problems he hardly had time for her, the idea of an independent job that came with an attached house began to look like the essence of practical wisdom. Suppose something happened to the factory? It was not entirely impossible. Wouldn't a career of her own shift some of the burden from him?

Mangal was appalled. First, there had been the issue of the son, now the issue of a job. She had accused him of marrying her under false pretences, he could do the same. He had wanted a companion, not someone determined to lead her own life according to her own ideas. Did she think he could not provide for her? He had hung diamonds around her neck, he would hang many more. It wasn't that, she pleaded. Then what was it, he demanded. What kind of marriage would they have if she would not live with him? Was she saying she wouldn't? Of course she wasn't.

Stalemate.

V
1996–1997

I996 was the first year that Mangal saw losses. After cement was deregulated, the marketplace intervened and the whole industry rapidly became more competitive. He could not sell his cement at the prices that more efficiently run factories did. There was a factory in the Sawai Madhopur region that was fully computerized. He had heard that in a year, at the most they wasted four to five days. Four to five days! And he wasted between ninety and a hundred. A hundred days swallowed by equipment breakdown and maintenance. Everything had to be done manually. He simply didn't have the deep pockets to computerize his systems.

So far as cutting costs was concerned there was no flexibility anywhere. The prices were fixed for the machines rented for the extractions, and transportation costs were high. Losses began to spill over, mounting like ladders stretching to the sky in Mangal's uneasy dreams. If only he had better staff, his own lacked the work ethic. The engineer for example, a BSc graduate, would spend hours lazily locating the trouble when the kiln broke down. It was all very well for him, the money wasn't going out of his pocket. If he fired him, he would just have to start the training process all over again. A new person, new carelessness; sometimes even small fires broke out.

As Mangal stared at the latest figures he thought of his wife. Let her do those wretched exams. It wasn't easy to get into the civil services. If she failed, she would not be able to blame him, and if she passed, she would have an income of her own should something untoward ever happen. It was always better to be safe.

'What has made you change your mind?' she asked.

'Is it so strange that I want you to be happy?'

'No,' she said, 'it's not, but why now?'

'You are not going to give me a son, are you? You are doing something, I don't know what, but you are.'

She turned hot and nervous.

'Tell me.'

'I haven't done anything.'

'Swear on your daughters' heads.'

'Don't make me do that. It's bad luck. Anything else, but not that.'

Baffled, he stared at her and said, 'I love you more than life, would have covered you with gold and diamonds had my factory worked better, yet you keep secrets from me. How can I live with this?'

His voice, his mournful expression, his words caused tears to stream down her face. Her sobs became so loud that he said, 'Don't worry. I will not force you to tell me anything. How do I know what you do, where you go, how you manage? I only know that if there is no trust, there is nothing.'

'Don't talk like this, Mangal, don't, please. I have no idea why I have not been able to give you a son, I am sorry. Please forgive me.' She felt like a criminal when all she had done was assert control over her body. That could not be so wrong. How she wished she could tell him.

'I am still saying I want you to be happy,' he said at last. 'Maybe it is better. The factory is not doing well, but that you know. Take these exams, or don't take them, but it is entirely up to you.'

If only this factory would go to hell, she thought, they could settle down to some kind of normal life. She would make sure their daughters grew up to be capable independent women, and he would gradually realize they were as good as sons. He would have to, because it was physically impossible for her to have more children. The only person in the world she could be absolutely open with was her gynaecologist. This made for some loneliness, but that was a price she was willing to pay.

Tapti filled in the application forms and joined a coaching group. The tensions of her private life receded when she was in the classroom. Later she could only wonder how effective desperation was as fuel. In her pre-marriage days she didn't think she would be able to master such dull topics as current affairs, knowledge of the social customs of Rajasthan, problems facing Rajasthan, industrial development in Rajasthan, rural development in Rajasthan, the dialects of Rajasthan, demography of Rajasthan.

Most of the other students in her coaching class were men. A lot of them were there for their second, even third, try. These were pumped for all the information their experience gave them. What questions were asked, what should they wear, was English preferred, did speaking in Hindi have a negative effect, were men favoured over women, what hypothetical situations did they ask you to deal with?

Had she not been a mother at twenty-two, and then at twenty-four, had she not been faced increasingly with the shadows of her future darkening all too apparently in front of her, she did think that she too would have succeeded only after multiple tries.

The family responded in various ways to her success.

Her mother said, 'You will be secure for life. The pay commissions make sure that salaries and pensions increase to keep pace with inflation.' As the beneficiary of her husband's pension, Mrs Ahlawat knew what she was talking about.

Pride filled Mangal. He who had been so bad at studies, whose student life had been marked by third divisions, had a wife who cleared the competitive exams in her very first try.

Himmat sent flowers.

'Who are they from?'

'Sonal Bhabhi.'

'See? And you say she hates you.'

'They are just for show.'

'Even she must be impressed. You have succeeded where many don't. Brains, you have brains,' said her husband.

His wife knew what it cost him to say this, how little he had wanted her to have her own career, and how certain he must have been that she would fail. She put her arms around him, and rested her cheek on his back. 'One day you will be proud of me. I swear. One day you will not mind that I haven't given you a son.'

He sighed and said nothing. She looked into his sad face, kept her arms around him, and she too said nothing.

Another two years pass. By now Mangal is completely alone in the factory. Day by day he sees it bleeding and keeps this bitter knowledge to himself. Soon, it will turn around soon. He increases the blasting, breaking open the earth, gathering the limestone, taking it to the factory to be tested. The kiln is the heart of his production unit, revolving day and night. It can never stop, and when some malfunctioning occurs, or when the electricity trips, or the generators break down, or a fire breaks out, he goes mad with anxiety and temper.

Tapti becomes a Probation Officer, Grade 1, in the Department of Rural Development. Himmat has become a minister in the central government. He shifts to Delhi along with his father-in-law, better medical care there. A year later Bishnoi Sahib dies.

Mangal and Tapti go to Delhi for the funeral. 'You can leave the factory for one day,' says Tapti, 'as it is we hardly ever see you.'

There was a time when he would have retorted, and whose fault is that? And at another time he might have said, just wait till I have enough money, I will live like a king and you will never have to work. But the numbers on his balance sheets stop these statements from leaving his lips.

'You are very quiet,' she says on the train.

He roused himself. 'Am I?'

'Yes, what is the matter? It's not Bishnoi Sahib, is it? You hardly knew the man.'

'True.'

'But I can understand. Death makes you serious.'

'You are a serious girl, Tapti. Not happy to be like other women.'

She smiled at him and wondered whether he still minded the exams, the son, the everything, but she could never ask, because even if he did, what could she do? Nothing in her marriage was as she had expected. The ache, the dissatisfaction, the yearning for something more refused to be contained within boundaries, it stretched through days, months, threatening to gobble up years as well.

They go to Nigambodh Ghat straight from the station to find themselves among hundreds of people.

'If I had known there would be such a crowd I would not have come. I can ill afford it, god knows,' said Mangal, as he looked around for familiar faces.

'They would have held it against us for years. In the end who else is there besides family? We can leave once the body starts to burn.'

When Tapti gets near Himmat, she notices the lines on his face. She can only imagine how he must have had to run around during his father-in-law's last illness, he who had always been so dutiful and so tender. She turned to her sister-in-law, hoping to be able to condole with sincerity. But Sonal Bhabhi was in no position to judge such niceties, her tears were copious, her grief extreme. Amar and Shweta, on either side, held her closely.

The mourners were the most clustered near Himmat. All around people were commenting on the history of Bishnoi Sahib, the toll, first prison, then campaigning, then public duty, had taken on him. It was his son-in-law's devotion that had prolonged his life. The son himself was rarely in India, look there he is, come from America to light his father's funeral pyre.

Husband and wife catch the night train back to Ajmer. 'Did you notice how Bhaiyya didn't ask us to stay?' remarked Mangal.

Tapti had noticed. 'Maybe his wife told him not to. She can't stand me, I keep telling you.'

'It's probably me she can't stand,' said Mangal, but his spirits seemed lighter and Tapti was glad they had had this time together. Even physical proximity creates a bond.

'Who knows what goes on in her mind, we don't, that's for sure,' said Tapti. Her thoughts turn to the funeral. How will Himmat cope without his father-in-law, the man who had nurtured him, promoted him, set him on his path.

She had not been able to provide any of this to her husband. It would have made a difference, she knew. Why had Himmat chosen her? She was much prettier than Sonal Bhabhi, but compared to political and social importance, beauty was ephemeral. Even happiness seemed so fleeting.

As she glanced at Mangal, he placed a momentary hand on her knee, then withdrew it, there were too many people looking.

Six months later Himmat calls to say he is coming to visit. When he arrives, Tapti notices how strained he still looks. Ten years have passed since she first laid eyes on him in their college auditorium, eight years since her own marriage. Her youth seems a lifetime away.

'How is Sonal Bhabhi?' she asks.

Still grieving for her father, the loss was great, he had been like a giant tree offering shade to all.

'Now you will be the one to offer shade.'

'Not possible. Besides, in Delhi, all I do is work day and night.'

'So does your brother,' sighed Tapti. 'I hope your work is more successful than his. I think he is running in losses.'

'I know.'

'How come?'

'He came to see me. About a further loan.'

'And?'

'I helped him with the land acquisition, with the original bank loans. If I do any more, there are a hundred people waiting to go to the press, accusing me of nepotism.'

'There is nothing you can do? Really nothing?'

'If I could, you think I wouldn't?'

'What will happen?'

'He might have to sell.'

'It would break his heart.'

But business was not about hearts, she didn't need his silence to tell her that. As she remained lost in her thoughts, he took out a neatly wrapped parcel from his bag, 'Here. A small present from your Bhabhi.'

She took it, her hands trembling slightly. 'Thank my Bhabhi from me. She is too good. I do not deserve her.'

'It's little enough she can do for you. I have always known sisters-in-law to be close. At least in the village –'

Mesmerized she stared at the little packet. So far his gifts had never been personal. 'Won't you open it? She will want to know what you thought.' Slowly she undid the wrapping, not wanting to tear any of the wonderful paper. It was a bottle of perfume. Christian Dior's J'Adore. She could feel her face becoming hot. J'Adore. 'J' could mean she, or he or I, it didn't matter. The main part implied adore, and everything about the present suggested that she should take the name literally. Smell it, he said in a low voice. As he watched, she sprayed some perfume on her wrist, its fragrance wafted between them. Do you like it? he asked. She lifted her wrist, he put his own fingers around it, brought it to his nose and sniffed slowly. He nodded. It was nice, her Bhabhi would be relieved.

Aunt dies. Uncle refuses to leave his house. There is talk of Tapti applying for a transfer to Ajmer on compassionate grounds, but the bureaucracy moves slowly. The days go by. From a distance she sees Himmat as a star continuing to rise. She wonders whether she can ask him to interest himself in his brother's business. She is not sure whether Mangal would appreciate her intervention, but then husbands didn't always know what was best for them.

Any reference to Himmat drives Mangal into a rage. These references she considers so small, so insignificant, so innocuous that she in turn accuses her husband of hunting for reasons to get annoyed with her. He wanted his brother blocked entirely from the landscape, how was that possible?

'Blood will always be stronger than anything else,' she said, brought up on this kind of knowledge. 'In the end who else is there? He will support you when everybody else has gone.'

Mangal who had also been brought up on these sayings, changed his tack. 'So far he has done nothing. No time.'

'His father-in-law was ill.'

'Well, now he is dead. Now what is his excuse?'

'Maybe he doesn't know the extent of the problem.'

'And why doesn't he? Because he doesn't want to. That's why.'

'But tell me, how is it going?'

'When was the last time you were there? What do you care?'

Her husband was behaving crazily because he was so stressed, she decided. How could the children leave their schools, she leave her job and go and live in the cement factory? As it is, she too is running up and down the state, she comes to Ajmer for the weekends, just like him, just like him. Everything she said was treated like a missile from an adversary, better not to say anything.

At night Mangal pressed against her. She could sense his unhappiness, but she had grown wary of words so far as he was concerned. She slipped her hands under his kurta and felt the lean and muscular body of a man who still had the build of a farmer. He put an arm around her and sighed. They lay like that for a long time.

VI

1998–1999

The summer of 1998 was one of immense heat. The factory suffered, the incidents of fires increased, till there was one so large that to even Mangal it was obvious he could no longer go on. He needed air conditioning everywhere, along with adequate warning signals. For this he needed massive cash injections, he still believed this factory could be an astounding success, the conditions governing the cement industry were more favourable now than ever before. As usual he had been at the wrong place at the wrong time.

He has no more money to draw upon, he has borrowed from the market, he has defaulted on his bank loans. Whenever he visits his wife, she marks the weariness on his face. She grows more and more worried about him.

But he shares little with her. For a man to go on complaining to his wife was to sink lower than the low.

'What is it? Tell me, what is it? I can't bear to see you like this.'

'I might have to sell.'

His face is in his hands, she can see the strands of grey among the wiry coarse black hair on his head, hair that had always been thick and springy.

'Are you sure?' she asks tentatively, hoping he won't get irritated.

But Mangal is past that. 'I wish I wasn't,' he says. 'As it is I have delayed, and the more I wait the less I will get. All the debts are mounting.'

'Have you got a buyer?'

'No. I haven't really been looking. But I am not here to burden you with my troubles.'

'I am your wife. If you don't burden me, then who?'

Finally she does make a phone call to Himmat. Mangal needed to sell. Could he find someone? Only if it was possible of course, she knew he was a busy man with a hectic schedule. She was asking him on her own initiative, it was necessary to keep her request secret.

Tapti, he replied, when have I ever been too busy for you? Don't insult me like this – I have not given you cause.

She was glad the conversation was taking place on the phone, she didn't want him to see how visible her embarrassment had become.

A few months afterwards came an offer so good that Mangal was forced to consider it. Himmat had worked hard to get the Dalmias interested in the factory, and in this he was not helped by Mangal for whom the offer represented hope. 'The fact that someone is willing to buy shows it is a good proposition,' he said to Himmat who had broken the news to him in Jaipur. 'I can make a go of it, if only I had the money.'

Himmat stared at him. 'And who is going to give you this money?'

'Why can't the seth go into partnership with me? He can own forty-nine per cent.'

'It's either complete ownership or nothing. Besides they want to change the way the factory is run, the management, everything. They want to bring in the latest technology. The seth is not interested in loss making concerns.'

A cry broke from Mangal, 'I have been wanting to do that for five years! I don't need some seth sitting in Delhi telling me the best way forward. Once it is computerized, you see how much profit they will milk from this one concern. The one I started.'

Himmat remained silent. Who had asked him to leave the cement dealership where he was making good money? Ambition had been his downfall – and everybody was suffering along with him.

In his silence Mangal read contempt. 'You always wanted me to fail,' he said bitterly. 'Otherwise was it possible that no bank would help me, even when I was offering the factory as collateral?'

'You are crazy. This has nothing to do with me.'

'Oh no? If you wanted something, heart and soul, I would have fought alongside you, fought till my last breath. But you, you are cold and distant. You don't feel it here. It doesn't hurt you that I have lost everything.' Mangal struck his chest, struggling to keep back tears.

'One day, when you are less upset you will know how hard I worked for you to keep the factory. Now I have found you a buyer so that your debts do not increase. I know how quickly things get out of hand. Should there be a distress sale, you will get nothing. As it is you are in losses, the market is aware of that. I know it has come as a shock. You don't have to decide immediately. They are not in a hurry –'

'No, why should they be? Their factories are in profit.'

'Well, only if they are in profit can they afford to buy sick units. You should be glad they are even interested.'

When Mangal told Tapti the news, he looked so stricken that she said, 'I thought you wanted to sell. Before the situation got out of hand.'

'Needed. Not wanted.'

'Don't if it upsets you so much.'

'If you knew the state of affairs, you would never say that.'

'Won't a life with less stress be better?'

'This factory was my life.'

'But your happiness is more important. What is money after all? We will always have a roof over our heads. Always have food on our plates.'

'Thanks to you,' he murmured so low she could hardly hear him.

'There is no name written on the roti you eat, is there?' she tried to tease him.

'There is no need. After all everybody knows who is feeding whom.'

The sale of the factory was arranged discreetly, all the liabilities taken care of; the workers' salaries and the market debts. Mangal would even end up with a few lakhs. The Gaina Cement Works was a small unit for the Dalmia Cement Company to acquire, not even a speck of salt on their plate.

The business pages of the press announced that for sentimental reasons the Dalmias wanted to establish a presence in their erstwhile state. Though Marwaris had spread all over India, the patriarch of this particular branch wanted to help industrialize the region he had emerged from.

The handing over of the shares took place in the factory offices in Amberi. All morning Mangal signed transfer papers along with the new owner, writing his name numbly over and over again, in the places indicated by the lawyers, as accountants and managers stood around and watched. Everything went smoothly, hands were shaken and Mangal was now free to vacate the premises whenever he wanted. There was no hurry, said the new owners politely. Mangal nodded and smiled. His

wife would empty out their rooms in the guest house, he said as
he got into his car.

He drove slowly, down the bumpy slip road on to the main
highway. He had spent more than ten years here, ten years
in which tonnes of cement had been produced, many jobs
generated and his own ambitions realized. He hadn't imagined
that it was temporary, that had been his mistake. He had
become attached to the land, to his kiln, to the whole idea of
being an industrialist. And as the scriptures tirelessly iterated,
attachment was a straight road to misery.

He had nowhere to go. To live with his wife, eat her salt,
was to descend into nothingness. Instead he thinks of his
uncle's house in Ajmer, a place where he would encounter no
criticism, no judgement. Uncle lived alone, with just a servant,
at least he could be of use there. Tapti's words came to his mind,
'Your happiness is more important.' Couldn't she understand
that there was no question of happiness now? Happiness was
making money, rising above your circumstances, knowing you
were successful and everybody else knowing it too. At the Ajmer
bypass, he turns off and drives along the familiar streets to his
old home at the foot of the low hills that surround the city.

It is left to his wife to gather up his things, to dispose of
furniture, to hire a tempo and send whatever she can to her
establishment in Bhilwara. She hears about the handing over
of the shares from junior staff who help her, and wonders why
Mangal is so loath to tell her anything, why is he so reluctant
to involve her in such a significant event in his life. Perhaps it
is because his grief is too great. She doesn't know what else to
imagine.

She stands in the rooms that had seen the initial tenderness
of her marriage, that had observed the baby years of her
daughters, that had witnessed Mangal's dreams of success. If
coming here, and that too after so long, could cause her this

much pain, she didn't wonder that Mangal would rather leave behind everything than face what he had lost.

On the way back Tapti goes to Ajmer. She finds her husband sitting with Uncle in the angan reading the newspaper aloud. Once she gets him alone, she asks, 'What are you trying to tell me?'

'What do you mean?'

'Why won't you live with me? You want me to feel bad, that I am not looking after Uncle, but you are? He can also live in Bhilwara. I have applied for a transfer but these things take time.'

'He will never leave this house.'

'But what is stopping you?'

'My life is over.'

'You can always start a new venture. Doesn't have to be as big.'

'Stop trying to manage my life.'

This was the situation when Himmat paid a visit to Bhilwara some months later.

Tapti saw his jeep ride up to her doorstep. She was seeing her brother-in-law for the first time since the sale of the factory.

'Aren't we out of your way?' she asked.

'Not at all. I have come to look at my constituency. To see how it is doing after the sale of the factory,' he said.

She looked at him. The sale of the factory had devastated her husband. If Himmat should be concerned about anybody, it should be his brother.

'Have you seen Mangal?'

'Why? Where is he?'

'With Uncle. Didn't you know?'

'Sona didn't mention – she is the one who keeps in touch.'

'I don't know how many times I have said bring Uncle here, but he says Uncle cannot be moved.'

'What has got into him?'

'Don't ask me. You must know how his mind works. He doesn't talk to me, doesn't listen. The children keep asking, where is he? What am I to say? Tell me.' By now tears were trickling down her face.

'Please, please,' he murmured, 'please don't cry. Things will change, I promise you.'

'How? Can the factory come back?'

'Bas, I promise you. Don't you trust me? Have I ever promised you anything and not delivered? Tell me, tell me, my –, my dear.'

She looked up, his gaze remained focused on her face, and he didn't look away. Nor did he look embarrassed. They remained like that for some moments. Shortly afterwards he left.

One month later Mangal appeared. 'He took Uncle to live with him in Jaipur. Just when we had settled into our routine. Why hadn't he thought of him all this time?'

'Maybe Uncle wanted to go now.'

'How do you know what Uncle wanted or didn't want?'

'I'm just saying that it is possible. His health is poor, in Jaipur the medical facilities are better. Why do you get angry at everything I say? I will stop speaking to you.'

'You will?' said Mangal. He bore down on her, clutching her wrist. His eyes were red, red with anger, an anger he was drunk on. She tried to pull away, his grip tightened. Was he going to hit her? If he did she would walk out and never return. Never. She scowled at him, and as he stared at her light brown glittering eyes, his grip relaxed and he turned away.

All day she felt the residual pressure of his hand on her wrist. The minute he used violence she would leave. The very thought of being an abused wife made her shudder with repulsion.

The day passed, then another. He did not repeat his gesture, taking care to keep his distance from her.

'What do you think about a petrol pump?' asked Tapti one evening as they sat together, silent and withdrawn.

'What should I think? You are giving me a petrol pump or what?'

'I don't have that kind of clout,' said Tapti trying to joke. 'Not yet.'

'Then who does?'

'Your brother. He is very concerned about you.'

'Why does he talk to you and not me?'

'I asked him because I can't bear to see you like this. I met him in Jaipur when I went to attend that convention on rural development. He is the only one who has the power to do anything. Who else could I approach? My brother?'

'At least your brother has a clean heart.'

'Clean hearts don't get you petrol pumps. For that you need contacts, political or bureaucratic.'

'You have been doing a lot of research.'

'And why shouldn't I? It's our future, yours and mine. Once we have a petrol pump, it is easy money. Like you thought the cement factory might be. Here you can make money even while you are sleeping.'

Yes, it was clear he had to do something, because with only his thoughts for company he would go mad. The hours weighed upon him like stones, he was not even forty, was he going to be living in his wife's house for the rest of his life?

All these days in Bhilwara, Mangal had not allowed himself to think of his kiln, now rotating to the command of others, an abler command. Nothing in his life had equalled the immensity of the cement factory. It had given meaning to everything he had ever been or done. The people who kept saying money wasn't everything didn't know the first thing about business. There was no point even hating the Dalmias. They had done what industrialists do, sensed a lucrative proposition and cashed in on it. How had they even heard of his unit? It wasn't big as cement units went. Himmat must have managed it somehow, and thought he was helping him.

It took a few more months, but Mangal eventually put his signature on papers that made him the owner of a Bharat Petroleum petrol pump, eight thousand-odd square metres, three diesel points, two petrol points, on the Jaipur–Delhi highway. The needs of both trucks and cars would be met, and there was enough space to expand. His profits could be used to establish a dhaba as well as a better quality restaurant. He could add a small service centre as well.

One crore rupees was the negotiated price. The next step was a bank loan. That was arranged by Himmat.

'See, it was possible to arrange a loan. If he had done that with the factory, I needn't have lost it,' he told Tapti.

That may be so, said Tapti, she had no idea of how these things functioned. But the factory was gone, what was the use of brooding over that which did not exist? This too was an excellent option, many people would kill to have it. And it was more of a certainty. Easy money. Once the site was allotted, he could spend the rest of his life watching money speeding into his bank account. Later he could always diversify into something else. One needed a solid foundation, that was all. There was a future for him in the new millennium, there was.

VII

2000–2004

Mangal was thirty-eight when he moved to the highway. That was a fine age, claimed everybody, young enough to bring enthusiasm and energy to a new venture, mature enough to tackle problems wisely. But if there were no problems with this petrol pump, neither was there any scope for either enthusiasm or energy.

Rising early, he was in his glass-fronted, all-purpose room overlooking the road by seven. At night he moved to the back of the building, where he slept. His petrol pump was open twenty-four hours. He chose a relative to assist him, once again established enough to be the rope that pulled various clan members out of their village poverty. This boy cooked for him on a kerosene stove, taking what he needed from the glass-fronted, all-purpose room, where a cupboard contained the stores, and a small fridge the perishables.

Tapti on her way to visit her husband. He would never call her, she would have to be the one to go, the one to break the defences he had built around himself, the one to convince him that it was their love that mattered, not some silly factory.

It is the first time she is going to see the petrol pump, there
are several bottlenecks due to roadworks, but by next year the
Rajasthan government has promised that the Delhi–Jaipur
highway will be so silky smooth, people will think they have
died and reached Singapore heaven.

She looked at the landscape. All around her were cars, buses,
trucks, motorcycles, the occasional bullock cart. Low growing
kikar trees with their prickly branches and tiny feathery leaves
bordered the road, parched looking fields stretched beyond.
In the midst of all this lived the chief minister's brother, light
years away from any centre of power. It was perhaps easy to
understand her husband's angst, but then it was absurd to think
that everyone in a family was created equal.

The petrol station was easy to find, situated prominently
on the highway as it was. Tapti's hopes rose as she took in the
pleasant aspect; in the midst of trees a row of pumps and a front
office painted white. Through the glass panes she can see the
figure of her husband. He seems to be handling some cash, and
this pleases her. At least here was an immediate solution to
their problems and money would hopefully act as a salve to the
wounds of losing the factory. She opened the door and went in.
He shut the drawer before he looked up.

'What are you doing here?'

'What do you imagine?'

He stared at her, at the little suitcase she was holding. 'This
is no place for a woman.'

'If it is a place for you, it is a place for me.'

She remained standing there, waiting for him to do
something about her presence. Slowly he took her case and led
her to a small room at the back. She looked around. His clothes
hung from nails on the wall. On a recessed shelf was a mirror,
some toiletries, his towel was draped across a rickety chair. A

door led to a tiny blue-tiled bathroom. The floor was rough
cement.

He gestured around, 'I told you.'

'It's fine. Next time I come, I can get a few things to make
it cosy.'

'No need. This is not a posh place in some posh colony. It
is a farmer's room − I am the son of a farmer − nothing else.
Get used to that.'

'I was used to that a long time ago. But what is wrong in
making yourself more comfortable?'

'Where do you see the scope for comfort? Nor am I the
type to need it.'

She turned away, as usual pitting him against her baffling
expectations. 'Arre, now you are going to sulk?'

'Always you misunderstand me. I come to be with you.
Then I get this.'

'What do you get? I didn't ask you to come.'

'I thought here at least you won't fight with me, but I was
wrong. If you don't want me to come, I won't. Ever.'

'I didn't say that.'

They sat silently, she on the bed, he in the chair. He looked
at her, slightly hunched, staring at her chappals, her glass
bangles making soft tinkling sounds as she moved her arms. In
a few moments she had changed from bright to miserable. Why
did he always make her unhappy, when his intention was the
opposite? When she wasn't there, he longed for her, when she
was, he fought with her.

'All you will get to eat is dal-chawal. The boy doesn't know
much else,' he said by way of apology.

She nodded. She had seen him cooking, crouched over
a kerosene stove, to one side of the small room. He had not
answered when she had asked his name. Too shy. Looking at

him, she wondered whether her husband had been like that when young.

They ate in a little patio, sitting on plastic chairs dragged from the all-purpose glass-fronted room. The rising moon shone on them, in the distance she could see fireflies flitting through some bushes.

'When I was a child, I used to see those in our compound,' she tells her husband.

'Here you can see them every night.'

'Nice.'

'Yes. Nice.'

'Pretty.'

'Yes. Pretty.'

There was nothing much to do afterwards. The light was put off, they lay down. The sheets smelt of cigarettes. 'I love you,' she murmured. He groaned slightly and reached for her under her clothes.

Afterwards he grew more expansive. 'You only were in favour of this petrol pump. Now you say you miss me.'

'But it is doing well? Money is coming?'

'Hoon.'

'Soon you will make enough profit to invest in another, hopefully in Jaipur. Bhai Sahib will help with the allotment, I am sure. You will be a petrol pump magnate.'

'You are always talking about him. He is like a maggot in your brain or what?'

'O-ho, I have not come here to quarrel with you. Slightest excuse and there you go.'

She put her arms around him, and he held her closely on a bed so narrow, that either they lay entwined or fell off. She felt the bond between them strengthened.

'Now at least say you are glad I have come,' she whispered into his shoulder, as his grip on her intensified. In the dark

Mangal can pretend everything is as it used to be. He thinks of the money he is going to give her tomorrow, money for the house, money he has not been able to give for a long time.

The next evening she prepared to leave. The sun was low in the sky, and she could hear the sound of birds coming from the few trees bordering the fields towards the back. It was quite rural, not a bad place to be. As she picked up her suitcase, her husband pressed a bundle of ten thousand rupees into her hands. She looked at the wad of notes. It had been a while since he had been able to contribute towards expenses; they had decided to invest the extra received from the sale of the factory, and he must have minded that the household ran on her earnings. She got into her car, rolled down her window to wave to him, but he had already turned his back to talk to the boy, far closer to him in his daily life than she was.

So Mangal continued with his dull and daily routine at the petrol pump. Gloomily he amused himself by cheating his customers.

'How much?'

'Five hundred worth.'

After two hundred he stopped.

'Arre, can't you hear? I said five hundred.'

'Sorry, sir. Do you want your tyres checked?'

As the driver bent to check the air in his tyres, the pump cranked into motion, and there it registered three hundred.

The distraction meant that just a hundred was added to the previous two hundred, and two hundred went into Mangal's pocket.

Each time he conned someone it was with a straight face, a frank and genial expression, a friendly smile, a flourish as the bill was made, torn off and handed over.

Every month he calculated how much money he had made by this method. It came to thousands. He wrote the amount

down in code. Sometimes, feeling depressed and discarded on
the Delhi–Jaipur highway, he took out the code and looked at
it. As he stared at the figures, he felt a sense of achievement; he
could, given half a chance, manipulate things to his advantage.

As a business, the petrol pump provided a steady income,
but it didn't satisfy. It had no audience, could generate no
appreciation. The money he purloined through skill and
intelligence provided a frisson that ceased to operate once he
lay down. Tapti's visits offered some respite, but once she was
gone, it was back to the same old thoughts.

When he slept he found some relief, in the morning work
occupied him, it was when he was in his room that loneliness
overtook him. This was not a loneliness that any person could
assuage. It was a loneliness in the world, the dislocation of a
person who has lost his way, and doesn't know how to find it
again, who doesn't know which way to turn.

His companions were those truck drivers who were regular
on this stretch of road. He had put charpais under trees where
they could punctuate their long haul with food and rest, had
hired a cook and opened a small dhaba. At some distance was
a secluded spot, bushy and shady, it was here that poor village
women lurked, offering themselves on worn and dirty durries
for anything between five and twenty-five rupees depending on
their age and beauty.

Along with the truck drivers, to his astonishment, came
social workers, talking about AIDS and the need to ensure safe
sex. It was not his place to provide an outlet for free condoms,
he told the weedy looking boy who was trying to establish some
kind of rapport. What did it matter to him how this business
was conducted? Even the suggestion that he was aware of it was
insulting to a man of his stature.

Later he heard that the female contingent of the NGO
had gone to the nearby villages to talk to the women. Had they

no shame? This was not an activity you could just come and discuss openly. He knew how sex in the village worked and it didn't work like this. And sex for hire even less so.

Tapti came the day before their anniversary. As she put her hand on his and reminded him of the occasion, he looked forlornly back. 'What marriage?' he asked. 'What have I been able to give you in all these years?'

'You have given me all that you had. That has been enough.'

'I am stuck here. Apart from you, as usual.'

'Your life is not this petrol pump. It is just what you do for a living,' she said.

'What life do I have other than this?'

'You have your family, you have us.'

'Whom I see, how often? I can count on one hand the years that we have lived together. But you wouldn't listen, you insisted on working.'

'And aren't you glad now? At least you didn't have to worry about us when you were selling the factory.'

'What are you saying? It is my job to worry about you.'

'My job also gives our children a settled home.'

'Girls – marry – go away – make their own homes. Now if I had a son –'

'Are you back to that nonsense? This is the twenty-first century, and the sex ratio in India is the lowest in Rajasthan. This is how we treat our girls. Abort them in cities, suffocate them as soon as they are born in villages.'

'Ask anybody. They will say I am right.'

'Look at Indira Gandhi.'

'Look at who her father was. You think Mridula is going to become PM?'

'Why not? Girls are precious gifts to a nation.'

'You sound like a parrot. Did Bhaiyya say that?'

'What, now I don't have a mind of my own? Instead of trying to appreciate your daughters, you bring in all this rubbish.'

As the words left her lips, she knew they would be badly received. Why couldn't he meet her halfway? Didn't her efforts to better their relationship merit that? She had never once reproached him for anything, not the disastrous factory scheme, the years apart, the financial insecurity, the failed dreams, the hours spent travelling to this benighted, soulless place. So didn't she deserve more than this talking to a wall, this heaviness that pressed down upon her with the weight of boulders.

He turned his irritated, unshaven, red-eyed face towards her and demanded, 'Don't you know, he will say anything his advisers tell him to. What about his own family? What would they say in the village, to see a minister's brother treated like this? Or his first wife? Divorced for no reason, just to further his ambition. Or Ram Babu – denied by his own father.'

'Oh, who cares about him?' said Tapti. 'We are not like that, why even bother mentioning such stuff.'

Next morning, when her husband was in the bathroom, Tapti stepped into the veranda. Though it was early, the roar of vehicles down the highway was unremitting. The nearer sound of birds was overlaid by that brutish, insistent, ugly noise. She shut her eyes, feeling dislocated by the divisions in her life. She was in her mid-thirties, her girls would grow up and leave, her mother would die, if she didn't have her husband, who did she have? He was committed to this place, that meant she had to be committed too. After a night of sex and some closeness she was more able to see through her husband's eyes and understand his resentment of all the things Himmat had and he didn't. Yet circumstances could never be totally similar. Without Bhai Sahib would they have been able to get a petrol pump?

Mangal emerged to catch the dreamy look on his wife's face.

'What is it?' he asked, jealous of looks he could not account for.

She was just wondering, why didn't he hire a manager? Then he could spend more time in Jaipur?

'I can't afford one.'

'Somebody from the village? You already have one boy.'

'Can you see him as a manager type?'

'Someone with education?'

'Who will cheat me.'

'At least try. I don't like thinking of you here by yourself.'

'Maybe I will make friends with the farmers around here. After all I am from the same stock.'

Tapti had a momentary vision of her husband's friends trooping into her Jaipur drawing room. Farmers, in their white dhotis, kurtas, heavy footwear and weathered skin, gold studs embedded in their ears. A rustic language she would barely understand, and Mangal, Mangal would keep up the village tradition of hospitality; he prided himself on that.

'I have plans,' Mangal continued, 'plans that involve staying here. Everyone will see it is not necessary to rely on contacts to make money.'

'Why? What do you mean?'

'I intend to expand.'

'Here?'

'Where else? Do I have acres all over the state?'

'But it is in the middle of nowhere.'

'When I have finished, nowhere will become somewhere.'

'Tell me how.'

'You will see.'

～

Gradually she realized his objective was to buy land around the petrol pump and build a recreation centre. Fast food joints, water slides, rides, amusement park type things.

These schemes alarmed her. She saw in them another route, less circuitous than the last, leading to disaster. What was it about her husband that allowed him no peace? The petrol pump was doing well, couldn't he let things be?

Did she always have to doubt him, he asked. That wasn't very nice of her. He drew her closer, gripping the bare waist above her sari. She leaned into him. They had enough, she pleaded, what was the need to expand? Where was the money going to come from?

That was the beauty of dealing with farmers. They weren't out to rip you off. You could buy their land at a reasonable rate, and everybody was happy. Of course he needed investors, but he was sure those would be forthcoming.

At once she visualized the demands that would be made on the brother. The expectations, the disappointment, the rage. 'Money isn't everything,' she murmured. 'Besides you are doing well.'

'Well? What is this little petrol pump business? It has no importance, and no one considers me anything.'

It was a matter of perception. Worth didn't come from business, big or small.

He didn't need her philosophy, he said. He only wanted a chance to develop the area. Were he to build a mall, prosperity would descend on the whole region. He knew farmers, he knew how to talk to them, he knew what they wanted from life.

She moved to another concern, would he be safe at night? Dacoits could come any time, after all he was open twenty-four hours, petrol pumps were known to have hoards of cash, and he was completely without protection.

'Oh, I'm not worried. We Jats know how to take care of ourselves.' His face was flushed, there was hope in the eyes she had seen so often wild with despair. She only wished that hope was more contained within the limit of his resources.

He was tender enough to specify some desire for her return. 'There is also something I want to show you.'

'What?'

'A surprise.'

He looked positively arch. She spent the next two weeks in anticipation, trusting the surprise would not be unpleasant. With Mangal she had never been able to predict anything with certainty.

Her mother objected to this trip as she had to all the others. Just thinking of her daughter alone in some remote, godforsaken place made her so anxious she could neither sleep nor eat till she had her home again.

'I have to go,' was all her daughter would say, which was no explanation at all. 'Just tell me when managing Mridula and Mansi gets too much for you.'

The mother looked offended. It was never too much for her. But why this second trip in the same month? Was her husband pining for her? That she would never believe.

'Why? You think I am so incapable of inspiring love?'

Mrs Ahlawat said nothing. If visiting her husband could make Tapti look, however fleetingly, gay and youthful, who was she to stop her?

'Ma, of course it is all right. What do you think could happen? He has even bought an Innova so I can travel in comfort.'

'About time he did something for you.'

'Yes, so then. I must do something for him too. The fact that things are working out has changed him. All these years it was thwarted ambition that made him so unreliable. Don't worry, Mama, if I can't trust my husband who can I trust?'

'Beta, all these years, and you are still a simple girl.'

Perhaps that is the way all mothers view their daughters, seeing the unblemished innocence they had as children, pristine despite the damage the world has done.

'Close your eyes.'

They were in the little room at the back of the petrol pump. Mangal had waited till they were alone, stoking her anticipation by withholding even a hint of what the surprise was.

Obediently she closed her eyes. Whatever it was, must be nice, he looked so much younger, almost like a boy, perhaps the kind of boy who commits mischief in the village, perhaps like Lord Krishna when he stole butter from people's houses. There was something of that in his look, something illicit.

She heard him open a drawer, then the sound of a key inserted into a padlock, the slight creak of the steel lid of his trunk.

'There,' he said, pulling her hand towards something cold and hard, 'you can look now.'

A Cobra Derringer rested beneath her fingers.

She wanted to sink down on the bed, bury her head into the stale sour smelling pillow and never look at the world again.

'What's the matter? Aren't you pleased? I got it to protect myself. Didn't you say you were worried?'

'So you would return to the safety and love of your home.'

'I told you I can't.'

He looked at her, her thick hair twisted in a bun, her pink and white skin, the young eyes. 'I am doing this for you. I want you to live like a queen.'

'I don't want to live like a queen.'

'Nonsense. All women do. Look, it's really quite simple, and quite safe. Are you afraid? Why aren't you looking? Arre, you can't be so silly. Here you put the cartridges, here is the lever to lock it, you pull the hammer back like this, and there, ready to go.'

No point hanging on to unrealistic expectations and futile discontent. At the click of the hammer she removed her head from the pillow, ready to deal with the death held so lovingly in her husband's hands. 'It's so small,' she marvelled unwillingly, 'I had no idea this was what you were thinking of. Suppose someone snatches it and threatens you? What about dacoits? Will you shoot to kill?'

Her eyes were moist with fear as she looked at him. He smiled, the smile of a man with a lethal weapon, as he brushed aside these words of warning. 'I'll show you how small it is,' he said. Looking at her, he slid off his pants, parting his shirt so that his erection was clear and visible. 'See, this is how small it is.' He placed the gun next to his penis, the shiny steel barrel thicker but not as long. The base of the pistol was embossed with wood, he cradled it in his hand, nuzzling his balls with the barrel, while at the same time using it to flick his penis up and down.

'See how compact it is.'

She put her head back on the pillow. It was disgusting, what he was doing.

He threw the weapon on the bed, and stepped towards her. 'Which pistol do you prefer?' he whispered, pushing the hair away from her ear.

After the shock, his body pressed warm and heavy upon her.

'Have you put it away?'

'Only when you tell me which pistol you prefer?'

'This one,' she sighed, gripping him, 'always this one.'

He pumped away inside her, and she moaned and arched, while the pistol glinted innocently from the corner of the bed where it had been thrown. He had not loved her like this in a long time, there was assurance, and afterwards, tenderness as well. Could buying a pistol do so much?

It could, and it did the next day too, in the morning and then in the evening, just before she was leaving.

'The pistol wants to give you a goodbye shot, to remember me by,' he murmured. And she had let him, and all through her journey back home his smell and his hands were upon her, as well as the memory of the passion they had shared. That the emotion had been heightened by a gun made her uneasy, yet here she was, wrapped within an embrace that had not entirely left her, wanting to prolong the pleasantness before she reached home, where it would fade into a domesticity that had nothing to do with any man.

VIII

2002–2004

Once he moved to Rajasthan, Himmat Singh Gaina was allotted government accommodation in Civil Lines, Jaipur. He had first visited this area as a supplicant to Bishnoi Sahib, first bumped into his wife outside the gates of one such house. He could now say he had returned Sonal to the home he had taken her from.

Living in Jaipur also allowed him greater contact with his brother's family. Himmat's conversation proved scintillating by virtue of the names he dropped, names of power figures at the centre, S and R and MM and NM and SP and MSY and so on. Tapti wondered whether Bhai Sahib's name was taken with the same panache in other households. When she asked, he merely laughed, leaving it to his wife to say that by making him head of the party in Rajasthan, the IPPP was hoping to make good their 2000 losses in the next elections. That's how valued he was.

Tapti felt she was at last experiencing the family intimacy she had always longed for. In all these years, it had been, oh, if only we were in one place it would be so nice, the children are growing apart, and so on, noises made with a certain amount

of conviction. Now that both families found themselves in
the same city, it was all conviviality; phone calls, outings to
restaurants and film halls, visits, even discussions of future
holidays together.

As time passed, the children began to feel less enthusiastic
about these meetings. Their aunt was distant, they said, and
Amar and Shweta never even looked at them, so what if they were
older and from Delhi? It was only their uncle who gave them
attention. Tapti remained silent in the face of such complaints,
not liking to show how much she shared their opinion, but in
fact it was only their uncle who gave her attention too.

The habit of being reticent about her professional activities
was by now ingrained in Tapti, but Himmat persisted with
questions that demanded detail. How was her tourist village
scheme getting along? Had it generated any revenue? Yes, it
had. Other states, Madhya Pradesh and Himachal in particular,
were thinking of using it as a model. They had invited her to
supervise pilot projects. These accomplishments evidently
pleased him. It was all his doing, she gracefully said.

These conversations, so harmless on the surface, caused a
series of dissatisfied ripples that spread across her daily life. To
have a man so interested in her work, to have him remember
responses, was to understand what it might be like to live with
someone who was proud of her achievements, before whom it
was not necessary to belittle one's own work.

Eventually the chilliness between the two families became
more obvious. Tapti was uncertain of the sequence of events
that led to this, but it was clear that they were no longer
welcome. We told you they were snobbish, said her daughters,
every negative opinion confirmed.

Their mother blushed at the memory of their last visit.
Himmat had politely escorted his sister-in-law to the gate
where her driver was waiting. Courteously he held the car

door open, she bent to get in, a movement that revealed a considerable expanse of gleaming slender back, a back that a low-slung sari emphasized. She felt a slight caress as fingers slid against her skin. The driver started the car, she rolled down the window and stared at him, he stared back. The girls chattered on, unaware.

All night she thought about it. In one way, that he should touch her was shocking, in another, it seemed an inevitable strand in the tangle of connections that had grown between them, starting from the day they had met.

She had not protested, she had even responded slightly by remaining frozen for a second, only an involuntary second, but still.

Prudence said avoid future meetings. It would be easy, because he was so busy, and his wife eternally jealous. Her many insinuations were accompanied by gay little laughs, it's amazing how relatives insist on clinging, my husband is so family minded he manages to find time for everybody, but of course it is up to us to not take advantage.

When invitations to their house ceased, she couldn't help admiring her sister-in-law's instincts, those of a bloodhound. Sonal with her X-ray vision had penetrated certain grey areas, judged and taken retaliatory action to guard the sanctity of her home.

Tapti was glad when some weeks later Himmat phoned and asked her to meet him at a small resort on the Delhi–Jaipur highway. It was just thirty minutes out of town, wouldn't take her long. Yes, she said, she too had been missing their visits, but she wasn't sure whether this was an appropriate place to meet? Would he like to come over?

He needed to see her alone, he had something to give her. He promised he wouldn't bite or attack.

In all the years she had known him, he hadn't bitten or attacked. Did he intend starting now?

No, quite the opposite.

People had such dirty minds, if they saw her with him alone, they would jump to conclusions.

He had deliberately chosen this destination with her reputation in mind. The suites were at the back, she just had to walk down the path from the car park, the number was III. He could personally fetch her if she wanted.

No, she laughed, trying to sound casual, there was no need for that. After all they were old friends, weren't they?

He agreed. Old friends.

She had never been with him alone. There had been the moment when he had caressed her baby's head along with her arm, and the moment he had held her wrist while smelling the perfume he had given her. Later she had decided these gestures were merely a brother's love.

The evening arrived. She dressed, applied sparing drops of that same perfume preserved all these years, then drove nervously down the highway, every turn of the wheels suggesting the transgressive. Try as she might, she could not be calm, and this agitation of her spirits, this slow heating of her body confused her. Nothing had happened and already her embarrassment was overwhelming.

She locked her car and walked towards the back. There were ixora flowering on either side of the path, the massive red clusters intense against the green. Further away she could see a peahen with some beige fluffy balls, her chicks, by her side.

The place was sylvan, drenched in birdsong, drawing her hesitant feet further along the path, when perhaps she should turn around and go home. But the deep unhappiness that was always gnawing at her drove her recklessly on.

No. III it said on a brass plate. She knocked, the softest knock possible, the door opened and he drew her inside.

Her hand lay hot and moist within his as she started to protest. Why were they meeting like this? It was almost as though they had something to hide.

Because there were eyes everywhere. This place belonged to a friend of his, here privacy was guaranteed.

Her distress grew.

'Forgive me, Tapti,' he said quickly, 'but it is impossible to get your attention when we are together.'

'Why do you need my attention? I mean you have it, but . . .' By now her face was on fire. He had used her name, it gave the situation gravitas.

'Would you like some tea?'

She nodded. The bile rose to her throat, she sat down on the edge of the rexine sofa and watched Himmat go to the door and bring in a tea trolley. He set out the cups, spoons and strainer, poured, added milk and sugar. In her entire association she had never seen him do anything remotely domestic. When she remarked on this, he said there were sides to him of which she was not aware.

Holding her cup she managed to ask, why had invitations to his house ceased? Cut off without a word of explanation, was that being brotherly?

Her Bhabhi was preoccupied, that was all. It was to assuage any hurt that he had called her here today.

'You can do that on the phone,' she said.

'I wanted to see you, no, that's not quite accurate, I needed to see you. Needed, you understand?'

Her spoon rattled around in her cup. She wanted the tea to get cold, so she could drink it quickly and leave. She began to talk nervously of her house, they owed it solely to him, she was grateful.

There was no reason to feel so obliged, he said. All he had done was expedite her home loan and make sure they got an allotment in the public draw, these things were often rigged. Should anything happen to him, she would always be secure. That had been his main concern.

She raised alarmed eyes to his face. What would happen to him? Mangal talked like that too. He had bought a pistol, he had insisted.

Mangal? Bought a pistol? Why?

'The petrol pump is open twenty-four hours. There are only him and his boy there, with quite a lot of money in the safe. What's to prevent dacoits coming? He showed it to me. Cobra Derringer, he said. A .38 Special.'

'Has he registered it?'

She had no idea. Should it be registered? Yes, obviously.

Himmat Singh Gaina gazed upon the face he had brought into his family. 'We can deal with that later. I have a surprise for you. Close your eyes.'

She stared at him. The last time somebody had asked her to close her eyes, it had been in order to delight her with a pistol.

'Don't look so anxious. It is something you will like. I went to a great deal of trouble to get it.'

'You or your secretary?' she attempted to joke, her body rigid.

'For this – only me. Now come on, close your eyes.'

Eyes shut, she heard the rustle of paper, the tiny snap of a box being opened. She felt a chain going around her neck, and then his hands clumsy under her hair trying to fix a clasp. Eyes still closed, she reached up, 'Should I help you?' but no, 'I want to do this myself, turn your back to the light. There. Now tell me, honestly, do you like it? It can be exchanged.'

Dangling down her chest was the biggest diamond she had ever seen. A huge solitaire, set in a simple square of white gold.

Questions, questions leapt about frantically, where did he buy
it, how did he buy it, was it real, was it for her, yes, it must be, it
was around her neck, wasn't it, but why?

'Well?'

'It is beautiful. But how can I wear such a thing? Everybody
will wonder where I got it from. You had better take it back.'

'That's why the chain is long. In case you wish to conceal it.'
She struggled to pull the necklace over her head, but he held her
hands. 'I won't let you return my present.'

'I can't.'

'I searched and searched for a stone as beautiful as you. A
stone that will keep its lustre for as long as you have kept yours.
The best selection was with wholesale diamond dealers.'

'But suppose it brings bad luck? You have to try out
diamonds first, didn't you know?'

'I checked all that with the dealer. He says when diamonds
are flawless, there is no question of bad luck.'

He drew closer, lifted the pendant, removed her sari and
slipped it within her blouse. 'This is where it should remain
hidden.'

The stone felt like a metal pebble against her hot skin. 'You
are my husband's brother,' she whispered, as she raised troubled
eyes to his face.

'Tell me, how much does that matter to you?' he whispered
back. 'One word and I am out of this room.'

The pendant lay against her breasts, her sari palla had fallen
to her feet. He slowly stroked the bare skin above her neckline,
his hands caressed the soft flesh of her arm. 'One word,' he
repeated. 'One sign, one gesture.'

With eyes that were wet with tears, she got her trembling
hands to her blouse hooks, and with great difficulty undid the
first one. He completed the rest.

After they had finished, she lay next to him, shyly aware of her nakedness. She pulled her sari from the floor, and lay shielded under the flimsy material. His hands were smoothing the hair around her face, his lips were dropping kisses up and down her body. Now he moved the material aside, 'You are mine,' he said in a low voice.

A slight chill crept over her, no more than an underlying current of a different temperature in a warm ocean. 'Hardly yours,' she murmured.

His grip tightened. 'Mine. Against all sense and reason, mine.'

She let it be. Men were like that, wanting to possess, could she change their nature? She was now a mature woman, she knew the two hours she had just shared with Himmat Singh Gaina were about more than sex. She started smiling to herself. 'Lot of planning went into this, huh, with the diamond and all?'

He buried his head in her shoulder and sighed while his hands wandered over her breasts. She found it amazing that the hands on her body belonged to someone she had always seen as distant.

'So? How long have you had this in mind?'

'Whatever desire I felt, I spent years suppressing. Years.'

'Then? What happened? Suddenly you decided – what?'

'Do you regret it?'

She tapped him on the thigh. 'I am not going to tell you anything unless you answer.'

'Each time I saw you I went away with an ache in my heart, thinking it was a mistake to even visit. Then of course there was all the work, and I would forget, but only until next time, when the same thing would happen.'

'Then?'

'Then, what? I came back to Rajasthan. I saw you more. To see you always with other people, my family, your family, always

I was dissatisfied. I bought the diamond, yes, I knew I should not, but I thought I am over fifty, life is going, for once I can give her a present she deserves.'

'You were so sure I would accept your gift?'

'I was sure of nothing.'

'Why didn't you start with something smaller?'

'I gave what my heart told me to.'

'Such filmi dialogue.'

'Does it seem like that to you?'

This time it was she who pulled his face towards her, she who opened her mouth and pulled his tongue inside, she whose heavy breathing preceded his, she who expressed a desire for him, newly created in this room.

She drove back slowly, her mind as refracted as the surfaces of the hidden stone. Several times she glanced at herself in the rear-view mirror and saw the inadvertent smile on her face. How had she suddenly stopped resisting? As he put the diamond around her neck, some part of her had succumbed, it was too hard to beat against him so continually. The touch on her back had left her far more agitated than this evening's assignation.

Before going home she visited Birla Mandir. The external factors governing her life had just become a hundred times more convoluted, but her spirits felt lighter than they had in years.

Now sitting in a corner of the temple, surrounded by cool white marble, the gladness of those hours lingered with her. In front of god, she felt pure and whole. This had to be kept secret, she accepted, that she should feel ashamed, she didn't. Ultimately she saw what she had received as a gift.

~

A year passed. How often did they meet? If lucky, once a month. With the stratagems concealment demanded, it could not be more frequent. For Tapti it was as though each meeting was their last. Sometimes she encountered him on TV, sometimes in the newspapers. When she came across him like this, it gave her a strange feeling to gaze at the public face of the man she had seen naked and amorous.

Should the IPPP win the next elections, Himmat would become chief minister. Scandal could ruin him. There were her children as well. Within the narrow ambit of the bed, it was all sex and its tender aftermath. Outside it was nothing.

There was one small problem. His face was so similar to her husband's that it resulted in some slight moral confusion.

'I wish we could meet at night,' she said.

'Why?'

'Then I do not have to see your face so clearly.'

'It is so like his?'

'What do you think?'

'Once you are here, you have to forget everything beyond this room. Everything.'

'And it is so easy to do this?'

He turned her face towards him. 'If you don't want to see me, I will cover myself.'

He pulled the edge of her sari over his head. He looked so funny, so strange, so inappropriate to her sense of him, that she pulled it off. 'Better to do this,' she said shutting her eyes. He got up to draw the curtains across windowpanes of frosted glass, and in the dimness of the room his touch was infused with even greater fervour.

In the shadows she could imagine him as her husband, and for a brief treacherous moment, visualize a life of fulfilment instead of misery.

'I prefer it like this. There should not be so much light on my shame.'

'You don't look ashamed. Not a bit. You are the most alive person I have met.'

'Am I?' She smiled and her thoughts went to that rather dour creature, his wife. It didn't take much to seem alive next to her. How often did they make love? But she wouldn't ask, because she didn't want the same question put to her, and besides, no matter what he said, she would not believe him.

She traced his eyebrows, the lines of his nose, his lips and chin with her finger. Every interaction with him left her with more to give. More to give her children, mother, and most of all, her husband.

In the end, replete with plenty, she could think of her petrol pump meetings with a heart full of fortitude. She would bring some cheerfulness to her husband, no matter how difficult it might be. Everybody should benefit.

This was always her resolution, a resolution which sometimes faltered when faced with the reality of Mangal's life. There he was, toiling day and night at the petrol pump, single-mindedly focused on the rupees he was gathering.

All her suggestions of commuting from Jaipur, appointing a manager, a relative if he didn't trust anybody, of finding something closer home, met with rejection and the accusation that she didn't want her husband to amount to anything.

Meanwhile Mangal kept collecting money with the aim of acquiring land around the petrol pump. 'You see,' he boasted to his wife, 'you see how much I will accumulate. My recreational park will be a tourist destination.'

This was all Mangal talked of, and always Tapti was thrown into a panic which she tried to mask by silence. Many times Mangal didn't notice, when he did, it was accusation time again. She didn't trust him, she didn't share his dreams, so far as she was concerned it was all right to live in a shed next to the highway for the rest of one's life.

'Who is asking you to live in a shed? Live with me.'

'Live off my wife? No, thank you.'

When he bought his first plot of land, he took her out to see it. 'Look. It is registered, it has the seller's thumbprint on it. I want none of the trouble my grandfather had with land. Now you will trust me, or no?'

Tapti stared at the fields before her. The yellow flowers of mustard plants waved about in a sprightly fashion. She looked at the green expanse, half closed her eyes, and was taken to the hills surrounding her childhood home, the garden with bougainvillaea spilling everywhere, a magenta so bright it hurt the eye, creepers climbing up the pillars of the veranda, a roomy house with enough space to hide and grow. A bicycle bell rang as a friend drove up her driveway, her father's voice greeted her on his way home from office. She shuddered. Once before she had seen this vision in the midst of the barrenness of Amberi, she was seeing it now and the promise it held out was only to be distrusted. She stared at her feet, planted on the mud banks that bordered the field. He wanted a mall here. The middle of this wilderness seemed an unlikely place, but support was what was required of her, and support she struggled to give.

'It is an unusual proposition, a mall among all these fields.'

'Yes, not everybody can think of these things.'

'It seems a little small, but I am sure the designer will take care of that.'

'Naturally. And the parking is going to be underground.'

'You will construct down as well?'

'Have to. Don't have enough space otherwise. I believe they do this kind of thing in Japan and Singapore.'

'Ah. I hope other farmers prove willing to sell.'

'Don't worry about that. Let's go and celebrate.'

'Where? Come to Jaipur. We can celebrate there.'

'Yes, I can even go to my precious brother with the plans. What do you think?'

'I think we can consider that when we have enough land. But for now?'

'For now I have some bottles of beer in my room. And tandoori chicken from the dhaba. That's all we need. We are simple people, no five star-shar for us.'

She followed him, the dust of the fields rising from her sandals and getting in between her toes. Did he need more money? she asked, as she took tiny sips of coke from her glass, coke that had to last until he had finished the bottles he had stashed away. She could borrow from her provident fund. How much would he need to buy another field?

His silence meant he would eventually consent. She might have liked a more enthusiastic response, her hard-earned money after all. Yet what was he to do, it was not easy for him to deal with this change in his fortunes. In the cement plant, he had been full of hope. We are building India, he liked to say. My father did his bit during World War II, now through industry I'm bringing prosperity to this backward dump.

Whatever the petrol pump was, it wasn't industry. Not that it was doing badly, for the first time in a long while they had no money worries. She had thought when she mentioned Mangal's need for an occupation to Himmat that she was establishing the basis of a happy life for all of them.

How deluded she had been. Happiness was not for her. When it did come, it came as a thief in the night, clandestine, stealthy, unacknowledged. How easily she had fallen into her lover's hands, as though that were her destiny. When she was with Himmat, she consumed his love with a hunger that disconcerted her. He couldn't declare his desire enough, a desire he had felt from the moment he had first seen her. Saying this he had raised her feet to his lips kissing each painted nail with such intensity she almost believed him.

He was going to be electioneering soon. She should come, it would be perfectly legitimate, she could talk to women who would not open up to him. Though it would be hard to be alone, surrounded as they would be by people, but just to breathe the same air as her would be enough.

'Again you are maroing filmi dialogue!'

'Every word is true.'

'Really? Don't campaign then. Stay in Jaipur and breathe the air I breathe.'

'All right.'

Jokes apart, she said, she would do anything to help him, anything.

Anything?

Almost. He shouldn't push his luck.

To have her in his life was luck enough.

Later in the month she gave her husband a cheque for two lakhs. If it would bring him peace of mind, she said, he could have all she possessed.

The field would be registered in her name, he said. There was no question of using his wife's hard-earned money without giving her a return.

It turned out that subsequently other farmers raised the price of their land. 'The minute these people smell money, they go mad. Simply mad,' said Mangal.

'You did say farmers were reasonable people,' she tried teasing.

'Once they get corrupted, even they get greedy, but not as greedy as builders. No, not as greedy as them. But then everybody has to live, I suppose.'

'Thank god I can help you.'

'Yes, and thank god you have such a tolerant husband.'

'What is it that you tolerate? That I work? That I support you in whatever way I can? That I want you to succeed? Very kind of you, so much tolerance.'

They stared at each other, her eyes full of tears, her voice verging on the hysterical, his eyes crazy, his voice grating and abusive. How had an ordinary conversation turned into this battle? The movements had been so swift, so confusing and treacherous that even though their words still hovered in the air, neither of them could tell.

When she appeared with the next lakh, he took the money silently, and though she waited anxiously for either appreciation or criticism, she got neither. She was both relieved and sad, wondering whether this meagre communication was preferable to none.

IX

2004–2005

It is the year before elections. The United India Party
approaches Mangal Singh Gaina. Would he be interested
in contesting? He was a Gaina, and a Jat, just what they needed
to counteract the appeal of HSG. They were thinking of the
Amberi seat, where he once had a cement plant, and where
there was goodwill towards him.

Mangal said he would consider it. He would have to juggle
his petrol pump business, and he needed a little time to make
arrangements. But just as he was discussing the matter with his
wife and brother-in-law, the UIP turned cold. It is all for the
better, Tapti had said, why bring rival political factions into the
family, they only want to exploit the Gaina name, why do you
think they approached you, when there are so many other Jats
with solid credentials?

He contacted the UIP, what happened, till now you were
very keen, you said who better than me to fight from Amberi?
Has someone tried to malign me?

They had laughed, it was a high command decision, they
had just been putting out feelers, that was all, nothing to take
seriously.

He wondered whether Himmat had had anything to do with the withdrawal of the offer. At the thought of this possible betrayal, his heart contracted. He was too proud to ask, too proud to seem hurt, or to let anybody know how much his spirits had soared at this unforeseen opportunity.

Election time draws near. In three months Rajasthan will go to the polls.

Elect a Government that Works was plastered on every billboard, every hoarding, every wall of every town, village and city in Rajasthan, with Himmat Singh Gaina's face alongside the IPPP symbol of a bird. As president of the Indian Progressive People's Party, he could be the first Jat to become CM of the state.

Would Rajasthan be convinced? The people were sophisticated discerners of which side their bread was buttered, an instinct honed over centuries of deprivation, when a little butter went a long way. The state needed many things, which no government, working or not, had been able to supply. They needed roads that wouldn't be washed out with a single monsoon's rain, schools with teachers who actually taught, hospitals with enough doctors, a working infrastructure that would boost tourism. Rajasthan had treasures that needed to be exploited, Rajasthan with its monuments and havelis preserved over centuries, Rajputana whose kings had managed to resist through guile, betrayal, treaties, bravery and courage the ravages of conquerors dotting the history of the north Indian plains.

The new government would focus on every aspect of development. For conferences, festivals and sports, Jaipur would be the ultimate destination. The road between Delhi and Jaipur would be a six-lane highway, unlike the present potholed, rutted affair: the usual story of a chain of open mouths swallowing government money in the process of construction.

To attract manufacture, they would create economically favourable zones.

One thing that HSG promised repeatedly in speeches, interviews, meetings and campaign slogans, was a determined effort to root out corruption. A Government that Works meant an end to kickbacks, bribes, nepotism, cronyism, under the counter deals.

There were sceptics who thought HSG was taking on too much. Who could remove corruption? Running as it did up and down the system. People may respond to calls of transparency, honesty and credibility, but they themselves were the first to bribe when faced with the intricate nightmare of Indian bureaucracy, designed to milk everyone who crossed it.

The youth wing of the Indian Progressive People's Party was enthused by the possibility of a new India, a place where merit was recognized. Over the years HSG had looked after them as family, knowing the value of loyalty, trying to set them up with jobs, facilitating loans. Now he told the local cadres, they must win. People rewarded you if they believed you had their interests at heart, and if they were organized they could reach every voter in the state.

A professional from Bombay was hired to make DVDs which would be shown throughout Rajasthan. TV advertising was too expensive, these DVDs would have a similar impact at a fraction of the cost. They would focus on IPPP achievements. The poor of every caste would feature, every religion would be represented. Here for example is HSG at the Ajmer Dargah. Standing next to him is the khadim, plump cheeked and light-eyed, who spoke of the secular nature of the IPPP, even while eyeing appreciatively the handsome figure in the cheque handed over.

These DVDs would be unleashed two to three weeks before the election. It would be hard for the ruling party to do something equally effective in the short time they had before voting began. In villages with no electricity IPPP workers with portable gensets, portable TVs and portable players, made sure all sections, all castes, got a viewing. Rajasthan had 8000 villages, the IPPP workers were determined to cover them all. Along with the DVDs, two Bombay films would be shown, free entertainment for the masses.

The remote areas of Rajasthan were covered by rallies, with warm up speeches by a Muslim, a Rajput, a Brahmin, a Jat, a Dalit, and the candidate of the party, followed by HSG wherever possible. In twenty-nine days the IPPP organized sixty-four rallies, where Himmat was the central feature. There he was in his white kurta pyjama, descending from his helicopter, on to a huge field in the middle of nowhere, up to fifty thousand gathered from every neighbouring village to hear him, see him, even climbing up on treetops to get a better view. Pictures in the local papers showed him walking through crowds towards waiting jeeps, while people rushed at him, trying to greet him, touch him, his security men close and discreet.

As polling approached, liquor was distributed.

The day before voting, all electioneering came to a halt. Himmat Singh Gaina arrived home, lakhs of people still swimming before his eyes, all indistinguishable from each other, as he would have been indistinguishable, had fate not pushed him from his village.

42,591 polling booths across the state. 3.7 crore voters. Again and again he had emphasized, it is your duty as citizens to vote. Put your chhaap on the bird to enable us to soar. Now it was in the hands of the gods.

Mangal sees Himmat's face on election posters. He sees the DVD that the IPPP workers showed the villagers from whom he had bought his fields. It could have been his face on the UIP posters, had his brother not somehow managed to convince them to withdraw their offer.

His brother had given him a petrol pump, and thought he had shut his mouth forever. Compared to how much money one could make as a politician, it was peanuts. Now he felt like a child banging on a door, crying to be let in, but always reasons given as to why he would be kept away from the centre of influence, power, importance. His brother didn't even respect him enough to take him campaigning, forgetting how devotedly he had once worked by his side.

One day, flicking through the newspapers, he saw a picture of his wife. What was she doing there? He stared at the grainy photo, read the print beneath. Apparently she was addressing a contingent of women – how to develop villages into tourist hubs, what would it mean for them to open their homes – the increased income. How could something so trivial be an election issue?

Was she allowed, as a bureaucrat, to do this? Surely not. Who had given her permission to speak in public? Why had she not informed him? Was he so little in her life?

The day before the elections Tapti came. To take him home, she said, his name was registered there.

'What makes you think I want to vote?'

'Your brother might become CM.'

'I can see the idea is making you all wet.'

She turned to leave.

'Where are you going?'

'Home to my daughters.'

'Not to him?'

'What has happened to you?'

'How do you explain this?'

A copy of *All India Times* was presented to her, opened at the offending picture.

What was it that he wanted her to explain?

It didn't suit her to play stupid. What was she doing, campaigning? Did she remember how she had stopped him from having a political career? Said that two brothers should not be in politics, the Gaina name was being exploited, and other such rubbish. And now? Did her office allow her to parade in front of photographers? God only knew what else she was hiding from him. Where was she spending her nights?

Her face grew red, evidence of guilt if he needed it. She put her hands up to her ears to shut out his voice, going on and on with his coarse words, his filthy insinuations. Why was she married to him, why?

'Well? What do you have to say for yourself?'

What did she need to say for herself? She was not in politics – she was not standing for election – couldn't he see the difference – all she had done was talk to village women as she frequently did, she hadn't dreamt it was anything worth relating.

'Even my wife he will use. What experience do you have in canvassing? When there are others –'

'He must have thought you were too busy. You always say you can't leave this.' Her voice trailed off.

'Have you seen the DVDs?'

Of course she had seen the DVDs, when on one rare and clandestine night, early in the campaign, he had called her to the resort. She had watched the films, with her head against his shoulder, his fingers toying with the pendant, wandering to her breast, rubbing against an aroused nipple, every image on the screen blurred by her desire. Yes, she had seen the videos.

'And did you notice how he ignored the development I brought to Amberi? Nothing about that, nothing. He will never mention my name even if it kills him.'

What on earth was her husband going on about? Had a mad dog bitten HSG that he should talk about Mangal's role in development when all he had contributed was one factory that had collapsed into losses, and needed to be sold to pay its debts? God had given her husband a lot of intelligence, you could see it gleaming in his eyes, eyes that envy was now marking with the ugliness of the devil himself.

Mangal went on muttering. Who did Himmat think he was, using his wife? He had a good mind to tell him what he thought. A good mind.

Finally the visit ended. He would not come to vote, and the weary wife returned home by herself.

25 November. The posters with Himmat Singh Gaina's face on them, plastered by the thousand in every town, mohalla and village retained all their freshness when the election results started coming in. Every room at the party headquarters had TVs on. District by district, who was trailing, who was leading and by how many votes. Bhadra, Nohar, Tibi, Ganganagar, Hanumangarh, Sangaria, Kesrisinghpur, Karnapur, Bikaner, Churu, Ratangarh, Sikar, Jaipur rural, Jaisalmer, Ajmer East, Ajmer West, the results flashed on the screen, alongside loud and excited commentary by psephologists, political commentators and journalists. What would it mean if the IPPP won, what would it mean if they lost, what would it mean if the State Legislature was hung.

One by one the votes were counted, booth after booth being tallied. On and on, for twenty-four hours, went the counting, 200 constituencies, 143 general seats, 33 for scheduled castes, 24 for scheduled tribes. HSG had contested from Ajmer West – Ajmer East was reserved for an SC candidate – otherwise he would have fought from both constituencies just to be sure of his seat.

He need not have worried. He won by a margin of 44,000 votes, safe, secure and comfortable. At the final count the

IPPP had an absolute majority. HSG was called upon to form the government. In various photographs, party functionaries beamed with pride as did the leaders of the IPPP youth wing, men in their forties. Youth goes a long way in Indian politics.

There was wild celebration. Fireworks exploded, laddus distributed, TV vans rolled up to the head office, interviews were sought, the crowds became denser. Vendors did brisk business in lemon soda, channa, peanuts, bhel puri and sweet potato chaat. The throngs outside Himmat's house thickened as people set up demands for darshan.

IPPP ki jai, they cried, IPPP ki jai.

It was HSG's glory moment in the press. The news section, the magazine supplements, pictures of his village, pictures of the school where he had studied, pictures of his family. Here was a success story that spelt Opportunity and Hope.

He had proved himself without the advantages of political lineage, or the appeal of name and family. In electing him, the people had elected one of their own, he announced. He would justify that faith if it was the last thing he did.

For the first time in Rajasthan's history a Jat was chief minister. Once the swearing in was done, he moved into the most prestigious address in Jaipur, 8 Civil Lines, next to the governor's house.

Himmat Singh Gaina proved to be a very visible chief minister. He was frequently seen on TV, talking about foreign investments, about international collaboration to help green the desert, about attracting industry and creating jobs. When he was in Jaipur, he started a weekly Jan Sunwai. From three to four thirty in the afternoon every Saturday anybody could meet him, rich, poor, farmer, city dweller, anybody.

From morning they started coming, crowding the road that led towards Raj Bhavan. They had to pass through security, give their names, show their letters of complaint. Once safety was assured, no one was to be denied entrance. At three sharp, the chief minister emerged, along with secretaries from various ministries. One by one the supplicant groups said their piece, handed over their complaints, which were then passed on to the staff concerned.

Unfulfilled expectations, partially realized schemes, system failures: these were the complaints. Children in our district are not being taught, no teachers. We have not got our pension, we are widows. Free laptops were promised the girl child, they have not come. We are homeless, we were promised housing. Under NREGA we only got twenty days of work instead of hundred which is the law, and even then our wages have been delayed. The road to our village, just outside Jaipur, is still unfinished after two years, very difficult in the rains.

The highlights were televised.

Tapti invariably put on the TV to watch these. This way she could feel some connection with the man. They hardly met nowadays, he was so busy and certainly more visible than ever before. She did not insist, as afraid as he of prying eyes waiting to rip open the shroud that covered her life.

From time to time there was correspondence. But he was not a man who expressed himself well in letters, and she was always careful to match his brevity with her own, never to be a burden, never to initiate contact, but only to be alive and responsive to him when he turned towards her.

Gradually the waiting wore her out. Remember, she said to the lover who loomed large in her mind, remember how I used to say I would be satisfied with the crumbs from your table? And you said why crumbs? The whole feast is yours? And now? Now you have a brand new life, and the crumbs you let fall would not satisfy an ant.

Sometimes she thinks it is better to break off than be kept hanging like this. Though her misery will be great, the slow anguish of thwarted expectation will not be hers. The surgeon's knife is a metaphor that often flashes through her mind.

Previously her days had had a wholeness and integrity of which she had not even been aware. Now she often felt unreal, as though someone else were living her life.

When she was with her husband, she tried to focus only on him. Frequently he asked what are you thinking, and there was always this infinitesimal pause before she could produce an innocent answer. What did it matter that she hardly ever saw her lover, she still had something to hide, she still led a life that was mentally and emotionally fractured.

With Himmat, she feels most herself, because from him she has no secrets, she can chatter, laugh, flirt, she can display her body, she can demand attention, love, caresses, promises, all unfettered. Outside the room, the happiness of those moments becomes submerged by caution and concealment. The weight of it wore her down.

From the newspapers she learns how he is reaching out to other CMs in IPPP governed states, he wants to strengthen the IPPP on a national level. Three months pass. He is travelling, he is in Delhi, he is in Ahmedabad, he is in Bombay, he is everywhere but next to her.

They notice the change, her mother, her husband. They accuse her in different ways. Why does she look so miserable, asks her husband, wasn't she thrilled now that her hero has won the elections? Her mother says, you are so quiet, you don't smile any more, what has happened? Too much work pressure?

Judging by the continuing comments, her efforts to look normal do not succeed. Maybe this constant pain is what is known as a breaking heart.

Finally, with much persistence on her part, they manage to meet at their old rendezvous.

'You have forgotten me,' she says. The tears she has kept under tight control come pouring forth. He holds her, kisses her, makes love to her, but with a difference. Even in these few hours, he cannot be completely hers. She wouldn't have voted for him, she tells him, if this was how he was going to behave.

'Oh? Who would you have voted for?'

'Your rival. The incumbents, the United India Party.'

'Come here.'

She has been putting on her clothes, winding her sari around her, when he pulls her towards him, drops her palla from her shoulders, undoes the hooks of her blouse and bra, holds her breasts in his hands, pressing on her nipples with his thumbs in a way that arouses her, and murmurs, 'Who would you have voted for?'

'It's a secret ballot,' she sighs.

'And if Mangal had been standing, who would you have voted for?'

'Him, of course. He is my husband.'

'And I? What am I?'

She turns her head away, he forces it back, 'Well?'

'You know what you are, what you have made yourself.'

'I want you to tell me.'

'What for? So you can be even more conceited?'

He slips off her blouse, unties her petticoat, pushes her back on to the bed, demanding that she tell him what he is, but she won't because in this resistance she senses his fuller attention.

'We will travel together. I am going abroad soon, come with me,' he murmurs.

'Are you mad? On what pretext? What about my children, my mother, and –' She stopped. She didn't want to say, my husband, because she had decided that her soulmate was in fact this man. At the same time she realizes that from now she must not give herself to him fully, even though in fact she wants to throw herself at his feet.

They part. He promises he will see her more often, but on one condition. She must never, ever cry. At this she smiles. She will promise him nothing, she says.

It was inevitable, despite all precautions, that she be seen. And seen by the unlikeliest person, her brother, a man who hardly ever came to Jaipur, who travelled down this highway perhaps once a year. But it is rakhi the next day, and he is driving down for the occasion. It was his duty to protect his sister, that was what the thread she tied around his wrist every year signified. And he would protect her. From what his mother had said on the phone, it seemed things were not going well in Tapti's life. This had surprised him, he had thought that since the husband was prospering, the stress in the family would ease. Musing on this, he pulled into a resort about half an hour from Jaipur and wandered with his young daughter towards the cabins, searching for a clean toilet. That was when he saw a figure in the evening light who looked like his sister. This sister-like figure, head covered, face obscure, hurries into a car parked inches away, reverses and speeds off.

Though he lingers, he sees no one else. He walks towards the back, his footsteps crunching on the red gravel, but all the cabins seem uninhabited, their curtains drawn, doors closed. Still, he is certain a man is involved. Though that is difficult to believe, nothing else makes sense. He will confront her later.

In his sister's house it was all gaiety. They agreed they did this too little, there should be more visiting between the families. It was only at night, when his wife and children were in bed, that

Ram Pratap accosted his sister. The colour rose in her cheeks, her face grew hot and flushed.

'Who is he?'

She kept saying nobody, nobody, what was he talking about?

He was talking about seeing her at the resort, near the cabins towards the back, scurrying towards a car. She must have arrived in Jaipur just before he had.

He was mistaken, she had just gone out to do some rakhi shopping, but her stricken demeanour gave her words the lie, as did her downcast eyes.

The mother, looking on, grew as confused as her daughter. After Ram Pratap left for Delhi, she started. She wanted no lies. Who was he? Who?

Why was everyone obsessed with this mythical man's identity, asked Tapti. Whoever he was, and she was admitting nothing, it was her business, and hers alone.

The mother ignored this. She was not making a moral judgement. That was between Tapti and her conscience, she was only concerned about her safety. Suppose her husband got to know? Had she not heard of honour killings? Her daughter must break it off at once. Having said this, she began to quietly weep.

'Stop it, Mama, stop it. I am sick and tired of tears, my own, yours, everybody's. Do you want that I should be miserable all my life? Why don't you make a sati out of me, throw me on my husband's funeral pyre?'

'Beti, how are you talking? Your happiness is my one desire, but it cannot lie outside the house. It is too risky. What will people think, your daughters, if you are found out?'

'I will be the judge of that. I am a grown woman, Mama, I do not need permission for what I do.'

X

2006–2008

Ever since Ram Pratap's visit, the tension in Tapti's household had increased dramatically. The mother's dire predictions were relentless, dangerous, you don't know what you are doing, though your husband is difficult, this is not the way, honour, children, shame, disclosure almost certain. Today Ram Pratap, tomorrow anybody.

Denial does not stem the plaintive tide, but neither does Tapti corroborate her mother's assumptions. So the monologue went on, battering, searching, seeking.

Why was she alive? She could resist her mother – the whole world with pride, stubborn silence, with assertions of autonomy, if only she felt more secure about his presence. Months have passed since the last meeting. Nights are for his family, car rides are with his secretary, and the days devoted to his public duties. He tells her he has a cell phone number exclusively meant for her. Often it is switched off, or the number is unavailable. She ceases to believe in its existence.

She informs him she no longer feels safe at the resort. She has been seen. Her family was making her life hell. Almost every day she had to hear things, and for what?

He promises to look for another place. She waits and waits, but there is no arrangement for them to meet, nor any suggestion of an alternative place.

Did he not care for her any longer? Was it better for desire to be fed sporadically, thus keeping the low level of pain constant, or was it better to endure the clean agony of separation?

These were questions that troubled her, and though she kept pushing them from her mind, it was fatiguing to have to do this constantly.

It is 2008, ten years since Mangal had sold the factory, twenty-five since he had started it. Along comes an invitation, it is founder's day, and on this special occasion we are paying tribute to all those who had anything to do with the Dalmia Cement Corporation. We request your pleasure as chief guest for the celebrations.

This is followed by a phone call. He must come, he absolutely must. His was the vision that created the factory, this twenty-fifth anniversary will not be complete without him. Will he please do them the honour of inaugurating their newly created archives? 'We can send a car to pick you up from wherever you like. Ajmer, Jaipur, Delhi,' goes on the voice.

'There will be no need for that.'

'Your presence will mean a lot to us, sir.'

That night the factory rose before his eyes, along with a great longing to see the place. So what if it was someone else's? The petrol pump he was now managing had also been someone else's. Circumstances changed, fortunes changed. Going back after ten years would be interesting if nothing else.

The evening before the event he drove to Jaipur. Though his wife greeted him with her usual tenderness, he sensed a change in her. Quieter, almost dull.

'Is anything the matter?'

She looked startled. 'No. What should be the matter?'

'You tell me. You are the one looking so dead.'

'And you are the one imagining things.'

They left it at that.

The sun was beginning to rise when he started out next morning, dew still dotting everything. He drove down the familiar way in anticipation, the road connected his past life to his present. Now it was widened and freshly paved. This carriageway had been in the making for at least ten years, a highway linking Delhi, Agra, Jaipur, Ahmedabad, Bombay, and bifurcating towards Udaipur, Vadodara, Surat and Rajkot. A road that made commerce easy, that would have saved him much time had it been built as originally planned. But then, what in India is built as originally planned?

The landscape had changed too. All around him was a low growing type of acacia. The locals called it videshi babool. Some MLA had brought saplings back from Australia to green the landscape, a tough hardy plant that grew within minutes of its seeds falling, a plant that produced neither fruit nor flower. Even animals wouldn't eat the leaves. Here and there he could see branches that villagers had left to dry before lugging them home for firewood.

Finally he turned on to the narrower road for the final five kilometres to Amberi. How smooth this road had become, better even than the highway. The random bougainvillaea that Tapti had planted along the hillside is in brilliant full bloom. Down the centre is a neat row of oleander, pink flowered branches waving at him. His heart begins to feel heavy. The success of the factory is evident even before he has entered the main gates.

Beyond, towering above the landscape he can make out not one giant machine but two. They have managed to add another kiln. Very good. Very good for them. An arched gate before him announced *Dalmia Cement Corporation Limited* in curved raised gold letters. He is stopped by security.

'Name?'

'Mangal Singh Gaina.'

'Who are you coming to meet, sir?'

'I am the chief guest,' said Mangal through gritted teeth.

He felt humiliated. Chief guests should be met at the gate, not be forced to show their credentials.

A paper is consulted, a phone call made, and he is directed to the guest house. There to the right, the home he had built is now a neat whitewashed double storeyed building, set jewel-like within a garden. Did they not have a water problem that they could afford to have so much grass? How was his bore well doing?

Some men are waiting for him at the entrance with a garland of marigolds and a tray. They do arti and put a tilak on him, for god comes in the guise of a guest, and is to be honoured in a similar fashion.

This was the home he had done his best to make beautiful for his wife, but it is as different as a mud hut from a palace. Air conditioners hum, marble floors gleam, barefoot bearers in smart uniforms proffer water and soft drinks, TVs beam into the glass-panelled foyer, pots of flowers line the outside, the grass that glimmers in the angan is so well tended that there is not a single weed or brown patch.

A small machine with blinking green lights is on the wall next to the receptionist, incoming staff press their thumbs on it to have their lunch registered and its price cut from their salary. Mangal thought of the free meals he had hosted in this very building. Well, that was how industrialists were made and men like him destroyed. He had always had an open heart, always. That was his problem.

Would sir like a tour of the factory? Of course, said sir smiling, he would love to see how they had modernized the place, there must be many differences, no?

Oh yes, sir. They were growing, putting up a third plant thirty-five kilometres from here, the kiln had to be near the raw material, or the transportation costs would kill them. But sir would know all such problems, continued the junior engineer deferentially, this factory was his inspiration, he had done all the groundwork.

Mangal glanced at this boy, in his twenties, glowing with the pride associated with a successful concern. His managers had seldom been able to reflect such pride, they were too ridden by the stress and anxiety that permeated the whole factory.

'What is that?' he asked pointing to a spire of water that soared above some trees.

'Oh that? That's a fountain in GG, or Gokul Gardens, our special park in the middle of the campus. GM Sahib's wife is very fond of gardening.'

As had been his own wife. He saw her face bending over the heavy pink blossoms of the madhumalti that grew in the angan. Our home is like paradise, she had said, it looks sweet, it smells sweet.

'This place must bring back memories,' remarked the junior engineer chattily.

Mangal nodded.

'On the other side of the garden are the staff quarters. Would you like to see them, sir?'

Quarters that he had also wished to construct would only make him more miserable. 'Let's go to the offices and factory first,' he said smiling, 'I want to see how many changes you have made, after all the future lies in technology, especially in industries like cement.'

The engineer flushed in his enthusiasm, 'You are absolutely right, sir. That is how to turn a loss making concern into a profitable one. Without profits, how can one continue?'

'Exactly. I knew when the Dalmias bought the plant that I was leaving it in good hands.'

With this mutual understanding established, the junior engineer and the former owner walked into the offices near the kilns. Mangal was taken up to the control room, and asked to leave his shoes outside the heavy glass doors. As the junior engineer ushered him in, the air conditioned atmosphere, the pristine purity of the marbled room, the glistening polished free surfaces hit him forcefully. Opposite the entrance were pictures of gods and goddesses festooned with jasmine garlands and illumined by small LED spotlights. Flanking them were photographs of the owners, Dalmia patriarch, matriarch and sons.

In the centre of the room, stretching through its length was a curved row of gleaming monitors, with blinking red, green and white signs and numbers. Here lay the heart of the whole enterprise. Involuntarily Mangal drew near and gazed at the black screens. These were what could have saved the factory.

A senior engineer who had joined them started explaining, 'We know at once the precise spot when something goes wrong. Our ground engineer tackles it immediately, no time wasted. The biggest change has been from analogue to digital. The production of cement has been revolutionized just in the last decade.'

Of course, said Mangal, he was aware of these changes. There used to be a manual control panel here, but that was long ago.

'We have a photograph in our archives, sir. When you go to inaugurate it later this evening, you will see.'

Yes, said Mangal, he was interested in the archives.

As they left the control room, they asked politely, And what was sir doing now?

Sir was now entirely devoted to social work. He worked with agricultural issues like land acquisition.

The engineers immediately looked respectful. Social work occupied a higher moral scale than working for money.

The rest of the visit passed in a daze. Mangal inaugurated the archives, he sat, honoured chief guest, in the front row of the Dalmia Rang Manch. He was given a bouquet, he was invited to say a few words, which he did. He spoke of legacy, of the importance of innovation, of his pride in seeing the factory functioning so efficiently, of the responsibility that went into keeping it efficient.

Where had those words come from, those meaningless, insincere words? His predominant feeling was pain, and the desire to escape. Somehow he managed to sit through the variety performance by the staff and children belonging to the factory school. He excused himself from the community dinner, he had many hours on the road before he reached home, and they, looking understanding, thanked him for his precious time.

Courteously a group of factory staff escorts him to his car, they thank him again for his invaluable contribution. There is no driver for them to summon, no driver to store the large basket of gifts that they have prepared, so they stand around and smile and urge him to visit any time. Mangal thanked them, reversed and drove out of the compound. In his rear view mirror he could see them, still standing there, waiting, watching, waving, gracious hosts to the last.

As Mangal drives, his eyes film over. Tears trickle down his face once the arched gateway of the property is behind him. He tries to control himself but soon it becomes dangerous to drive. He pulls over to the side of the road, sinks his head on to the wheel and cries and cries till his insides are hollowed out.

His heart was breaking. This is what he had wanted, this vision, this dream. But someone else had come to build on his foundations. They had added their own beauty, but it had been his originally.

If only he had been able to ride out the losses for a few more years. He too would have computerized the systems, seen the changes that technology could bring. Instead of testing limestone twelve times for its composition, simply X-ray it. How much time this saved! Time is money, nowhere more true than in business.

Slowly he restarted his SUV. Grief stricken or not, he had to reach Jaipur tonight. Almost five hours. His wife was expecting him. She had timidly suggested he not go, it might be distressing, but he had rejected the implication that he was not man enough to see his former factory.

On and on he drove. On either side of him were fluorescent factory signs, gleaming momentarily in the darkness. Lights from passing trucks flickered in and out of his car. Their drivers were his cohorts now, the ones who would stop by, often after midnight, to eat and sleep for a few hours on the cots he had provided. They all drove to schedules, and chewed gutka to keep awake. Vehicles from the Gaina Cement Works had at one time plied this road. Who even remembered that company now?

Finally the demands of his body dictated that he stop at a wayside restaurant. He chose the same place where he had eaten with his brother, Tapti, Ram Pratap and Mrs Ahlawat when they had initially come to see the factory. Sagar, it announced in huge pink and green letters.

A bus with a wedding party drew up near the entrance. His gaze fell on the bridegroom, this boy throwing his weight around, ordering dinner for everybody, dressed in white embroidered satin, with seven strings of pearls hanging from his neck, heavy gold studs in his ears, his hands and feet covered with mehndi. Ten to one he had not seen his bride, but what did that matter? He had seen his own on many occasions before marriage and much good it had done him. In the end it made no difference to the success of the match. These things were decided by one's karma, not by seeing or not seeing.

And yet that evening he had felt buoyant with optimism. It was on the table over there, by the water tap, that he had exchanged his first intimate glance with his fiancée, a moment when happiness seemed around the corner.

He would spend a few hours in Jaipur, then return to his petrol pump next morning. That was where he belonged. His dream of a mall seemed flimsy and evanescent against the solidity of the factory he had just left.

In Jaipur his anxious wife plied him with questions, what was going back like, were the creepers in the angan still there, was the factory running well, what is the guest house like?

His answers are brief; marble floors, central air conditioning, guest house computerized, everything computerized, third kiln. Dual carriageway to the factory from the highway. Creepers fragrant and blossoming, bougainvillaea profuse, colour everywhere.

She grew silent in the face of these details. Clearly the factory was flourishing, what must it have been like for Mangal to actually experience it? If only he had listened to her and not gone. When she tried to comfort him, he shook her off, I'm all right. They were very nice, treated me with a lot of respect, did arti, didn't know at the gate I was coming, apologized later.

How was the food?

It was getting late, he hadn't wanted to stay.

So, he had eaten nothing?

Sagar. He ate at Sagar, he said reluctantly, not wanting to mention the place that had once figured so strongly in his imagination.

She looked at him, then looked down. I remember Sagar, she said slowly, when we went to eat there, the first time I saw the factory, before we married.

Involuntarily he shifted closer to her. She had said, 'I remember Sagar,' and those words now made him repeat all he had said earlier, as though he were relating it for the first time, fresh details of the marble, the velvet road, the punching system for those who ate lunch at the guest house, the control room, the bank of computers. She heard him this time round with a feeling to match his own.

For the remaining hours of the night, his sleep was restless and disturbed. At dawn he got up, made himself some tea and left for the petrol pump, each kilometre putting more distance between the cement factory and him. Soon, he promised himself, he would forget. The trip had been rife with memories, but that was the last he was going to have to do with any of them.

∼

In all this time Tapti has not seen Himmat even once. When she gets in touch with him, his promises are profuse, but there is no concrete suggestion as to how they are going to meet. She really has only one choice. Love needs food, and this was a love that was being starved. If she has to suffer, she might as well suffer as a virtuous woman. A love based on this kind of fear could only live within narrow limits, and those limits grew narrower each time they met.

Since his election, his own dread of being discovered had obviously increased. She had noticed how much more preoccupied he was with who was likely to see them, who would guess and who would leak those guesses to the press. She had always considered herself the one more at risk, now she had to recognize his own sudden aversion to it. What had happened?

Did his wife suspect? Why was he so reluctant to meet her? He was the one who had initiated this, now she was the one who had to pursue him. Was this fair? Before hanging a solitaire around her neck he should have factored in his public life.

Those false assurances. 'Nothing can separate us. On the day you put a garland around my neck at your college function, I reciprocated with my own garland. How else have you been close to me all these years?'

She sets up a rendezvous in a small hotel in Pushkar. He must come, this will be the last time she will demand anything from him. He does not protest, and she thinks he too will be relieved when it is all over. She had told many lies in order to be absent from home, and they weigh oppressively on her. It was all beautiful when they were together, away from him she grew weak and guilty. Her double life lurked in the shadows of her mind, burdening her with its secrets. She resented feeling such a criminal. Every time they met she wanted to discuss this with him, but their meetings were so hurried, so driven by the urgency of his passion, and her own responses, that no discussion ever took place. After this, her love would have to be interred in the remoter recesses of her heart. There to flower or wither, as time dictated.

The hotel she has chosen is charming in a rustic fashion. There is a restaurant below, with tables facing the lake just beyond. Strings of coloured lights are threaded through the surrounding shrubbery, winking on and off, like simulated fireflies. She arrives first, and settles down to wait. It is a pleasant room with floors of white and green terrazzo, and lamps of bronze latticework. The cover on the low double bed is a melange of thread and mirror work. The wall hangings are embroidered, the cushions bordered with dangling shells. The room is so pronounced in Rajasthani motifs, that it could effortlessly decorate a tourist brochure. One can have too much of magenta, red and yellow, thinks Tapti as she looks at colours that have formed the backdrop of every single office she has ever worked in. Now they will colour the setting in which she will part from her lover.

Her face in the wooden carved mirror is still beautiful, though disappointment has edged her eyes and tiny creases have begun to invade the smoothness of her forehead. She knows that he will only come when it is very late, but she has the promise of a night before her, and though this is farewell, it is also the first time they will have the luxury of more than a few hours. A honeymoon feeling, the same excitement and anticipation, the same need to look pretty and be found desirable bubbles up in her.

One by one the shutters of the shops around come down and the crowds dissolve. Cursorily she turns the pages of a book. The moon rose bright and shiny, refracted prettily in the waters of the lake.

He came late as she had anticipated, wrapped in a shawl that covered half his face. Seeing him after so long, the words she had prepared left her and she could only look at him. Her breath came fast, her lips parted of their own accord, her body felt heavier than normal as she rose to unwind the shawl from his neck. Everything was alive and intense, brilliant and lovely. Surely to live in occasional happiness was better than none at all.

His arms were around her, his face next to hers, she could feel his breath. They stood like this, silently, before he pushed her towards the bed, and slid his urgent hands into her petticoat.

She tried to stop him, 'I did not call you here for this.'

'No? Then why did you call me?'

This was not an easy question. If you want to break up, silence and distance will do as well.

'Well, tell me, why did you call me?' His hands were now inside her blouse, brushing the diamond that lay between her breasts, his solitary, super-expensive badge upon her.

'I want to give this back to you.'

He didn't even hear her, and soon she began to moan in a way that embarrassed her, but she couldn't help it, while he revelled in every sound she made. When they finished with the sex, the cocoon that held them together slowly splintered and dug its shards into her skin. Her tears then came, as involuntary as her earlier sounds.

He patted her cheeks with his handkerchief. Enough, enough, he murmured, trying to block from his memory another crying woman who had lain in his teenaged arms. In everything they were dissimilar except for one fact – his desire had led him to steal something that was not his.

'I should never have touched you,' he said mournfully. 'It's made everything worse instead of better.' She could not help but agree. It was better not to act upon one's feelings. Though what was the use of saying that now? It was done.

'Don't lie,' she teased, trying to lighten her own mood. 'You were dying to touch me. Do you really regret it?'

He was silent. His best loves were these secret ones that caused the women pain and guilt. He was much better at being a politician than a lover. He put his arms around her and sank into her willing body once more. Outside, the restaurant lights were being switched off. In the dim room the lovers were barely visible.

Three times that night they made love, a love that grew progressively sombre. When she asked him whether their few meetings had anything to do with his wife, he said it was nothing like that. He just didn't have the time.

She accused him of being a coward. He didn't defend himself. There were so many people involved, what could he do? What could she say to that? There were so many people involved in her life as well.

Their complaints interchanged. Yes, she said, he shouldn't have started anything. She had been perfectly fine the way she was.

Then he was the one to ask, did she regret it?

That was the trouble. Even now she could not say that she did.

In the end they stopped talking. Words were useless. All that mattered was the way they touched each other.

It was still dark when he rose to leave next morning. His car would be waiting on the outskirts, he was going to drive to Delhi, and he would have many hours to think of the night, and the fact that this was indeed their last encounter.

She was right, of course, it was too dangerous to go on. Again he thought of that far off love on the roof. She has emerged from the crevices of his memory to reproach him along with Tapti. Why should personal happiness be denied one who was so successful? But this sacrifice was the price he had to pay. It was a strain to be constantly watchful, to guard against his own instincts when they were together in front of people. If it was risky for her, it was a thousand times more risky for him. All kinds of insinuations by his political opponents, pictures in the newspapers, phone taps, stolen SMSes, technology could do anything these days. Every day he visualized the leaks that could destroy him. His government could fall by this one indiscretion.

Gradually, surrounded by the soothing sound of his powerful SUV, thoughts of her left him and he began to concentrate on the day ahead. Kapil, his secretary, was going to meet him in Delhi. There was an IPPP sammelan at the national level. Issues of leadership would be raised. It was too soon yet, but maybe ten years from now, when he was in his late sixties, maybe then, if the Rajasthan story continued to be good, then maybe the seat of the nation. But for now, say nothing to anyone, who will stab whom is never known, just make yourself indispensable, make yourself synonymous with clean politics and progress.

On the way back to Jaipur he will visit his brother's petrol pump. If he facilitates his brother's ambition, surely things will become easier for everybody in the family. How much, he wondered, would that ambition cost him?

Mangal was inconveniently placed right on the highway, and this was a road he travelled often. He never allowed his driver to stop there, not for petrol, not for tea, not for anything. Seeing the pump caused him an uneasiness that irritated him.

It was quite a large place, well, he should know, he found it, but it seemed to have grown larger. Since everything was over with Tapti, he might as well pay his brother a visit on the way back. It had been so long since he had seen him.

Dawn. The hills he had grown to love became clearer in the greying light of day. They looked inscrutable and majestic, how many kings and rulers had they seen, how many struggles for power witnessed, how many forts supported on their high hilly tops? They would still be there when all of them were dead and gone.

The sun rises higher and he can see the rippling silken fields of ripening wheat, with women, along with the odd man, bent tenderly over them. Some fields are naked, they have been harvested.

The green and gold of the waving stalks were the colours of his childhood. Wheat dominated their lives, it was their major crop. He had lived close to the land, and he had always known what to expect from it. These colours, this hope, how could they ever leave him?

Away from Ajmer the hills receded, but still he saw the odd one – we are with you yet, with you, with you, sang the fields, the scrubby kikar trees, the high forts and temples, as his car sped smoothly down the road. He saw the earth chequered in indecision – should I curse you with dry, arid scrub and rock, or bless you with greenery and rich brown fertility? Promise, withdrawal, promise, withdrawal till they were well away from Ajmer and the land dissolved into the flatness of the north Indian plains.

Three days later a security convoy stops in front of Mangal's petrol pump. Mangal hides his surprise, obviously he knows when his brother travels the Delhi–Jaipur highway, but that he would never stop by is something he has grown to expect. He doesn't even bother thinking of explanations, they are too far apart for him to imagine he will find one.

To what meharbani does he owe this visit? he now asks.

Himmat was passing by, he wanted to know how he was doing.

Really?

A slight blush on the older man's face. Mangal sends for water, tea, cold drinks for everybody, brother, secretary, driver, security men.

As Mangal showed HSG around, he said casually, 'You see all the empty land behind the petrol pump. Once you drive down that little slip road, you have room to do a lot of things.'

'Like what?'

Oh, he had his own expansion plans. He had already bought land from some farmers. Others too were willing to sell. Surely his brother was in sympathy with wanting to rise in this world.

Buying land from farmers? What would they do without their land?

They were very eager to sell. Couldn't wait to get their hands on the money.

What exactly were Mangal's plans concerning this land?

'I want to build up the place. Make a high-class hotel, boutiques, some eating stalls, with Raja Burger, Asli Pizza, maybe a chaat wallah, a chola wallah, food for the road, people in a hurry. And attach a restaurant to the hotel, for those who have time.'

But what was Mangal going to do for money?

He was thinking of a collaborative effort. It would attract business too. Not like the cement factory of yesteryear, when the interest on the loans and the fixed salaries ate up any profit he might have made. This, thank god, didn't depend on limestone. Just hungry tired people driving down the road. There was never going to be a shortage of those. Would Himmat like to come to the back and see the fields? If he had the time, of course, he could also see where his brother lived.

Yes, Himmat did have the time. This was where Tapti came on all those weekends, this was probably where Mangal had sex with poor village girls, if he knew anything about his brother.

Himmat was showing a lot of interest in his set up, thought Mangal. Despite himself, his voice grew warm and persuasive as a sales pitch emerged.

'It takes vision to bring civilization to a desert,' he volunteered. 'Not everybody can do it. Here we are uniquely positioned, we have the trust of farmers, yet we have the outside contacts to develop the area.'

'They may not want their area developed.'

'They cannot want what they do not know.'

There was a silence. In Mangal's mind many thoughts were swirling, thoughts of what their combined strengths could do, he the businessman, his brother the politician. These had been his dreams once, and he hesitated to voice them again in case they met with scorn. His eyes were on his brother's face, the face that gave away nothing.

'Maybe if you operated out of Jaipur, it would be better for your family,' was all Himmat said.

'My family? What have they to do with anything?'

'It has everything to do with your happiness and theirs.'

Mangal could make no response to this. 'I will let you know when my plans solidify,' he ventured.

'Yes, do that,' said Himmat, turning to get into his car with a gun wielding guard in the front seat. The convoy roared out of the dirt road on to the main highway.

'It's not very much land, sir, just one acre or so,' ventured Kapil.

'You don't know what farmers are like over their land. They are willing to kill for it. Arguments over an inch can lead to murder.'

The lonely night passed for Mangal as had so many others. He had sent the girl home, he didn't like them spending the night, they reminded him of the village, of smoke, but above all, of poverty. It was better to be alone, under the stars, where he could weave those fantasies of a future that seemed brighter, more within reach, now that his brother had visited and seen for himself the fields he had bought, seen that he wasn't just talking, he was taking initiative as well.

As he stared at the sky, he was reminded of his own young nights under stars as brilliant. Only when he had been sent to Ajmer to follow in his brother's footsteps had they begun to dim, obscured by the many other lights flourishing in the city.

Dogs barked in the distance. How sound carried in the night. He could hear frogs and crickets from the undergrowth just beyond his single room unit. He turned on his side and stared at the latticed shadows thrown by the woven ropes of the charpai. His pillow cushioned his face, his feet rested on a thick woven sheet that would protect him from the slight chill of early morning.

At this very moment his brother would be sitting in a palace, surrounded by servants running at his slightest command. He would travel in planes, go abroad, he who, like himself, had been the son of a farmer. How was it that when one brother shone, the light did not reflect on those belonging to him?

His brother could have been more responsive about his development plans. He knew how people in power were encircled. He had after all seen something of this when they were canvassing for Bishnoi Sahib. It didn't take much to imagine how many times his brother's feet would have been touched, how many boxes of sweets would have been laid at his door, how many, many men, young and old, would surround him, just begging to be allowed to serve, loud with gratitude and oaths of loyalty. That they would be mostly Jats, would be apparent from their names, their looks, their voices. Every other Jat in the world would benefit, but not him, the lone outsider.

When he had started his cement factory, and they were still in profits, he had been able to wear designer brands, been able to buy his wife jewellery, but more than being flush with money was the precious conviction that he was on the road to success.

That very road still stretched seductively before him, but now he was older, and more marked by failure. He couldn't do it alone, he needed the backing of the powerful. He wanted no favours – just loans.

His inadequacy pressed down on him, suffocating him. He was in his forties, if he was to do anything with his life, it had to be now. Politics had been denied him, and he hadn't really minded, thinking it better to make it on his own. Now he was determined not to be satisfied with the meagre pleasures of running a petrol pump.

XI

2008–2010

M angal on the phone to Tapti. 'Find me an architect.'
'From where?'

'Don't you have government architects? I want someone who knows how to get permissions, one who has contacts in the press, and with business houses, one who knows how to attract investment, I need plans, a model, an estimate.' Tapti finally selected a man bristling with ideas, a man also working for the Commonwealth Games, she told Mangal.

Yes, that would do, he said.

A site meeting was arranged.

The architect was enthused by the project. We will integrate the fields into our scheme of things. They could have a rural theme, if the client so wanted. The client wasn't sure, he wanted to escape the rural, not embrace it. And where were the boundaries of the site? There at the back they could see those fields, he had bought two of them. It would be about an acre. Was more land needed?

No, no, said the architect. He could work within one acre. Later, with more land, they could expand, but one acre was a good place to start. Split levels could accommodate many shops and restaurants. His boys would take photographs, measurements, and mark the trees. In six weeks the initial plans would be ready, once it was finalized, the model would follow.

His fees would be ten per cent of the whole project, but for now he wanted fifty thousand advance and a further fifty thousand once he delivered the drawings.

Maybe your brother could lay the foundation stone, joked the architect on the way out. Then it would be a full-on family affair. Something for the press to make much of. Mangal smiled a tight constipated smile, his thoughts circling around the fifty thousand rupees he would have to give this man.

The plan that took Mangal's fancy included glass-fronted shops, central air conditioning, a grassy angan with a marble fountain, and seats all around. He managed a loan with the petrol pump as collateral. The income from the petrol pump took care of the interest. In two years he had to pay back the principal, but by then the complex would be running. The contractor was given an advance, work started, and the clock began ticking.

These were heady days for Mangal. 'Look,' he told Tapti, 'I shall bring development to the area. These farmers will be grateful to me. Their sons will find employment here.'

Tapti stood next to him, looked at the dust rising from the open craters, looked at the girders that were being erected, looked at the piles of bricks, the loads of gravel, the sacks of cement, the cement they had once so unsuccessfully tried to manufacture, and hoped that this time at least her husband's dreams were going to come true.

The distant fields undulated with growing crops. This was the serene land her husband had violated, but buildings have to be built, shops constructed, and in doing so, jobs were generated, and who could say this was a bad thing?

Unaccountably the money ran out within a year. The complex was far from ready. Mangal began a serious assault on his brother. He was the rich and powerful one, whom industrialists vied to please, whose bank accounts were bursting with crores.

His time in Jaipur increased as he lay siege to this citadel. In his car were the architect's sketches, in his dickey a model of the complex, part of which was already completed.

As he drove to Raj Bhavan, he looked with annoyance at the lush tree lined roads, the bungalows set back in their gardens. When he approached 8, Civil Lines, it was to be confronted by high walls with coils of barbed wire straddling the top. He stopped in front of the closed gates and honked. One of the uniformed guards strolled over and tapped at the window.

'What is your work?'

'To meet Himmat Singh Gaina.'

'Himmat Singh Gaina?'

'CM Sahib.'

'Do you have an appointment?'

'I am his brother.'

'Please enter.' The guard pointed to a small side door.

Inside, more security. There was a gate within a gate, there were guns, there were khaki-clad men, there was a plethora of questioners.

What did he want?

To see Himmat Singh Gaina, he repeated.

'CM Sahib?' they repeated.

The same.

Did he have an appointment?

He didn't need an appointment. He was the CM's brother.

Phone calls were made. The security man said with a faintly derisive tone, 'Doesn't have an appointment. Says he is CM Sahib's brother.'

Mangal stood, calm and steady. He would not feel humiliated. It was they who would have to apologize once they found out who he was.

'Name?'

'Mangal Singh Gaina.'

'ID?' said the man.

Mangal produced his driving licence. The papers he needed to show his brother were then taken out from their folder, each item examined with witless intensity. The model remained in the dickey, that impressive model which would move the least development prone to admiration.

'You can enter.' The car would have to remain parked some distance away on the road, apparently security didn't appreciate anything too close.

He was escorted by a guard up the long driveway, flanked by rows of trees and flowering bushes. Birdsong could be heard. The grass was a fine, delicate, uniform green.

'Real brother, sir?' asked the guard.

Mangal nodded.

'First time coming, sir?'

A head waggle that could be interpreted in any way. He was taken into what seemed a guest room. Would he like some tea?

No. He was being treated as a guest instead of a family member, and hospitality in such circumstances was unacceptable.

'Someone will come,' and he was left clutching the plastic shopping bag that contained his architectural drawings.

Ten minutes. Fifteen. Twenty.

He got up, then sat down. Next time he came it would probably be like this again. He became conscious of the fact that he had never been to his brother's house. The door opened and his sister-in-law appeared. He can barely decipher the smile on her face, it is so strained.

'Pranam, Bhabhi,' he says bending towards her feet.

She draws away. Why hadn't he told them he was coming?

Sonal's face looked alarming, the grimace on it seriously contorted. Her eyes flickered over the packet in Mangal's hand. Had he come to give his brother something? It was such a shame but CM Sahib was not available right now, he was in a meeting. Then he would be leaving Jaipur for Delhi on the evening flight. Was there any way she could help?

The cordial note, the politeness bewildered Mangal. His sister-in-law had always treated him with kindness. It was true they hadn't met for a long time. Had that offended her? Women were changeable he knew, warm one day, and cold the next. But surely this was too extreme?

Yes, he said, he had plans he wanted to show his brother. Plans he had paid one lakh for. Done by a very good architect. The model looked even more impressive. The work was nearly complete.

His sister-in-law held out her hand. She would show them to CM Sahib.

CM Sahib again! The man was his brother – not some CM. Clearly she wished to distance them. With an effort, he said, 'You have to see the model to understand.'

'The plans will be enough for now,' said Sonal.

And Mangal was forced to be content. He bent to touch her feet before he left.

She drew back, no, no, she laughed in a brittle fashion. 'What is the use of showing respect by touching my feet?'

'What do you mean, Bhabhi?'

'He has done so much for you, and still you want more. You two can never be satisfied. Sticking to us like leeches. No shame. No pride.'

Each word hit him like a stone. He stared at her, she stared back, her lips trembling, tears in her eyes.

He turned to leave, this meeting worse than anything he could have imagined. His sister-in-law had gone crazy. They were keeping it a secret. Or no. She hated him, she was making her husband hate him too. His brother would meet him and explain.

Moodily he drove over to Moti Doongri. The affront he had received needed solitude to digest, and once home, his wife would persist in wanting to know what the matter was.

He bought some fried potato chaat from the vendors at the foot of the hill, ate it without pleasure while climbing the steps that led to the temple just below the fort.

What was he doing in this city? It was inconceivable that he would be so isolated in the village. There may have been the odd feud, but so what? Nothing basic had been wanting. They ate well, they were regarded with fear by their women and children, and these equations had carried on from generation to generation.

Yet the outside world had opened his mind, given him defeat but triumph also. For someone who had come from nowhere, he had managed to run a cement factory for ten years, he had a successful petrol pump, with enough resources to borrow money for development.

At home his wife kept on with her patient questions till finally he burst out, 'Even Sonal Bhabhi treats me like a beggar. All these years I was her younger brother, and now she has become Mrs CM she is so proudy. And why is she saying you are like a leech?'

'Why? I don't know. I told you we don't meet any more. She suddenly took a dislike to us. Mridu and Mansi were very upset.'

'Proudy Mrs CM, I'm telling you.'

She laughed uncertainly, looking at her husband slumped in his chair, his head thrown back. White fluorescent lights cruelly lit the rough stubble on his chin, the unhealthy yellow tinge of his complexion, the lines that snaked down to his mouth.

If only he would stop trying to be a big man. First the cement plant, now this wretched tourist complex, half built, waiting forlornly for cash injections, waiting as the factory had once done. What was he thinking, she wondered. She didn't dare ask. Like hers, his suffering would have to be borne alone.

Mangal, in fact, was thinking of how he would accost his brother. It was not possible that Sonal Bhabhi's opinion was shared by him. The woman was deranged. In the village her face would have been covered before her younger brother-in-law, and her voice would go unheard. He regretted leaving the plans. They may be lying in the trash even now. Tomorrow he would go to the CM's house first thing. If necessary he would say he had an appointment, making it impossible for his brother to refuse him without embarrassment. After so many years in politics, he must have oceans of black money, just sitting in his various lockers, waving its charms seductively, out of sight, out of reach. Naturally his brother would deny any possession of wealth. Who could prove black? That assumption of innocence maddened him in advance. Though no one walked alone in this country, he, the brother of a chief minister, was being forced to do so.

Five o'clock next morning found Himmat Singh Gaina walking briskly on the jogging path that wound around the compound, thoughts, strategies, plans taking shape as he picked up speed. It had taken him years to find the uses of being by himself, now he found these hours necessary rather than strange.

The breeze was cool. The hoarse cry of peacocks could be heard as they strutted boldly on the grass. His uncle had often told him how he used to stare through the gates of the Ajmer

Club; so much space used for something as useless as grass.
Now he was in a bigger house, with even more grass.

As he reached the front of his house he heard voices coming
from the direction of the driveway. Among the bird twitter, the
harsh peacock cries, came the harsh human cries of his brother,
a sound that sluiced away the goodness of the morning. That
voice with its ceaseless demands, was the voice he would be tied
to by blood as long as he lived.

Mangal. Always violently yearning for what was beyond his
reach. It is your grandfather in him, his uncle used to say. He
also had so much anger, for any small thing you could feel his
stick, his chappal. That is why I ran away. But run where you
like, family karma will follow.

His steps slowed as he turned towards the gate. He had to
meet him, it could not be said that the chief minister turned
away his brother.

Their eyes met. Himmat made a gesture towards the
security men and Mangal was let inside. Walk with me, Himmat
offered, it is so pleasant in the mornings. Mangal fell into step.
Did Himmat know he had come the other day, Bhabhi said he
was busy, he had left his plans, she had promised to show them
to him, he had not heard, so had wondered, he had been unable
to get him on the phone, hence this morning visit, when brother
could not be so busy. He had the model in his car, if he cared to
examine it, everything would become clear. One lakh was what
he had paid to the architect. A Jaipur man, also involved in the
Commonwealth Games, the structure was almost completed,
would he like to come and see it on his way to Delhi? Financing
was what he needed, just enough to complete the initial stage
necessary to generate revenue.

The plans, said Himmat, were already on his table. He hadn't
had the time to look at them, absorbed as he was in hammering
out the Jat OBC bill. Mangal would be interested in that. It

would at last give Jats the equal status that was their right, after all a considerable portion of the state was Jat, and this should be reflected in policies.

The walk finished. Would Mangal like to come inside? Have breakfast with them? His Bhabhi would be very pleased to see him.

Mangal hesitated. 'I don't think so. She acted very strangely yesterday, said impossible things about me, my family.'

'She feels strongly,' murmured Himmat.

'Give her my pranams. I cannot be fighting with women. When will I get an answer?'

Soon, soon.

By when? His loan was finished, he had given the petrol pump as collateral.

'The petrol pump was for your security.'

'Don't worry about my security. Isn't there always the mud hut in my village? I can take my wife and children there.' Mangal turned to leave, almost running down the driveway, the air of those spacious grounds would suffocate him if he stayed a moment longer.

One week later Mangal is back in Jaipur. The ease within the house dissipates as soon as he arrives. He knew he unsettled his daughters. Fate had seen fit to deprive him of a son, mating him with a wife who refused to breed as much as necessary. His uncle had been given Himmat because his own son had died, who had he been given?

He had instead these girls to whom he could not relate. His wife said to be patient, they were typical teenagers, but this was a concept he was unacquainted with.

That evening it was Mangal who put on the TV in time for the CM's weekly Jan Sunwai, held on the front lawn of the CM's mansion. Looked at objectively it made very boring

viewing, who could bear to watch this week after week? It was
another publicity ploy, that much was clear. There were a lot
of farmers, for drought threatened the region. He had already
heard mention of better storage, irrigation facilities and water
conservation on the news.

Those people were bowing before Himmat, like devotees
in a temple. And his brother too, the ultimate politician,
dressed in a starched white kurta-pyjama, acknowledged the
god-like status being accorded him by an expression of noble
solemnity on his face. He knew he was proud of keeping his
election promise, I will always be close to the people.

Mangal could see his face lit by the falling light of
evening, could see the hordes gathered in front of him,
could see various men collect petitions, could see how they
were shepherded, group by group before the chief minister.
Security men stood behind, dark suited in all that white. He
wondered how they would prevent an attack should someone
assault him from the front? Maybe there were security men
dressed as farmers among the crowds. Himmat himself still
looked like a farmer, thin and wiry; his body belied his age,
fifty-eight.

You are unnaturally quiet, remarked his wife. His silence
alarmed her, normally there was far more raving in circumstances
like this.

'Am I?' was all he said.

Next morning Mangal opened his eyes as usual at five. Careful
not to disturb his wife, he doubled the sheet over himself, the
accumulated AC of the night making him cold. He felt under
his pillow for his watch, a Rolex, a present from his brother. As
he held the heavy Swiss precision links in his hand, cool from
the night, his eyes grew wet. It had been the best present he
had received on his fortieth birthday. No one else could please

him like his brother, no one else had the key to that place in his heart that made him feel special.

If only he could have understood why that hand, that voice had stopped reaching out to him, he might be more accepting of the situation. Did he embarrass his brother? Was his presence a political liability? How could he accept this, when the Indian political scene was littered with embarrassing relatives, far worse than him, acknowledged, loved, accepted? When he saw Himmat's picture in the papers, smiling, looking deferential, bending his handsome head over this leader or that, they looking up to him as though he were the son they had never had, his heart squeezed bitterness and bile into his blood system, corroding all his faculties.

He turned his head to shake the lacerating feelings away, trite because of extensive familiarity. It was inconceivable that he should live the rest of his life hounded by these demons, but years had passed and the demons had only become more entrenched. He stared at the second hand of his beautiful steel watch, every tiny tick making him aware of his wasted life.

All day the oppressive misery persisted. It had been there so long, he couldn't imagine being without it. Once he became a business magnate, once his name was heard with respect all over Rajasthan, that would be the day when he would be free of this pain.

'Maybe I should sell your jewellery,' he said to his wife the next time they met. He had come to Jaipur, and as he said this, he noticed the expression on her face change. Immediately he was alert, 'What is it, don't want to part with your precious diamonds?'

'No, not at all. All I have is yours, you know that.'

'Yes, yes, I was just mentioning. In case the worst comes to the worst.'

He hadn't really meant to touch her jewellery, that was the last thing he would do. Then what devil had led him to mention it? Just to be sure he could. If he really wanted to sell it, nothing could stop him, but perhaps it would not be a bad idea to go to her locker, check on how much she had.

He woke early and by six he was on the road. As he approached his petrol pump, he saw his dreams of a sophisticated complex on the side of the Delhi–Jaipur highway evaporate like dew on desert leaves. The workers had vanished, leaving gaping holes in the half built structure, the rods of the building stuck straight out of concrete planks. It looked palpably incomplete and incredibly ugly. His failure was visible every time he turned his head. Before construction, his dreams had been able to drift sweetly above the smooth soft green of the landscape. Now they were disturbed and hideous.

With Mangal gone, Tapti felt lighter. Away from him she could function better and this made her feel sad. Pictures of an alternative life, of peace between husband and wife, of happy daughters, glimmered in her yearning head. This is what everybody she knew had. Why was it impossible for her? She had tried so hard with her husband, had his interests at heart, but when had he ever listened? For how long had she been telling him that there was always the option of coming to live in Jaipur, they owned their house, Mridula and Mansi were sixteen and eighteen, soon they would be independent. What was the need for any complex by any roadside? But he was stubborn, and her way of looking at things only made him angry.

She wasn't even sure what the problem was. If this project was so good, surely with time, patience and perseverance other ways to realize his dream could be found. He had already spent lakhs, he was in a position to buy land from farmers, even at enhanced prices. The existing complex could surely be finished cheaply in some way. He used to say he would build stalls gradually, and rent them out to fast food and souvenir joints.

Now he wanted crores, and Himmat wasn't giving it, was that the problem? But it seemed preposterous that Mangal could even think his brother was in a position to finance this venture. Was it encouragement he needed, involvement, contacts? When he had conceived of it on his own, bought land, got a good architect, embarked on building, why was he so adamant about support now?

Should she phone Himmat in order to understand the situation? They had not been in touch since that night in Pushkar. Gone was the waiting, longing, yearning. All she felt now was a dreary lassitude, but there was the odd day when her spirits were lighter. In some years, and with iron self-discipline, she might recover. If she called him, might he not think she was begging on behalf of her husband? That would sully whatever there had been between them. She would have to call Sonal Bhabhi, no matter how unfortunate that choice might be. There was no one else.

Mangal heard from his brother far sooner than he expected. Minister Sahib was busy, otherwise of course he would have come himself, said Kapil. He had given this matter top priority, but he simply didn't have the kind of money the brother was demanding, nor could he arrange it. Even an introduction to developers would be seen as a political favour, and it could backfire.

When he had got him the petrol pump allotment, he had given him something people would kill for. For the rest of his life money would come running towards him. Did Mangal not realize how lucky he was?

But it was a sound business decision, explained Mangal into Kapil's unmoved face, and he did believe that one of the present government's election planks was encouraging industry in the state. Besides, it was almost finished, as Kapil himself could see. Once the initial block of shops was up, the revenue generated would finance the rest. Look, look at all the land around. It would provide employment, it would serve good quality food, not stuff like roadside dhabas. Pizzas, burgers, dosas, Western and Indian fast foods, all this would be a big attraction, and food chains would pay to come there. Even Kapil could see the possibilities.

Yes, said Kapil, he could see the possibilities.

It was not so easy, said Mangal. Kapil would know of course that banks did not easily sanction loans for such projects, nor was he a fool, wanting to depend upon his brother more than was necessary. He didn't accept for a minute that Himmat didn't have the money. One couldn't mastermind elections the way he did, without access to serious cash.

He had the income generated from the petrol pump. True, it was his brother who had helped with the allotment. But did that mean he could never think of anything else? That all growth was banned? It was like asking Himmat to remain a junior minister forever – would he like that? His brother had an entire office at his disposal. If he couldn't consider a personal investment, then he could help with floating shares, getting financial ratings – that kind of thing.

Essentially, said Kapil, Himmatji was a public servant, not a businessman. Ethics forbade him to participate. This was an election year, he had to be careful, one misstep and the Opposition would seize it.

'Bhai Sahib plans to stand for another term?'

Kapil looked at him. Why would he not? For five years the man had been chief minister. His schemes had proved popular, the reservation for Jats especially so, the Jan Sunwais were a success, complaints were seen to be redressed. True, Rajasthan had a tradition of removing incumbent parties, yet with HSG the IPPP stood a good chance of being re-elected.

Tapti would have recognized the tight smile that greeted Kapil's pronouncements, but Kapil had gazed too little at the changing terrain of Mangal's face, and when he went back to Himmat, he could report that his talks with Mangal had gone well. The man seemed to understand, there had been no shouting, screaming or loss of temper.

Mangal spent much time agonizing over what Kapil had said, seeing his words as taunts underlining his lack of contacts, initiative, resources, access to money. If Himmat wanted, he could float a public company, why didn't he offer to help? They could have shared the profits, planned the different stages together, behaved like brothers instead of strangers.

His thoughts return to his wife's jewellery. Pawning it would buy him time. There were moneylenders who specialized in short term loans. She need not even know. Most of it was kept in a bank locker that either of them could operate.

When their application for a locker had come through at the Punjab National Bank, they had both gone to deposit the jewellery. He remembered her climbing up a small stepladder to put her boxes away in a long narrow steel opening, eight inches by two feet, remembered the lock she had snapped on as an extra precaution. It's not as though you have stuff worth crores, he had teased, but you never know, she had said.

Over the years she had bought jewellery whenever she could; it's for the girls, she had said, as an excuse for her own fondness. Put together, it must be of considerable value. He knew she kept the locker key in her Godrej steel cupboard drawer. He would go tomorrow and take it while she was in office.

Two days later Tapti wakes to the cold muzzle of a pistol pressed against her forehead. It is her husband. He searches her face, she stares back in terror.

'What is it?' she whispers.

'Where did you get this?'

The diamond pendant is in his hand.

'What do you mean?'

'Where – did – you – get – it? Answer me,' he hissed.

'I – I bought it.'

'How much did it cost?'

'I – I have forgotten.'

'Well, I had it valued. Only a rich man could have given this to you – a very rich man, you hear? How many do you know?'

'What are you talking about?' she croaked.

'Don't pretend to be innocent – all these months – why months? All these years – how many years? How many? Tell me.' At each word he pushed the pistol harder into her cheek, working it around until it came to press against the hollow of her throat.

She shook her head gingerly.

'Still pretending! The jewels I gave you were not enough? You did it with him, didn't you? Whore that you are. And whores have to die.'

'You are mistaken. Ask him.'

'Him? He is going to tell the truth? Yes, I mounted your wife – because I own everything you have.'

'Please – please put the pistol down. I can explain.'

Back and forth he moved it under her chin. She closed her eyes.

'Answer. How many times? Or have you lost count?'

'No times.'

There is sweat on her upper lip, her mouth is parted, she is breathing heavily. In her dark dishevelled hair, he notices

the silver strands. They irritate him and he yanks her from the
bed in order to slap her more easily. He can see the redness he
leaves across her cheek, the tears in her eyes. Her silence feeds
his fury. This time he feels the bone beneath his clenched fist.
As he raises his hand again, she stammers, 'He – he – yes it was
he.'

'What did you do to earn it?'

'Nothing. Nothing happened. I swear.' Her eye was
beginning to swell so that what with the tears and the snot and
the bruise she looked truly ugly.

'I know him. He does not give something for nothing.'

'He tried – but I – I did not agree.'

'Liar.'

'No. Not lying.' The words were hardly audible.

'When did he do it, where did he do it?'

He moved the pistol lower, between her breasts, gripping it
hard so that she wouldn't notice his trembling hand.

'Please, please, I can't talk like this.'

'You'll have to.'

'In his house.'

'When?'

'Last year.'

'Why didn't you tell me?'

'How could I? It would spoil your relationship.'

'Where were the others?'

'I had gone alone. He had called me. Wanted to discuss
some business, he said. I thought it was to help you. I went.'

He continued to stare at her. She stared back, willing him
to believe her. Her face was wet, for the briefest moment he felt
like wiping it. 'Nothing happened, nothing, nothing, nothing.
I promise.'

'So that's why Bhabhi hates you,' he said slowly. 'And all
along you made out it was she who was the jealous bitch.'

At this she turned her head away. He shoved her on to
the floor, and slumped on the edge of the bed. She crouched
before him and held his feet. 'On my daughters' heads, I swear,
nothing happened.'

'Why did you keep the necklace?'

'He wouldn't take it back. I tried.' Her grip tightened.
'Forgive me. Please forgive me. I stopped going to their house,
I avoided anything to do with them. Ask the girls – whether we
ever met – ask Ma.'

Women were killed for far less in his village. To see him
dithering like this would have brought the contempt of his
elders on his head. He gave her a kick, 'Get away – just go.'

'No, I will not. If you do not believe me, why should I live?'

He kicked her again, then again. His feet were bare, as
they always were in the house, and as he kicked, her soft lumpy
body moved then settled, moved and settled. She had her
arms around her head, but she made no other move to defend
herself. In the end it was he who left. She heard the thud of him
descending the stairs, then the slam of the front door and the
sound of his car reversing.

When she didn't hear anything for one minute – two –
three – she collapsed where she was, curled foetus-like on the
floor.

Mangal gets into his car. He needs to leave Jaipur as soon as
possible, the whole city is poisoned. He drives mechanically,
weaving in and out of traffic, seeing and not seeing at the
same time. He turns on the radio thinking it might help him
concentrate, but the sounds are so much babble, he turns
it off.

Away from Tapti, he can imagine killing her more easily.
Why had he taken the precaution of removing the bullets from
his gun? But the discovery of the diamond, his suspicion, the

turmoil in his soul, had deprived him of all certainties and he hadn't wanted to make a mistake with such a lethal weapon.

Now he thought he should have kept one bullet for her and one for himself. Where their honour was concerned, Jats were willing to sacrifice everything. It didn't matter who they had to kill, how close the family member, it was only through asserting their manhood that their reputation was preserved.

But that would leave his brother free to enjoy the remaining years of his life. No, Himmat would have to face the consequences, it was up to him to make sure he did.

He thought of their meeting a few days ago. How easily Himmat had talked, how well he had dissembled! As a politician you had to be skilled in pretending, after all didn't you perform for lakhs, crores of people? What was a brother? It would be child's play to deceive one who had spent a lifetime looking up to his older sibling.

Once he made up his mind to kill them both, he felt more tranquil. It would be preferable to catch them together during an assignation and shoot. Then he would escape. Who was going to go after him when they saw the dead bodies of the chief minister and his sister-in-law? To avoid scandal, they would hush it up, this VIP should not be seen in such a compromising situation. He would plan his strategy once he reached what was now his only home. He would never spend a night in that Jaipur house again.

He was free from everything, all family, all obligations, all duty. With their deaths, his work would be done. It was strange how his mission had changed within these few hours. It felt like years ago that the success of his shopping-cum-recreational complex seemed important. He had thought he was working for his family's future. That had driven him to look at his wife's jewellery, that had enabled him to uncover the truth about his life. Otherwise he would have gone on living a lie, the falsehoods increasing with each passing day.

She had said she had met him privately once only, accepted the diamond because he had forced it on her. On reflection this seemed hard to believe. Why would he suddenly press a diamond on her? There must have been something between them, some indication. Would he ever think of giving jewellery to his sister-in-law? Never in a million years, not even if she were Miss India herself. His brother's wife was sacrosanct.

Rage again rose in him and with it the sound of his hand against her face. He should have slapped her more, but it seemed strange to be battering his wife, leaving a mark beneath her eye for all to see. How would she explain it? Though it was no concern of his. She was nothing to him now, nothing.

How would he ever know where she went or what she did? Why had he been so happy to break from the tradition of village wives, covered women, eyes on the ground, voices low and respectful when they addressed their husbands, no matter how independent they were otherwise. He had never known a wife to think differently from her husband while he was growing up, never; it was against nature, against tradition, against everything the shastras held sacred. He thought of his brother, the gratitude he had felt initially at his choice of wife. All misplaced, all showing the fool he was. How clever Himmat had been to send him far from home, so he could prey upon his family in any way he liked. His brother had been the one closer to his wife, the one who advised her, the one who lived in the same city. True, Tapti visited, but that was to keep him quiet. Yes, she had asked him to come home, but she had known he wouldn't.

He had never doubted his wife's loyalty. No matter how much they fought, how bitter the words between them, how they pulled in opposite directions, he had always relied on her love for him. Now, in place of that certainty, was a monstrous engulfing darkness, and for a moment he was in so much pain he felt he would collapse and die. Taking quick shallow breaths, he pulled up to the side of the road, and blindly walked up and down the soft shoulder.

Finally he got back into the car. As he drove, he became more and more certain that his wife had lied about Himmat. She had only told him enough to remove the pistol from her body. If she had told him the truth, he would have killed her. But what had she gained? Only days.

Once he had taken action, it wouldn't matter whether he spent the rest of his life in jail. He assumed he would. It wouldn't even matter if he got the death penalty, nothing would matter once these people were wiped out.

The first thing he did when he reached the petrol pump was to lock himself in the back room with his pistol. Slowly he caressed the solid gleaming instrument, the short barrel, slowly he rolled the lustrous gold bullets in his hand. One for him, one for her. Power, he held power, he held justice. It felt good to be the master of life and death.

The next day and the next, and the day after, his wife did not call. Each moment confirmed her guilt. No matter what the circumstances, what Himmat had said to persuade her, what she had done had struck at the root of his life. Why should he go on struggling against his destiny, hoping for success, for a legacy to leave behind? His own needs were minimal, how much did a farmer's son require? All the luck in the family had gone to one man, and that was a man for whom everything was not enough.

He tracks his brother's movements through the newspapers. At the moment he is in Delhi. Briefly he wondered how he would do it. Enter his house, try and find him? Too clumsy and uncertain. During his morning walk? Aim and shoot. The deed was done.

But this way of killing didn't seem right. He needed distance between Himmat and himself, he wanted the man in a more neutral situation, where there was no question of greeting, talking or welcoming. It would have to be at the Jan Sunwai, when there were crowds about, when his brother would be standing in front of many people, absorbed in his role as saviour of Rajasthan. It would be nice to see him fall when he was so full of himself.

Nobody would stop him from entering the Jan Sunwai. He would deal with the security issue by reaching the CM's residence before daybreak and throwing the pistol over the wall. During his walk with his brother he had noted the thickness of the bushes towards the back of the garden. A good cover area.

He cradled his gun possessively – now his path to a more meaningful future. He ran his fingers over the smooth metal casing of the bullets. They looked innocent, colourful and pretty as wrapped sweets.

The idea of killing them together in their assignation spot now seemed highly impractical. It involved more waiting, more stalking than he had patience for. Since they knew he knew, they might be cautious. Weeks might pass. Until he acted, he was consumed by hatred. He could think of nothing else but the naked body of his wife in the bed of another, see nothing else but him putting that necklace on her, fondling her breasts, drawing her closer, entering her as though she was his to enter. What else would he do? You could buy a lot with a diamond as expensive as the one he had given. How long would he spend on her? And she, how would she respond? Again that stabbing cruel shaft of pain that made him rush to the bathroom and retch into the toilet. He squatted on the floor, and vomited again. Everything he had ever felt for his wife was being thrown out.

It was late that night when he started for Jaipur. He would do it while she was sleeping. He wanted none of the drama that had been enacted the last time, none of the lies, the pleading, and above all, he didn't want to see her face. By the time her body was discovered, he would be back.

The road was quiet, the moon was shining big and brilliant. It was Buddh Purnima, he remembered his boy telling him, and everything was gilded in silver light. It was soothing driving in the darkness, none of the constant negotiation with traffic that one was forced to do during the day.

It was two in the morning when he reached Mahavir Udyan. Stray dogs could be heard barking. His car headlights picked out the empty streets, bits of trash lying here and there, the shut gates of houses, the high walls. It was a good neighbourhood, one of the best in Jaipur. How had she managed to get a plot in such a place? In a draw, she had said. Public lottery. Why had he been so willing to believe her? These things were rigged, her lover must have arranged something. There was no way a civil servant of the middle rung could have won a plot in such a locality.

He was approaching A-1/43. He turned off his headlights and stopped outside. He had the house keys in his pocket and he now unlocked the gate, and walked softly up to the main door, its key dangling from the ring in his hand.

As he stepped on to the wide porch, he found he needed to sit down on the swing to collect himself. The perfume of the raat ki rani pervaded the whole garden. He remembered how Tapti had wanted fragrance night and day, he could see the madhumalti spiralling up the side columns of the veranda, so

that you entered the house to the accompaniment of pleasing
smells. There were a few clouds in the sky, the moon was now
lower, round and beautiful. Its loveliness increased the sorrow
he felt for the life he might have had. He had only longed for
the fruits of his own hard work, nothing impossible. His wife
had been at the centre of many of his desires and now he felt
completely hollowed. He looked at the pistol in his hands, this
was what he was going to be remembered by.

He imagined taking off his shoes, walking barefoot up the
stairs to their bedroom, seeing his wife sleeping. He would aim
the pistol at her heart. It would be difficult to find the exact
spot under the sheets, never mind, he would shoot once –
twice – in the general region. Then he would run down, grab
his shoes, jump into the car and drive away.

Now do it. Open the door, go up, step by step, get it over
with. Then tomorrow the rest of the plan.

But his feet were weighed down by iron blocks. He rubbed
the jagged edge of the key against his palm, rubbed it and
rubbed it till the hurt penetrated and he stopped. He got up
and without thinking of what he was doing, walked towards the
gate and into his car to drive away from the house, filled with
an even greater repugnance than before.

He drove mechanically, unaware of what he was looking
at, unaware of the traffic that was now slightly heavier. All he
wanted was to reach the petrol pump. Plan tomorrow and then
finish. Here, he knows, there will be no hesitation, no weakness,
none of the multiplicity of feelings that had attacked him on
the porch of his wife's home.

Once he arrived, he parked the car in the paved area and
unlocked the door to his room. He sat with his pistol on
the edge of the bed, his legs dangling, too restless to try and
sleep. The sun emerged intense and red above the fields in the
distance, lighting the cement waste at the back of the pump.

The next day finds him determined to focus on what lies ahead. The burden of that fruitless expedition to Jaipur troubles him. He tells himself that what he did, or rather, didn't do, could from a certain perspective be seen as magnanimous. He had spared a woman, he had considered her daughters.

What is bothering you, Bhai Sahib, are you all right, asks his chief assistant. Yes, he is fine, says Mangal, looking tenderly at this caste brother brought from the village, in many ways his closest companion. Upon lying down he falls asleep immediately.

The next morning he gets up when it is still dark. A quick bath, the water is cold and he shivers. His service staff have been told he has important work somewhere, they will manage the pump. He knows he will never return. This is a price he is willing to pay. As it is he has no home, and after today that will be literally true. He looks around, mentally saying goodbye to the man he was.

On the highway he accelerates till he reaches one hundred and twenty kilometres an hour. The road is as empty as it can ever be, only a few trucks, a few buses, a few cars. He stops at a petrol pump very like his own for tea and a piss, washes his face, and reaches the city limits as the sky is turning a gentle grey.

When he reaches Civil Lines, it proves easy to walk along the broad quiet roads adjacent to the house, easy to toss the pistol swaddled in an old black cloth over the high walls into the secluded, bushy corner he had noticed earlier. His actions are not marked by anybody, and he feels destiny smiling upon him.

The sun rises. Who knows, his brother might be taking his morning walk round the jogging path, not for chief ministers the stress of public spaces. The light is golden now, the glistening dew makes everything seem cool and fresh.

He drives a few kilometres, stops at a dhaba near Moti Doongri and drinks more tea. He orders a hot kachori, but

after a few bites, finds it sitting so heavily in his stomach that
he feels sick.

Mangal now needs to kill the hours till two thirty, which is
when the gates will open for the Jan Sunwai. A film hall that
runs morning shows proves to be an obliging timepass. He
watches three hours of an old Shah Rukh Khan blockbuster.
The noise, the songs, the dances, the chase stun him pleasantly.

The lights come on and he goes to another theatre. There
the film is more recent. He settles down to watch *My Name Is
Khan,* a salted, buttered tub of popcorn in his hand. He eats, he
watches Shah Rukh Khan travel the length of the US to prove
his innocence, rejected by his family, alone, misunderstood and
preyed upon. In the intermission he buys a veg burger.

At two o'clock Mangal makes his way to 8, Civil Lines and
moves slowly along with the crowd. Once he has entered, he
waits till he recognizes one of the house staff, greets him in a
warm and friendly fashion before walking towards the back.
The Cobra Derringer is where he had thrown it in the morning.
The gods are with him; he feels that strongly.

The Sunwais were held to one side of the front lawn, and
Mangal sits in a corner with the farmers, that stock from which
he has emerged. They take him back to his childhood, those
faces, that way of sitting on their haunches, those turbans,
that tranquil air that suggests they can stay immobile forever.
There are a lot of them, the monsoon has been poor and
famine threatens the region. So much for the vaunted changes
in agriculture, thought Mangal, so much for better irrigation
facilities, water conservation, hybrid seeds. Maybe the next
CM will manage things better.

A rustle, a heave as the CM appears exactly at three. He is
accompanied by his staff, the secretaries for agriculture, rural
development, law, education, food, disaster management. They

take care of the petitions handed to them. A month had been
allotted for each case, should the recipient not get redressal,
they were entitled to appeal again.

As the meeting begins the supplicants are lined up. One
by one, they edge nearer. One by one, their cases are disposed
of. HSG is only thinking of the matters at hand when he looks
up and sees his brother. What could he be doing here, to make
what demand, what quarrel, over what issue?

The pistol's snout glints as it is uncovered. Their eyes meet.
Mangal raises the gun and empties three golden beauties into
the older man. The chief minister falls, blood oozing from his
chest. For a moment he stares at Mangal, then his eyes flicker
shut. Security men quickly cordon off the area, the crowds are
hurried out, a siren begins to wail. The ambulance that is always
in attendance can be heard up the driveway. More security men
surround Mangal, his arms are pinned behind him, his weapon
snatched. There is no need for this, Mangal has made no move
to leave the spot. His gaze is fixed on the slowly spreading
red stain on the front of the white kurta. Not many present
know that a brother has shot a brother, all that will come later.
Himmat doesn't die at once, but as far as Mangal is concerned
the story of the Gaina brothers is over.

Acknowledgements

Many people helped with the research involved in this book. In Delhi they are Jamal Kidwai, Safi Rizvi, Vimlaa Mehra, DIG Prisons, Mani Shankar Aiyar, Khinv Raj and Ritwik Agarwal. In Chandigarh it was Aruna Choudhary, MLA from Punjab.

In Ajmer Anuradha Marwah was guide and mentor. It was through her that I interacted with people in the city as well as the surrounding villages. They are M.K. Marwah, Kirti Pathak, Vasudev Devnani, MLA North Ajmer, members of the Ajmer Adult Education Association, Badri Prasad Pancholi, Indira Pancholi, Sheila Upadhayaya, Sanjay Palod, Mahavir, Saroj, Sulakshana Sharma, Vikas Sharma, Mathur of the kirana shop, Ram Swarup Chowdhury, the Jat headman of Tajpura and the villagers of Tajpura, Irnia, Gundalli, Pratapura and Sampla.

My writers group, Janet Chawla, Anuradha Marwah, Deepti Mehrotra, Sujatha Mathai, Charty Dugdale, Amy Kazmin, Gopika Nath, Mala Bali and Inbar Ushpiz heard versions of this year after year with great fortitude.

I thank my agents, Ayesha Karim, Lucy Luck and Shruti Debi. At Penguin Random House I thank Meru Gokhale, Arpita Basu and Anushree Kaushal. Julian Loose's comments over two years have made this novel what it is.

For five years Ira Singh has listened to accounts of Bhai-Bhai. The debt I owe her is incalculable.

My husband, Nidhi Dalmia, is the plinth upon which I build any edifice; I thank him.